The Tides of Kadavar

THE TIDES OF KADAVAR

THE TWELVE PALADINS VOLUME ONE

BY C.E. WOOLDRIDGE JR

I dedicate the works of my imagination to the son, and all sons, who will never have the chance to have their own.

Preface

This book is the culmination of years I have spent with friends and family alike. It is the by-product of all the fun we have spent sitting at the table, rolling dice, and having nightly food runs. By any amount or measure, I hope you, the reader, will enjoy the tales in these pages, and the pages beyond it.

I have spent over a decade building the world, its history, and the people that live in it. Like some of you out there, I spent a good amount of my youth playing tabletop RPGs of all flavors. After a short career as a player, I became more interested in taking the role of the narrator of these wonderous stories. Every person that I managed to be the narrator for said that I had a knack for detail, and an unbound limit of imagination.

Each time I became the narrator, it took place in this very world you are about to step in to. My promise to you is originality and a well-oiled machine. For where ever the wheels may take us...

I suppose we shall have to see.

Introduction

First and foremost, the overall goal here is to have fun.

The pages are packed with life, adventure, and monsters. I really prefer the monsters and the bad guys to be terrifying. If they weren't then why bother. I wanted to capture the essence of a good fantasy story, and I feel that I have made a real contender here. But I will let you be the judge.

There are swords and magic, but as you delve deeper, you find the characters also reflect some real issues that can be found in our own version of humanity. There is racism, discrimination, corruption, mental illness, religious adversity, and several other topics.

The people of my world have different skin tones based on their subrace, and that means color, in case you are wondering. I am one of those that believes that there is one human race. In that light, the people of my stories will always be referred to by their cultural identities or nationalities which is the way that things should be.

P.S.
The List of Chapters and Illustrations is in the back of the book. Enjoy!

"...and most importantly, make sure to be kind."

Priest of the Twins

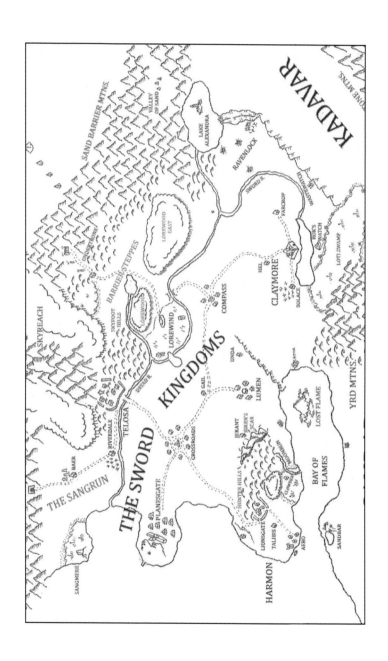

PROLOGUE
LEGACY

It was the middle of the night. The moons and the stars were invisible. The sky was blanketed by rain clouds. The drops of water from above lazily fell to the earth below. The weather had remained an irritating drizzle, but it was more favorable considering that a full-on deluge would have been worse.

The weather had remained the same since before the daylight disappeared. It was a direct reflection of the two people that now headed northeast on the road to a place called Shalestone.

The two people were paladins, warriors serving the will of the deities. It was a man and a woman, both humans, and together they were husband and wife. The man wore a suit of intricate chainmail that was made of lavender metal links, and there was a design up and down the center of the torso that looked like a spout of silver waves. The woman had a shield strapped to her back that was emblazoned with the holy symbol of Undine and Nielda, the Twin Goddesses of the Moons.

The symbol was a large circle, inside the circle was a smaller, pale blue circle that shared a border with the large one. To this effect, the remaining portion of the larger circle formed a crescent moon, and it was colored lavender.

In the woman's hands was a basket that carried their six-month-old son. The woman's heart, as well as her husband's, was much heavier than any rainfall they could experience this night.

The boots of their armor splashed on the wet mud as they made their way along the road, and they walked by many lamp posts that stood to light their way. By now, the two of them could see the town upon the horizon.

The woman knew the time was coming closer and closer, and she had to push away her emotions so that she could find the strength to do what needed to be done. Then the woman stopped in her tracks.

Her husband turned to come to her side.

"I was hoping for a much longer peace this time," the woman said as she stared down at the covered basket.

"I know. I feel the same way," the husband agreed.

Their faces were wet from the sprinkling rain, but the husband could see his wife's eyes fought back the tears.

"We can at least rest easy knowing that Targen and Vivica will take care of Henrick," he assured her.

She embraced him by standing closer and leaned against his chest. He, in turn, embraced her with a hug.

"When we are done, we will come back, and spend the rest of our days with him," he said.

"Okay," she replied.

The two of them continued their walk in to town. The landscape of the town was made up of tiny hills, and the roads were lined with short wooden fences as the avenues sought to wind around to meet each of the homes. At this hour, and with the weather, there was no one else walking around.

The small hovels that served as the homes for the dwarven people were dug into the earth, the outside of each home was made of a solid, smooth, stone wall, and a slanted wooden awning. The doors that entered each home varied by design depending on the clan that lived there. Some doors were square while others were round.

Before reaching the front door of each home, there was a small *dooryard* as it was called. A tiny area in which the different people would decorate, or garden, or something of the like.

Each of the homes, somewhere above the hill in which their hovels were dug, a chimney stuck up out of the ground, but tonight, only a few of them were producing smoke.

After a few minutes of walking, the husband and wife found the dwarven home they were looking for.

The stone wall of the entrance was chiseled with straight lines and squares. The door was square in shape, and upon the door in the dwarvish language was the name *Skullbright.*

They stepped through the gate attached to the fencing around the dooryard. The dooryard of this residence was mostly plain grass, but upon the stoop of the home was a stone statue of a humanoid holding a shield between its hands and the tips of its feet. The couple knew the depiction of Himokar, the Giant God of the Mountains.

They both stepped under the awning to protect themselves from the rain for just a moment as they prepared one of the hardest decisions of their lives.

The woman got down on her knees, and gently sat the basket before the door. She only placed a hand on the covered basket, and she felt the warmth of her son who lay beneath the thick blanket.

The rush of emotion with the moment at hand nearly overwhelmed her. She thought to take her son back with them, but she knew she could not. She knew that her son would not be safe.

The woman then produced a rolled piece of parchment that was tied closed with a single piece of twine, and she placed it on top of the blanket. With her hand back on top of her son, and the piece of parchment, she closed her eyes, and let out a trembling sigh as she mustered up the courage to do what she needed to.

"Okay. I'm ready," she said as she stood back up.

The man reached over, and hammered his gauntlet upon the surface of the door, creating a series of resounding thuds that assuredly would find its way to the sleeping ears of the dwarves that lived inside.

At the end of the knocking, the man and woman quickly turned and departed.

They disappeared in to the night.

It was a short moment before the door to the dwarven dwelling came open.

A stout dwarven man stood before the doorway of his home. The sight of a mysterious package on his stoop immediately caught his attention. However, before he decided to tend to the basket, he picked up the parchment that was on top.

He rustled his light brown beard to scratch at an itch before he rolled the twine off the paper. He stood there in the doorway, and let the cool, rainy air blow into his warm home as he read the note to himself:

Targen and Vivica,

I could think of no one else to watch our son. You have been the most warm-hearted of people. Skald and I must leave Henrick in your care. Our duty has been called for once again, and the risk has been no greater than it is now. When, and only when, Henrick is old enough and strong enough, tell him that we have gone to Terra Nix. That is where our quest takes us.

Your friend,
Sonya Gronthjerte

"Oh, most dire," the dwarf mouthed to himself.

He placed the paper on a nearby table, and then he picked up the basket, and pulled the blanket to peak at the infant's face inside. The dwarf stared at the sleeping child, and silently vowed to his departed friends that he would raise the child as his own.

He then promised to the child as he brought him in, and closed the door, "Come on, lad, you'll be a dwarf in no time."

CHAPTER ONE
THE WOLF AND THE LION

Captain Fenri stood near the mouth of the large, ship-sized cave waving his arms in motions that told his crew to hurry. The phrases "Come on, lads!" and "We gotta go!" echoed off the earthen walls as the syllables left the boundaries of his thick black beard.

His crew, the crew of an infamous pirate ship known as the *Wailing Wolf*, had just returned to their secretive home in the Bay of Flames after stealing a precious item from the country of Harmon, and stealing such an item had invoked the wrath of the Harmon naval force.

Captain Fenri, as well as his crew, knew that they were going to be hunted. So, they needed to sail back out to keep the discovery of their home nonexistent, but more than that, they had been *instructed* to go back out.

The homes that were carved out into the cavern walls exploded into action as a hundred pirates were beckoned by their captain. The crew hurried back to the Wolf, bounding around the gangways that had been built to connect the homes, and made the ship ready to set sail once again.

As the last man passed by the captain, a voice called out, "Samuel."

Fenri turned to regard the familiar voice. It was a man of similar build and an unmistakable resemblance, save for the twenty or so more years this person had on the captain. The two met eyes as the older man walked up and placed a hand on Fenri's shoulder. "Sam," as he called the captain by first name, "We'll be watchin' over yer loot should ye return, but when ye do, you'll hafta fight fer it."

"Aye, pop. I'd expect no less," Fenri shot the old man a grin.

"Just come back safe, and give ol' Longspur some hell will ye."

The captain scoffed a bit as he began to walk away. "Ha, we ain't be sinkin' that monster of a ship. The other ones, though, can't say the same for them."

The older man yelled, "Just come back safe! Ye hear me!"

Captain Fenri took off on a sprint and nearly bounced up the brow to his ship. Soon, the mooring lines were removed and the ship was well underway. The crew of about 100 pirates knew their jobs like professional sailors. The Wailing Wolf had her helm manned, crow's nest filled, the oars in the water, and cannons on standby.

The captain figured that the battle would not happen for another day or so since Admiral Longspur's ship still needed to find the Wolf. However, the Bay of Flames had a bottleneck, because there was only one channel in, and only one channel out. Even though the bottleneck was many miles wide, if the Harmon ships were spread out, the Wolf would be discovered very quickly.

The pirate leader was anticipating that there would be ships sent into the bay to herd the Wolf out, but he would not delay the inevitable and risk fighting the galleon with less of a crew than what he had now.

The swift brigantine tore through the water as it emerged from the cave mouth. The oars heaved the ship out beyond the cove. The crew maneuvered the Wolf through an alleyway between the stone cliffs that surrounded them that would eventually lead them out to sea.

In this alley, the ship had to ride the strong currents that flowed through it. The crew used the oars at this point to keep the ship steady and accurate before splashing into the winds of freedom.

It was out beyond the cove, beyond the secret lagoon, and the alley that the crew found winds blowing to the west. The pirates raced about the ship, working lines to get the sails down, then the oars came in, and the Wolf started to gain speed.

By this time, the sun was at its highest point. The skies were clear with not a single cloud in sight. The winds brought the surrounding seas to life, and the ship listed comfortably as it traversed the deep blue ocean. It was a perfect day to mark the first day of summer in Golterran.

As the collapsed volcano known as Old Flame, and the location of their cove, became a distant picture behind them, the captain decided it was time to talk to his men. Upon the quarterdeck, he stood behind his helmsman, and first mate, Constance.

Constance was a young, blonde-haired man, always shaven, and as salty as Fenri. The two have been together for more than 10 years now.

The captain called to his first mate, "Conny, gather the lads."

"Aye, Cap'n," was his response.

Constance went to the ladder that led down to the main deck, but he never went down. From atop the ladder, he yelled across the deck, "Oi! Cap'n's Call ye bilge rats! All hands on deck!"

The pirates scuttled about like a swarm of crabs, and some yelled down to the decks below. After a few minutes, the 100-pirate crew of the Wailing Wolf was assembled.

Captain Fenri casually strutted over to the top of the ladder to look down upon his crew.

"Lads," he started. "Y'all be knowin' the peril at the other end of the bay. While the moment is still before us, if ye be wantin' to take the small boats and leave, go now. Ye'll not be seen as a traitor in me eyes this day. Take yer chance, and go now."

His crew remained silent and unmoving. His crew knew him well, and that he lived by his words, and his actions. If any man would leave his service today, they would indeed survive, and not be a target of his wrath.

Constance, standing beside his leader, came in with his voice, "Cap'n has lost his bloody mind. Thinkin' us blokes are the leavin' kind. Aye, mates?"

His question was answered with many "ayes" in return.

The first mate continued, "Ye ain't no foolin' us. Mates are goin' to die when the battlin' comes. We the Wailin' Wolf, we stoled the treasure of Harmon. Who from the cove can beat that?"

Another round of "ayes" followed.

"If there be any group a maggots that can be taken down the navy, it's us!" Constance's voice grew louder with each part of his speech.

A round of cheers ensued, then it settled down to silence as Constance raised his hand. The First Mate then turned to his commander and said, "Cap'n, what say ye?"

"I-," Fenri had begun, but then heard something from above.

"Cap'n! Ship off the bow!"

Fenri and Constance rushed through the crowd to get to the front of the ship, and it was there that they stared beyond to the horizon. It was a ship, but its mass was nothing compared to what the Admiral's ship was. Even without a spyglass, the captain could tell it was a frigate. It didn't matter, though. The Wolf had been spotted, and that was evident as the other ship began to steer towards them.

The captain turned to face his crew, and shouted, "Wolf den!"

The silent, watching pirate crew exploded into action, moving to and fro about the deck. Some packed the cannons, while some disorganized the main deck, and others headed below decks. The crow went into a crouch inside his half-barrel shaped station so that he would not be seen, but not before pulling the colors down.

Once the preparations were in order, everyone went below to the second deck. The topside had been shuffled around and torn apart to make it look like an empty ship that had been raided. Constance and Fenri were the last ones down.

Down below, the pirates readied the cannon igniters, which would be fed through small, drilled holes in the main deck above. To this effect, it was made so that the guns could be fired without anyone being above deck.

The *wolf den* was a trick straight out of the captain's playbook. It would allow them to get all their cannons off as a preemptive strike against curious ships. It is a trick that has worked in the past, and none usually live to spread word of such a tactic.

Fenri and Constance stood at each side, port and starboard, of the ship looking through a small peep hole should the need to fire come.

Long moments passed.

Constance signaled to Fenri to come to the starboard side of the ship. Both of them could discern from the crashing of water that the Harmon craft was close. The captain signaled to his other men with a fist going into an open palm which told them to lock the door to the main deck, but to be ready to spring it open.

The bow of the other ship could now be seen. His next hand signal was a fist with the index finger pointing to the sky, and his men readied the igniters, holding them inches from the cannon fuses.

The other ship then came alongside of the Wolf, and it wasn't before too long that the smashing thud of gangways resounded in the deck below. The Wolf was being boarded. The pirates below could hear the tapping and dragging of boots, and indiscernible talking.

These indicators told the experienced crew that this was indeed a ship from Harmon. Fenri looked once again through the peephole, and he knew the other ship was lined up perfectly.

Captain Fenri and his crew then turned their eyes to the doors leading up to the main deck. The doors rattled as if someone was attempting to open them.

Fenri then gave the command that dragged a thumb across his neck. The pirates lit the fuse for the five cannons. A short moment of quiet hissing passed...

The muffled voices of the soldiers at the door could be heard, "The door won't budge."

The doors continued to rattle.

Another soldier chimed in, "Hey, do you guys smell something burning?"

BOOM!!!

All five cannons hit with devastation and violence that shredded the Harmon ship's deck completely into a cloud of splinters and smoke. The second deck door of the Wolf was unlocked, and it went flying open. Pirates charged up with a cry of battle, and they took the boarding party by surprise. The main deck of the Wolf had become a mass of chaos and sword fighting. Pirates and Harmon sailors battling each other through the fog of dust and cinders.

Captain Fenri casually rose up from the shadowy depths of the second deck. He had the head of his favorite battleax, *Betty*, resting on his shoulder. He looked back and forth across the melee with a smirk as if he was having a day at the park. Fenri adjusted his brown leather tricorn to a comfortable position, and he scanned across the gap between the ships for *his* target as the smoke cleared. The gangways were all gone due to the cannon fire from a minute ago, but that wasn't going to stop him from reaching the captain on the other ship.

He weaved through the fighting like a snake in the grass, dodging blades, and taking enemies down as he passed by his mates before reaching the Wolf's quarterdeck. From here, he unsecured a line that was attached to the mast, and this line had no other purpose than what he was about to do. With a running start, he heaved himself into the air and swung himself to the other ship like some of his crew had already done.

The battle had nearly started, but it was going well for the crew of the Wolf. Many sailors were dead on deck. Salt water and blood mixed with the shuffling of boots and shoes. The Wolf's crew had only suffered from cuts and bruises. Fenri and his group of men on the Harmon ship cut down all who approached them, and they slowly inched their way across the shattered deck as the navy sailors continued to lose ground. It wasn't long before the sailors were overrun, and only the Harmon captain was left above. The pirate crew didn't even look at the officer in the blue and gold uniform. They left him for Captain Fenri to duel.

"Fenri, you dishonorable cur, using such a ruse," the Harmon captain insulted Fenri as the pirate leader reached to the top of the ladder to the Harmon ship's quarterdeck.

"Ye be mistakin', lad," Fenri told him. "I had no honor to begin with, but I do commend yer intelligence in fallin' for such a ruse."

The retort enraged the Harmon captain into attacking. The Harmon officer rushed forward, and came at the pirate captain with a combination of thrusts and slashes. Fenri dodged the attacks while parrying a couple others.

Fenri returned the favor by coming at the officer with quick, heavy strikes that played into the weight of Betty's head. The ax was a bit slower than the sword was, and so the pirate's weapon missed its mark.

Having given each other a small introduction to the ballad they were about to play in, the pirate and the naval officer clashed again. It was the wild swings of the unpredictable fighter versus the discipline and trained spirit of the soldier. Swing after swing, and clash after clash, Betty and the cutlass kissed each other in a clanging cacophony over and over.

Each man tried to use what they knew to gain the upper hand on the other, but neither one was letting up. They danced and exchanged blows, but they seemed to be equally matched, and not one attack would find flesh.

But the pirate was holding back, and as the anxiety of making the kill became too great, Fenri decided it was time to change it up, drop the wild fighting, and revert into the training he and his crew had gotten from the Sultan of Sandar.

In the next moment, Fenri feinted by leading with a Betty uppercut, but he let it go wide on purpose.

This caused his opponent to take the bait and flinch. Fenri followed through with a pivot on his foot before delivering a devastating roundhouse kick to the officer's face.

The officer's composure faltered, and he stumbled backwards, nearly falling on his butt, but the officer caught himself inside of a kneel. The officer returned to his feet in an instant. During that time, Fenri had taken a wide stance, leading with the left foot, and held Betty in both hands with her head pointed straight to the sky and her bladed face pointing at the pirate captain.

The two captains became locked with their eyes on each other.

Fenri scoffed at the other captain, "Ha. Yer pretty good with a blade, I'll give ye that, but this ends, here and now."

"Then you are a moron," the officer shot back. "No doubt this plume of dust and smoke has caught the eye of the *Lion* by now. My ship is merely delaying the inevitable."

"Hahaha," the pirate busted out laughing at the officer's doom-saying so hard that he had to catch himself with his hands upon his knees.

When Fenri regained his composure, his eyes met with the officer one last time. Only this time, the pirate captain's eyes shimmered with a pale lavender light.

"Ye don't know what destiny is, lad," was what Fenri foreshadowed to the man.

With inhuman speed, Fenri rushed towards the officer with Betty held straight up once again. The officer tried to anticipate the direction of the coming attack, but he truly had no idea while he struggled to track the pirate with his own eyes.

The pirate took the flat, backside of his ax, and slammed it upon the top of the officer's head with a resounding crunch that completely stunned him. He then twirled with a wide and powerful backswing, leading with Betty's blade and drove the ax to sink three-quarters of the way into the neck. The body fell limp upon the quarterdeck. Blood flowed all over the planks, and Fenri had to use a firmly placed foot on the corpse to pull Betty free from her dinner.

The Harmon troops were dwindling in numbers by this time, and the pirates were now searching every deck of the Harmon ship for stragglers. The battle was growing to a close.

After the Harmon ship had been scoured, a pirate poked his head out, and yelled to his leader, "Cap'n, they got lots o' powder in their holds."

Captain Fenri smirked. Gunpowder had to be one of his favorite things in the whole wide world. He loved how it smelled when it burned, and he especially loved how it made evidence disappear when it exploded.

Fenri called across to the Wolf, "Conny!"

Coming from the Wolf's main deck, the First Mate appeared with a waved hand, "Here, Cap'n!"

"Let's get a fire going!" Fenri shouted to him.

The rest of the crew heard the words, and all cheered over their victory. Without being given new instructions, many of the pirates went below the deck of the Harmon ship, set up new gangways, and created a human chain to quickly haul the barrels of gunpowder from the holds to the main deck.

When the Captain of the Wailing Wolf tells the crew to get a fire going, it means to pile the main deck with as much gunpowder as possible, and from a safe distance, turn the ship into a giant incineration. The crew of the Wolf was infamously known for not letting enemy ships stay afloat.

The pirates had gathered all they could on to the ruined deck of the Harmon ship. It was now time to get back on the Wolf and get to a safe distance.

As usual, Captain Fenri was the last to step foot back on the Wolf. "Get these gangways off my ship, lads."

"Cap'n!" a call from the crow again. "*Lion* off our port."

Fenri held a closed fist in the air, "Hold. Leave the gangways."

The captain's timing couldn't have been better as the first of the three gangways had already been kicked into the sea.

Fenri went to the port side of the ship and looked to the horizon. Constance by his side, they both saw the large, four-mast ship in the distance.

Captain Fenri knew his ship would be outmatched by the giant galleon. The wolf den trick would not work on that big of a ship, but the brazen pirate leader couldn't stop thinking about how much he wanted to destroy that ship. Time was becoming short, and he had to come up with something that could put his men out of harm's way long enough to figure something out.

He looked back at the gunpowder barrels on the Harmon ship.

Staring back out at the Harmon flagship, he ordered his First Mate, "Conny, get the powder on the Wolf. We're gonna play the long game on this one."

"Hoy, ye stupid blokes! Cap'n's got more tricks! Get that powder o'er here," Constance ordered the pirates.

As Fenri continued to stare at the Harmon ship on the horizon, he managed to look down at the water, which was now a calm and smooth surface, and there he saw the reflection of the two moons, Undine and Nielda.

Fenri scoffed, "Ha. Let's see what ye girls have for me."

CHAPTER TWO
KINGDOM OF THE SWORD

Today marks the 1st of Kindletar. It is the first day of the first month of the summer season, and it is the day after the Summer Solstice. On the continent of *Golterran*, the seasons are divided into quarters. These quarters begin with a single day that marks a solstice or an equinox, and then after that, a three-month cycle begins. A month is then subdivided into three 10-day weeks referred to as *tendays*. After the winter season, an additional, standalone day is added to mark the New Year.

This year is the first year of the Fifth Age. This age has been named by the Solian priests as the *Age of the Salamandar*. The dawning of this new age came about when *Mount Magnus* erupted. The eruption caused itself to collapse into a dormant volcano that is now known as Lost Flame. The news of the volcano's collapse reached all over the continent, and in the hearts of those who truly believe in the God of Fire, only words of doom fill their beliefs now. The belief of doom, however, does not belong to all who act as representatives for the God of Fire. *Sol*, as he is known, is not only the Salamandar God of Fire, but he is also the God of War.

Terra Sanguinar, the Land of Blood, or more commonly known as the *Sword Kingdoms*, is one of six major regions in Golterran. It is here in the Sword Kingdoms that an entire country is home to those who pay tribute to the God of War.

The country is known as the *Kingdom of Claymore*.

The people from Claymore believe in Sol so much that the collapse of Mount Magnus has yet to hinder their faith. In fact, most of the people here scoff at doomsayers, and they find it derogatory to think that Sol would let his people fall into darkness. In Claymoran society, it is believed that through war, violence, and action, peace can be obtained. It is also through this belief, that an individual's honor can remain intact both in life and death. Every citizen of Claymore, from their earliest years as a child, is trained in the use of weapons, and taught the ways of tactical mastery.

All the other holds of Terra Sanguinar are privy to this knowledge, and it is because of this knowledge that there has not been any aggressive action *towards*

Claymore in nearly 300 years. It is also because of this information that crime is non-existent in the Kingdom of the Sword. Almost everything is punishable by death.

However, not all citizens of Claymore are born here. People from other kingdoms travel to Claymore to make a living because of its safety and security, and just as every citizen is not from Claymore, there are also those who don't follow the Path of the Salamandar.

The Salamandar appreciates those who choose him as their patron deity, but Sol is not a god of blind worship. He is a god that favors discipline, honor, and uncompromising martial prowess.

The 1st of Kindletar was a bright and shiny summer morning. Just as it had been for countless years before. The first day of a tenday was known as *Moonday*. Moonday was a day in which the regular members of the Claymoran Army were given a day of recreation, and it was on Moonday mornings that Henrick Skullbright, a Sergeant of the Gold Brigade in the Claymoran Army, would always choose to go for his regular jog around the Castle-City of Claymore.

Members of the Gold Brigade were enlisted soldiers who had been sponsored by the Darkbane House, one of four royal houses in Claymore. There was also the Red Brigade for those sponsored by the Blade-Briar House, the Green Brigade for those from the Vicidian House, and the Blue Brigade for those from the Odoko House.

The brigades were each housed inside of large, two-story barracks that had the roof and the doors painted to match each brigade's respective color. Each floor of the barracks had 250 bunks lined from one end to the other in perfect military fashion. These bunks were two high, and thus, each barracks housed 1,000 personnel.

These troops were also the king's personal army, if need be. The city's guardsmen and patrols, although trained like the Brigades, did not play a part in this number nor did they live in the barracks with the rest of the soldiers. In fact, being a guardsman was actually the job of a regular citizen.

Sergeant Skullbright lived on the bottom floor of the Gold Brigade barracks, and his bunk and locker were located near the center of the floor. At this time, he had just finished putting on his leather shoes and light, tan-colored clothing for the exercise he had planned. He attempted to do everything as quietly as possible, including the opening and closing of his footlocker, so as to not wake up his fellow brigade members that were sleeping nearby. Respect for others was also a highly valued sentiment in Claymore. When Henrick was all dressed and ready to go, he got up from sitting on the side of his bunk, and strolled down the center aisle and headed out the yellow-painted door.

Outside, the sergeant observed the morning sky. It was light blue without a cloud in sight. Rays of sunlight, which came from the east, beamed over the top of the white-gray bricks that made up the 20-foot walls of the inner city, and those walls casted shadows over the barracks as the structures were tightly nestled up to them. This made the morning air outside the barracks cool and crisp.

In the center of the inner city was Claymore Keep. It was a three-story structure made of similar white-gray bricks, but bricks were large and sharply cut which gave the structure a more polished look. The first floor was built wider than the floor above it, and the difference of width made it so that clay roof tiles could run along the surface at a shallow angle. These roof tiles were painted with a vibrant crimson. The consistency of the keep continued as the second floor was wider than the third. For the most part, the walls of the keep drew a symmetrical square, but in each corner, there was a tower that traversed to each floor. The keep was where the king, and his ensemble, resided. It was where all of the officers of the Claymoran Army lived, it is where all of the kingdom's political meetings took place, and on the top floor, it was where the throne sat.

Tucked along the western and northern walls of the inner city were the royal houses, and the houses were more like mansions. The construction of these mansions was very similar to everything else in the city, and each house was decorated with the colors that represented each of the families. Furthermore, the sunlight had already begun to grace the royal houses.

Henrick determined the near-perfect weather to be the factor for a good day to go for a jog. As a warm up, he went through some light exercises such as jumping jacks and pushups. When he was finished, he followed the avenues through the inner city until it brought him to the Sword Gate, the southern gate that exited the inner city, and entered the Sword Ward in the mid-city.

On the other side of the Sword Gate, Henrick looked left and right, which was east then west. The sun completely provided light across the mid-city, and he could see the wide street that nearly went the length of it. The citizens of Claymore, who were mostly human, were already milling about the city, and from what Henrick could see, nothing exciting was going on. He continued his walk, crossing the street from the gate, and into a section of the city known as the Sword Ward.

The Sword Ward was the city's public training grounds. There were several obstacle courses throughout the ward, there were clearings designated for sparring, and then there was a beaten track that went around all of it. On the eastern end of the Sword Ward, there was a small structure made of metal that was known as the *Church of Steel*.

The Church of Steel was a place of worship for those looking for Sol's blessing. Sometimes, and even now as he eyed the peculiar place, Henrick had to wonder if he was the only one in the whole kingdom that tried to avoid visiting that place. The man just never found the idea of religion interesting. His adoptive parents always had a statue of Himokar in their dooryard, but he never once saw them stop to regard the thing.

The sergeant ignored any form of calling from the church as he stepped onto the track. He took the counterclockwise route on the track before he began to increase his pace. As he made his way around the circuit, he found others on the track that had the same idea as him, both males and females.

He got through a couple of laps before his body found a rhythm. On his way to completing another lap, his eyes scanned the rest of the training grounds. At one moment, he saw a group of *odum*; the native, dark-skinned humans of Golterran.

The term "odum" was a derivative word from their old and lost language of *oduman* that translated to "one place" which also implied the meaning that there was only one place in which the odum were from.

The odum on the field were wearing the blue House Odoko tabards, and they were all locked in wrestling matches. The blue house practiced heavily on wrestling and martial arts, but they also had a focus on using large weapons, such as greatswords, greataxes, pikes, glaives, and the like.

The wrestlers were lost from sight as Henrick made another lap on the track. He began to make the first turn on his next lap, and he couldn't help but notice a nearby officer. It was an odum man dressed in chainmail, and he wore the black and red, four-section tabard of an officer. In that short moment, Henrick was able to see two red circles side-by-side, which identified him as a lieutenant, on the man's left breast, which was a black section of the tabard. The right side was red and had the design of a sword on it. The officer looked directly at the sergeant, but the officer never said anything. When Henrick came back around, the lieutenant stepped out onto the track.

"Sergeant," the officer addressed Henrick with an open palm raised in his direction.

"Aye, sir," Henrick replied while panting from his exercise.

"You have an urgent letter back at the barracks. You need to go read it," the officer said.

"Aye, sir," Henrick answered.

Before the sergeant could begin to step away, the officer had a question. "Have you seen Sergeant Bellum?" the officer asked.

"I have not, sir," was all that Henrick could offer his superior.

"Very well. Carry on," the officer said before walking deeper into the Sword Ward to do his own inspection of the grounds.

Henrick did not waste any time, and he headed straight back to the barracks.

Once Henrick had returned to his bunk, he found an envelope with a wax seal. The seal, to which Henrick recognized, was General Hormac's. General Hormac was the top-most ranked member of the Claymoran Army, and the right-hand to the King. Henrick sat down on his bedside and tore the envelope open. He read the letter with his eyes, and kept the words inside his mind:

Sergeant Skullbright,

You have been selected to join a small team of witch-hunters. You will be led by Captain Thor Spearfall, and you will muster with him before the Keep's doors on the morrow before the sun has risen. Come in your House's uniform.

Respectfully,
General Hormac

The letter took Henrick by surprise, he had heard rumors floating around about this special unit, but even he wasn't sure if they were true or not. In his unexpected stupor, he did not hear the approach of one of his friends.

"You got one, too?" the familiar voice spoke.

Henrick looked up at the man standing at the foot of his bunk.

His name was Kendo; he was a man of House Odoko, and stood at six-foot-seven. The man was bald, and clean shaven, but that youthful look did nothing to deter the fact this man was a muscular tree stump with a greatsword slung on his back.

"Uh, aye," Henrick was similarly surprised by his friend's visit. Henrick was about to ask Kendo about getting a letter, but he noticed it in the man's large hands. "Do ye know who else got one?"

"I asked the lieutenant that gave me mine. He said that Sirus and Lars were on his list as well," Kendo explained.

"That makes sense, the lieutenant that found me was lookin' for Lars," Henrick added. His mind also tried to consider who else might have gotten a letter.

Kendo then suggested, "You should get cleaned up. I'll find the other two. We can meet up at the Brand for lunch."

"Aye, that sounds like a good idea," Henrick agreed.

"Good. I will see you there," Kendo said before departing.

After a moment of stripping off his sweaty shirt, and taking off his shoes, he gathered his soiled clothes, a bar of soap, and his towel from the rack at the foot of the bunk. He placed them in a small basket he had in his footlocker, and then he walked back out of the barracks.

In the south-east corner of the inner city, and behind all the barracks, was a large, stone-built, man-made pond that pumped water in from the nearby Star Fall Lake. The water then traveled through the city by way of an aqueduct, passing through grates in the walls, and eventually returning to the lake. The edges of the pond were traced with a wooden deck. Upon looking at how the whole thing was made, it actually seemed more like a swimming pool. Furthermore, the pond was where the enlisted members of the brigades bathed.

Henrick made the short walk from his barracks to the pond, and once he was there, he went to the closest open area he could find. He then placed his items on the ground so that he could strip himself down to his birthday suit. He then picked up the dirty clothes and the soap before carrying them into the water with him.

The water was all natural, and all that natural feeling came with the crispness of cool and clean water. He kept a hand over his genitals so that the cold-water torture would be lessened in his mind, but he was always reminded that it never worked that way.

From what Henrick could see, even before getting in the water, he was not the only one out here using the pond. Many soldiers of Claymore, male and female, were out here doing the same thing he was. Since personal respect was a highly valued piece of culture in Claymore, the bathing pool was something of a hallowed area. A place where privacy was sacred. However, that didn't stop some of the soldiers from taking a peek at each other.

Henrick splashed around a bit, and put the bar of soap to work. He hand-scrubbed the important parts of his body, and agitated his soiled clothes in the water to get them clean. The whole process took him about 15 minutes, and he usually didn't like to spend any more time than needed at the pond. It was cold, after all.

When he was done, he got out of the pond, and retrieved his towel to wrap his waist. He preferred the rest of his body to air dry, and while he was doing that, he wrung his clothes over the pond to get the water out. After a little bit, his body was mostly dry, and he managed to get the excess water out of his clothes. With everything in his basket once again, he headed back into the barracks, and to his bunk. He used the towel rack at the end of his bunk to hang his towel, and his damp clothing.

Next, he began to gather clothes from his footlocker. He grabbed a pair of shoes, tan pants, a purple tunic and a clean pair of undergarments. He put the underpants on, but then placed the other items on top of his footlocker after closing it. Henrick figured that it was still morning for a couple more hours, and so he was going to take a nap before heading out for lunch.

It was in no time at all that the noon hour had fallen upon the castle-city. All of the avenues were brightly covered in the sun's light, and as it was a summer day, the temperature had risen significantly. The heat of the sun, however, would be the least on anyone's mind who ventured into the *Coin Ward*. The

Coin Ward was the northern section of Claymore's mid-city, and it was the location to all of the city's shops, artisans, inns, and taverns. The Coin Ward was identified by the golden roof tiles on every structure there, but on top of that, it was also the busiest part of town.

As for the collection of inns, taverns, and bars that littered the Coin Ward, there was one that was truly unique from the others, and that was a place called the *Brew and Brand*. The Brew and Brand was one of only a few places in the entire world where the famous *Boulderbrand Ale* was crafted and sold. The dark and creamy ale was made from a recipe only known by the Brandybore Clan of dwarves from Undertrone, and it was a member of that clan, Ul Brandybore, that ran the establishment.

Inside the Brew and Brand, a customer could come inside and be assaulted by the smells of cooking meats, smoking pipes, and distilling alcohol. Strangely enough, the aroma was one of the things that made people come back. The wood finishes all around the room were tawny, like the inside of a mahogany, and it allowed customers to see every detail of the place.

In one of the corners of the lobby, there were stairs leading to the second floor. The upstairs had chambers for travelers to stay in, but even though the Brew and Brand had lodging, it was the lobby downstairs that made the most money. The lobby served as the restaurant and bar. It had ten round tables with four chairs each, and the bar near the back of the room was complemented with fourteen stools.

At night, the place was known to be busy. However, during the day it was a decent place to get lunch. And it was during the daytime hour on the 1st of Kindletar, that four of the Brew and Brand's best customers had decided to walk in for their typical lunch gathering. Although, the purpose of their gathering today was far from typical.

Henrick was the first one through the door, and as he placed the first steps into the establishment, he could see that other patrons were already here, and the tavern's personal bard had arrived as well. Henrick was dressed in the clothes he had set out earlier, and he had a belt with a short sword sheathed on it.

Following behind him was Kendo, and the large man had to duck slightly as he came through the doorway.

Behind Kendo was Lars Bellum. He, like Henrick, is a member of Gold Brigade, and the two of them spar on a number of occasions. Sergeant Bellum had dark, medium-length hair, and sported a goatee. Lars was also an *aerin*, just like Henrick.

The aerin of Golterran are the lighter-skinned humans that trace their heritage from the long-lost continent of Lumia. The term *aerin* is a reference to the Goddess of Wind and Freedom, Aerith.

Bringing in the rear, was a man who wore leathers and a dark gray cloak with the hood down. His name was Sirus. He was known as a ranger of incredible skill. He used to travel the continent as a mercenary before Claymore's General sought to hire him as a tracker, permanently. Sirus was the leanest of the group, and he kept his straight, brown hair tied back in a ponytail. He was half-dryad, his golden eyes served as evidence, and his flesh resembled tones that were similar to the wood of a birch.

As the four impressive warriors came into the establishment, Henrick led them to the closest table on their left side. The men sat there and waited to be served. As they did, their eyes wandered around the place. They took silent account of the building's interior construction even though they had been there countless times before. Of all the tables inside the place, only one other was being used. It looked like a human couple had come in to do the same thing that they were about to do.

The kitchen of this tavern was located in the basement, but that did nothing to stop the aroma of cooking beef, carrots, and potatoes from escaping out into the main area. It was from these scents that the warriors could guess what was being served for lunch.

The four men finally moved their eyes to the other great thing about the Brew and Brand, and that was the entertainment. It was a dwarven bard who went by the name of Furl Stonebrow. He played at this establishment quite often, and when he didn't, he would sing ballads at other parts of the city. At the moment, the blonde-haired, middle-aged dwarf was sitting on a short stool on the tavern's stage, and was tuning his lute for a coming song.

While they waited to be served, the men began to whisper amongst themselves with a gentleman's bet as to what song Furl was to play today.

"What say ye? Bet he plays *Mountain Warrior*," Henrick started the coinless wager through his peculiar accent.

"I don't think so. It is the middle of the day, he is to play Gold Plain Melody," Kendo whispered in return with his odum accent.

"Maybe he will play..." Lars came in next, but he was never one to enjoy a good ballad and so he paused. "...something heavier than the Gold Plain."

"Bah," came the grumbling from across the lobby. "I can hear ye lads. And I'm afeared to let ye know that today'll be a new song."

The four warriors drew curious looks at each other after shedding their eyes towards the bard. Similarly, the people at the other table were curious as well. The moment that followed was when Furl began to strum the strings of his lute.

Stone Princess, Stone Princess, how your vigil has been long.
Watching over the valleys, the weak, and the strong.

The infamous tavern waitress, Snerva, came across the lobby from behind the bar on the far wall after Furl began his playing. She approached, her long golden braids swayed as she walked, and when she came to the table of the four friends, she asked the anticipated question, "What can I get fer ye, gents?"

Silent and guarding, in the shadows I hide,
Waiting for cries, in the time that I bide.

"Whatever's cooking down there," Lars spoke first.

"We got cow steak, carrots, and boiled 'tators today," the waitress listed, also in a peculiar accent that was close to Henrick's.

With the fires of war, I am the speaker of peace
And through my voice, the sand I will crease.

"Fantastic, one plate for me," Lars said.

"Aye, me too," Henrick piped in.

"I'll take two," Kendo raised his hand as the waitress's eyes followed around the table.

"Potatoes and carrots, no steak though," Sirus said, drawing awkward looks from the two aerin men. He could only glare back to fight off the mocking gazes.

Stone Princess, Stone Princess, how your vigil has been long.
Watching over the valleys, the weak, and the strong.

"And a pitcher of Boulderbrand," Henrick requested.

With a nod of agreement from each of the four warriors, Snerva took her leave to head to the kitchen. In the first moments waiting for their lunch to arrive, the men sat back and enjoyed the rest of Furl's song.

I cared for you once, and now you're gone.
The people you rallied, were a family of one.
But time has passed, your memory of none,
Now you're a part, of the mountain and the sun.
Stone Princess, Stone Princess, how your vigil has been long.
Watching over the valleys...the weak...and the strong.

The somber melody of Furl's song held a hint of sadness, and left the people in the tavern almost speechless, but when the people at the other table came out of the emotional daze, they began to offer a clap of approval. It wasn't long after that that the four warriors joined in the celebration.

"Thank ye," Furl spoke to his crowd. Without another word from the bard, the stout minstrel began to play one of his more known ballads, the Gold Plain Melody, which was a lyric-less song that was a little more upbeat and delightful.

"So what'd'ya guys think?" asked Henrick. "About the new job?"

"Witch hunting, and killing magicians?" Lars spoke of the thought in their minds. "Can't say. Never really had to fight one before."

"Aye, same here," Henrick said.

"I've encountered a few in my days as a mercenary...magicians that is," Sirus began, drawing the attention of the other three. "Bandits, outside of Claymore, tend to keep them around for extra firepower. But just like an arrow, spells can miss their target."

"That's good to know," Henrick nodded.

The waitress had returned to their table with the pitcher of the dark Boulderbrand ale, and a few tankards to go with it. "Food'll be here shortly." And then she took off again, going back to the bar area. The blonde, busty aerin woman drew the attention of the men as she traversed the lobby floor, and not the first time either.

"I wager we'll be doing this hunting in response to what happened at Rok's Watch," Kendo said as he poured the first pint.

Kendo's statement grew curious looks on the faces of the other three.

Rok's Watch was an old outpost that Claymore used to station troops and keep eyes on the southern shores of the Starfall Lake. It also sat on the northern border of the Loti Swamp.

"What happened down there?" Henrick questioned as he took the ale next.

"Sergeant Faldor, from Red Brigade, was stationed there," Kendo started. "While he was there, orcs from the Yens attacked. It would have been a great battle, but a witch came from nowhere, and destroyed the orcs with a single spell, and then she turned on the tower. As fate would have it, Captain Spearfall was there, but he was not able to defeat her."

The mention of Captain Spearfall drew the others into the story even more. He was Claymore's champion, and an expert when it came to hunting down and killing those who wielded magic power of any kind. Not to mention, each of the men already knew that Spearfall was going to be their commanding officer in this small band of mage-slayers.

"What did the witch do to 'im?" Henrick said.

"He said she didn't fight back. That the mere sight of the Cap' forced her to retreat into the nearby swamp before he could catch her."

"Running away?" Lars felt a bit skeptical about the story, considering this witch brought death, with a single spell, to a roaming band of orcs. He poured his pint after finishing the statement.

Sirus dismissed the pondering, "We all know what kind of a rep' Spearfall has in this land. In other lands, even as far as Telosa, his name is known." The others nodded in agreement to the sound reasoning, especially in bringing up the dryad capital to the distant northwest. After filling his cup with ale, Sirus looked around at his buddies, "Are we to assume that we are a party made to hunt down this witch with him? It would only seem the most likely of goals in our formation."

Henrick, Lars, and Kendo nodded at the notion.

After that moment, Lars said, "In the end, though, it would be an honor to fight and kill by his side."

Kendo raised his mug before the others in preparation of a cheer, "To battle, and victory on the road ahead." The other men joined in the celebrating words and softly tapped each other's cups before taking the first sip of their drinks.

"To battle," the other three said simultaneously.

The minutes stacked on for a while before the waitress returned with their meals. When the meals came, they were served on a metal dish, and each plate held a beef steak cooked to medium-well, a peeled and boiled whole potato, a whole boiled carrot minus the green stalks, and a fluffy bread biscuit. Sirus's plate was missing the steak as ordered, and Kendo had two plates in front of him. The pitcher still had enough for another round or two. All and all, the meal was to be a good one.

Lars presented the required gold coin currency to the waitress. She then said, "Enjoy yer meal, gents." She was then gone again, off to focus on another task.

"To great food," Lars said, bringing about another cup-tapping celebration.

Nearly an hour passed by the time they had finished their meal. Once finished, they gathered themselves and departed the Brew and Brand. Stepping outside they took a quick look around the avenue outside of the tavern, assessing their surroundings to make sure nothing was out of place or disturbed. If it's one thing they teach the people of Claymore: it is to always expect a fight. The kingdom's own history is why every citizen must serve a minimum of two years in the Army. To this end, everyone in Claymore is a soldier to some extent.

This knowledge keeps the neighboring lands from invading them. To date, Claymore has played a role in every major conflict in the Sword Kingdoms. They were the best, and everyone knew it.

Their vision peered west down the main road of the city, and they could spot the fountain of the Coin Ward that stood a short distance from the north gate. Satisfied, and with nothing to warrant their curiosity, the four men followed the mid-city road to the east. After the road bent southward, it sent them out of the Coin Ward, and towards the *Rose Ward*.

Rose Ward was one of many residential areas inside the castle walls, and this one filled the entire northeast quarter of the mid-city. It was also identified by the color of the roof tiles which were more of a red wine than a red rose.

As for the homes in the city, most of them had two floors. The first floor was constructed of gray masonry walls, an entrance door on one or two sides, and some of them had windows, but not all of them. The second floor was made with wood framing, and the walls were made of white plaster. The roofs came up at a point like the letter A, and they had small chimneys, which came from potbelly stoves, poking out from one side

In the southwest corner of the Rose Ward, there was a large grassy clearing known as *Rose Park*. It was a fairly large recreational area where citizens and families could come to relax, play games, or anything else that might suit their need for self-enrichment. The park offered thinly-paved walkways, benches, a field, and a pond. But the park was famous for two of its more notable features. Those features were the abundance of red rose bushes, and the Crown Balcony.

The red rose was the kingdom's favored flora, and it was the major contributing factor to the park's beauty and popularity. Unsurprisingly, it was how the park got its name. The flower had the kingdom's color, and its thorns represented the act of warding off trespassers. Warding off the dishonorable.

Above the west side of the park was the *Crown Balcony*. It was a convex surface that reached out from the wall that separated the inner city from the mid-city. In a much older age, the monarch of Claymore would use the balcony to address the entire kingdom. According to history, it was rarely used, and that same tradition had made the people here forget about it.

The attractions of the Rose Ward did little to slow the progress of Henrick and his friends. They continued south on the road, and completely passed the park and the wine-colored roofs. This brought them to a three-way intersection.

From the crossroad, they could see the east gate. It was a couple of thick, round top, wooden doors that when together were 10-feet-wide, and they stood about 15-feet-tall inside of a stony archway. A bulky tower was built over the top of the gate, but it only stood about 12 feet higher than the city walls. Inside the tower, the gate commander and a handful of marksmen were housed.

To the south of the east gate, there was another residential area. This one was known as the *Temper Ward*. It had fiery orange roofs, and its real estate filled the entire southeast corner of the mid-city and traveled west until it met with the Sword Ward.

Before Henrick and his friends looked to the west road, they stopped for a moment to regard the statue at the center of the intersection. It was a life-size statue of the first monarch of Claymore, Samuel Blade-Briar. The statue faced towards the east gate with a battle-ready stance, and a greatsword in hand.

Henrick and Sirus stood by on the road as Lars and Kendo walked over to regard the face of the statue. Once there, their gaze fell to the base of the stone statue, and to the plaque of gold.

"*Samuel Blade-Briar, Slayer of Darkness, Chosen of Sol,*" Lars read the words of the plaque aloud. They had seen the statue and the plaque a hundred times before, but today, Lars read it as if trying to invoke the man's long-lost blessing. A brief moment passed over the two and then he continued, "If only legends like him were still around."

Kendo replied with a scoff, "Ha! If men like him were around, maybe there would be someone to fight." The moment of reverence continued. "But, to become the champion to the God of Battle? That *is* legendary."

Lars could only agree, "Indeed."

The men regrouped before they continued their journey through the city. They followed the main avenue by heading west from the intersection. After a couple of minutes, they reached the Rose Bridge.

Below the bridge was the stream that ran from the bathing pool by the barracks, and the man-made aqueduct carried the water to a grated section of the south wall.

The bridge was constructed with four sanded stone pillars, two at each end. These pillars were chiseled to have the etchings of rose bushes on them. Between the pillars, the rest of the bridge was made of polished wood framing, and it had been stained with red wine.

After their footfalls thudded across the surface of the bridge, they passed through a large doorless archway that led into the Sword Ward. This archway was part of a divisional wall that completely segregated the Temper Ward from the Sword Ward. It stretched the gap between the outer wall and the inner wall, and the aqueduct ran adjacent to the wall on its eastern face.

As the four friends entered the Sword Ward, they quickly eyed their next destination as it came into view.

The Church of Steel.

The hallowed place for those in service to Sol. The structure was made with thick wooden framing, and it had to be in order to support the metal plates that served as the walls. The steel in which the plates were made came from the weapons of fallen soldiers. The church was a small structure and only had the capability to fit about 20 or 30 people at once. The building has stood ever since the aerin and the odum acquired the castle in ancient times, and the resistance from corrosion comes from the duty of the priests whose tasks includes coating the church with oils.

Of the four men, Henrick was the least excited about making this stop. He did not care for the idea of religion like his friends did. However, out of respect for his friends, he would go inside and sit while they participated in a sermon from High Solian Morgan.

One by one, the four men entered through the metal entrance door. It swung open without a sound. A sign of the oils' presence, but the men were loud enough with the shuffling of their feet.

The place was one chamber. There were no back rooms, and no doors that led anywhere else. The inside had a dark ambience about it. Each of the braziers on the walls flickered with green flame. The floor had a brown rug that traveled from the entrance to the stage at the opposite end. On each side of the rug, there were five pews that could seat about three people each. On the stage, there was a narrow altar that was made of steel like the rest of the place.

At the back of the stage, there was an eight-foot-tall metal statue that had been shaped, welded, and constructed to accurately resemble the Salamander God. It was a serpentine creature, but it had a humanoid-like torso. It had arms that held a greatsword, and a long head with wiry whiskers coming from under a pointy nose. From the back of the torso and to the end of its long tail, there were spines that made the thing look even more menacing.

The church was empty save for the visitors and the three priests that were currently working this day. High Solian Morgan was at the altar. He was an older man with a large frame, and he was a mix of odum and aerin lineage. He had loose, curly, salt and pepper hair, and a beard to match. He wore a black robe trimmed with green, and upon the left breast of the robe, Sol's holy symbol was sewn on. It was a green triangle with the design of a black flame in the shape.

The High Solian priest eagerly waited for his appointment with the men.

Off to the side was Cleric Mitch. He was an aerin man, and seeing as he was the youngest of the priests, he was busy applying oil to the statue. Standing to the side of the High Solian was Cleric Landar. He was also an aerin man, but his age was somewhere in the 30s. Both of the younger priests wore black robes without any trimming or symbols, and they had belts on the outside of their robes with maces hooked to them.

Lars, Sirus, and Kendo walked down the center aisle between the rows of pews. They approached the altar; Morgan wasted no time in beginning his service. Henrick, however, took a seat at the first pew near the door on the left.

Morgan spoke aloud with a deep and confident voice, "What manner of deed brings you before the gaze of the Salamander? In what manner do you believe that the Fire God should spend his blessings on you?"

Kendo spoke first, "We are here to gain Sol's blessing for the coming battles." Kendo said.

"We have a new mission: to slay magicians in defense of the kingdom," Lars followed.

"Our wish is to find glory and victory on the battlefield," Sirus finished.

Morgan replied, "To kill a magician is no easy task. Very well. A blessing I shall grant you. For *He* revels in the victories to come. And should you die on the fields of battle, *He* shall welcome you to the City of Brime."

The *City of Brime* was a fabled city made completely of copper on the plane of *Kor Magnus*, and Kor Magnus was the place in which patrons of Sol would go to find their eternal rest.

Morgan concluded with, "Now join me in a moment of meditation, and steal yourselves for the coming confrontations."

Like all the previous times Henrick had been here, Cleric Landar would always approach him, and this time would be no different. Even now, the man of average build tried to sneak through the shadows as he made his way towards the entrance, but Henrick already saw and expected the priest. Cleric Landar has been working at the church for as long as Henrick has been serving in the army, and each time the two came into contact with the other, Landar gave Henrick a short interrogation.

"It's been a while, Henrick." Landar greeted in a whispered voice as he took a seat across the aisle.

"Landar," Henrick acknowledged the priest with a whispered voice but never looked.

"Sol favors you; you know. Becoming one of the best ten fighters in the army of so many is no small feat," Landar complemented. "Will you not join your fellows at the altar and *revel* in this moment?"

"Ye never skip a beat," Henrick said nonchalantly. "If Sol favors me so much as a warrior, then he should understand why I don't bow before 'em. Besides, ye know I'm not the religious type in the first place."

"But why? Why not stand outside if it is so? Something must be bringing you in here?" the priest argued.

"I'll not argue that I like fightin', but the thing that brings me in here is to wait fer my friends to be done." Henrick said.

"The more you deny Sol, the closer you come to losing a battle, and losing your life." Landar proclaimed as if his words were etched in stone somewhere.

"Ye want to speak of favor?" Henrick finally put his gaze upon the cleric. "What kind of war-god needs a church?"

Henrick's statement cut through the air and made the cleric sit up a little straighter. Landar then got up and walked away with agitation in his steps. Henrick was glad to be rid of the cleric's attempt at conversion, but as the patient soldier relaxed in his seat again, he found his gaze upon the statue of the Salamander. Henrick spotted a glint in the eyes of the metallic statue, but after a few blinks it was gone. His curiosity made him scan around the church for the source of such a trick, but in the end, he couldn't find an explanation.

The sermon then came to a conclusion. The four men gathered outside, each of them filled with a renewed motivation to move on with their mission. Even Henrick felt that, but that was because he broke the cleric's demeanor.

With their time at the Brew and Brand, and their journey through town, the sun had descended by a couple hours as the light of day was well into the afternoon. With preparation still to be had, they decided to head back to the barracks. They continued their way west towards the Sword Gate, but they stopped short when they noticed that one of them was headed in the opposite direction.

"Henrick. Where you headed?" Sirus asked.

"I'm gonna stop by the park, I'll meet ye guys later." He replied.

With shrugs and nods, the men went their ways. Henrick crossed the Rose Bridge, and as soon as he was able to, he turned left. He found the first paved walkway that entered the park, and took it. The walkway then came to a fork that led left and right. He chose the left path, and in this direction, the walkway ran along the bank of the pond in the park.

This pond was also man-made, but it was not connected to the stream or the aqueducts, and it was actually created to look more natural. As he traced along the bank, he took in the sight of the small fish that could be seen in the crystal-clear water. After a couple minutes, the walkway became the divider between the pond and the large grassy field. Eventually, the walkway took him away from the pond, and as it did, the side that was not open to the field was lined with countless bushes of red roses.

A short distance later, he began looking for a bench to sit on, but many were already being occupied. During his search, he found something that he really did not want to find. It was a chocolate-colored tabby sneaking around the base of the flora. He continued on his way, and paid the gazing cat no mind as he did not want any feline attention. His quest for a place to sit had taken him a little longer than it normally did, but he found one that was empty, and after sitting down he followed it with a deep sigh.

"Big day." Henrick whispered to himself, reflecting on the opportunity that was presented to him today. He was ready, he told himself. In his mind, he was already there. Charging through flames to kill the enemies of Claymore.

Strangely enough, the lands had been peaceful since he joined the army. He came to Claymore approximately nine years ago, and became a citizen by working as a serf to House Darkbane, then five years ago he joined the army with recommendations from the female-led royal house. He joined the army to be able to fight battles, and only now, after so much training and watchstanding, does he get to do it. The excitement, and the suspense of it all were almost surreal to him at this moment.

Then he thought back to the conversation at the Brew and Brand. Could there really be a witch in Claymoran lands? Slippery enough to escape the blade of Captain Thor Spearfall? He relished the thought of doing battle with a challenging foe. And he couldn't wait.

Hours passed by as Henrick enjoyed the scenery of the park and all people doing their activities. The sun had become significantly lower in the late afternoon, and the shadow cast by the inner walls behind him brought a familiar chill with it. As the shadows began to deepen, Henrick began playing with the thought of returning to the barracks, but then something caught his attention.

It was an aerin woman, with brown locks of unkempt and wild hair that came down to the middle of her back. She had emerald green eyes, and golden skin that was bathed by the sun. She wore a suit of leather armor, and from the skin that was visible on her arms, she had seen her share of combat. While the sway of her physique attracted Henrick's male attention, his attention to detail couldn't ignore the fact that he had never seen her before in the city.

As she walked by, the two locked eyes for a second, and during this, Henrick felt an unusual thump from his chest. Suspicion was sinking in. She attempted to casually continue her way by, but was interrupted.

"Pardon me," Henrick beckoned. She turned to regard him. "Would ye mind sittin' with me?" He waved his hand toward the empty space on the bench. "I've just...never seen ye before."

She humored the man by sitting down. She then offered her hand to him. "I'm Serena."

Henrick took her hand for the shake. "The name's Henrick Skullbright." Her hand seemed soft compared to his, but they were far from delicate. He could feel a coolness from her skin, and he thought it was probably from the late afternoon air, but he noticed her hands held scars.

"*Skull bright*? That's not an aerin name, is it?"

"It's dwarven," he stated. "I was raised up north."

"Ah. That explains the accent" she concluded. "Did you grow up inside the mountain?"

"Not quite. There's a village at the base o' the mountains called Shalestone."

"I see. Well then, Henrick," she began. " I've actually lived in these parts for a while, but I don't frequent the city much."

His gaze came upon the scars on her arm again, "Are ye a mercenary of some kind?"

She brought her own eyes upon her arms, and replied with, "Oh no, you could say that I'm a hunter, but only if the game is big enough."

Henrick spoke with a cool smile, "Very nice. I respect takin' down giant beasts. I've not had that pleasure meself, but I assume they can be quite unpredictable."

"You have no idea," she returned the smile, but there was a hint of a hidden meaning in her words, but she was glad that this soldier did not pick up on it. "Do you come through the park often?"

"Aye, it gets me-" Henrick began but he was cut short by a call in the field.

"Sergeant Skullbright!" a voice came from across the field. It was a voice that both Henrick and Serena recognized.

And with that Serena stood from the bench quickly, "It looks like you spoke too soon."

Henrick and Serena stood up from the bench. The warrior took two steps forward as he tried to identify where the call was coming from. He then made a quick glance back at Serena, but she was gone. It was like she had vanished. He suddenly looked up and down the walkways, and the field to see if he could spot her. He could clearly make out the other citizens in the area, but there was no Serena. He had to wonder how she did that.

The source of the voice then spotted its quarry, and called once again, but with a raised hand this time, "Sergeant, over here!"

Henrick could clearly see that it was Captain Spearfall shouting for him. Henrick came away from the bench to stand before the large captain of 35 years. He was muscle-bulky, and wore his chainmail like it was a second skin. Despite the many battles and kills the man had under his belt, he did not wear a single scar on his body.

50

Once before the captain, Henrick came to attention and saluted, "Aye, sir."

"Henrick, no more courtesies from now on. You're on my squad." Spearfall declared pointing to himself with a thumb.

"Sir, uh, right." He dropped the salute and came out of attention.

"Come with me, and let's talk." The two began walking north towards the nearest gate on the inner wall that led to the keep. They traversed through the grassy field in Rose Park. "The reason I have personally come to get you is of most importance. This is my briefing to you. A scout returned home no more than an hour ago, and reported to the King that a witch was sighted to the east, near the edge of the Kadavari Wastes."

"Pardon for askin', sir, but is this the same witch from Rok's Watch?" Henrick asked.

"Unfortunately, there is no way of telling until we get there, but the description matches." The captain answered. "We are going to meet with His Majesty early in the morning to begin our trek to the east. I've already informed the others for the most part, we are to travel light, and maintain mobility. Bring food and tools for survival only, and that's it."

The serious tone from Spearfall was filling Henrick with a great amount of pride, because he was about to embark on the greatest journey of his life to do battle with the enemy, and a fierce one at that. The captain supplied his subordinate with a few more details about what is to be expected on the road, and probably during the encounter.

As they talked, the officer guided their journey to the *Rose Gate*. Before they could enter the inner city,

Spearfall mentioned that he was heading to the keep to meet with General Hormac and King Marc Blade-Briar to discuss any loose details. He also advised Henrick that he should go on to the barracks, and prepare for tomorrow.

Henrick departed Spearfall's side and went on to the barracks. He followed the road through the inner part of town south, and this took him between the keep and the barracks.

The entrances to each barracks were on the narrower sides of the structures. As with the layout of the city, each barracks was identified by what brigade was housed inside. That same color could be found on the roof tiles, and on the framing of the entrances and windows. The barracks that Henrick stayed in was the building that sported yellow.

He went inside his barracks. Once he was at his bunk, he began to stuff his backpack with all the survival items that were standard issue for the army: a bedroll, a mess kit, a small tent, a tinderbox, a peening hammer, a handaxe, a waterskin, and a coil of rope. Just as he did earlier in the morning, Henrick went about his prepping as quietly as possible.

Some of the other Gold Brigade soldiers were sleeping, some were off to the side playing dice or chess on top of their mattresses. At the eastern end of the building, he could see Sirus and Kendo gathered around Lars and his bunk. Henrick was out of earshot from them, but he could imagine they were talking about slaying the witch or something of that nature. All of them seemed motivated in their quiet deliberation. Henrick felt the same way, and he couldn't wait to start.

Before long, he was done packing, and soon made his way to sleep.

Morning came, but this day was not as grand as the previous. It was cloudy, and the clouds were a hazy gray. The water had already begun to sprinkle a bit by the time the recruited men and women mustered with Captain Spearfall before the keep. They were organized by two ranks and five warriors abreast. Henrick and his friends were four of the warriors that stood in the rearward rank. The captain took a quiet and visual account of the soldiers to assure that none were absent, for he would not stand for it.

Henrick, as well as the others, looked at the keep as they stood before the large iron doors. Above the doors, and hanging from hooks upon the second-floor wall was the flag of Claymore. It was a black flag with a red stripe down the middle, and inside the red stripe was the design of a sword with the tip of the blade pointing downward.

Everyone's eyes then fell upon the captain as he began to speak, "Alright, listen up. For some of you this will be your first time seeing your king. You will be respectful. His Majesty has the throne because he defeated the other three houses in combat. Lack of respect could be met with a challenge under the *First Law*. Do not forget that because he will win."

The First Law, in short, was Claymore's justice system. Every citizen had the right to invoke ritual, honorable combat against any person who they believed to have wronged them or another. The ritual had to be done before a city official, or an officer of the army, in order to maintain the ethical judgment of honor, otherwise killing someone outside of the ritual was considered murder.

As the idea of the First Law filled the minds of the warriors, the captain continued, "I needn't remind you that you *ten* are the best we've got for the job at hand. Once the king is done with us, we make for the west gate and depart immediately. We got a witch to hunt. And – "

Spearfall was then cut short at the sound of trumpets. The sound came from inside the main hall of the keep. The large, iron double-doors heaved open with a resounding clank, and the King of Claymore, Marc Blade-Briar stepped out from the portal, and right behind him to his left, was General Hormac. Both of them walked with no guards to their side, no protection at all, for these two men didn't need it. Their gait exuded an air of leadership and fierceness.

Before the king and the general could stand before Spearfall, the captain called, "Attention to His Majesty." He, and the ten warriors standing behind him, came to the erect military stance.

"Come to ease, soldiers." King Blade-Briar commanded. "Gather 'round me, now. Courtesy is not necessary. Not now." The warriors broke ranks, and gathered near the king in a half-circle to listen to his words. "I can't stress the importance of your task. My belief is that this witch is the same one from Rok's Watch, and we've found her hiding spot. You *are* the eleven best soldiers in my military, so do not disappoint me." His tone of voice rang with unbridled confidence and it was inspiring, but at the same time, it was serious and intimidating.

The warriors were enamored by the king's strong appearance. He was a white haired aerin man of about 55 years. He wore a steel tiara on his head, the center above his brow held a diamond-shaped ruby, and the bands were intricately detailed to look like swords wrapping around the head with the hilts meeting the ruby. He wore the *Flamemail*, the burnt red-metal suit of chainmail that had been worn by every monarch before him since the days of Samuel Blade-Briar. He carried the royal flamberge over the red cloak on his back, and even in his older stage of life, he was still perhaps the strongest man in Claymore. The king looked more menacing than anything else, and because of that, none of the king's words escaped the ears of the warriors before him.

"I expect each, and every one of you, to do what is necessary to ensure the safety of the people here at home, including my own life. Don't stick around any longer than is required to get the job done. Understand?"

A vocal, "Yes, sire!" came from all the soldiers of the group.

Henrick, in that moment, glimpsed something. He was staring at the king like everyone else. He thought his eyes must be betraying him, but in the fraction of a second, it appeared as though the king was engulfed by a dark shroud, almost like smoke or mist was bleeding off his body. Just as quickly as it had appeared, it was gone, and he began to feel dizzy and reeled back.

Lars spotted the peculiar movement, and caught Henrick before he could fall backwards. "You okay, man?" he asked as he held Henrick by the arm to keep him from hitting the ground.

"Aye, I think I just need some water," Henrick replied.

The king stepped forward to regard Henrick, personally. "Do not let the stress of the mission deter you from survival, Sergeant." The king then regarded the group. "That goes for everyone."

Another round of, "Yes, sire," came about.

"You all are dismissed," commanded the King. The warriors came back to attention as the king and the general departed for the keep doors.

As soon as he was gone from sight, the warriors came out from their erect pose, and looked upon their commanding officer for the mission. "Alright, gather 'round. Meet at the west gate in an hour. Our horses should be ready, and we can get this hunt going. Anything else?"

Kendo raised his hand. Everyone regarded the large man as he began the popular Claymoran Army phrase, "We bring the fight..."

Everyone else finished, "...every day and every night!"

CHAPTER THREE
WHISPERS IN THE KEEP

The torches in the dimly lit dungeon flickered as air wafted throughout the space. It was a sign that the entrance door from above had become open. The place reeked of urine, defecation, spoiled food, and rats. It was a place where people of interest were kept for interrogation, for not even common criminals were fortunate enough to make it to this dark hole of suffering.

The clanking of the dungeon door closing echoed off the walls, and the sound of footfalls followed behind it. The creature descending the stone stairway was black, completely black. His clothing, his skin, even the peculiar vapor emanating from his body was black, but in this foul place it would be hard for anyone to see it. The dark humanoid's eyes glowed white with malice and hatred. When the creature took its first step into the dungeon hallway, the torches among the walls suddenly went out.

The five prisoners slunk away from the barred windows of their respective cell doors. This was not the first time these people have felt the presence from this dark wanderer. Each of them quivered in fear, their whimpers just barely leaving their lips. Fortunately, they would be spared from the necrotic torture this day.

To this end, the prisoners welcomed the sight of the usual guardsman that checks up on them, and no matter how many times they complain about their mysterious visitor to these guards, it only paints a picture of insanity. So, they become ignored.

The shadowy figure walked to the rear of the dungeon, which fashioned two prison cells. The left one held a dryad prisoner while the one on the right was empty, and nearly clean, comparatively. The dark humanoid went to the vacant cell on the right, and walked inside, closing the door behind him.

At the back of the cell, he ran his night vision eyes to the center point where his hands would also find the camouflaged stone button. He pushed against the rocky mechanism with both hands. To the right of the dark one, on the adjacent wall, a hidden passageway was revealed.

The passageway traveled a few yards forward, and then it took a bend to the left for another few yards before arriving at a small stone room. The room had only two furnishings in it; a pedestal in the center, and a mundane cabinet off in a corner.

The dark humanoid entered, and went straight for the pedestal. Its attention was focused on it, and paid the other decoration no mind. He took a deep breath, and began to cast a spell upon the darkened crystal ball that was displayed upon the surface.

"Insuno vox transitum, Umbra Hadara," the white-eyed creature muttered in the draconic tongue. The verbal components of the spell were perfect, and the hand movements fulfilled the somatic requirements. With the spell complete, the dark orb began to glow inside with swirling clouds of purple.

"Umbra Hadara, can you hear me?" the creature spoke again, but this time it was in the gibbering tongue of Abyss.

A suspenseful moment filled the air, but it was soon over when a voice, in the same abyssal language, came from the sphere, "Scarm, why do you contact me? It is, too, early."

"Indeed, Umbra," Scarm replied with bearing. "But I have come to notify you."

"Of what?"

"A gathering of humans is heading for the Shelf," the shadowy figure explained. It brought a moment of silence from the voice inside the crystal, which urged Scarm to continue. "Are your assassins still in the nearby swamp?"

"I am not going to divert their task for a scouting party," the voice of Hadara came in, but his tone was of disinterest.

"It is not just a scouting party, Umbra. It is the one known as Spearfall that I have relayed in my previous reports. And in his company, he has ten of this city's *greatest warriors*."

There was another silent moment, but Hadara eventually answered, "I will inform my men, and let them make the decision. Do not forget, we have the Black Lotus to deal with as well. They also pose a threat to us in the coming battle."

Scarm suggested, "If they are such a threat, why not let me conjure a nightwalker among them, and this city. Be done with both."

"You will do no such thing, Anima Scarm," Hadara ordered. The Umbra continued after a brief moment, "Be mindful that Planesgate has an eye on Claymore, to use magic of that magnitude would warrant their investigation and response. If Sanguinar is to become ours once again we must do this...strategically."

"Fine. What of Lumen, and Skyreach?" Scarm asked.

"Your place is there, Anima. Don't worry about anyone else, but yourself," the demeaning tone almost infuriated Scarm at that moment.

Suddenly, the crystal ball lost its glow, and returned to its idle state.

Scarm would have to wait another week before it could fully recharge itself in the darkness. He stood there, his palms now on the surface of the pedestal, lurching over slightly, and angrily keeping himself calm.

"Perhaps you should wear the mask, Umbra. Discover your own anxiety in resisting the urge to kill these blood bags," Scarm muttered to himself.

Since taking on his current assignment nearly a decade ago, Scarm had grown impatient, and resentful. Even with his heightened anxiety, the only thing that kept him going was his own agenda. Once this charade was all said and done, he would kill Umbra Hadara, and take his rank. Those were the rules of ascension among his kind, but equally, his hatred for his commander was white-hot like the glow of his eyes.

Scarm was then brought out of his reflective stupor, and his attention was immediately drawn to the waft of air that pushed into the small room. The familiar sound of the dungeon door echoed through the dungeon once again. The anima silently moved back into the secret passage, and peered his eyes into the dungeon's hallway through the cell door's window.

It was a Claymore guard, torch in hand, stepping down into the dungeon. He walked to the first cell on his left. Scarm could see the prisoner's hands holding on to the bars of the small window. Scarm could hear the whispers of the prisoner, but could not make out the words. When it seemed like the guard did not care about the hushed statement, the hands reached out.

"Get back in there, scum," the guard demanded while swatting at the filthy hands. The prisoner regressed back into its soiled home. The guard proceeded further into the dungeon, but stopped short when his torch suddenly went out. "Hmm? Stupid torch," the guard cursed.

The now-blind guard used his memory of the dungeon layout to turn back, and head for the exit. Anima Scarm watched the guard intently, and as soon as guard's disadvantage came to mind, the dark humanoid's homicidal tendencies flooded in.

Scarm emerged from the secret passageway, and pushed in the large stone button. The door activated to close, and the sound of stone sliding on a poorly oiled track was enough to arouse the attention of blind guard. The guard scrambled as he hastened his search for the first step, and drew his sword. The guard still could not see, and for some reason, he had not found the stairs yet. Adrenaline and fear took over the human's brain when the sound of a cell door opened, and then closed with a smack of enthusiasm. Scarm drank the fear building in the human. His psychotic lust became unchained. The dark humanoid felt giddy, and aroused by the murderous deed he was about to commit.

"Digitus Mortis," came the draconic words from Scarm as he pointed his hands at the guard.

A streak of black lightning shot forth; sparks of white energy sizzled as the spell cut through the air. The dark magic struck the blind guard in the back. The electricity tore through the man's armor, and he could feel his life force evaporating like boiling water. The human fell to the floor, dead, dropping his sword and torch to the ground with a clank. His limp head crashing against the corner of the first step of the stairs. Hushed bellows came from the cells of the prisoners.

With the corpse on the ground, Scarm retrieved the soldier's boot knife, and proceeded to stab repeatedly where his dark magic had struck. He then dropped the knife on the floor, and walked over to the nearest prison cell. The dark humanoid used a minor spell to unlock the door, and then opened it.

"You are free to go," he told the prisoner in the common tongue of aerinese. The shadowy man then ascended the stairway, and exited the dungeon.

A long minute passed before the broken-minded dryad realized that its cell door was open, and the dark creature was gone. It stepped from the prison cell and saw a crack of light from above where the dungeon door was left open. A moment later, the prisoner was gone.

CHAPTER FOUR
A SHADOW IN SKYREACH

The dark-skinned giant of a man took the stance known as *Cova's Maw* as he stood before the wooden practice dummy. One by one, he would slowly jab and punch at the wooden dummy, and occasionally he would weave his attacks between the three pegs protruding from the face of the dummy's body.

Sometimes, instead of punching, he would slap the pegs with open hands in an upward motion as if deflecting an imagined attack. As he rounded out his routine, his pace would quicken, but just as soon as he became lightning quick, he would slow back down so that he could maintain control, and focus.

His practice took all of his attention, and he paid little mind to the diminishing sunlight that shimmered across the cloudscape. The sun was not so easily forgotten high atop the Skyreach, the tallest mountain on Golterran, but its presence and warm rays did nothing to beckon the monk.

After a few more rounds of his fighting routine, he decided to take a break. To his left and right, many other wooden dummies stood along the stone tile walkways. Behind him was a small handmade pond with a large boulder sitting at the center. The man decided to go right. The tiled walkway formed a square around this pond. On two sides, there were the practice dummies, another side had a neat, and well cared for flower garden. On the fourth side, there was a clearing that led to the edge of a cliff. To this effect, it was a natural balcony of sorts where benches had been made so that anyone sitting could overlook the landscape below. In the corner of the walkway where the balcony met a side with dummies, there was another walkway that led back to the temple.

The muscle-bound man walked to the balcony with calm and measured strides. The bare feet of the 275-pound man were as silent as the gentle breeze that blew by.

The man walked by the benches, and stood before a short wall made of cobblestones that ran the border of the balcony. The wall served as a means of warning since the edge of the mountain was only five feet away. He focused his eyes on the world that lay beneath the altocumulus clouds. Through the cloud breaks, he could see the treetops of a vast forest known as the *Viridian Shade*.

The odum man then sat upon a nearby bench, but then returned his facing towards the open sky. As the man sat there, he allowed his body to calm down, and he turned his mind to his next form of practice.

He raised his right hand with an open palm facing upward before his face. He closed his eyes, and focused on the elements around him, and more specifically, the water elements. His mind reached out to the clouds, the pond that lay behind him, the sweat running down his body, and whatever molecules may be floating on by in the breeze.

As the man began to open his eyes, he could see the water particles come together in a dance of swirls to form a small orb of blue glowing energy that floated above his hand. This icy magic power was the signature technique of the *Uireb Nen*, the ancient martial arts of the dryashu, the ash dryads. And as he had been told many times by his master, he was the only half-dryad in all of Terra that knew how to use it.

Some time had passed as he continued to maintain his concentration on the small bit of energy he had summoned. The two moons of Terra, *Undine* and *Nielda*, began to show themselves as the light of the sun continued to fade away, and as the sky turned to twilight, the man soon found himself in a lull, and then his mind had gone elsewhere.

"*Yobo*," the voice called out to the man by name.

The man was not a man; he was a boy. He was paralyzed in the shadow of a giant overlooking the broken bodies of his father and mother. He could only see black and white and red. He was slumped over on the floor, in the entryway of his house, and couldn't move because his fear wouldn't let him.

"*Yobo*," the voice echoed again.

The boy's eyes managed to watch as the shadow carried a child out the door. It was the boy's sister, but there was nothing the boy could do against the demonic red eyes of the giant. The giant was soon gone, and the silence of his house would begin to haunt him.

"*Yobo*," the voice came a third time.

When the man came out of his disturbance, the blue energy became chaotic in an instant and soon exploded into a puff of icy mist. The man soon had his wits again, and noticed someone standing to his side with a hand on his shoulder.

"Yobo," the visitor called a fourth time.

The man, Yobo, looked to face his teacher, mentor, and master. He was a dryanix, a snow dryad. He had a pointed flare at the top of his ears, he was much leaner, and shorter than Yobo was. The dryad was shaved bald, but he had a long white goatee. His skin had woody textures, and his flesh resembled color tones that were close to a yellowheart.

"Master Asulus," Yobo called him by name and then followed by speaking in feylic. "I did not feel your approach."

"Lost in thought again?" the teacher asked, continuing the conversation in feylic.

"Yes," was Yobo's response.

Master Asulus came to sit on the bench beside Yobo, and then said, "Yobo. You have been atop this mountain for a very long time. More than a decade now. Through the Uireb Nen I believe that you have gained much strength in body and mind. I have noticed shivers in your walk, and this tells me your past has returned to your eyes."

Yobo could only lower his head to the sentiment, a weight of disappointment washed over him in that moment, but Master Asulus was not blind to the body language.

"Do not bother your mind with doubt," the master continued. "This means that there is little more I can teach you." On that note, Master Asulus stood back up before returning to the tiled walkways. "See me back to the temple," Master Asulus requested.

Yobo joined his Master. Side by side, Yobo was close to two feet taller than his master. The two of them headed towards the abode in which they called home.

"I have been waiting for the moment to tell you this, Yobo," Master Asulus began. "And it would seem that the time has come for you to expand on your knowledge of the Uireb Nen." The master took a moment of reflection before continuing. "We have taught you the ways of the ancient dryashu that has survived for countless generations. You know our techniques, and have done well sparring against the other students. However, the application of knowledge into power is something that you have yet to experience."

Yobo remained silent, and focused on soaking in all that his mentor had to say.

Master Asulus continued, "In the lore of the dryashu Uireb Nen, there were monks known as the *Gunn Drambor*."

"What is the Gunn Drambor?" Yobo asked.

"In translation from the old tongue, the term means *angry dragon*." Asulus answered, and then there was a pause. "They were monks meant to harness the Uireb Nen with anger and hatred rather than discipline. As the last Gunn Drambor, I have been training you to take my place."

Yobo's demeanor of sincere interest turned grim, and it actually caused the young man to stop in his tracks. Anger and hatred did not sound anything like his master. The entire time he had known Asulus, he was always kind and happy. Sure, there were moments where he had to be stern with the tall man, but it never became a situation of extreme emotion. The words took Yobo by surprise, and he had to wonder just what anger and hatred the small dryad held inside.

Master Asulus took a few steps ahead of his student before stopping himself.

"*Take your place, master*?" Yobo questioned.

Master Asulus scoffed at the notion with a happy smirk, "Hah. I am 173-years-old, Yobo. My time is drawing near, and time is what keeps all living creatures in check."

With his master's joyful tone, Yobo relaxed a bit. The two of them continued on their walk home.

"Tomorrow, you will start your trials to become the Gunn Drambor," Master Asulus proclaimed. "But I will warn you, Yobo, the center of power for the Gunn Drambor is pain. Similar to the pain that you carry now. The trials will take you to the darker parts of your mind. And it will expose you to elements that thrive on your pain. If you can master your pain, and harness what is in your heart, you will become a being of unconquerable fury. However, as you have mastered the basics of the Uireb Nen, heritage dictates that you must discover your missing knowledge on your own."

By this time, the master and apprentice had arrived at the doorstep of their homestead. It was a large and wide, single story, wooden building of octagonal shape. The place was painted in olive green, and trimmed with a deep purple. At the doorstep, there was another dryad that sat in a chair, and quietly observed the two approaching while also remaining observant of the area within sight. The entrance to the place also had lanterns hung from hooks at both sides of the doorway.

Master Asulus and Yobo came to regard each other at the end of their walk.

"In preparation for your trials, I want you to take a moment, and test your limits with *Hesin's Cure*," Master Asulus advised. "And not that little snowball you made earlier. You're going to be a Gunn Drambor. Let your past empower you."

"Yes, Master," Yobo said with bearing, although he really wasn't thrilled thinking about his past.

The two departed. Master Asulus went inside the wooden structure referred to as the temple, and Yobo made his return to the training grounds. During his trek back, the odum monk took note of how dark it had become. The stars were out, and the skies were clear enough that with the naked eye the Scarlet Tear could be seen. It was an enormous cosmic field of red gas, but to the people of Terra who believed in the *Beginning of Time*, it was said to be the grave site of the first star destroyed by Yamino.

The Scarlet Tear was not the only sight to be enjoyed this evening, the two moons of Terra were also out. Undine was a moon of bluish hue, currently beginning her third quarter, and in her waning gibbous phase was Nielda, a moon of lavender.

The moons are said to be of identical size, and thus they are the perfect representations of the Twin Goddesses of the same names.

To have the Twin Goddesses as his audience, Yobo almost felt invigorated by their soft glowing light. By some measure of imagination, the large odum man thought that he should try to make sure that Undine, the Goddess of Water, would be pleased with his ice magic.

Once Yobo took his first steps back onto the training grounds around the pond, he took a moment to formulate what he was about to do. He knew that to push the Hesin's Cure farther than he ever did, the spell would require a lot of water to pull off, and with that information at hand, he decided the best place to try and conduct this was atop the giant rock in the middle of the pond.

The man made no splashing sounds as he calculated his steps through the cold water, but after a short moment, Yobo arrived at his destination and climbed atop the boulder. In all the time that he had spent in these training grounds, he had never once taken a step into or through the pond, because before this point he had never needed to.

Looking down upon the surface of this boulder, he found it surprising that there would be enough room for him to take the stance required for Hesin's Cure. Beyond the surface of the giant stone, Yobo looked below to the water beneath him, but in that moment, an idea flashed before him, and soon he turned to regard the cloudy, moonlit sky beyond the cliff edge.

How much water did the clouds hold? He thought as he looked out at the horizon, but it didn't matter to him in the grand scheme of things. He was going to start his trials to become a master of the Uireb Nen. In his mind, he needed to put everything he had into the spell.

Yobo took the stance that he needed: feet and legs were low and wide, his left arm and palm stretched in front of his body while facing the stars, his right arm and hand tucked at the side of his torso with palm aiming at the space above his left hand.

This was *Cova's Maw*, the basic stance of the Uireb Nen, but this was also the somatic component required to increase the power of Hesin's Cure, just as it was designed to.

Yobo closed his eyes for a moment to center his mental energy for the task at hand. The man did not burden himself with the ideas about the Gunn Drambor, and sold himself on the premise that the only thing that needed to happen tonight was Hesin's Cure.

When he felt ready, the monk opened his eyes, and began to use his knowledge of the Uireb Nen, and started to collect elemental energy into a small, glowing, blue sphere just like before. This time, however, the Cova's Maw was put into action, and in no time at all the sphere had grown in size by four times.

At this point, this was the limit Yobo had been taught with this spell. He had done it countless times, and to get the icy spell to this point was no chore to him. Unlike before though, this time he needed to make it even more powerful, and for that he needed more water. Yobo reached out with his mind and his feelings to the resources around him, both near and far. He felt as though he was performing the new ritual correctly, but the elements did not want to obey him.

A very strong breeze suddenly enveloped Yobo during his concentration as if nature itself was telling him *no* in defiance. The man continued his search for the key that would drive the elements to his cause. For a long moment, however, the elements would not come. Fear of doubt and failure began to seep into the cracks of his mental shell as he attempted again and again to gain the power he needed to test his limits. Those emotions took the wheel, and took his mind elsewhere.

"Piss-eye." An echo of a negative memory rang in Yobo's mind. He was a boy. He bumped into a stranger as he darted through town. The stranger could only offer a racial slur to someone of half-dryad descent. Someone with yellowish eyes like the Yobo's.

The Hesin's Cure energy flickered in a flash due to the disturbance, but the monk maintained his concentration against the new threat of his post traumatic reminiscence. Now, he had a battle from the inside, as well as the outside.

"Your parents had it coming, boy." In the man's mind, he could almost see the giant shadow again, talking to him from the other side of the training grounds. The shadow's words were burned into memory. Words that would never be forgotten.

Yobo's memory flashed. He felt the giant silhouette kicking him square in the face, and being left limp on the ground to grasp for his parents' corpses as his face swelled up. The events of that day still felt fresh. The monk's topaz yellow eyes grew narrow, and his brows furled. His teeth gritted and his muscle became tight against the vivid replay for he knew what the giant would say next. The beast held his young sister over the shoulder, the giant padded her unconscious body on the butt with his enormous blue hands and said, *And don't worry about her, she'll feel great when she gets older.*

Beyond the Hesin's Cure in his hands, Yobo could not see the rest of the training grounds. Everything had disappeared into a featureless landscape. This memory had not surfaced so intensely before, or at least not since he was adopted by Master Asulus. Yobo's breathing soon turned to angry grunting, and his chest puffed every time he drew in breath

The half-dryad monk's breath came out as steam as the temperature around the pond, and the training ground dropped significantly.

Yobo then turned to regard the echoing words of the giant shadow, and it was like he could see it in the corner by the training dummies. The monk was not the small insect of a boy he used to be. Now, he was trained in the Uireb Nen, and in his hands he had the key to salvation from this foe.

Not too far away, Master Asulus, and the other monks who called the Skyreach their home, watched from outside the doorway as Yobo began to surpass limits that not even the other students thought was possible.

It soon became difficult to see anything at all as a strange fog rolled in. The monks that had lived here the longest had never seen fog atop the Skyreach before.

Master Asulus, however, knew exactly what was happening.

———————— ◯ ————————

From all around the mountain of Skyreach, the clouds that spanned the skies were drawn to the top. The pond that surrounded the large boulder became weightless as thousands of water droplets hovered in suspended animation before being forced into the Hesin's Cure made by Yobo.

The simple brown saam that Yobo wore did not offer much protection against the biting and stinging cold that hung in the air. As the Hesin's Cure technique grew to almost twenty times the size, the monk had to elevate his hand to make sure there was room for it, and the soft blue glow was transforming into an intense bright white.

Cyclones of water and snow swirled around the giant globe of magic, but it would not be for much longer. Yobo could sense the height of the spell's formation reaching its peak. The monk then felt himself return to reality with a clear mind, as if the spell pulled all the negative energy from him. His concentration was now on this overwhelmingly large sphere of icy magic, but to his dismay, he wasn't sure what to do with the spell at this point.

It was at that moment that his eyes fell upon the training dummies nearby. The giant shadow was gone, and with that, his intended target, but it was the only logical choice, he thought. With his coiled right arm, he threw his palm forward, reinforced by the magic of the Uireb Nen, and smacked the giant ball of ice magic. The enormous Hesin's Cure flew at the training dummies, but it all seemed like it was happening in slow motion. And then...

BOOM!

The magical grenade exploded with a sharp cacophony. The release of magical pressure took Yobo off his feet, and off the boulder. He went flying backwards until he came slamming against the floor of the clearing behind him, but his body continued to slide through until he crashed into the short wall. The wall did what it could to warn of the cliff edge, but it was crude and decorative at most. The rocks of the wall broke apart from each other like stony shrapnel as it tried to slow the momentum from the flying human, but it wasn't enough to keep him from rolling right off the cliff.

The training ground became completely encased in ice, from the dummies to the edges of the clearing. The magic was so intense that the ice magic crept its way, albeit slowly, to the doorstep of the monk's home.

"*Master!*" one of the younger monks gasped at the sight of their human companion's departure.

"I saw it," Master Asulus said. "You all stay here. I will check-"

Master Asulus cut his words short as the lamps outside of the citadel suddenly went out. The master monk narrowed his eyes at the peculiar phenomenon. From where they all stood, the temperature had not changed, and the lamp oil was filled every time that the monk's would relieve each other from the door watch.

The cloudscape had returned below the peak of the Skyreach, and the red glow of the morning sun painted the sky above the horizon, but the sun had not risen yet. The clouds mimicked the purples and magentas of the fading night. Splashes of white and gold could be seen at the farthest reaches of the eye.

When the piercing light of rays finally shot across the world below, it brought its warmth upon the face of the monk. From this comforting warmth, he was able to wake up from his inadvertent slumber. Yobo opened his eyes against the blinding light of the sun in his face, and when he did, he could not believe where he was.

He looked around on the surface in which he lay, and he turned his face towards the sky to realize that he was almost thirty feet below from the training grounds. The natural stone that he happened to land on was just big enough for his body to fit on, and the slight slant of it probably stopped him from continuing his rolling flight.

The only thing the monk could make up in his mind was that he was lucky to have not been tossed from the mountain completely, but then he also couldn't have anticipated the release of his magical attack. What a blast it was, he thought.

The monk returned his gaze to the sky, and the orange rays of light soaring across the sky.

"I've been out for a while," Yobo said to himself.

The monk then stood up, and turned to regard the natural stone wall of the mountain face. In his mind, he began to mentally mark footholds in the stone wall, and charted a course to get back up. But as he plotted, a thought had struck him.

If he was down here the whole night, how come no one had come to find him? The thought spun his mind into action. He wanted to hurry up the wall, but was convinced not to rush it because one wrong move could be a much farther fall.

One by one, he moved his hands and feet along the surface of the mountain. Coming off of the platform down below, his climb instantly made it disappear, and then Yobo felt as if it was just him, this mountain, and the open air below.

Instead of giving into fear, he felt some sort of calm as he made his way to the back up, and it was this calm that allowed his calculated movement to become smoother and smoother. It was in no time at all that Yobo had reached the training ground, but as he returned, he remained on his hands and feet.

From the clearing with the benches, the man scanned over the frozen arena. Almost every feature was covered in glossy white ice. The training dummies were shattered and broken from the expended force of the spell. He then glanced at the nearby garden which was blanketed with frost.

Where was everyone? The thought continued to plague his state of mind. It was a normal morning routine for the students to come out and greet the morning sun with a round of meditation, but no one was around. It was eerily quiet. This absence of noise drew Yobo's eyes to the path leading to the temple, and even from where he was at, he could not see anyone sitting outside.

In that short moment, the sun had risen a bit more, and the increasing heat felt like Lumina herself was telling Yobo to move on. And so, he did. Yobo crawled on all-fours as he traversed the icy tiles.

Mysterious vacancy pounded on Yobo's mind as he went. All of the monks would have been awake by now. It had been that way for more than a decade. Of course, he could forgive them if they didn't meditate given the state of the training grounds, but still. Where were they?

As Yobo got closer to the building, he finally stood up as he came clear of the icy ground. When he was on his feet, the monk found something else missing. He could not even smell the vegetable broth that was normally cooked for breakfast, and that was an aroma that permeated across the entirety of the temple grounds.

With all of these indicators missing, Yobo's instincts started to kick in. Master Asulus told him that the trials would start today, and perhaps, he now thought, they had already begun. If that was the case, he would be ready for anything.

Yobo slowed his pace and measured his steps considerably so that he could assess the area around him. On a typical day, the leaves of the many willow trees around the temple would rustle and sway with the wind. There was no wind, the trees rested silently, and the air was quite still.

Yobo continued to inch closer to the doors of the citadel, but he stopped and took another look around to make absolutely sure that he did not miss a detail.

He scanned over the chair that the watchstander usually sat in, and he was hoping a hidden lead might show itself. Nothing jumped at his attention, and there was only a metal striker leaned against one of the legs. He then looked at the lamps around the doorway. They were unlit and probably cold. Yobo got closer to the doors, but he became more worried as he did. In all the time that he has lived on top of the Skyreach, he has never heard or seen the training grounds so silent and empty.

Yobo crept up to the doors of the temple and grabbed the handles. He took a deep breath and then opened them, allowing the sunlight behind him to filter its way in around his huge frame. The brilliant light and its warmth could do nothing to aid Yobo in that moment, and it only showed him the truth of cold reality. The doors opened into a large common chamber with many doors leading into small bedrooms. At the center of the chamber was a hearth with some sitting pallets around it.

That wasn't what Yobo saw, however. He saw every single one of his dryad companions, his friends, and his family torn to pieces. Glistening amber liquid, the blood of dryads, covered the floors and the walls. Some of the dryads were missing limbs while others were garroted or eviscerated. Or all of the above. Green and yellow gore was splashed all around, and the bodies were in such bad shape that he could not make out who was who.

Yobo's breathing became heavy as adrenaline started to pump into his veins as he tried to fight off the emotions building into his eyes. The gold-eyed human measured his steps as he entered the temple in a quiet manner. The thought going through his head now was that the assassin could still be here. The cold substance on the floor clung to the bottom of his feet.

As Yobo made his way through the chamber, he looked down upon his slain family multiple times. Still, he could not tell who was who.

"Aw, man," the man let the trembling words slip out. He fought back his fears. He could sense an echo of his past coming to haunt him, but he had to remain focused. He needed to keep his mind on the task at hand. But every time he would look down at the dead dryads, he could only feel that there was just too much in common with his past, and now, present. The feeling was quickly becoming overwhelming.

Yobo traversed to the first door on the left side. This was his room. He opened the door, and slipped inside once he saw that it was not occupied. In his room, he went next to his sleeping pallet and grabbed his quarterstaff that was leaned up in the corner.

Back out in the common area, Yobo went door to door, and made sure that no one else was inside the citadel. To his relief, whoever did this was no longer around. As that notion settled in, Yobo came out of the last room, and looked upon the devastation that was before him with unblinking eyes. The weight of grief crashed against his demeanor. His eyes began to swell, and then water. He finally slumped against an adjacent wall, and sobbed uncontrollably with his hands over his knees as he tried to keep himself up.

"*Aaah!*" Yobo screamed into the silent rooms of the temple.

The man continued to whimper in sorrow for a long moment. Through the watery shell of tears, he looked around the room attempting to make sense of who was who again. Yobo sought to identify his master, but there was so much carnage that none of the dryads looked unlike the other.

Eventually, he stood up, and began to compose himself. He got his body moving again, and he was reluctant to wipe the moisture from his cheeks. His feet sloshed around the floor as he went room to room to gather supplies. He kept his mind busy with what he was doing, but during his foraging, a thought crossed his mind.

He needed to leave before the dryad death-curse took effect.

The death-curse was one of the things that he learned from Master Asulus, and from his dryad mother when he was still a boy. *Nekratal's Curse*, it was formally called. A curse placed on all of dryad-kind by the God of Undeath which evolved expired dryads into mindless, feral undead. To this effect, all dryads have adopted cremation as a funeral rite.

Then his thoughts went beyond the curse. Beyond the Skyreach and the temple. He realized that he needed to find his way to Telosa, and warn the other dryads of what had happened here. Perhaps, they had some insight on what could have caused this kind of disaster.

Between all the rooms, including his own, he was able to gather a backpack, a water skin, a blanket, a hammer with a piton, a hatchet, and a sack of dried fruit and mixed nuts so he could eat on the road.

When Yobo arrived at Master Asulus's room, he threw the backpack, with all the contents inside, onto the bed. He then sat upon the side of it, and took note of a folded parchment upon the small night stand. The human might have ignored such an item if it did not have his name written on the face. He opened the note, and it was a short list of things, but for what he was not exactly sure.

"Telosa, Snow Fang, Hemagorgon, Suldo's Stand, and Black Lotus," Yobo whispered the list aloud to himself, but of everything that was written, Telosa was the only thing he knew of.

Yobo refolded the note before stowing inside of his backpack. He gathered his items, began heading out of the temple, and returned his face to the shining sunlight of the morning.

On his way out, he thought of the funeral rites in dryad culture, and the man was not about to let his family's memory be tainted with the thought of them roaming the top of the Skyreach as the living dead. He took the two lamps off the nearby walls. He placed one in his backpack, and placed the other on the ground before the open doorway. He then reached for the metal striker that was nearby.

In no time at all, Yobo opened the lamp and ignited it. Judging from the lamp's weight, it still had a full belly of oil. The monk then took a step back while the flame of the lamp was still exposed. He took the stance of Cova's Maw, and used his knowledge of the Hesin's Cure to begin drawing in the fire energy that was being produced by the lamp.

Master Asulus had taught him to fire and water with the Hesin's Cure, but after showing the younger man how to use fire magic, he warned him to never use it unless absolutely necessary. The reasoning was because fire magic has the potential to harm more than the intended target.

To the tall odum man, this was a necessary reason. As the flame drew into a sphere of sweltering fire above his hand, the oil of the lamp was being burned at an alarming rate. As soon as the lamp's fuel ran out, and the flame turned to smoke, Yobo launched his fire-version of the Hesin's Cure into the main chamber of the temple.

The fireball collided with the farthest wall, exploding and igniting most of the large room in an instant. Once the fire had a good blaze going, Yobo grabbed the chair by the doorway, and dragged it off to a safe distance. He sat and watched the blaze as it consumed his master, his family, his friends, and his home. But the fire was consuming more than what was inside the wooden structure. The monk's mind wandered. Just as it had wandered many times before.

Yobo was trapped inside his own turmoil. Why did this have to happen to him? Why again, he asked himself in the silent burning. Why must his family always be taken away from him? Not even the intense flames of the temple could match the hot anger that was building inside of him at that moment. The faces of his parents, his sister, his master, his comrades, they all flashed before his eyes, and then there was nothing but the blaze before him.

It was like the searing heat was a reflection of everything in his life. Everything was always being destroyed. Everything that he cared for was taken away. Again. Images of the giant shadow looming over his dead parents flashed in his eyes as if he was there. He clenched his trembling fists before he snapped to his feet. He was no longer a boy at the mercy of fate. He knew how to fight now. He knew the ways of the Uireb Nen. And his master was right, he was going to use his abilities out of anger and hatred. At that moment, he could feel nothing else, and his anger sought what it needed for freedom.

His emotional state then reached its boiling point.

"*Raah!*" Yobo roared as he twisted, grabbing the chair with both hands, and launched the chair into the roaring fire. His eyes stared out at the blaze, unblinking, and his breathing became heavy as his frustration became unhinged. "I will find them. I will destroy them."

With the roaring fire as his resource, the monk used the Hesin's Cure to draw in more energy, and unleashed it upon the trees nearby, he then made his way down to the training grounds where he continued upon his path of destruction. Laying waste to the training dummies and then eventually to the garden.

"Where are you?" Yobo screamed out.

But there was no response. There was only the sound of cracking and sizzling fire.

Satisfied that his quarry was not on the mountain, Yobo returned to come before the temple. He then stomped off to the left, guiding his strides through the burning trees, and beyond that, Yobo could see the starting point of his descent. It was a natural stone staircase carved into the side of the mountain by the dryads.

Yobo took the first step down. He left flame and smoke and ash in his wake, and he swore that's what he was going to leave once he found the assailants.

He departed the Skyreach, and began his hunt with revenge heavy in his heart.

CHAPTER FIVE
THE WITCH OF THE WILDS

It had been three days since the unit of mage-slayers left Claymore, and for three days, the rain did not yield. During their first day and night, the soldiers stopped in Solace, a small farming village, to rest, and to replace a horse that had begun to limp. In Solace, there was a small army outpost that provided security for the farmers. The usual conflict in this village was the occasional bold predator from the wilderness, and in rare occurrences, orcs from the nearby Yrds would make the extra-long journey to raid and pillage.

After the group had gotten rest and woke up the next morning, they continued the press onward. Based on what the reports had said, the witch of Claymore was spotted near Rok's Watch. The journey from Solace to Rok's was a bit longer as the team had to follow the bank of the Starfall Lake south, and then to the east. The road was also a bit less beaten, which slowed the trot of the horses.

The troops had to spend their second night in their tents, but at least they were kept dry, as opposed to being out in the rain directly.

The soldiers got back up before the first light of the third day. The sunlight over the past few days seemed like a thing that did not exist. The rain never lightened up, but the men and women could only think ahead, because at Rok's Watch was actual shelter for the horses too. With several hours on the road already, they could not wait to arrive.

Captain Spearfall was at the head of the band, Henrick, Sirus, Kendo, and Lars made up the four leading behind their commander. The soldiers formed two ranks of horse riders, with the remaining six behind the four friends.

"Captain, is it true that Rok's is a whole palisade now?" Lars asked their leader.

"Aye, Sergeant," the captain replied while keeping his eyes forward. "After the witch attacked, General Hormac sought to make a few upgrades to the place. The place needed it though, the place was turning into a dump."

The others that could hear the conversation nodded with acknowledgement.

"See for yourself," the commander added.

It was then that the ten soldiers behind Thor looked ahead to see the shadow of Rok's Watch coming up over the horizon. Even with several miles between them and their destination, the warriors could tell the place had become a bit larger.

Rok's Watch was nestled almost two-hundred feet from the bank of Starfall Lake, and on top of a very shallow hill. From this hill, and the newly built watch tower, the watches could see farther into the distance of the surrounding area.

After a moment of quiet trotting, the mage-slayer troops arrived at Rok's Watch.

The walls of this place were about ten feet tall, made of wood, and reinforced with iron hardware. The outpost as a whole was in the shape of an oval with the three-story watchtower in the center.

The metal portcullis was raised by some of the militia that was currently stationed out here, and this allowed the horse riders to come inside the perimeter of the walls. Also, inside the walls of this place were several masonry buildings, five in total, no doubt to provide shelter. The place also had a large stable, and a blacksmith.

As Thor rode by, the many troops regarded him with humbling faces and salutes. Many of them knew the exploits of the man, and felt honored to be in his presence. Thor shot shallow nods at the men as they all shared suffering at the hands of the falling rain.

Thor's troops rode their horses directly into the barn-style stables before dismounting. Their boots came splashing down into the mud below.

"Thor," came the call from the entrance.

The others tried to half-listen while tending to the mounts. The man at the door was clad in a chainmail suit with the Claymore tabard pulled over it. Some of them could see that he wore the same rank as their commander.

"Jaren," Thor came to meet the man with a hefty handshake.

"You're back so soon, and with troops," the tone in Jaren's voice was almost questioning.

"The General sent us out here. Apparently, someone has spotted the witch again," Thor explained.

As the two captains talked, they began to walk out of the stables, and into the rain. It wasn't long before their voices became distant and vague.

"Who was that?" Henrick asked.

"That was Captain Borg," one of the female warriors answered. "He is the commander of this outpost."

"You know him, Launa?" Kendo asked the warrior.

"Aye, I used to be stationed here," Launa replied. "He's a good fighter."

Captain Spearfall then reappeared at the entrance. "Grab some food and drink, we leave in three hours. The witch isn't here, and Captain Borg has not heard from Wastewatch in 2 days.

When Thor turned to leave the stables once again, he rejoined at the side of his friend Jaren a few strides away. The two of them began walking towards the southern rampart of the outpost.

"Who are these warriors you've brought with you?" Jaren had to ask.

"Handpicked by Hormac," Thor answered plainly.

Jaren didn't look at his friend, but he wore a perplexed expression on his face.

"You mean you had no say in the matter?" Jaren asked another with a hint of jest in his tone.

"Apparently, they were all contacted by letter as well," Thor continued. "And I was given just over a day to prepare for the ride."

The two of them then climbed the wooden stairs to the top of the rampart. Up here, the two captains had a rather clear view of the vast swampland that lie to the south. Even with the rain, they could see far into the distance.

"You best watch your back, Thor," Jaren said while staring out into the swamp.

Thor looked at Jaren, but found his fixed look to be a sign of actual concern.

"As I said, two days ago was the last time that we had a check-in with Wastewatch," Jaren said. "Before that time, there was no word of the witch out here. Based on what you have told me, and the amount of time it takes to ride out this way, something just doesn't smell right."

"When you put it that way..." Thor let the rest of the notion ride, and he almost could not believe that his friend had a sense of paranoia about him. "How have things been out here?"

"Just take a look," Jaren said, waving a hand before the sight of the swamp. "We've not seen a troll in a month, and my warriors are getting bored with nothing to fight. Maybe I should have some of them go with you."

"If something has happened to the ones at Wastewatch, I doubt numbers will win the battle," Thor said. "We'll go out there, investigate, stay the night, and return on the next day."

Jaren nodded. "Can't believe I'm saying this, but at the first sign of trouble you should try to get back here."

"You have my word, brother," Thor could only agree with his friend's notion.

As planned, Captain Spearfall and his ten warriors departed Rok's Watch, and they were already several hours into the ride. It was after these hours that the rain began to break, and this was the first telling sign that they were close. The trotting of the horses became easier as the earth below became dry, and it was a moment later that the place known as Wastewatch came into view.

Captain Spearfall raised his fist to bring the other riders to a halt. As soon as the air became silent, Thor, and his crew, surveyed the area from a distance.

The area in which the warriors held was still shaded by the overcast clouds above, and this cloud cover continued towards the outpost. It was immediately after the outpost that the landscape fell away, and emptied to a bright and sunny desert beyond. The light in the distant background wasn't as bright as it could have been through. This probably meant that the sun was well into its descent.

Aside from the structure before them, the rest of the rocky grassland around them appeared calm and undisturbed. It was also possible that a threat was lurking about, and had yet to show itself.

Thor, as well as the others, thought that even at this distance they should be able to see people moving about at the outpost. Unlike the others, however, Thor knew that the place had a basement.

"Alright," Thor said to get everyone's attention. "Henrick and Sirus, you're with me. The rest of you hold tight, and if you see anyone else approach, ride in."

A round of "Aye" came from the other warriors.

Thor dismounted. He then took his sheathed, curved longsword from his saddle, and strapped it around his back. Likewise, Henrick gathered his longsword and round shield from his horse after dismounting. Sirus took the bow from his back after sliding off his horse.

"Henrick, you take point," Thor directed. "Me and Sirus, we'll follow single file."

From several hundred feet away, the trio of warriors from Claymore approached the otherwise silent outpost. Weapons became drawn, and their minds came to the ready. During this time, the warriors would occasionally look to their sides, and they half-expected a gnoll or some other kind of monster to show itself.

The danger never came.

Henrick, as the point man, kept his eyes mostly ahead. As the outpost became closer, more detail was becoming visible, and it was unfortunate what he could see. Hiding behind shallow crevices and rises in the landscape were the corpses of those who had stood watch out here by the wasteland.

"Bodies, sir," Henrick called out."

Thor's vision turned forward, and confirmed what his subordinate saw.

"Aye," Thor responded. "Keep forward."

After several more minutes, the trio broke into the perimeter of the outpost. There were rotting corpses spread across the grounds. More than a few crows began to flap their wings and take off as their meal became interrupted. The place reeked of decay and death.

Thor instructed. "Hold right here."

As the two men obeyed their orders, Thor stepped out from the single file formation to kneel down at one of the corpses. The captain looked over the body, and tried to make sense of the damage. Between the festering of rot and the crow's appetite, it was difficult to discern what had killed him. Thor got up, and ventured to the next body, and the next. It was all more of the same story, and the story was a mystery.

The captain's eyes then looked at the watchtower, the top of the masonry tower was shattered and crumbled, but that was normal as the tower has been that way for nearly 200 years. An amalgamation of stone bricks and wooden beams sat atop the structure, but it wasn't the top of the tower that got Thor's attention. It was the still usable basement that came to his mind.

The captain retook his position in formation.

"There is a basement in the tower," Thor explained. "We need to see if there is a body down there. Move forward."

The three warriors were on the move again, and they progressed to the single wooden door at the base of the tower. Once they were there, Henrick raised his shield and sword while taking position in front of it. Thor came around him, and placed his hand on the door handle. Lastly, Sirus moved in closer so that he could let loose an arrow right over Henrick's shoulder if he needed to.

Thor nodded to his two partners to which they nodded back in acknowledgement. Thor gripped the door handle tightly, and yanked the door open in one swift motion. A light cloud of dust burst forth from the entrance of the tower, but that was the only thing that came. The inside of the tower was silent, and it was dark.

The captain looked at one of the nearby corpses, and found a torch in its hands. He pulled it free, and fetched a piece of flint from one of his belt pouches. He placed the torch on the ground and used his curved sword to strike the flint. After a few attempts, the torch came to life with fire.

With the torch in hand, Thor brought it to the entrance of the tower, and used it to reveal the other half of the stone and wood implosion. The collapse of the upper sections filled the first floor, but there was still enough room to walk in, turn right, and go down the stairs to the basement.

"Okay. Shield at the ready. I'll be right behind you with the torch in hand," Thor said to Henrick. "Sirus, you stay up here. If we are not back up in ten minutes, regroup with the others, and go back to Rok's."

"Aye," Sirus replied.

Henrick and Thor entered into the Wastewatch tower, and began to descend into the basement. The stairs curved as they went deeper, and the two warriors, even while wearing armor, attempted to move as quietly as possible. Henrick's hands were shaking because of how tightly he was gripping his sword and shield. He was just waiting for something to jump at them. Thor, however, had remained calm, and was doing his best to make sure that the both of them could see ahead with the torchlight.

At the top of the stairs, Sirus watched as the torchlight disappeared from sight.

Henrick was surprised that a place like this would have such a deep basement. If he could have guessed the depth at which he was at currently, twenty feet would not have been far off.

Step by step, they descended. Every once in a while, Thor would look at the torch, hoping that the thing didn't go out, because he knew that of all the things that might be hidden down here, trying to go upstairs in the dark would be the most difficult to defeat.

After another half-circle of stairs, the two warriors finally found the basement chamber of the tower. It was a single room with several wooden beds, and a cooking spit in the middle. The ceiling was about ten feet high.

The light from Thor's torch revealed what he was not hoping to find. It was another corpse, but this one appeared to be better preserved than the others. Not even a single rat was found down here.

Thor moved through the room, and to the body. It was located beyond the closest bed. He kneeled and brought the torch in closer for a better look. The clothes and armor covering the torso was immensely stained with dried blood as well as the floor all around.

"This one's been stabbed in the heart," Thor said. "But not before a larger blade got into his gut. Someone finished him off."

Henrick remained silent, and waited to hear more from his commanding officer.

Thor got up, and used the torch to light the cooking spit, and then offered the torch to Henrick.

"Go let Sirus know that we are clear, and to get the others over here as well," Thor instructed.

Henrick sheathed his sword, took the torch, and headed back upstairs.

Thor remained downstairs, and sat down on the bed across the room from the corpse. He thoughtfully stared at it, and played different scenarios in his head.

"Gnolls don't use swords or daggers," he whispered to himself aloud. "There hasn't been any Black Lotus activity for a while. I know Serena wouldn't do this."

The seasoned warrior ran his hand through his hair as he pondered on other situations that might have occurred here. This time he stared at the dusty floor, and almost expected to find an answer in his empty stare.

"Orcs would never travel this far," he continued. "Was this planned? Could the Vicidians be behind this?"

Thor then brought his eyes upon the roaring flame of the spit as if it was going to give him the answer that he sought, but the answer would not come. When the answer would not show itself, he got up and began to go upstairs.

When he came upstairs, Thor could see that all his warriors were still accounted for. He walked around to the back of the tower until he came to stand at the edge of a great cliff, known as the *Kadavari Shelf*, no more than thirty feet away. From here, he stared out into the golden vastness of the *Kadavari Wastes*.

The dry and cracked landscape of *Kadavar* traveled beyond the range of the human eye, and the horizon was always blurred by the moving dust and sand that dominated the environment. A strong wind blew up the side of the cliff as if warning the captain to go no further.

"Can't say I've been out this far, sir," Henrick said as he came to stand next to Thor.

The rest of the warriors joined in the reverence as well. Five warriors on each side of their captain, and all of them standing and staring out into the wastes. The golden hue of the place grew dim as the daylight was waning.

"Kadavar used to be covered in water, ye know," Thor extended some historical knowledge to his warriors. "It connected the east of the Sword Kingdoms to the ocean, in the most ancient of days."

The warriors continued to stare off in the wasteland in silence acknowledgement of the captain's words. Their own version of imagination conjured images of what the place might have been like with a body of water.

"Alright, listen up," Thor began. "Something happened out here. All the warriors stationed out here are dead. I've already ruled out gnolls, orcs, and the Black Lotus. There is one dead in the basement of the tower, and he was stabbed in the heart after taking a blow to the gut. So whoever did this is making it personal. If anyone has an idea, I'm willing to hear it."

Thor looked around at his subordinates for any insights, but he didn't really expect any of them to answer. After a moment of silence, Thor continued.

"We'll camp here tonight, and leave tomorrow," he said. "Two people per watch. No fires outside the basement. It's possible whoever did this is still around, and we don't want to take the chance of being caught flat on our feet. Let's get to it."

At the word of the commander, the warriors sprang to life. They gathered the bodies, including the one in the basement, and piled them outside and behind the tower. The cooking spit in the basement was tended to. The horses were tied up near the entrance of the tower.

Sirus, being half-dryad, did not require the amount of sleep that the others did, and being the ranger that he is, he decided to climb the ruins of the tower to be a lookout. Near the top, he managed to find himself a nest of sorts where he could completely conceal himself as he meditated.

As the twilight hour struck, the cloud cover above remained, and it left the farther areas of the nearby landscape especially dark, but you could also tell that the moons above were attempting to break through.

The hour had become unknown to Henrick, but he found himself back in the tavern in Claymore. The sunlight peered through the windows, and the usual customers came to and from the Brand. His ears recalled the sound of the Stonebrow's song, but only the melody for he could not actually see the bard.

The warrior looked around as he felt awkward in this most familiar establishment. He wanted to get up from the table he always sat at, but he was not able to move. Just as frustration was starting to set in, Henrick viewed the arrival of a peculiar warrior.

It was a humanoid of some kind. It had teal-colored skin, and he wore thick plated armor of a dark-colored metal. The creature was bald-headed, but due to the numerous spines that protruded from its head and face, he wasn't sure the thing *could* grow hair. It had orange eyes that only suggested an old and ancient anger.

As this strange warrior passed by Henrick's table, he began to show the same dark and cloudy mist that he saw upon the king. This sent Henrick back in his chair as he continued to watch. The teal-skinned creature sat down at a table directly across from the door from Henrick's table, and then it made eye contact with Henrick while sporting a devilish grin.

The warrior then became completely engulfed in the black mist to the point you could not tell exactly what it was anymore. The most distinct feature now was the sinister, glowing, white eyes. All of a sudden, and at an unprecedented speed, the dark form went through the table and charged at Henrick.

Everything went black.

Henrick woke up. Sweat beaded on his face. However, it wasn't the dream that had woken him up. Standing over him was his friend Kendo, nudging him with a hand.

"Henrick, are you okay?" Kendo whispered as he witnessed the sweaty face.

Henrick raised his eyebrows to accommodate his sigh of relief.

"Aye, had a strange dream," Henrick said, continuing the whisper.

"Okay. It's your turn for watch," Kendo said.

Henrick got up from his sleeping pallet, and took note of the still burning cooking spit which provided enough light for him to start putting his gear on. Moments later, Henrick emerged from the basement, and to the entryway of the ruined tower. Kendo had remained downstairs as Henrick was his relief.

The air was cool and dry tonight, and it looked like the cloud cover had finally broken. The moons were out; Nielda was in her waning gibbous phase while Undine was entering into her third quarter. The soft pale glow made the outlying landscape somewhat visible to the human eyes.

Outside the doorway was Lars, who was also starting his watch.

"How ye doin'?" Henrick asked.

"Not too bad," was Lars' response. "Still waking up." It was after that sentence that Lars let out a profound yawn. "What do you think of all this?"

"Ye mean comin' all this way for nothin'," Henrick added. "Not sure. I know we were all lookin' fer a fight with a witch. After seeing this place though, the captain seems to think it was something else though."

"It does seem weird, but there is a lot of land out here," Lars began. "Witch could be hiding anywhere, but as you said, I doubt the witch would resort to using weapons."

A moment of silence came over the two warriors as they let the information sink in.

It was after this moment that the sound of footfalls came from the side of the tower, and it was soon that Captain Spearfall appeared in the moonlight.

"Not sleeping, sir?" Henrick asked.

"Not tonight, gentlemen," Thor answered. "My thoughts have been dwelling on the situation here, and I agree, our being here is quite strange."

"If I may, sir, what is that sword you carry?" Henrick asked.

At the completion of the question, Thor took the blade out of its wooden sheathe, and let the moonlight shimmer across its glossy texture.

"It's a sandaran water blade, only the royal guard to the Beru-Lai in Sandar are given these weapons," the captain explained. "Very sharp, and they never succumb to rust or dullness."

In the minds of Henrick and Lars, the weapon seemed impressive, but the question lingered.

"How'd *you* get one, sir," Lars asked.

"I...," the captain began but then stopped. Out of the corner of his eye, Captain Spearfall caught movement in the darkened environment around them.

The movement of their commander's gaze towards the west caused Henrick and Lars to look in the same direction on the note that something was not right. When the warriors peered at the nightly horizon, they could not see much except for ten pairs of glowing white eyes floating almost one hundred feet away.

Henrick recognized them, or at least felt something familiar about them. He looked upon the encroaching dark humanoids. They carried the same mist as the king did, and appeared to look like that creature from his dream. He then looked at Captain Spearfall and Lars to understand that they could see them as well.

What Henrick did not understand, however, was that he could see them through their dark, smoky visage. He narrowed his eyes and focused his concentration. The black mist changed into a cloud of lavender, highlighting the opponents against the nightscape, and he could see the dark, spiked armor covering their forms from head to toe.

"Of course," Thor said to himself aloud with an angered tone of realization.

"What are they, sir?" Lars asked.

Thor then spoke in feylic, the language of the dryads, "Keep yourself hidden, Sirus." It was in hope that the ranger could hear him, and respect his call. The words were not elevated in volume for the captain knew that the ranger's ear would catch them.

Henrick and Lars looked to each other in confusion as they did not understand the words.

"Lars, go wake the others, now," Thor said in a controlled tone.

As soon as Lars departed and went down the stairs, four of the dark humanoids evaporated into a floating mist, and sailed towards the tower. Captain Spearfall attempted to keep an eye on the movement, but it was only Henrick that was able to see the entire thing unfold.

The dark, animated clouds flew right by Thor and Henrick. Henrick swung his sword at the traveling mist, but his blade went right through it. The dark mist descended the stairs.

Thor, although out of the way of Henrick's sword swing, ducked away from the tower entry as he caught a glimpse of the dark mist just as it was going by. He regained his footing, and stared back out to the other six humanoids that remained.

"You can see them?" the captain asked Henrick without taking his eye off the opponents in the distance.

"Aye," Henrick answered with only a second of hesitation.

"Good," Thor said before a second's pause. "Fight like hell."

At the conclusion of his statement, Thor rushed out into the battlefield to face the dark humanoids, and Henrick was right behind him.

As the gap between the combatants began to close, two of the dark humanoids rushed forward to meet them. In the shining moonlight above, the warriors from Claymore could see that their enemies had long jagged blades for weapons.

To the eyes of Thor, he could tell right away that those weapons were the ones that killed the warrior that was in the basement of the tower.

The dark humanoids engaged the humans at the same time. Once engaged, the fighters came to their stances.

Thor's opponent was first to move, and made the experienced warrior draw up his sandaran sword in a horizontal fashion. Thor used the strength of both arms to block the downward strike of his opponent, but as soon as the clang of metal rang Thor was already making his move.

The dark humanoid maintained pressure on Thor's block, but it did nothing to stop the incoming kick to the shin. The dark humanoid reeled in pain, and the warrior from Claymore pushed the jagged blade aside. Thor followed up with a sidestep, then swung his sword upward, cutting through the earth below, and making the blade uppercut through the armpit of the dark humanoid and continue on to decapitate it.

The dark figure fell limp upon the ground, lifeless, and then it dissolved into a pile of ash.

Thor brought his sword back up in a vertical and ready position, and the warrior took note that there were no stains of any kind upon his weapon. The captain shot a grin at the remaining dark creatures.

The remaining creatures did not step forward, and Thor began to question the peculiar passiveness. The captain took this moment to see that Henrick had had similar luck in defeating his opponent, but when he turned his gaze to the collapsed tower, he took a mentally grim note that none of the other warriors had come out.

In those few seconds of looking back at the tower, Thor looked back at Henrick to notice that two more of the dark warriors had moved in on him. One fought Henrick from the front while the other fluidly flanked him. Before Thor could realign himself to the new opponents that were about to engage him, he witnessed a long knife slip through the back of Henrick's armor.

The dark humanoids reluctantly revealed their strategy to Thor, and instead of becoming focused on the opponent in front of him, Thor leapt backwards and found the second opponent creeping up on him.

The move was unexpected, but the dark humanoid brought its two short blades up to block the leaping side slash. The jagged blades, however, were not constructed like the sandaran sword was, and the masterfully crafted sword cut through the metal before slicing through the top half of the dark humanoid's head.

As the dark one fell and turned to ash, it was the remaining combatants that flocked to Thor's position. Thor raised his sword up once again to block a downward strike against him, and followed through with a powerful front kick to the abdomen that sent the next dark fighter back several feet. The other dark creatures barreled upon him in succession. The next attack came at him in a thrusting jab that nearly missed his neck, but Thor was the quicker one.

In the midst of his dodging, another blow came at him from the back, but the equally strong sheathe managed to absorb the deadly chop, however, the force of the blow caused him to stagger a bit.

All the movement in the darkened landscape while fighting off the dark humanoids began to set a wave of confusion in Thor's mind and it was at this moment that he lost track of all his opponents. Everything was getting blurred.

Adrenaline had taken over, and Thor came out of his stammering with a series of fast and quick blade swings. A couple of overhead chops came from him as he had located a target. The attacks became parried, but then Thor pointed the tip of his blade down before slithering it back upwards until he punctured his sword through the jaw of a dark humanoid.

In the midst of overcoming the blind fighting, and relying on instinct to get himself out of this mess, it was the short victory that left the experienced warrior open. Thor felt the chilly metal blade find its way under his left shoulder blade, and suddenly the great warrior had lost all of his strength, and found that he could no longer hold his sword.

From the side, Captain Spearfall had his face crushed by the weighty boot of another opponent. Thor fell to the ground writhing in pain, but he would not let himself call out in anguish. He would not give his enemies what they wanted.

Lying on his side, Thor could see the dark warriors reforming the line in which they had started with except one of them came to stand over him. The glowing white eyes of this demon looked down to meet the glossy coat of Thor's.

Thor wasn't sure he could speak at that moment, but at the same time he had nothing to say to this dark warrior. He could feel the life energy inside him dissipating. His body became numb as the blood flowed from his wounds.

The dark warrior crouched down to get a better look at him.

"Before you die," the creature said in a guttural version of aerinese. "Know that your homeland will once again belong to the Lord of Darkness."

Thor's panting was getting heavier with each breath.

The dark warrior that was over Thor produced a long knife and thrust it between the ribs of the captain, piercing his heart. In that exact moment, Thor's eyes went wide and motionless.

The dark warrior stood back up, and rejoined its companions. They each turned to mist, and traveled off into the dark wilderness.

Several hours later, the morning sun had begun to come over the horizon, and it was this moment that

Sirus had been waiting for. Heeding the advice of his commander, he had decided to remain hidden, but the time to move had come, and so he stood up from his perch atop the broken tower, and peered over the nearby land.

With bow in hand, and an arrow at the ready, he was prepared, hopefully, for anything he might see, but thankfully, the area was clear of any movement. He remained at the ready, and spent the next couple minutes focused on using his half-dryad ears to seek out any hidden threats.

When Sirus was convinced himself that the area was secure, he began his climb down from the tower. As soon as his feet touched the ground, the ranger part of him began to scan his locale.

He first moved to the entrance of the tower before kneeling down. From here, he was able to pick out the various footprints from his companions, but strangely he was not able to find any others. He followed the base of the tower around to the other side where the horses were tied up, and they were all accounted for.

Sirus moved back to the tower entrance, and looked down the dark stairwell to the basement. He had thought about going down to investigate, but his thoughts were fairly certain as to what he was going to find down there. His gaze then fell upon the two bodies that lay out in the distance.

Bow still at the ready, the ranger calculated his movements out into the open field. He turned to face many directions as he attempted to spot any would-be targets.

As the ranger approached the bodies, he began to find prints on the ground that were not standard issue for Claymoran soldiers. He kneeled down, and ran his hand across the edges of the print. Sirus could tell that the boots were heavy with a thick metal toe on the front of them, but then he found two more prints, closer to the bodies, that were lighter and almost unseeable.

Sirus pondered about this for a moment, but then shrugged the notion off until he could finish his investigation of the area. The ranger then made his move to the first body. It was Captain Spearfall.

The captain had suffered minor wounds at the hands of enemies, but when Sirus crouched down, he saw the two penetrating marks on the body. The ranger was stricken with disbelief that the famed Thor Spearfall had been slain.

"They are called *the shade*," a female voice came from behind him.

In a single, fluid motion, Sirus stood up and drew his bow before aiming it at the figure that was now standing over Henrick's body. Sirus was astounded that whoever this person was, was able to approach his vicinity without a sound.

The person was an aerin woman in leather armor with a brown hood over her head. She had a belt with several pouches attached to it, and a quarterstaff in hand.

"Who are you?" Sirus said.

"I..." the woman began, "would put your weapon down before you upset him."

The woman pointed with her eyes to an area over Sirus's leading shoulder. The ranger followed the woman's gaze until he noticed a large striped feline crouched in the dry grass about twenty feet away.

The situation in which Sirus was now in left him stammering in silence. In the interest of his own safety, however, he managed to lower his weapon.

Sirus asked again, "Who are you?"

The woman stepped away from Henrick's body, and towards Sirus for a few steps.

"I thought it was obvious," she said to the ranger. "I'm the *Witch of Claymore*."

Sirus felt skeptical as he narrowed his eyes at the woman, "You've got to be kidding me."

"Shall I *show you*?" she asked, but also jested. The hint in her voice was not hidden.

"No, no, that's ok," Sirus said while sneaking a peek at the tiger once more.

"If you're the Witch of Claymore, then what are you doing here? Come to finish the job?" Sirus asked.

"No. I've come to take that one away," the woman said while turning to regard Henrick's body with a pointed finger.

"Henrick? What do you want with his body?" Sirus asked with a concerned tone.

The woman thought about the question for a second, and then said, "That part, I will show you. Come on, Sand."

The woman moved back over to where Henrick's body was, and her feline companion joined her hearing its name. Standing over the warrior's body, she kneeled down, and placed her staff on the ground.

Sirus, convinced that this was not going to be a combat encounter, replaced the arrow in his quiver, and placed his bow on his back. He walked over to the body as well, but tried not to get too close to the giant cat.

"How do you know what those things were?" Sirus asked.

The woman answered while reaching into a pouch, "This is not the first time that I have seen them, and they killed the last group that was sent out here. They are very dangerous, and for whatever reason, they can only survive in the dark."

In the midst of her speech, the woman produced a diamond that was half the size of her own hand from a pouch on her waist, and placed it on the ground.

"Help me turn him over," the woman asked Sirus.

The ranger did crouch down, and help flip Henrick's body so that he would be face up.

The woman began searching her pouches once more. The next item she produced was a strange ball of tangled roots to which she took the diamond, and pushed the shining gemstone inside the ball. After that she placed the combined items on Henrick's chest, and then stood up.

"Okay. Give me some space," the woman said.

Sirus managed to stand up when she did, and upon request, he did back up a few feet.

The woman then looked at her feline companion with a cocked head, "You, too, buddy."

With a grunt of lazy resistance, the tiger moved away from the woman and the body.

The woman took up her mundane staff from the ground, and with both hands held the item at a downward angle so that the tip was pointed at the diamond-stuffed root ball. From this point, she closed her eyes, and reached out to the life forces of nature.

With her empathic abilities, she could sense the dry, but still-breathing grass, the tiny creatures that

111

hide in the earth, the smooth air that now began to breeze at the woman's call, the blazing sun of the morning hours, and small amounts of water that was hidden from sight. She reached out to all the elements of nature, and prayed silently to the Twins, so that the gift of life magic may be granted.

From the side, Sirus was witness to one of the most amazing displays of magic he had ever seen. His eyes were wide in disbelief.

The root ball began to float above the body of Henrick, and it began to spin, and it spun so fast that it was hard to tell exactly when the material began to dissolve into green particles of magic.

The breezing air became nearly violent, and kicked up a dust devil in its wake, but Sirus could not take his eyes away from what was happening. The particles of green magic surged with electricity as it traversed over Henrick's body. The wind then stopped, and the dust was left to fly in all directions. When it was all done, the woman opened her eyes, and Sirus moved in closer. The two of them could see that Henrick was breathing again.

Sirus' mouth was hung open as he tried to wrap his head around what just happened. For the third time, Sirus asked, "Who *are* you?"

"My name is Serena, and I'm a servant of nature," she said.

"You're a *druid*," Sirus stated.

"Of the *Ember Grove*, yes," she added. Serena then pointed her eyes over to the body of Thor. "Your commander knew that as well."

Sirus looked at the body of his commanding officer. He felt skeptical over Serena's claim that Thor knew of her, but he remained silent as he returned his posture towards the woman. In the next few seconds, the ranger had accumulated so many questions that he wanted to ask Serena, but he wasn't even sure if they mattered at this point.

The ranger had reached a conclusion all of a sudden. He, and his companions, were sent out here to hunt a witch, but according to the witch herself, Thor was already aware of what she was. Sirius wondered if this druid and the captain had been working together when the orcs attacked Rok's Watch. He must have seen that she was not a threat. It made sense. Thor, under the command of the king, was tasked with coming out here to hunt Serena, and brought the warriors with him anyway with that knowledge in hand.

"We were sent out here to die," Sirus voiced the grim realization out loud. The idea of such an act infuriated the mind of the half-dryad. "Thor brought us out here, knowingly that *you* were not a threat, and then my friends got ambushed and died," Sirus said with an elevated tone and an angry waving gesture.

The nearby guttural sounds from the tiger assured that the next segments of dialogue remained professional.

"Perhaps, in the face of your anti-magic society, Thor felt obligated to come out here anyway," Serena shot back with narrowed eyes.

To Sirus, the notion was logical. If it had been revealed that Thor was harboring a magic user in Claymore lands, he would have been considered an enemy of the kingdom.

"I suppose you have a point," the ranger agreed, his brows still lowered.

"You have one, too," Serena pointed out. "Someone sent you people out here to die, and now there are two of you to expose the truth."

Serena's statement brought Sirus' eyes down upon Henrick.

"So, what do you want with Henrick?" the ranger asked.

"I wish I could say, but that is for the Twins to decide," she said. "I was merely sent to retrieve him, and nurse him back to health."

"I see. Do you need help with him?" Sirus offered.

"Should be fine, that's what I got him for," Serena said while pointing a nod at Sand.

"Henrick really isn't the thanking type, so in case he remains consistent, thanks for helping him out," he said.

Whatever the moon goddesses wanted with his friend, Sirus decided that it would probably be best not to get in their way, but the ranger wanted to make sure that his friend would be well equipped when he was feeling better.

The ranger walked over to where Thor's body was. He picked up the exotic blade the captain had, and relinquished the wooden sheath from the back of the corpse. With the items in hand, Sirus returned to the side of the druid. She had just finished getting Henrick on to the back of Sand.

"Here," Sirus handed her the weapon after sheathing it. "Make sure he gets this when he wakes up."

She took it, and put it on her own back.

When she was done, she noticed that the ranger had moved back to Thor's body.

"So what's your name?" she asked.

"Sirus. Sirus the Hood," he answered.

"And what will you do, Sirus?" Serena asked another.

"I'm going to bury my commander, and then return to Claymore," he said. "I was sent out here on a hunt, and the hunt is not over."

CHAPTER SIX
CALL OF THE TWINS

Henrick stood in a dark, featureless environment. A bright spotlight shined down upon him, but when he looked up, there was no source of the light. He looked around in pitch blackness, but he saw nothing. He looked himself over wondering how he was able to feel alive after having been delivered such a deadly blow, but it took him a second to realize he was wearing his clothes, and not his armor. The confusion began to permeate in his mind.

The sound of rushing air suddenly whizzed by him, but there was no breeze upon his skin. The sound swirled all around, and he looked in every different direction when he thought he could pinpoint the source of it. His thoughts reeled from the constant stimuli. He thought the noise would drive him insane, but then it all went away when a figure appeared before him.

Given the shape of the figure, it was a woman. She had no face, and no distinguishing features. Some broader details like the length of her hair were notable, but she was like a ghost. A cold silhouette outlined in pale blue. Even though the landscape was dark, Henrick felt as though he could see through her.

Henrick's eyes then fell down to an object she carried in her hand. It was a heater shield. Vanilla white, outlined in gold, and emblazoned with the holy symbol of the Twins. He found it strange that the object was as solid as himself.

Then the thought occurred to him: was he actually dead? Perhaps this was him passing to the afterlife. He couldn't help but wonder what a godless warrior such as himself had waiting for him. But that same notion drove him to contemplate on why he would even bother with such a question. He was a warrior, and he had a warrior's death. If that was true, however, where was he? Perhaps he *was* alive. Perhaps this was another strange dream. He did agree with himself on the growing number of strange dreams he has had of late.

The mind games in his head came to a stop when the woman began to approach Henrick. He attempted to back up, but instead he ended up bumping into something. When Henrick regained his footing and pushed off, he turned to see what had halted his retreat.

It was another strange figure, but this one appeared to be a man. His figure was ghost-like as well, except Henrick could clearly see the suit of lavender chainmail covering most of his body.

The two ghostly figures moved to stand side-by-side before they continued their slow march towards their corporeal target. Henrick back peddled, and when the anxiety of their haunting pursuit refused to end, the man just turned to run away into the dark landscape. As he turned to run, he skidded to a stop. The featureless environment was gone in a flash, and he found himself standing upon the edge of the Kadavari Shelf, and the nightly hour was still upon him as it was when he fell in combat.

Henrick looked around and saw the collapsed tower of Wastewatch. The landmark confirmed his location, but he wasn't able to stain his eyes with the tower for too long. He then looked out into the wasteland, but it wasn't there. Instead, he looked down upon a great sea, and as his vision scanned over the horizon, he could see a series of plateaus rising above the water.

He took in the sights and tried to comprehend what was going on. None of it made sense to him. Then there was a flash of purple light in the sky, and shortly thereafter, a meteor fell from the sky above and crashed down somewhere by the plateaus. There was another flash, and suddenly, the wasteland was there. Barren and lifeless. Desolate and arid.

Henrick suddenly felt as though someone was trying to tell him a story through all the images that he had been shown so far. The story was not over, though. As he continued to watch the horizon, a darkness began to creep its way across the cracked earth of the wasteland.

In an instant, the clear night sky was enveloped by thick cloud cover. The moons were forbidden to look at the world below, but the shimmer of the Twins upon the clouds managed to keep Henrick's eyes from being blind in the dark.

The creeping darkness was then upon the face of the cliff down below. It floated to the top where Henrick was standing before it began to roll across the landscape to the west. He turned around, and suddenly he was viewing the City of Claymore from the outskirts of the city. He looked on in horror as dark and corrupted magic raged over the walls, and the screams of the people filled the night air.

Henrick was not able to do anything but stand there and watch. He looked down at his clenched fists trying everything he could do to break free and run to his people, but there was no result.

The sound of the rushing air came once again, and beckoned Henrick to look. When he finally did, he could see the lineup of the dark humanoids again. His eyes returned to his hands, he noticed he had regained his sword and shield, and found himself charging the battlefield.

The first of the dark creatures he remembered vividly. The creature's form was outlined in a lavender glow that allowed the warrior to see the creature in the dark environment.

Henrick knew that he had done well against this first round opponent. Every time the wicked blade of the shade came after him, he would parry the blade. He would then use the edge, and face, of his shield to deal massive damage. It was the House Darkbane fighting secret, after all.

One by one, the warrior would deflect the incoming attack and send it away or lock it up. He even managed to convince the dark one from thinking it was learning the warrior's technique, and when the opening presented itself, Henrick switched it up, blocked with the shield, and went for the shallow but deadly jab to the face.

Henrick felt, however, that he was not in control of the scene, and instead he was just along for the ride. He stood his ground, just as before, which meant he knew what was coming next.

Against the rollercoaster of emotions washing over him, Henrick was forced to stand there and wait as the other dark humanoid appeared before his eyes. Meanwhile, the unseen slipped in behind him, and sent a long cold blade through his left kidney.

His strength was lost, and it was a breath later that everything went black.

Just as he thought the nightmare was over, he heard a female voice.

Get up.

Henrick woke up. His head was covered in sweat caused by the disturbing dream he just had. At the moment, however, he wasn't sure he had left the dream completely for wherever he may be, his eyes could only process pitch black.

Unlike his dream, his nostrils caught the scent of earth, and he could feel the cool dry dirt between his fingertips as he pushed himself up into a sitting position. His back ached in the spot he had felt the knife go in.

When he reached behind himself to feel the wound, he was astounded to know that there wasn't one, and it was at that moment he took note that he was no longer wearing his armor. This drove him to another realization. His weapons were gone, too.

Henrick looked around in the darkness as if it was going to help him to see, but it never did. He remained in his sitting position for a moment longer as he tried to mentally work out the other aches in his body.

It was in the following moment that something reached out to him. It wasn't a hand or something that he saw, but a sound that rang in the environment around him before reaching his ears. It was the sound of a single drop of fluid splashing against a pool of some kind.

With his sight unavailable, Henrick was able to imagine the sound that echoed, and he began to wonder if he was inside of a cave. He assumed that his guess was right, and it restored his belief that he was very much alive. The warrior from Claymore sprang into action and rolled himself on to all fours. He began feeling around on the ground towards the direction in which he thought the sound came from.

After shuffling around in the dirt for a few minutes, Henrick's hand felt the presence of a wall, and it was a wall that was also made of earth. With the wall as his support, he managed to push himself to his feet.

Once Henrick made it to his feet, the warrior's mentality kicked in, and he began to ponder about how he could have been put in this cave. His mind debated about the thought of being captured by one of the dark humanoids, but that thought disappeared as soon as it had come up.

The sound of a single drop rang in the air once more as if it was beckoning Henrick to stay focused. The warrior was completely unaware, but the peculiar sound erased his warrior instincts in a flash, and so his mind dwelled on the source of the echo.

With the cavernous walls as his guide, Henrick felt his way down the dark passageway of the cave network. It wasn't long before he noticed the flickering light of a torch bleeding in his direction.

When Henrick came around the bend of the passage he was in, he noticed a person with their head down, sitting in a chair in the middle of an intersection. However, as soon as Henrick got close, his eyes beamed at the sight of a large feline getting up from a lying position, and stepping out from the darkness of another passageway. The feline came into the intersection, and nudged the person in the chair awake. The person raised her head to reveal her familiar face.

"*You*," Henrick stated as much as questioned.

Still sitting in the chair, the woman made a waking stretch with her whole body before getting up. She then stared at the man's blank face before rolling her eyes.

"Don't tell me you forgot my name," the woman said.

"I met ye fer about two minutes," Henrick shot back, "and that was several days ago."

"It's Serena," the woman reintroduced herself, "and it's been closer to a tenday."

"A *whole* week?" Henrick exclaimed.

"Come with me," Serena said. "Oh, and don't worry about my tiger, Sand."

Serena began down one of the tunnels after plucking the torch from the nearby wall.

"As it stands, he's the least scary thing in the world now," Henrick added.

Henrick followed the brown-haired woman, and in the midst of following her, he did manage to admire her hypnotizing gait once or twice. But even with the small distraction, he had to wonder what her involvement was with the events that had transpired back at Wastewatch. He wanted answers, but he figured he should wait until he was done shadowing her.

One after another, the two humans and the tiger passed through intersections, and the complexity of the tunnel system made Henrick feel lost. In all the time that he had spent patrolling the Sword Reach, he never imagined an underground system like this existed.

It was after a few more minutes of traversing the cave tunnels that the three had stepped outside in the open air of the night. It was a clear night and the moons had already set. The light of the distant stars and the vague glow of the Scarlet Tear shimmered across the local landscape.

From what Henrick could tell, this cave was nestled at the bottom of a crater. The immediate surroundings were elevated by rocky outcroppings, but there were a few pathways out. The cave itself was dug into a shallow stone cliff.

Nearby, to his left, there was a small pond with a gentle run of water coming down from above the rim of the crater. Henrick went over to the pond, went to his knees, and began shoveling water in his mouth with his hands.

Once he had gotten his fill, he sat back, and stared at the pond for a moment. From here, the surface of the water turned into a flash of reminiscence. Images of the recent battle and his nightmare replayed in his mind. In the next instant, the images were gone, and his mind returned to the ever-pushing determination of his mission.

"Where are we?" Henrick asked.

"About half a day from the Shelf, and north from where I found you," Serena explained. "If you climb out of here and look west, you can see the river leading to the lake in the distance."

"Was I the only one ye found?" Henrick asked. Although, he was certain of what the answer was.

"You were the only one that wasn't dead," she replied. She came over to the pond, and sat next to him.

"Damn," Henrick cursed. "To think that those creatures...we never had a chance against 'em."

"Those creatures are called the shade," the woman said.

"The shade?" Henrick said rhetorically to commit the name to memory. Then his mind fell on thoughts of Claymore. "Where're me things? I've gotta get back to Claymore."

He looked to her as he spoke, but his gaze was not met, and she kept her eyes towards the body of water.

"Not yet," she said. "I can tell your body still aches. Rest until tomorrow, then you can leave."

It was as if her words carried some sort of tangible power, because as soon as she brought up the pain,

Henrick's ache seemed to reappear. He grabbed at his side, but slowly and gently.

"I suppose another day of rest couldn't hurt," he agreed.

Get up!

Henrick woke up at the sound of the strange voice calling to him again.

It was after his conversation with Serena that he went back into the cave to get some sleep. He was led by the woman to a different chamber that had a thick sleeping pallet on the ground, and it was in this other chamber that Henrick got more rest.

Unlike the first chamber in which he found himself in, this one had air that was filled with the sound of sputtering sleep. The torch that was set in this chamber still had a flame going, and the warrior from Claymore soon discovered a litter of creatures that were not there when he went to bed.

Piled all around him on the pallet was a litter of young tiger cubs. His eyes went wide and a small amount of panic set in as one of Henrick's closely guarded secrets was about to come to life.

He was mildly allergic to cats.

A little at a time, and one by one, Henrick worked the tigers. He picked them up and moved them aside without disturbing them too much. He did this as many times as he needed to in order to get to a sitting position.

Once he made it up, he then used his arms and started to push himself up and off the sleeping pallet. This maneuver caused many of the still sleeping cubs to roll around until they clashed in the middle with furry cuteness.

Henrick continued to push himself up until he was finally standing and free of the kittens. At the foot of the pallet, he tried to brush off as much of the dander as he could with his hands, although he really couldn't see it.

In the midst of him doing this, however, the noise of the whipping clothes caused a disturbance on the other side of the chamber. Henrick's peripherals caught sight of it and his eyes beamed at the movement. There were three adult tigers who had raised their heads at the sudden noise, but after realizing that it was just their guest, the tigers rolled back over.

Henrick walked over to the entrance of the chamber with his back towards the wall, and grabbed the torch off the wall. He moved with a purpose to get away from the felines as his eyes were already beginning to dry out and itch

He continued through the passageway until he came to a five-way intersection. Henrick became completely flabbergasted. He thought this might be the intersection from before when he found Serena in the chair, but that intersection had four pathways.

He stepped to the middle of the intersection, and made a motion to look down each of the dark, earthy halls as if one of them would give him an answer. He continued to spin around but then realized that he lost track of which path he had just come from.

He threw down his arms in defeat, and let the torch fall on the ground. He continued by placing his hands on his waist, and once again looked down each of the pathways for some hint, but again, nothing came to him. He lowered his head in defeat before closing his eyes as he dwelled on his predicament.

As Henrick came to open his eyes once more, his head was still drooped, but his focus fell on the still lit torch. The flames were being pulled in the direction of one of the tunnels. He grabbed the torch and headed in the direction by which the flames pointed. A short while later, he found himself winding through a curved tunnel that descended further into the earth, and the deeper he got, the louder a familiar sound got.

It was the sound of a droplet splashing into a body of some unknown substance, and just like before, it was as if the sound beckoned him. Deeper and deeper the tunnel went. How deep he had gotten, he was not sure, but his curiosity seemed to cut through the ever-aware demeanor that he usually wore.

A moment later the tunnel leveled out, and became flat once more, but more to Henrick's awareness, he could see a bluish light coming up from the tunnel ahead. Drawn to the peculiar glow, the man continued.

After a long jaunt of a straight away, Henrick soon found himself in a large, round chamber at the end of the tunnel network. The chamber had no other ways out and the curved, dome-like ceiling was about 15-feet-tall.

In the floor of this chamber was a circular pool of water, and at its center was a large blue crystal that glowed with energy and warmth. From somewhere in the ceiling, water had found its way inside the chamber. Droplets fell and tapped upon the apex of the crystal which made the resounding noise that had been calling for Henrick's attention.

The warrior from Claymore found its way back to the front of Henrick's mind, but he already knew that he did not have his weapons and armor so he would have to take his situation and roll with it.

But it wasn't the formation of the chamber, or the potential presence of magic in the crystal that snapped Henrick out of his curious stupor. It was a feeling. It was the presence of a dark energy. He had no way of knowing, but he knew that that was how it felt. It was similar to how he felt when the shade attacked. But this thing had no dark mist bleeding from it, and somehow, it felt benevolent.

He looked around the chamber, hoping to spy some sort of camouflaged monster waiting for him to turn his back, but each time Henrick managed to exploit his supernatural sense and reach out with his feelings, he kept feeling the presence from inside the crystal.

Henrick looked behind himself and noticed that the pathway in which he entered this chamber was no longer there, and that brought him to question his unknown ability. He returned his attention to the crystal.

"What are ye?" Henrick asked aloud while staring at the blue crystal.

As the final syllable left his lips, the water in the round pool began to ripple as if a tremor shook the foundation of the chamber, but the chamber never vibrated. Soon after, the water began to swirl, and the swirl picked up momentum until the acceleration turned into a contained water spout. The spout continued to increase in speed, and eventually it met with the ceiling.

Watery mist sprayed all over in the chamber, but it didn't last long as the water spout began a new trick. The spout stopped abruptly, and the suspended water was pulled to a single point above the tip of the blue crystal before it formed into a humanoid shape. The watery transformation then took on more detail and less transparency until finally Henrick could see what the creature before him truly was.

The creature had the form of a naked woman, her skin was ocean blue, her eyes were completely white with no discernable pupils, and her hair was jet black and ran the length of her back with a small red starfish decorating the top of her bangs. Henrick was awe-struck by the presence of the magical creature, and his *male* side of the house definitely sized the woman up. He had never encountered a being like this before, but he also couldn't look away from her and her supernatural beauty.

Her figure floated above the blue crystal and from this point, the two met eyes.

"Henrick, Son of Skald," the female creature spoke with the most soothing of voices before taking a bow. "I am the envoy of the Twins. Nielda has chosen you as her champion."

"Her *champion*?" Henrick questioned. He was surprised by the bluntness. "But I've never been a patron to her, nor 'ave I been a patron to any of the known gods."

Henrick paused for a moment, and when the woman did not continue, he did.

"Is that why I can sense the dark creatures that attacked me?" He asked.

"Yes," the creature answered. "With your appointment, you have been given several gifts in which you must discover, and master, on your own. The gift that you have already discovered is the ability to sense extraordinary darkness in others."

"While that *may* explain that, I usually don't be takin' a knee to things of make-believe," Henrick said. "For all I know, I could be showin' the first signs to summon arcana in this world. If ye ain't got some sort of proof, then I might hafta disappoint the ol' moon lady?"

In the following moment the blue woman glared up at the ceiling, but it wasn't like she was looking at it. It was as if she was looking at something beyond it. It was after a few seconds that the creature returned her gaze to Henrick. She began to wave her hands before her body as if she was casting a spell of some sort. Water splashed out from her fingertips as her hands weaved the somatic components.

When the spell had come to a completion, the blue woman had made a shield materialize before the two of them, and it was a shield that Henrick recognized. The shield floated down to Henrick, and once it was there, he placed his still burning torch on the ground as he grasped the shield from its lower half. It was the white shield with the symbol of the Twins from his dream. The one held by the ghostly woman.

To see this item before his eyes was maddeningly impossible to comprehend. For how could this item possibly have been known to anyone else when he saw it for the first time yesterday? Inside of a dream no less. He swallowed the lump in his throat as valid proof was provided. He secretly scoffed at the idea of becoming a believer in one of the gods, but how could he deny them now? The woman said he was *chosen*, and so it begged the question.

"Why 'ave I been chosen?" Henrick asked with his belief in check.

"Each of the gods may designate a champion to carry out their will," the creature explained. "You were chosen at the precise moment that the previous champion fell. That was 25 years ago"

The words rang in the mind of Henrick, because that was exactly how old he was, but what did that mean? Was he chosen at birth? He already had it in his mind that he would need to look elsewhere for that sort of information, so for the time being he would stick to the matters at hand.

"With regret, the planet Terra is dying," the woman said grimly as she continued. "The squabbles between the other deities have blinded them to the dangers at hand, but in order for you to safely pursue the preservation of your world, you must stop the ancient enemy of Claymore."

Without a second thought or a hint of hesitation, Henrick already knew the answer.

"The shade," he proclaimed.

"Abyss has his eye on Claymore, and your quest is to stop the shade from encroaching on Terra Sanguinar," she stated. "Do this, and your path will be clear."

"*Encroach*?" Henrick echoed aloud. His brain cut that word out of the entire sentence, and he lowered his eyes as he ran the information through his head. In conclusion, he knew it meant only one thing. "The shade plan to invade Claymore, and they 'ave already made the first move."

"Already, you possess the wisdom necessary to complete your quest," the woman said. "Now you must go, and carry it out."

Sensing the end of the dialogue, Henrick had one final question, "What is yer name?"

The blue woman did not provide the answer, and instead said, "May the light of the moon guide your path."

At the end of the final syllable, the woman turned into a watery form, and shortly thereafter, gravity took over and the water returned to the pool. Unlike before, however, the crystal no longer provided the blue glow that it did.

As the light faded away, Henrick looked around in the now dark chamber, and was relieved to see that the torch was still burning. Now, with shield and torch in hand, Henrick made his way back up through the tunnel network.

Back up the winding tunnels he went until he had returned to the intersection by which he had started. When his steps carried him up enough to look into the intersection, he noticed that Serena was there waiting for him. Her eyes fell on him, but she waited for him to start the conversation.

"What kinda creature was that down there?" Henrick asked her.

Serena explained, "She's a water nymph; a protector of the seas, and a creature whose beauty can blind mortals. I see you were given a gift."

He came to a stop before Serena, and held up the shield to show her the symbol on the front.

"A gift from Nielda," he stated before returning his eyes to her. "So ye've met the blue lady, too?"

"Yes," she answered. "I have been instructed to help you with your mission."

Henrick lowered his eyes a bit, staring at the ground while he milled through his thoughts and trying to figure out which order they should go in. He ran the events that had led to this point through his mind and from what he could figure, the most direct path to challenge was the road back to Claymore.

While Henrick tossed himself around inside his own skull, he almost didn't realize that Serena had taken a few steps forward, and presented an item of uniqueness before him. The warrior looked upon the wooden sheathe of Spearfall's sword as it was held in Serena's hands in a gesture of offering.

"The captain's sword," Henrick whispered aloud.

He did not draw the weapon, although he really wanted to. Instead, he took the sheathe, and strapped it to his back with the handle rising over his right shoulder. Henrick then slipped one of the leather straps of the shield over the sword's handle to secure the shield to his back.

"We can get the rest of your things on the way out, if you'd like," Serena offered.

"Aye. We're gonna need some of it going to Claymore," Henrick said.

"What's our plan when we get there?" she asked.

Henrick answered with, "Gonna hafta find my sponsor, and then, get an audience with the king."

CHAPTER SEVEN
EXILE

The early parts of the night had fallen, and the cloud cover above hid the stars from the citizens of Claymore. The roads of the outer city were dotted with burning lamp posts, and the silhouettes of people were like tiny ink blots against the already darkened scene. The cool breeze that blew across Starfall Lake made for a comfortable summer night.

The sight brought a great sigh of relief from the mouth of Henrick as he continued to approach the east gate. As he prepared to cross the boundaries of the outer city, he noticed that his partner had fallen out of step with him. He turned to regard Serena as she stopped in her tracks.

"What's the matter?" he asked her.

"Mmm. Civilization is not my thing," Serena answered. "I'll camp out here for the night. Besides, I don't think anyone in there will welcome *him*."

Both Serena and Henrick turned their eyes to Sand who was at her side. The scent of water was absent from the air, and it didn't seem like it was going to rain. Henrick figured she would be fine since she had been living outside for some time, and because of that, he accepted her decision.

"Alright," he added. "Give me 'til noon tomorrow. I'll meet ye at the west gate."

Serena returned a nod, and then the two parted ways.

Henrick continued towards Claymore, and his trek took him through the outer city. This part of town was a collection of various folk. All the citizens here were Claymoran warriors just like everyone else, however, some were farmers, some just wanted to live with little to no responsibility, and then there were those that were completely impoverished.

Over the last few years, Henrick has made many patrols through the outer city, and has seen the population of the poverty-stricken grow substantially. The taxes inside the city continue to rise, more buildings in the mid-city have become vacant, and those smart enough have already left the kingdom all together. Many have blamed the kingdom's problems on the King and the House Leaders, but the leadership from inside the throne room always assures the people that all these decisions are necessary in order to build upon the kingdom's defenses. He never really believed in those decisions, but after seeing the upgrades at Rok's Watch, it did become hard to argue the reasoning.

However, every time he saw the terrible shape that the outer city was in, just as he saw it now, he became filled with a mixture of emotions. He wished there was some way to avoid the outer city altogether, but at the same he wished he could do something to help these people.

The road through the outer city and to the east gate was only a 10-minute walk. Normally, the guards at the gates would ask for identification papers, but wearing the uniform, and rank of the Claymoran Army was a way around that situation.

Even with his uniform on, one of the guards at ground level approached Henrick.

"*Henrick?*" one of the guards called out, this one was female.

"Amelia, how ye doin'?" Henrick asked the female warrior with her name.

Amelia wore the tabard of House Darkbane. She was the youngest sibling of the Darkbane family, but she was also too young to uphold the role of a House Leader. To this end, she was bound by tradition to work as an enlisted person until she came of age. She had platinum blonde hair and eyes that reflected the blue of the lake's surface.

"Never mind me, you're all dirty," she noted his tattered and stained uniform.

"I got separated from Captain Spearfall's team, been on the road for a few days," he answered. "What day is it?"

"It's the 1st Aeresday of Kindletar," Floor answered.

"Thanks, I gotta go report in," Henrick said. As soon as he finished his words, he began walking forward once more. The two guards moved aside, and went back to their post without a bother.

Henrick did not feel too lightly about holding secrets from his fellow warriors, but he had to weigh his words carefully. He wanted as few people as possible to notice that he was back in the city, and he did not want anyone asking about Thor Spearfall or the others until he arrived at his destination. So far, his journey back had been uneventful, and he was looking to keep it that way.

Once he had made it through the east gate of the city, he soon found himself in a most familiar place and was once more face to face with the statue of Samuel Blade-Briar. With his friends gone, however, Henrick had no time to stop and stare at the stone idol.

He traveled west through the city, passing by many people, even at this hour, and Henrick paid them no mind. His dirty uniform was noticed by more than one citizen, but it was nothing to fret about. He then passed by the Church of Steel before reaching the Sword Gate. The guards positioned here remained at their posts as Henrick approached and then passed them.

As Henrick entered the inner city, it was for a fleeting moment that he thought about stopping in at the barracks to check his locker for anything he might need, but he decided against it as there was a more pressing matter at hand.

Instead of going to his barracks, he went to the opposite end of the inner city and passed by the tall Claymore Keep. At the opposite end of the inner city, he looked for the Darkbane House. The two-story, mansion-like structure was built using the same materials as the barracks. The roof had yellow tiles, and the windows and doors were outlined with gold. There was a tall hedgeline that traced the perimeter of the mansion grounds, and standing before the property was the Darkbane flag: it was a satin gold background with a multi-pointed black sun and rays of light protruding outward of the same dark color.

As he approached the hedge line of the Darkbane House and stepped on to the gravel walkway, the resounding crunch under his boots had alerted the serf that was on watch just inside the entrance door. The door came open, and the light from inside the main hall poured out to illuminate the walkway further. Henrick and the serf met eyes. It was a male teenager, and the young man could only remind Henrick of his younger years.

"Evening, Sir, how may I assist you?" the serf asked.

"I need to speak to the House Leader," Henrick replied.

"Of course, please come inside, and have a seat," the serf said with a wave of the hand while opening the door wider. "I will go fetch the Lady."

Henrick stepped inside the Darkbane House. The main hall was furnished with several high-quality couches and chairs, and with some of the chairs being close to the door, he decided to go for the first one. He slouched over and held his body up by resting his arms on his thighs.

As he sat there and stared at the floor, he mulled over his thoughts. It had taken him almost two days to reach Claymore, and without a mount to bring him here, his feet were killing him. The urgency of his mission warranted a shorter sleep while on the road, and now that he was comfortable, the weariness felt even heavier.

His thoughts fell upon the information that he had gathered from the water nymph, and wondered how he might go about explaining such information to his sponsor. Henrick knew, however, that if anyone was going to believe him, it was going to be her.

He also was going to need her help if he was going to get an audience with the king. Henrick knew, and so did all of Claymore, that going into the throne room without an invitation is near to the same as issuing the Law of Combat against the king.

He continued to press on his mind for answers, because he had to find some correlation between the shade and the king. And why did the dark shroud of the king feel the same as the shade? It was that notion that baffled him the most, and he simply could not wrap his head around it. From what he could tell, the king was still human, but at the core of it, he understood that he was missing a piece of the puzzle.

Another thing he understood, without question, was that he had some knowledge that the shade were planning to invade Claymore, but he did not know when, and that piece of information was the principle driving him to try and make the best decisions quickly.

Then his mind fell on other aspects of the impending dialogue. The thought was fleeting however, when his eye became distracted by the sudden realization that the main hall had been rearranged and decorated differently than when he was a serf.

The wooden chairs, like the one he sat in, were by all accounts the same ones he remembered dusting off long ago. However, there was a new chandelier of candles in the lobby, and the boring yellow carpets that he swept in his years were replaced by black carpet. Metallic gold baseboard traced the bottom of the wood slat walls.

He noticed several new pictures had been placed on the walls of the grand hall, and it was this curiosity that got him to stand back up to take a look. He saw pictures of the Darkbane House leaders, starting with the founding leader, Sarah Darkbane with the phrase "The First Queen of Claymore" included on the bronze plaque beneath the picture.

Henrick followed the list of pictures down a ways until he came to the eighth and final picture that was up, and it was the one face he was familiar with the most.

"Henrick?"

The familiar voice of a woman beckoned Henrick's eyes to the middle tier of the staircase where he saw his friend Melissa Darkbane. She had long locks of golden blonde hair, sharp green eyes, and a facial profile that was renowned across the city. She wore a nightgown of gold, and her voluptuous features attempted to catch Henrick's eyes off guard, but success was only held for a second as she finished her descent of the stairs.

"Melissa, it's good to see ye," Henrick said but in a low tone.

"I would say the same, but your uniform has me *curious*," she noted.

"Aye, can we speak in private?" he asked.

"Oh! I see you're trying to season me up with that dirty man look again, eh," Melissa followed through with a flirty tone.

The thought of reigniting flames of passion with Melissa pulled Henrick's mind astray, but as his heart pounded harder in that moment, the thuds in his chest woke him out of his stupor.

"I wish...I could agree, but," Henrick began, but then he moved closer to her to whisper. "Thor is dead."

"*What?*" Melissa blurted out. She looked around the main hall to see if anyone was around, or listening. She then grasped Henrick's hand and began to lead him upstairs. "We'll talk in my room."

Upstairs the two went, and once they reached the second story, Melissa steered Henrick down a hallway. After a short way, the hallway made a bend, and then they arrived at the door that would lead them to their destination. Melissa turned the knob, swung the door open, and the two went inside. She then closed the door, and flipped the deadbolt. The door entered into the room at one of the corners.

"Okay, we should be good to talk in here," Melissa said.

Henrick looked around the room. The floor was mostly hardwood panels, but there was thick, soft carpet leading from the door to the king-size bed. The walls were designed in similar fashion to the rest of the interior found throughout the mansion. The carpet was stark white, and that made Henrick avoid stepping on it.

The bed, at the opposite corner of the room, had a cherry-stained frame with some sophisticated routing that followed along the planks. It was covered with purple blankets and had golden pillow cases.

Along the wall to the left of the door was a round table with a few chairs by it, and just beyond that was a pair of purple curtains that covered the windows on the next adjacent wall. The table had a silver platter with four silver cups surrounding a large glass pitcher with some tea inside of it.

Along the wall to the right of the door were several dressers, and on top of those dressers were the countless glass bottles of soaps, lotions, oil, and perfume. In the next corner after the dressers, there was a five-foot-tall mirror.

And in the center of the room was a large wooden tub with a water pump to bring hot water up from the boiler downstairs. The tub was currently filled with a steamy mixture of water and soapy bubbles.

Soon after coming into the room, Henrick made his way to the table and sat down. His beleaguered demeanor was obvious to Melissa.

"So what happened?" Melissa asked.

"We left Claymore, and took our time followin' the west coast," Henrick began. "We stopped in Solace, and Rok's Watch along the way. We made our way out to Waste Waste, and durin' the night, we got ambushed."

As Henrick told his story, Melissa made her way over to the table and took up another seat. She remained silent and allowed her friend to continue. As Henrick's words came to a point of suspense, he brought his eyes to meet her.

"What does yer family know of the shade?" he asked her.

"You were *ambushed* by the shade?" she replied as much as stated in complete surprise.

"Aye," Henrick answered. "We never had a chance against 'em either"

It was at this point that Henrick took the shield and Thor's weapon off of his back. He placed the shield on the floor, leaned up against his table leg, and then placed the wooden sheathed blade on the table as he continued.

"Me and this blade're all that remain," Henrick said grimly.

Melissa took note of the weapon on the table, but since she was the one that personally taught Henrick the Darkbane shield style, she couldn't help but notice the nonstandard issue shield he had placed on the ground. She took the shield in her own hands, strapped it to her left arm, and then took it back off to see the face.

"Slightly larger than what you're used to," she noted. "But the weight is lesser, and a sign of the Twins on the face? Don't tell me you're a believer now?"

"That's not the worst part," Henrick proclaimed. "While I was out there, I learned the shade're planning to attack Claymore."

Melissa paused and lowered the shield onto the table next to the weapon and tea set. Her eyes judged the man but only for a second. She took a moment to measure the weight of Henrick's words. His words were never questionable to her in the past, and not for a second did she believe that he was making this up, but news of invasion would be hard to sell.

When Melissa remained, Henrick continued, "What do ye know about the shade?"

"We have books on them. Old books," she began, staring out into the open air as she reminisced during her story. "My mother would read them to me from time to time, when she would teach me about all the vile things in this world we live in. The shade are agents of Abyss, referred to as the Children of Abyss sometimes, but they live out in the middle of the Kadavar wasteland. Their presence in Terra Sanguinar was removed almost seven hundred years ago."

"They can travel quickly in the dark, and natural light sources, like fire, disappear when their presence is nearby. Sunlight, however, will kill them, while magical light keeps them from stepping through the shadows."

"If the shade *are* coming here, we need to tell the king," she finished.

"I've been thinkin' about that during me way back," Henrick said. "I'm pretty sure the king sent us out there to die."

Melissa's eyes beamed onto Henrick as she warned, "That is a grave accusation to be making Henrick."

Henrick then stood up at that moment, and regarded her as he continued with animated arms, "Ye know Claymore just as good as me, Melissa, perhaps much more. There's been somethin' playin' in the background for years 'round here. The people have felt it, too. Crime has grown in the villages, and the lower class has been bled dry by high tax to the point of hunger and poverty. Claymore is weak right now, and it's a perfect time to strike."

At that moment, she almost felt embarrassed, for it seemed that Henrick had been keeping a better watch on the kingdom than she or the other house leaders. She was curious just how deeply he felt about the situation, and how he was planning to deal with it.

His logic on a long-term strategy to weaken the nation before attacking was smart, and she had to wonder if maybe he was right. Perhaps something is going on, and the army has been blind about it. But she also wondered how he would go about proving this theory to the leadership of the kingdom?

"The news of Thor's death will get the attention of the house leaders," Melissa explained. "But how will you plead your case against the king?"

"Before the group of us left, the captain said that a scout reported a witch, and that the scout reported straight to the king," Henrick explained. "Scouts aren't supposed to report to the king..."

"They're supposed to report to the general," Melissa finished the statement.

"A major breach in protocol, if you ask me," Henrick added.

Melissa then stood up, and took a few steps to stand before Henrick. The two of them locked eyes.

"I need to talk to the king," Henrick said.

"Fine," she said plainly in agreement.

She then leaned in, and wrapped her arms around Henrick's neck and pulled him in for a hug, but it wasn't a hug she was after. The two of them were suddenly locking lips in a kiss. The bristle facial hair of Henrick's that had been growing scratched at her but it only added to her arousal. His hands went down to her hips and he pulled her in tighter.

"But I'm gonna collect on this right now," Melissa said without pulling her face away.

"What'd ye have in mind?" he returned the playful tone.

She pulled away from him in the moment, having felt his excitement, and started to walk towards her bathtub. On the way there, she pulled the string on the back of her gown, and slipped it off, one shoulder at a time, exposing her naked, curvy figure.

She stepped into the still steaming water, and sat down in the tub while turning her gaze to Henrick. She moved her feet out of the water, and rested her calves on the edges of the tub as if she was opening an invitation.

"I'll let you figure that part out," Melissa said.

King Marc Blade-Briar sat erect in his high-back throne made of oak and red velvet cushions. His left hand rested on the arm of the throne while his right hand was outstretched to the hilt of the royal flamberge that stood on blade-end.

From the throne, a red carpet traveled nearly thirty feet between two pairs of stone pillars until it reached the wooden double doors that led into the throne room. The pillars had a pair of torch sconces, and on either side of the carpet, there were tables that sported various plates, cups, and cutlery.

There was a single window on each wall, except for the wall that held the doors. The windows were no more than a foot from the 12-foot-high ceiling, and about two-square-feet in size. Each window also had a red curtain that was pulled across it, but that did not stop some of the sunlight from outside pouring into the room.

At this particular moment, and sitting at the various tables were some of Claymore Army's commanders, and each of the house leaders, and General Hormac, who sat at the same table as the Blade-Briar house leader.

General Hormac was an aerin man with a bald head that had worn too many helmets throughout the years. He had brown eyes, a square jaw, and the creases in his face that showed him to be close in age to the king. He wore a suit of chainmail, and wore a white and red tabard that signified others of his station as the highest-ranking member of the army.

The man next to the general was Marc Blade-Briar the Second, named after his father of course. This man was in his mid-thirties and had short, straight, raven black hair. His eyes were black, and he wore the dark red tabard of House Blade-Briar. Marc the Second, like his father, was also very well built.

On the same side of the room, but at a farther table from the throne was Roland Hadoku. He was the leader of House Odoku, and he was the only odum that was in the room at the moment. The Odoku House always favored wielding a short and trimmed beard, and Roland was no exception to that tradition, although the same could not be said for his bald scalp. Like most of the men in Claymore, he was also very muscular. He wore the blue robes of his house as opposed to wearing armor.

On the other side of the room with a couple of the commanders, was Tyr Vicidian. He was a sanct, a human subtype with bronze skin that trace their origins to the eastern reaches of the continent. His

147

face had angular features, and he was the most lacking in stature between all the leadership. He was by far not the least dangerous in terms of combat due to his incredible dexterity and agility. He had straight brown hair that was tied back into a ponytail, and his eyes were as green as the solid green tabard he wore.

"Where is Darkbane, General?" the King asked without turning his eyes away from the door. His voice was deep, and almost brooding.

"She will be along any moment, sire," the general replied.

"This had better be good," Tyr commented.

"She said it was important," Marc the Second shot at the Vicidian Leader.

"Either way, you two bickering will not help the matter," the General said.

A loud knock then came at the doors of the throne room. After the proper three second wait, the doors came open at the hands of a couple of guardsmen, and standing before the open doors was Melissa Darkbane. She was wearing a suit of gold-tinged plate armor with the Darkbane tabard pulled over it.

Standing behind her, and slightly to the side, was Henrick. He wore his standard breastplate armor under the Claymore tabard, which was still dirty and beaten from before. However, the man did manage to shave his face. The two of them marched forward. Melissa's steps were coupled with the sound of clanking metal. Both of them walked on to the carpet leading to the throne.

Henrick exchanged looks with each of the house leaders and the commanders out of curiosity as they were curious as well. Then the interest between the various leaders began to peek as they exchanged looks and whispers between themselves. Tyr remained silent on his side of the room, and patiently waited for the dialogue to begin.

Halfway down the carpet, Melissa and Henrick came to a halt to stand before the king and his throne. It was at this moment that the leadership in attendance recognized something of far greater interest. Henrick was the only one, save for the King, who was armed.

Henrick looked upon the king from over the shoulder of Melissa. He used what he understood of his supernatural sense, which wasn't much, and attempted to reach out with his mind and feelings. He was trying to recreate the phenomena that he had seen the first time he laid eyes on the King. This time, however, the Sergeant did not find what he was looking for. Furthermore, the torches on the pillars were lit.

"Your Majesty," Melissa began her address to the king. "This is Sergeant Henrick Skullbright." She waved a hand in his direction, but did not turn around, and kept her eyes on the king. "He was part of Captain Spearfall's unit, and is the only one to have returned so far."

General Hormac rose out of his chair in an instant. The other leaders drew their eyes upon Henrick more closely now. The general marched to Henrick's side immediately.

"What do you mean you're the only one, Sergeant?" the General asked, and his tone was almost accusing.

Henrick turned his head to regard the general. He said, "It's true, sir. We were ambushed at night while we rested at Wastewatch."

149

The information of an attack against Claymore caused the other leaders to rise from their seats before they began to form a semi-circle behind Henrick and Melissa as they walked forward.

"Ambushed by who?" the general continued his questionnaire.

"Dark creatures known as the shade," Henrick stated.

The eyes of the skeptical leaders tried to judge the sergeant, but before they could draw their own conclusions another argument was voiced.

"That's absurd," the voice of the king reigned in the concerned eyes. "The shade are nothing more than a legend. They have not been seen for almost seven hundred years."

"My apologies sire, but I know what I saw," Henrick argued with polite bearing. "Had it not been for the moons, I might not have been able to see them at all." It was in the following moment that Henrick removed the shield and the wooden sheathe from his back. He left the shield on the ground, but held the resting blade in both hands for display. "I very much doubt the captain would let me take his weapon willin'ly."

"The captain has had that weapon for decades," Roland commented from behind, clearly recognizing the foreign sheathe. "For you to have this weapon is unlikely."

"I agree," Tyr added, following the thought. "Thor would never let anyone have that blade."

General Hormac snapped the sheathed weapon from Henrick's hand, and gave the weapon a closer inspection. He raised the weapon near to his eye level, and exposed the part of the blade that was closest to the hilt.

The afternoon sunlight reflected off the silvery metal in which the blade was made, and the streak of light was seen by the audience across the eyes of the general. The metallic composition was part of what the general was verifying, however, he was also looking for the stamp in the metal. After his inspection, he fully sheathed the weapon, and handed it back to Henrick.

"The blade has the royal stamp of the Beru-Lai, and the weapon is most assuredly made of arcanium," the General stated. "The weapon is Thor's."

"Then Thor *is* dead," Roland said, emphasizing his words with a wave of his hand.

The leaders looked to one another in somber agreement.

"Everyone else is dead. How is it that you survived?" the general asked.

"A hunter found me, and patched me up over three days. I can show ye the scar, if ye'd like?" Henrick offered.

The general then turned to the king. "Sire, the presence of the shade could be troubling."

Henrick moved to return the sheathed weapon to his back, and leaned over to pick up his shield. During that time, the king remained silent and unflinching in his seat. He watched Henrick's movements as if he was a hawk. Before Henrick could put his shield on his back, he discovered the king's gaze upon him. Their eyes met in quiet contention.

While most of the attendees paid their attention to the king and awaited the quick response, the Vicidian House Leader read Henrick's face.

"More to say, sergeant?" Tyr prompted the man.

At the completion of the question, all eyes fell back on Henrick, but he did not return his gaze to any of them, not even the general. The general, with his three decades of service under his belt, suddenly saw fire in the eyes of the sergeant, and then realized that the king was locked into those eyes.

"Speak, sergeant," the General commanded.

"The king sent us out there to die," Henrick accused after swallowing the lump in his throat.

Marc the Second stomped to stand in front of Henrick. Henrick remained unwavering in his position as the general remained at his side.

"You will watch your tongue, *sergeant*. Lest you have a death wish?" Marc the Second threatened through clenched teeth.

Melissa then made a step to Marc's side, and said, "I would watch your tone, Marc."

"Shut your damn mouth, Darkbane, I will *not* have you, or your pup, turn this throne room into chaos," Marc the Second nearly screamed.

"Surely your father is capable of defending himself, as a king of claymore should," Melissa pointed out. "Or perhaps, you know something about these accusations."

With no leg to stand on, Marc the Second backed off, and back-peddled to stand beside the general. The other leaders heard the whole exchange. All of them could see where this was going, and some of them had to wonder if their assumptions were going to come true.

General Hormac exchanged looks upon Henrick and the king once more after the Blade-Briar Leader had moved aside.

"In the last few moments, before the accusation had been addressed, the king and the sergeant, here, have been locked in a stare to which the likes I have not seen in a long time," the general began with a hint of formality in his tone as if addressing the room. "Here are the facts; Thor is dead, the rest of his team is dead, save for the sergeant, the sergeant has just accused the king of a treasonous act, and so far, the king has remained silent."

The other leaders, in unison, began to back away from Henrick and the general as they felt their most sacred law of Claymore would be cited.

"In accordance with the First Law of Claymore, Subsection Echo, the sergeant may challenge the integrity of the king through ritual combat until one of them is dead," the general said while continuing to look back and forth between the two would-be combatants.

"There will be no ritual combat," the king spoke.

The narrowed eyes of everyone then fell upon the king curiously.

The king continued, "The sergeant has come into my throne room spreading a fairytale about an ancient foe that no longer exists. He clearly has tried to put the houses against one another, and seeks to divide us even further should his doomsaying spread from the keep. In accordance with the Sixth Law of Claymore, I will instead spare the sergeant's life due to his ignorance, but to ensure that no more fiction is spread across the Kingdom I am going to expel him from our lands."

It was after these words that the king rose from his throne, but did not move his feet an inch. The king pointed a finger, and a scowl of contained rage at Henrick.

"I am giving you *three hours* to get your ass out of my city, and by the next morning, you had better be outside of my lands," the king declared.

The entire time the king had spoken to Henrick, the general watched the king with a discerning eye, and he could not believe that the situation was being sidelined as it was. In the early days of his rule, the general knew the king would relish at the idea of splitting heads with an overconfident subordinate.

But that was years ago, and apparently the times had changed. The general knew that the king was making a mistake, and when word got out about this meeting to the general population, it was going to generate more turmoil in the kingdom. For now, though, the general had to stand by the king's decision.

"Darkbane, get him out of here," the general commanded.

"Come, sergeant," Melissa said as she guided him towards the door with a pointing arm.

Once Henrick and Melissa were out of the throne room, the king sat back down.

"Vicidian. A word. Everyone else can leave," the king demanded.

With that, the commanders, Marc the Second, Roland, and the general departed the throne room.

"Yes, Majesty?" Tyr asked.

"You will have your artisans develop posters for that one; I want to make sure he does not cause any more problems in the kingdom," the king requested.

A smirk spread across the face of the Tyr, "And what should the bounty be set at, Sire?"

———————— ◯ ————————

Later that day, Melissa escorted Henrick to the outside of the west gate. Henrick had his backpack with his typical configuration of goods. Plus, he had the sandaran water blade, and the white heater shield strapped to his back. He had the look of an adventurer about him.

Henrick and Melissa took a look around for any prying eyes. The outer city of the west gate looked completely run down like the east side, and the people who were out and about didn't look any better.

As it seemed like they were okay to talk, the two of them then exchanged glances as if a long time would pass before he would be back. The two of them smiled at the memories they had together.

Melissa spoke first, "You did good in there. You didn't issue the challenge, but the king will be seen as weak, now."

"I was about to challenge 'em, Melissa, I was," Henrick said through a shake of his head. "But the King didn't take his eyes off of me. He knew that I was not supposed to be there. That I was supposed to be dead."

"The general saw it, too," Melissa added. "And I imagine the king's movements will be weighed very carefully from now on."

A moment of pause came about, and it cued Henrick to turn to the road going west.

"The shade are comin'," he said. "The king's words're not gonna to deter me from defendin' this place. I'll be back when I find the way."

"Might I suggest something?" she asked.

Henrick remained silent.

"Go to Lumen, they have a library there. Perhaps you can find something that will help us. And as much as I hate to say it, if the shade *are* coming, we may need to get some help from a wizard."

"What about the law?" Henrick argued.

Melissa shrugged at the notion, "We'll cross that bridge when we get to it."

Henrick nodded. "Aye then, I'll send word of my return."

The two of them then came together with a profound hug.

"Take care," was her last words before they parted ways.

About two miles down the road, Henrick took a pause in his trek along the road to look back at Claymore from a distance. As he looked back, however, he noticed he was being stalked from about twenty feet away along the road.

"Serena," Henrick called out.

"At least you remembered this time," she jested. "So, what happened in there?"

"I saw the king, and he saw a ghost," Henrick explained. "I told them what I knew, and I was exiled for it."

"Exile?" Serena said in disbelief, rearing her head back. "That doesn't sound like the *Claymore* way."

"It's not," he confirmed.

"So...who was that at the gate?" Serena asked without skipping a beat.

"Her name is Melissa, she's the leader of the Darkbane House," Henrick replied.

"Is that all? You two were hugging it out. Seems like fraternization to me," Serena goaded.

"If ye must know, we *are* friends," Henrick shot back with a smirk. "Which by the way, she suggested I go to Lumen."

"Lumen, huh? I've never been there," Serena said.

"Aye, me neither," he added. "Apparently they have a lot of books, and perhaps one of them holds the key to defeatin' the shade."

"Sounds like a plan. Like I told you before, I've been instructed to help you with your mission," she offered.

"Aye, I'll take all I can get," Henrick said.

"See, I knew you might say something like that, so I brought my friend." Serena waved her arm, and looked to her left. Coming up, and out of the tall grass was her tiger companion. "Sand is gonna help us, too."

"Bah. I almost forgot about him," Henrick exclaimed.

Serena scoffed at Henrick. "Ha. Now who in their right mind would forget about a 400-pound animal."

The comment brought a snarling yet playful roar from the tiger.

Henrick began to walk west with Serena and Sand in tow. She laughed as he had admitted defeat. The sun fell ever closer to the horizon as the hours in the day went by. It was going to be a several days hike from Claymore, but Lumen would be the next stop.

CHAPTER EIGHT
EARTH, WIND, AND FURY

It had been five days since Yobo took his final step off of the Skyreach. The winding stairs that had led him down from the mountain proved to be less daunting than when he had gone up them so many years ago, but none-the-less, he had made it down without losing his balance, and without much of an encounter.

On more than one occasion, Master Asulus would provide lessons to Yobo about the different creatures that lived among the trees of the Viridian Shade. Some of those creatures would sometimes find their way up into the mountain caves, or hide in burrows in the hills to the south. During his trek, Yobo wondered where all the creatures from his lessons were at, but then his memory and imagination brought on images of creatures he would rather not meet, and so he instead felt fortunate to have not run into any.

Throughout the five days of travel, he had seen much of the landscape in which he could only remember viewing from the great heights of his former home. The different forms of scenery gave him a therapeutic feeling. From the rocks of the mountains, to the overgrown trees of the forest, and the moss-patched hills. It all reminded him of the garden back at the temple. He and the other students were always in charge of taking care of it. It was a way for the masters to teach the students to be responsible with their gifts, and to care for all innocent things no matter how large or gentle they may be. The feelings made his journey enjoyable for the most part.

During other parts of his journey, he unknowingly found that his demeanor changed. He was no longer looking at the amazing world of Terra, and instead, he felt the pressure of revenge banging on the door of his post-stressed mind. The notion snapped him into a snarling realization, and it reminded him why he came down from the mountain in the first place. He looked down the road with violence clear in his eyes and determination in his heart. Over the course of the five days, Yobo found himself vowing to avenge his master and his friends. Each time his mind wandered in this direction; it became amplified by the trauma that plagued him.

It was through the cracks in his mind that fear and doubt seeped in, because even though his memory of the events on Skyreach drove him forward, it also led him back to the memories of his childhood. Yobo was countlessly stricken with the weight of his inner turmoil, but he knew that he had to push forward. He knew there was a price that had yet to be paid.

He had not come across any monsters on the road, but to Yobo, the monsters inside his mind made the journey quite eventful. The man was hoping to reach his destination to give his mind some distraction.

It was mid-morning of the present day when Yobo set off again, the sun shone upon his back and illuminated the way to the west. There were only a few clouds in the sky, the temperature was warm, but not hot, and the breeze rolling across the gold-splashed hills made the scenery move as if Yobo watched cresting waves across an ocean made of summer.

Here and there, giant boulders and other such rocks dotted the landscape to the east and north, but as the day went on, all of that seemed to fade away when Yobo finally reached the base of the Skyfoot Hills, a range of foothills surrounding the mountains of Skyreach.

At the bottom of the hills, the road continued west, and for a good stretch it carved through the landscape on a nearly straight path. After a couple more miles, the road turned to the northwest, and ran alongside the Dryad River. The golden, rocky fields faded into lush green plains on both sides of the river, but the everlasting presence of the summer solstice could still be observed by the various golden straws that appeared in the midst of the emerald blades. The river banks were smothered by cattails, but every so often, there was an opening between the plants. Through the openings, Yobo watched the soothing flow of the river as it ran to the west. The water was crystal clear, and he even managed to spot some fish swimming against the current.

His fish watching came to a pause when he noticed a signpost displayed on the side of the road. Yobo approached the sign, and counted three arrow-shaped signs and all of them pointed to the west.

Yobo noted that there were no arrows pointing to the southeast in which he had come, but he decided not to dwell on the notion too much. He returned his focus to the arrow-shaped signs which held names spelled in the feylic language. From top to bottom, the arrows read: *Telosa, Riverdale,* and *Baer.* The monk knew that he was headed to Telosa, and had never heard of the other places listed. Either way, his journey carried him farther to the northwest.

For the next hour, he continued to walk alongside the 100-meter-wide river. At the end of that hour, the road brought him to an intersection, and the north side of a wooden bridge that spanned across the running water. At this intersection, he found another sign. According to the arrows on this one, Telosa was north, the other locations were still to the west, and the arrow that pointed south had the name of the bridge, *Thunderbridge.*

The monk turned for the road that went north, and after about half-an-hour, the background of the scenery began to fill with the western reaches of the Skyfoot Hills. The immediate landscape was relatively flat, but it lazily climbed in elevation the longer the road went.

Eventually, the elevation leveled out, and as Yobo came to the top of the comfortable slope, he could see the dryad city at the other end of the prairie before him. From a distance, the location looked like a patch of dotting colors on the hillside. Yellows, purples, and cyans were clumped together inside walls of drab green.

The foothills surrounded the city on all sides, but beyond that, Yobo could see the dark green silhouette of the Viridian Shade rising above the peaks. Furthermore, the Skyreach Mountains stood above everything else like a blue shadow.

As he got closer, he could see the general layout of the city as it began at the base of the hills before climbing up in elevation. Winding roads and avenues drove deeper into the heart of the city. The splashes of color he noted from before were the painted roof trimming of the many buildings, and there didn't seem to be any sort of organization to the randomly colored town.

Yobo's golden eyes continued to scan the city, his eyes eventually came across a large, stark white structure near the highest point of the city at the top of the hill. The structure was easily the tallest one among all the others, and even more peculiar was the cross-shape that it held near its crowning point. At the center of this cross-shape was a large golden window or beacon of some sort, and with the bright, summer sunlight, it seemed as though the structure glowed with a bright, golden magic or a star.

By the time the monk peeled his eyes from the golden light, he found that he was about 200 yards from the main gate of the dryad city, and the city walls. The walls, and the gate, were made of a grayish wood that did not seem painted, and it all stood approximately 10-feet tall. The top of the walls were designed to have a wavy look to them, and the design would ascend and descend repeatedly all the way around the city. These curvy boards were also painted with a drab green.

Yobo saw that this wavy design was prevalent through the dryad town as all the roofs shared the design, but instead of green it was all the colors that he had seen from before.

Just as the gate had been given observation, the monk noticed a small structure on the outside to the right, and a post that flew the Telosan flag: an olive-green background with a purple head of an antlered deer.

Nearby, several guards were posted both outside the gates and on top of the walls. The guards had been watching the monk like a hawk as soon as he came into view, and as Yobo stepped closer and closer to the gate, the guards began to gather their weapons and prepare to challenge the approach of their visitor.

The dryad guards wore green suits of wooden plated armor on top of dark leathers, and they wore complementing open-face helmets that sported purple plumes. The guards exchanged looks and whispers with each other as the human continued on his course. When they all agreed that the human had stepped too far, four of them sprinted forward with their spears at the ready. The troops on the wall readied their bows.

The challenging dryads stomped in an audible warning to Yobo. The tall human was not expecting a conflict, but he did recognize the demeanor of the guards and so he stopped.

"Halt!" a guard sharply yelled at the top of his lungs in the human language. "Do not come any further!" The guard's spear remained at the ready in both hands.

The monk returned the volume, but he spoke in feylic, "My name is Yobo of Skyreach. I have- "

The guard then interrupted Yobo, and returned the feylic language, "Your name is of no concern to us. Leave these grounds, now!"

The guard's demands took Yobo by surprise, and he suddenly felt like he wasn't sure about what to do at the moment. His mind played back to the image of the note he had found, which was now in his pack, and he knew that this was where he had to be, but why were the dryads acting the way that they were? Without having a full understanding of the situation, Yobo decided that he needed to remain assertive in his quest.

"I am not leaving! The dryads of Skyreach have perished! I need to tell your people" The monk spoke aloud.

"*Skyreach*?" the guard said with an almost mocking tone. "No one cares about those traitors. And if they took in a *piss-eye* like you, then good riddance."

"What did you *call* me?" Yobo's words came out calmly, but he could feel his emotions flare up in an instant. The blood in Yobo's veins twitched as the slur rang from the dryad's mouth. His tone was like he wanted the dryad to say it again. As he made his question, he began taking measured steps toward the guard.

In a flash, Yobo's eyes took him to his hometown from when he was child. He remembered the many people that called him such foul words, but it was more than remembering, the many voices circled around his head like an echo in a cave. This sudden turmoil built upon itself until Yobo found himself reliving the nightmare of his parents' death, and his master's death.

The monk's buried anger began to surface, and it made the hair on his skin stand up straight as the adrenaline began to pump from his brain.

The guard could see the anxiety on the human's face, and with the number of guards still standing watch at the gate, he knew that the human would have to be a damn fool to cause a scene, lest the human was looking for a death wish. But the guard was okay, if that happened.

Full of confidence and bravado, the guard granted Yobo's request, "You are a *piss-eye*, mutt. Now get out of here."

Yobo took his backpack and quarterstaff off his back, tossed it to the side, and made himself ready for the oncoming attack by taking the stance of Cova's Maw. His hands were clenched into fists. The monk had sworn to himself that he would not be the young boy from his memories, and he would not allow these soldiers to insult him without a response.

The dryads noted the gold-eyed humans' stance.

The one that had been speaking thus far, spoke again, "It would seem this one means to violate our city, men. Let's not disappoint him." At the end of his sentence, the guard rushed forward, spear in hand.

The other guards at the gate began making profound movements. The ground guards moved to join their companion while the archers on the wall readied arrows.

The lead guard closed the gap, and knew that the human stood no chance against him, or his companions, and once he got into range, he thrust the tip of his spear at Yobo's chest. The guard's lack of understanding suddenly became his undoing as the monk dodged the stabbing point of the weapon, and then stepped into the body of the guard. Yobo grasped the spear, and then used the polearm to force the soldier to move how he wanted. The monk's strength was almost twice that of his opponent, and he used that difference in power to swing the guard around his body until ultimately tossing him aside like another piece of luggage.

The guard crashed against the grassy field before the city's gate. The ground released a cloud of dirt and dust as it became disturbed. Yobo flipped the spear in hand to get it into a throwing position, and he made it ready to throw at the now-prone guard. The monk coiled his arm and threw the spear at the vulnerable guard.

As the guard came to a sitting position, the spear punctured the ground between his legs. The guard looked over at the human with anger as if the reluctance of a killing blow was meant to mock him.

Yobo made a single stomp towards the guard with a puffed-up chest and yelled, "*Get up!*"

The monk was challenged in an instant, but not by the guard he had tossed. The other guards from the gate encroached upon him, and all three of them approached at once. Yobo was not about to let advantages take root against him, and so he doubled back to get his quarterstaff.

Once the blunt weapon was back in hand, the monk turned to find the three guards had come to their own form of measured steps as they slowly worked to circle around him. By this time, the initial guard had gotten up and joined his comrades. The battle was now four against one, not including the archers that still stood upon the wall.

The battle was steeped in suspense as Yobo exchanged glances with the guards, and kept his ears handy should a guard decide to move against him from behind. The monk's experience with the Uireb Nen has taught him to wait for the opponent to make the first move when outnumbered, and so that was what he did.

The anger continued to roil inside of Yobo, but as the span of time grew, the edge of rage began to dull. In Yobo's heart, he knew to treat life with respect, but he could not let go of the disrespect from these dryads. He wanted to punish them. He was no longer the little padfoot in the streets; he had the power to shove his fists in their face.

No longer would the unsureness of the situation continue. In his readied stance, Yobo lowered the bottom tip of his staff onto the top of his foot, and in a blurred movement, he used his foot to launch, and aim the other tip of his staff at the head of one guard.

The quarterstaff moved with such power and speed that the dryad had no time to react, and the weapon smashed him square into his nose with a resounding crunch. The guard's eyes went black in an instant while the staff bounced into a slow twirl in the air.

The sudden release of energy took the other guards by surprise. Yobo hopped backwards, and then pivoted on his feet to step inside of the spear that was pointed at his back. The monk used his giant size hands to grab the spear, and when he noticed another guard approach to diffuse the maneuver, Yobo yanked on the weapon, forced the attached guard to move, and used the spear to parry the next. After the deflective maneuver, the monk then shoved the one guard into the other resulting in a collision that sent them off their feet and rolling to the ground.

Yobo snapped his eyes to the sky and reached up to grasp his quarterstaff as it fell back down to him. His eyes then fell upon the fourth guard and prepared for the coming assault.

But no such attack came, and instead, the guard studied Yobo with narrowed eyes. It was the lead guard, and the dryad came to realize that perhaps the half-human knew how to fight. After all, the monk managed to put all of them on the ground without actually injuring anyone.

In kind, Yobo measured the guard with his own eyes and realized the guard was stalling. But the monk would not waste the opportunity to strike back at the guard that held such slurs in his vocabulary.

Yobo started a baton routine with the quarterstaff; spinning it in hand, then with two hands, then spun it across his back with wide arcs, and vibrant *whooshes*. In the final movements of his routine, Yobo made a full twirl with his own body to gain as much momentum as possible and then followed through with grabbing the end of his staff and whacking the guard in the side of the head.

The guard was amazed by all the movement, but when Yobo made the obvious change in his footwork, the guard noticed immediately and went for the duck.

The quarterstaff missed the blow. The guard stepped in, and went for the stab. The spear found meat in Yobo's underarm, and as the monk came to face the soldier again. The pointed blade broke out from under the skin just below his shoulder blade.

Cold lightning shot through his body all at once, and Yobo gritted his teeth in pain as the weight of the pointed weapon relinquished from his body in reverse motion. He could feel the blood running down his back and side, and the sting of sweat getting mixed into the wound. The flow of adrenaline came to a screeching halt, but only for a second.

It was in that second that the guard followed his attack with a front kick to the giant man's hip. In that second, Yobo had no strength to brace against the kick, and was sent to the ground. This time it was the monk's body that kicked up a cloud of dust and dirt, and his quarterstaff went flying away.

As Yobo came tumbling to the ground, reality snapped back into his mind, and he quickly scrambled to his feet, and prepared to be on the defensive. He had to ignore the fires in his body as he forced himself to use his upper body to get up. His whole right arm was quivering from pain. Every little mico-movement brought on stings and bites inside his muscles. He needed to get up quickly, though, as he feared the lead guard would be in pursuit.

But the pursuit never came.

Instead, Yobo saw the squad of guards back on their feet, standing side by side, and with their spears at the ready again. Except, they were still missing the guard that had blacked out.

"Come on, *half-breed*," the lead guard taunted before throwing nods to the other two dryads.

169

The two guards rushed forward to engage Yobo once more. They were filled with intent to stop the lone invader at any cost, and that cost was the monk's life. The soldiers could see that the human was favoring a side of his torso, and so they knew the advantage was on their side.

The tall monk had it in his mind to avoid using the side that featured his wound, but as the spears came at him, his trained reactions forbad him from committing to such a handicap. When the first tip jabbed at his body, he used the back of his hand to push the weapon out wide while simultaneously twisting in a semicircle to deliver a devastating roundhouse kick. The giant foot of the monk knocked the guard out.

Yobo completed the circle as he dove into a crouch. He didn't see it, but he could feel the other spear move the air above him. The monk brought his eyes up to lock on to the guard's, and from his lower position, Yobo pinched the haft of the spear in his armpit before rising up with his fist not far behind. The monk's whitened knuckles connected with the dryad's jaw, and took the soldier off of his feet before plummeting to the ground on his back.

Then it was just Yobo and the lead soldier.

The guards upon the walls pulled their bowstrings taut in anticipation. The suspense was short lived as one of the archers let an arrow loose. Yobo backflipped to avoid the arrow, and the several that followed it. When he landed on his feet, he found that one archer had withheld their shot, but the monk quickly noted the single movement before snatching the arrow out of its flight.

Yobo realized he had no solid defense against the archers, and he wasn't sure how many arrows he could keep up with until one found his skin. The throbbing pain in his side reminded him of his other issue as his blood-stained rags stuck to his body. It was at this point that Yobo lowered his arms as he did not want to further the situation.

"That's right, *piss-eye*. You're outnumbered," the guard said with a smirk. "Time to give up."

The slur echoed on the cavernous walls of his ear canal and rang repeatedly until the dark shadows of his memories and his past reappeared in his mind. They flashed across his vision in an instant, but he saw them all. Yobo could feel the tears swelling in his eyes as his rage was reemerging and quickly becoming overwhelming.

What was the reason for the dryad's spite? He had no idea. He did not understand it. But he knew what he needed to do to get rid of it.

Yobo took the stance of Cova's Maw, and quickly began to draw in the elements of water that filled the air around him. He didn't ask for permission, and he didn't beg either. He forced the molecules to come to him. Just like before. Floating just above his leading hand, the Hesin's Cure began to form, and form quickly. The elements that became bound to the monk's will shed light of blue and white. The orb grew in size, sparks of energy erupted from its surface, and the temperature dropped significantly.

All the guards were enamored by the spectacle of magical light, and were equally unaware that their surprise curiosity had left them visually paralyzed. The spectacle began to attract citizens outside of the gate, but not all of the people watching were struck by awe, though.

Bigger and bigger the Hesin's Cure grew, and the spell was nearing the same potency as the last one he let fly. As he fed his anger with the breaking elements around him, he noted the approach of two figures. They stepped out in front of the citizens before coming to stand at the side of the still-standing lead guard.

The figures were dressed in olive green saams, which were the ceremonial dryad martial art robe, and around their waist they wore white sashes. They were both dryad and seemed otherwise unarmed. Yobo then witnessed the two, in perfect unison, perform the Cova's Maw stance and followed with the Hesin's Cure in pure mastery. What came next though was alien to the human.

The cannonball-sized Hesin's Cure techniques were pulled back smoothly and slowly until the two dryad monks took the sphere in both hands. Then they made one-way motions as if spreading the magic of the sphere across their forearms. As the icy magic disseminated, the frosty magic formed upon their arms until it looked like their hands were deep inside a pair of gauntlets made of jagged ice. The two dryad monks then returned to the Cova's Maw.

As Yobo continued to be locked in his rage, the concept of what the dryads had done and not grasping that idea infuriated him. The human grunted with each exhale, and power swelled in his giant spherical spell. The large orb then grew in size some more.

The ground below Yobo's feet became slick with ice and the area around began to cover with snow.

The sphere shot out bolts of pure ice lightning, and sometimes these bolts would randomly strike and tear up the dirt and grass below.

"The center of power for the Gunn Drambor is pain."

Unexpectedly, the words of his late master echoed inside the walls of Yobo's mind, and just as the name implied again, everything that Yobo had learned on Skyreach came flooding back into his persona. The rage was gone. The hatred was gone. He suddenly wished it could have done the same for the wound on his back, though. However, his sour disappointment from his racist aggressor was not gone.

The steam from his breath soon became the instant reminder of the magic in his hand and Yobo's attention could only fix upon the guard. His respect for life stood in the way of his own feelings. Feelings that wanted to drop the icy bomb on the head of the guard, but he could not simply forgive the one who did not feel the same.

He moved his hand and held the giant, freezing sphere overhead, and yelled, "Call me *piss-eye*, *one more time!*"

The guard stammered with wide eyes, and it caused the two dryad monks to break their stance to regard the fool behind them.

"Did you *provoke* this man?" one of the monks asked. This one looked older and had dark green hair with silver streaks. His skin also has a greenish hue to it.

The guard could only nod and affirm his stance, "His kind are not allowed here."

"That does not permit you to act like an adolescent human. We are dryads. We are superior to them. Now, there is going to be an explosion. Get your men, and the people, out of here. You will be dealt with later," the older monk instructed with lowered brows and a pointed finger.

Without much hesitation, the guard moved to wake his partners up. He was quickly successful, and once they were all on their feet, they turned and ran for the gates. They began to usher citizens away from whatever was about to happen, but that didn't stop the people from crowding the walls of the city.

"Young man," the older dryad monk spoke loudly to Yobo in a neutral manner.

Yobo 's eyes regarded the dryad in silence.

"Use everything you have, and toss the Cure at me," the dryad suggested.

The human's eyes went wide in disbelief at the request. "Are you sure?"

"Of both, I am," the monk replied before making a smirk. The dryad monk then looked to his side, at his apprentice, "Purall. Ready yourself for an earth bullet. I shall deflect this to the sky."

The younger of the two monks, Purall, replied to his teacher, "Yes, Master Tresa."

Purall threw out his arms wide to dismiss the magic of the icy gauntlets. The dryad monk retook Cova's stance before and performed Hesin's Cure once more. Yobo watched the dryad execute the technique but the dryad used it to summon elements that had escaped his lessons from Master Asulus.

Purall used the spell to draw in the particles of the ground around him. Dirt and dust levitated off the ground before being pulled away to coalesce into a sphere of hardened, packed earth and stone. The expansive knowledge of the technique using a new element left Yobo's mouth partially open. All he could muster at the moment was why he didn't think of that. Which made the next technique even more unusual and equally impressive.

Purall changed up the Cova's Maw in such a way that the stance was completely flipped: his leading left side shifted to the back and brought his right side to front, his now-coiled left arm still held the earthy magic, and now the right hand was held out in front. In this advanced stage of the technique, Purall began to use his empty hand to call upon the powers of air.

The new complexities of the Uireb Nen stunned the mind of Yobo. Purall used his abilities to conjure up a second Hesin's Cure. This time his leading hand held the elements of a swirling, miniature, sphere of a cyclone, and if it hadn't been for the dirt and dust floating in the air, Yobo might not have noticed it at all.

The young dryad held a count of two Hesin's Cure, and at the end of it all, Purall flipped the technique around again to bring the earth sphere out front.

"Now, young man," Tresa called to Yobo.

"*Yah!*" Yobo took his Hesin's Cure from overhead and launched it at the older dryad monk with a cry of action.

Tresa took the shout as the cue to be ready for the incoming attack. He charged forward as if sprinting at the giant spell. It was only after a short distance that Tresa dove into a slide to get under the unexpected descent of the Hesin's Cure. With his ice-covered arms, Tresa reached up from his prone position and caught the orb from underneath.

Typically, magic did not have any physical weight, but the sheer magnitude of the spell warranted the weight that Tresa now pushed against. In this moment, the master monk's breath became steam due to the bitter cold air that surrounded the spell.

By all appearances, it looked as if Tresa had caught the giant Hesin's Cure, but it was soon becoming apparent that the orb was not going to get pushed away anytime soon.

Yobo flinched as if he was going to move to help, but he stopped himself since he had no idea what to do at the moment. Perhaps, he thought, this time his rage had gone too far, and the lingering emotions of doubt began seep into the corner of his mind. The tall man lowered his head a bit, and he felt disappointed in himself.

Purall noticed the face on the human. "Do not fret, young man. Suldo's technique is quite dependable."

The phrase, or word, or name rang in the memory of Yobo. He remembered something on the note that said *Suldo's Stand*, and he was instantly filled with a feeling of excitement and profound curiosity. What exactly was Suldo's Stand? He had to wonder.

And just as the tall odum man had finished the thought, the giant Hesin's Cure seemed to vanish in an instant. Yobo looked onward in astonishment at the mastery that this Tresa had with the Uireb Nen. The veteran monk held a Hesin's Cure in his hand as he made his way to his feet. This orb he held above the icy gauntlets was a typical size for practice and sparring, but unlike the rest in which Yobo knew, this orb seemed too heavily concentrated and unstable.

With the icy air gone and things suddenly returning to normal, Tresa's face became drenched in sweat as he focused on keeping the orb contained in such a small form. The compact energy released arcs of frozen lightning, but each of these wicked bolts became attracted to the icy gauntlets and danced across their surface without harming Tresa.

The older monk quickly turned to face west. He saw an area away from the city, away from the roads, and out towards a clearing. Master Tresa looked to the sky which held the descending sun, and with a great thrust into the air, he used Cova's Maw to launch the concentrated magic of the compact spell. As he did, the magic of the icy gauntlets went with it.

Not far into the spell's flight, it began to revert to its original size.

Purall wasted no time. He held up his leading hand as if aiming his earth Cure at the giant frozen one, and with the air Cure in his rear hand, he performed the typical launching maneuver of the Hesin's Cure. In this particular fashion, Purall slammed the air into the sphere of earth which sent both Cure's soaring off into the distance like a supersonic bullet.

The bullet pierced into the giant frozen ball.

BOOM!!!

The explosiveness of the magic with the shining sun in the backdrop made it seem as if the world was covered in the gleam of deep blue and white. The sound, although fleeting, was a cacophonous roar of deafening thunder that echoed for miles, and shook the foundations of the city walls. The citizens watching the spectacle unfold suddenly crouched and lowered their heads in fear that the spell's disaster might reach them. But it never did.

A large pile of pure ice boulders came crashing against the ground below once the sound had completely faded.

The three monks stood there facing the sunny scenery of the afternoon. A quiet had settled in the aftermath of the blast.

"I must apologize for my people's behavior," Tresa spoke while maintaining his neutral tone. He did not turn to regard Yobo as he spoke, but the human had already turned to look at him. "They do not trust humans, much less a human with dryad blood. Your presence means that one of the dryads betrayed our way of life. And I share their sentiment." Tresa then regarded Purall. "Go to the school, and bring me an extra saam."

Purall did as he was told, and departed for the city gates.

"I apologize for my actions," Yobo said with a guilty tone.

In the midst of Yobo's words, Tresa then turned to regard the human and spoke as he finished, "*Really?* I wouldn't. They were acting like children trying to understand whether or not a flame can burn."

Yobo understood the words and their meaning but found the choice of metaphor to be curious. He remained silent as he felt that Tresa would continue.

"But fire and destruction is why humans are not allowed in Telosa. It happens to everything that they touch. Even with your gold eyes, you are more human-looking than a usual half-breed." The master paused for a second before continuing. "Between the two of us, however, we do have one thing in common."

"The Uireb Nen," Yobo stated plainly as he sensed the direction of the dialogue.

"The Uireb Nen puts those that know and teach it at an impasse with our own kind. Dryads are raised and taught to distrust humans, but we who practice the art are also taught to respect all walks of life," Tresa then broke his cool demeanor with a smirk. The older monk shot his eyes back across the field to the boulders of ice in the distance. "It is incredible. The amount of power you are able to conjure with the Hesin's Cure. Master Asulus must be proud."

Yobo turned his eyes to the boulders as well. "I wish he was still alive."

"I saw the smoke from six days ago," Tresa admitted. "What happened?"

The human explained, "I used the Hesin's Cure much to the same effect as that one. The blast was too much, and I nearly got thrown from the mountain. When I awoke the next morning, they were all dead, butchered like animals. Master Asulus left me a note with a list of things on it; two of them were Telosa and Suldo's Stand."

Tresa listened to the story of Yobo's, and the dryad had already assumed the human must have burned the place down to keep the curse at bay. Secondly, using a Hesin's Cure that powerful could explain the sudden disappearance of the clouds the day before. Lastly, Tresa had to wonder if Asulus somehow foresaw his demise, and if that was the case, why didn't he send for aid?

Master Tresa reminisced about the several times he made his way up to Skyreach to visit Asulus. It was on one of those trips that he discovered the faithless monk teaching Yobo the art when he was still very young. From that point on, he knew that Asulus was teaching a half-blood the art but for what reason the late master would never share. He would always say, "...*until the dryad give up their way of life, life would have no meaning.*"

Of course, Tresa knew that Asulus always referred to the fact that in dryad society destiny was chosen at birth, and from that choice, each dryad was expected to follow their appointed journey for the rest of their days. Tresa could not imagine dryad society any other way, and the notion of a chaotic dryad society made him sick.

It had been a little over a decade since Yobo started training on Skyreach, and only now did Tresa begin to imagine what Asulus was getting at as he stood there next to the human. The master monk could not deny that through the Uireb Nen, the two of them had found common ground to stand upon. Perhaps that was the true wedge between the humans and dryad, Tresa then thought. Perhaps this half-blood was Asulus's key to closing that gap, or at least the beginning of something that would spark change. The many years of dryad wisdom suddenly painted Yobo in a new light at that moment, and Tresa thought that for a second he must be seeing the human just as Asulus must have all this time.

The feeling was unexpected, unknown, but it was an accepting feeling, and it brought a smirk to the graying dryad. No matter how he now felt about the big man, the traditions of the Uireb Nen must remain the same.

"I can tell with certainty that you *have* found Telosa," Tresa said, "and you have already seen Suldo's Stand."

"What is it?" Yobo asked with excitement.

"Suldo's technique is quite literal in which you *stand* your ground," the dryad monk explained. "It molds the elements of the Hesin's Cure into a variety of uses."

"Can you teach me?" the human nearly had a begging tone, and a clenched fist before him.

"The laws of Telosa forbid me from teaching outsiders anything about our culture," Tresa told him coldly, but followed with a lighter comment, "If you have learned anything from Master Asulus, I suspect he made you learn and experiment on your own. Between me and Purall, your mind has already been opened to a multitude of possibilities. It is up to you to discover them yourself."

Yobo respected the continuity between the Masters of the Uireb Nen, and the sense of honor and legacy filled him up with pride in that moment. In his own mind, Yobo would do his best not to disappoint those virtues. He knew that lurking in the depths of his being was that shadow of rage, but for the first time he found himself pondering on how he was going to conquer this fear he carried with him everywhere.

Yobo was content with trying to figure that out later. Between the conversation and thought-dwelling going on, he and MasterTresa almost didn't notice that Purall was returning from the city with another in tow.

This other person was a female dryad, roughly about the same height as Tresa and Purall, but she had long auburn hair, hazelnut eyes that held the power of youth and station, a slender figure covered with an elegant purple dress that just barely draped across the ground. Her skin had grainy lines like the wood of a birch, and held the light tone of such a tree as well.

As soon as Tresa noticed the visitor, he quickly turned to regard her while taking the proper bearing with a deep bow. When Tresa returned upright, he said, "Lady Hinora, I was not expecting you."

The woman's voice held the firmness of confidence and command, "I should always be expected when someone attacks my city. Introduce yourself, young man?"

"Yobo of Skyreach, ma'am," he introduced himself while also displaying a bow.

"You have manners," she took steps forward while she spoke. "At least Asulus taught you that much."

After walking by, Tresa moved to Purall's side to give their queen room.

Lady Hinora walked a slow circle around Yobo as she continued, "I have been following your progress believe it or not. The Queen of Telosa is meant to be a very skilled diviner, and I have learned your reason for coming down here."

Yobo remained silent and continued to meet the woman's gaze when she came to be in front of him.

"As anyone would expect from a human, you seek to kill, and to destroy," Hinora must have struck a nerve or something with the human for he lowered his eyebrows and picked up his chin a bit after that sentence. She then came to stop before Yobo and met him face to face. "Did you know that you are the first human in 200 years that has been able to converse with the Queen of Telosa?" She intently stared into Yobo's eyes as he remained silent, and steered the conversation based on what she could see in the man.

"I can see the revenge in your eyes. And your dryad blood will keep you focused on your hunt until you complete it."

Yobo narrowed his eyes as the queen played on her peoples' biases. He continued to remain silent and listen to her.

"The creatures you hunt are called the *shade*," the queen said to him. "They're a remnant of an old civilization corrupted by the Dark God Abyss."

The words of Lady Hinora made Yobo open his mouth a bit as he finally had an answer, but he refrained from showing too much emotion based on the woman's demeanor.

"How would I find them?" Yobo asked.

At that moment, she looked to the southeast, behind and beyond Yobo's large frame. It seemed like she was looking at something nearby, but her vision was currently much farther away. Thousands of miles away.

"I can see many things, Yobo of Skyreach," Hinora explained. "I cannot see everything, though. The workings of the shade are always hidden from those who rely on arcana."

She then raised a hand up to her side which cued Purall to step forward. He came over and handed Hinora a neatly folded olive saam with an equally folded red sash on top. Sitting upon the center of the items was a small red tincture with a label that had the feylic word for *healing*. Lady Hinora held the items up to Yobo as if offering them as a gift.

"My people will never agree to help humans survive, even if it means the end of days," Lady Hinora's demeanor suddenly became soft and concerning. "The shade, however, do pose a threat."

Yobo took up the clothing items, and his face was that of surprise against the change of tone from the woman. For a second, it put him off guard. It vaguely made him feel like she yearned for help of some kind, but thought that perhaps her station as queen forbad her from making such a request.

"That red sash is said to have been made by Hesin during the First Age, enchanted to never dull, break, or fray. Master Asulus was the last one to wear it, and now I am giving it to you."

"I am not sure how to thank you," Yobo said. He felt humble in that moment, and it almost made it difficult to meet her eyes again shortly thereafter. It was as if he could only look at the vibrant red sash.

Her powerful tone soon returned as if it had never left. She turned to walk towards her monks, and then faced Yobo again once she stood beside them. "Don't thank me, young man. You were chosen from birth, by fate, by destiny, to carry on the legacy of the Gunn Drambor. The weight of responsibility now rests with you. If you want to thank me, don't disappoint the ones that came before you."

Yobo offered a nod to the queen and to the other monks as well. The monks returned the nod. "I won't," he simply stated with a hint of determination in his voice. He moved to and fro to gather his items from the ground, and then he turned halfway as if meaning to leave but he noticed Lady Hinora move.

She waved and pointed a hand to the south, "Follow the road until you get to Planesgate. There, you will find your black lotus."

CHAPTER NINE
WHISPERS IN THE KEEP PART TWO

Down the steps, Anima Scarm descended into the depths of Claymore's dungeon once more. It was dark as pitch as it usually was since his presence had snuffed out the torches. It left the remaining prisoners to rot in darkness, and it was only complimented by the cool and damp, urine-tasting air. The prisoners lay silent as the white eyes in the dark passed by their cells. Ultimately, Scarm came to enter the cell that led to the hidden chamber.

Scarm did not hesitate in activating the switch. From what he had been gathering, the garrison in charge of the dungeon had yet to replace the guard that patrolled down here, and the *escaped* prisoner was killed on sight.

If there was one thing that Scarm counted on, it was the poor investigative skills that the people of Claymore had, and it was because of this incompetence that he knew that he had made the right move in dealing with that situation. So far, no suspicions had been reported that magic was the cause of death.

At the moment, however, Scarm was more concerned with how to deal with Umbra Hadara. He was not so much worried, but he wanted to find the right way to take a jab at the Commander of the Legion, especially since the Umbra's assassins had gotten sloppy.

It was unfortunate for Scarm that his current assignment was so physically separated from the politics of the shade nation of Lacus Perdia, otherwise the Anima could use this failure as a means to show the commander was weak. As the secret door came open, Scarm agreed to himself that no matter the outcome of the war, he would find a way to get Umbra Hadara completely destroyed.

The shade entered the chamber that contained the darkened crystal ball, and approached the pedestal in which it rested on.

"Vox transitum insuno, Umbra Hadara," Scarm incanted. Just as he did the last time, he cast his dark divination spell so that he could communicate with his commanding officer. The orb came to life as the swirling shadows danced within.

The Umbra's condescending voice came with the language of the shade, "Anima, why are you calling me so soon?"

Scarm decided that he would just cut to the chase, "Umbra, someone has returned from the ambush."

A short moment of silence fell over the chamber. The Umbra asked, "Then deal with it, or has incompetence outweighed you?"

"The only incompetence here is the trust placed with your choice of assassins. They are not thorough." Scarm shot back. "But a bounty has been placed on the survivor's head. His own people will hunt him down for us."

"Is it wise to rely on such measures?" the Umbra questioned.

"Does it matter?" Scarm continued his rant. "Apparently, relying on others to do the dirty work is a curse of mine at the moment."

"Hahaha," the Umbra's voice scoffed at the Anima's notions. "Beware little mote, your tongue is not as valuable as you might think, but soon we shall see if your fangs are sharp enough."

At the end of Umbra Hadara's words, the communication link suddenly ended, and it made sure that the shade leader got the last word in. Anima Scarm stood there and sweltered on the words of his commander. He felt nothing but infuriated. However, he knew that he had made his own successful jabs at Hadara, and that was enough to satiate his ever-trying patience in living among the humans.

Anima Scarm took measure of the conversation as he began his turn to leave the chamber. As soon as his dark, misty figure berthed from the secret door's frame he heard the sound of the dungeon door closing with a resounding click.

Scarm paused for a second, panic suddenly took over the usually calm and dark mind of his. He waited to close the hidden passage and peered his night vision through the dungeon lobby to see if anyone was coming down.

No one ever came down.

Scarm motioned to close up the secret door and the cell that held his secret. Once out of his cell, he walked to the other cells, and made a head count. The prisoners were accounted for. He then glared in the direction of the dungeon's entrance with concern. There was only one question that came to the mind of the Anima.

Was someone spying on him?

CHAPTER TEN
OUT OF THE BAG

The clattering of wooden mugs resounded on the tabletops of the local tavern in the small town of *Solace*. Tonight was an exceptionally busy night at the *Three Moos*, and that was because the local farmers had been spending most of their day tending to their fields. Unlike most folk on Golterran, Week's End in Solace was the day to get sloppy drunk for no other reason than to wake up late the next morning before returning to work. The place roared with games and blabbering chatter, and it smelled like month-old ale inside. The cool summer breeze that managed to sneak its way into the tavern every time the door came open did nothing to dissipate the smoky pipe cloud that lingered a few feet above the crowd's head.

All the noise, and the laughter, and the environment inside the tavern as a whole didn't matter to Henrick as he sat at the bar. His eyes were distant and his mind was lost in thought through the shallow and slow sips of his pint. His mind was heavy on the road ahead. Stopping in Solace was not part of the plan originally, but Henrick wanted to probe the locals and gather some information about the *Western Sword Reach*.

The barkeep noticed Henrick's reserved demeanor. "Ye lookin' lost there, friend."

Henrick came out of his stupor and looked up at the man. When Henrick first came in and got a drink, he didn't really pay much attention to the facial detail of the man who had served him, but this time he did.

He was an older man, Henrick was guessing probably in his fifties, with short salt and pepper hair. The barkeep had black eyes, scruff on his face from where he had skipped shaving for about a week, and was about as tall as Henrick but stockier in stature. The man's voice was deep and raspy.

Henrick sought the opportunity to get right to the point, "Aye. Anythin' out there in the Reach worth fightin'?"

"Hadn't heard nothin', but there were some merc types that wandered into town a few days back," the barkeep explained. "Said they were hunting some monsters. I don't really remember what all it was that they said, but they were headin' west into the Reach."

A few seconds following the dialogue, the door to the tavern came open, and a couple of militiamen came in. They were wearing chainmail and the Claymore tabard. One of the men remained by the door while the other one eyeballed the barkeep and crossed the floor of the tavern to get to the bar at the other end.

The barkeep met the gaze of the militia, and Henrick in turn noticed the barkeep's attention getting pulled away. Both the barkeep and Henrick looked at the militia now, and both of them noticed the roll of paper in the warrior's hand.

The roll of paper tumbled as it was dropped on the bar between the barkeep and Henrick.

"Post this on your board," the man instructed. "It's a bounty from the capital."

The barkeep grabbed up the paper just as the militia turned to leave the bar. Henrick remained at the bar for a short moment, but a shiver ran up his spine. He finished the rest of his drink in a gulp before getting up to leave the tavern himself. His eyes were fixated on the barkeep as the man began to tack the top two corners of the poster.

Henrick's time in the Claymoran Army and all the extra hours of survival and strategic instruction were serving him right. Just as Henrick placed a hand on the door knob to exit the tavern, he spotted his name at the top of the poster.

Once out of the tavern, Henrick turned to his left and began taking the road west through town. Before he got completely away from the tavern, he could already spot a handful of people getting up to take a look at the newest paper on the hiring board through the windows.

Henrick's pace quickened slightly. Once he felt that he was far enough away, his mind fell upon the matter at hand. The King of Claymore exiled him, and then apparently sought to have others do the work of finishing him off. The notion only made Henrick's desire to find a way back into that throne room even stronger. For now, he would keep that information as a note for later.

Henrick brought his eyes upon the road ahead, and silently admired the night life of this quiet village. The road was illuminated by lamp posts, and there was a run of simple wooden fencing on the shoulder between each lamp. Sometimes, the road would branch off and lead to a small house in which he could see candles burning in the various windows. The nightly breeze caressed the skin on his hands, and the wind had warm hints of summer between the cool elements.

The blades of the dry grass stalks rustled in the darkness, but he soon realized it wasn't from the breeze. Henrick came to a stop and his attention snapped to the direction of the noise. Out of the shadows with a quick hop over the fencing came Serena and her tiger.

The sudden presence of the large feline had caused a couple of nearby villagers to stop in their tracks as well, and they nervously waited for the animal to walk by as the trio continued to walk west.

Henrick paid the cat no mind as other things were more important than his own personal suffering. These thoughts were also painted on Henrick's face, and with the lamps flashing by, Serena could see it.

"So what did you find out?" Serena asked.

"Not much, but it seems there's a bounty on me head now," Henrick said almost plainly.

"You don't sound too worried about it," she proclaimed after studying his face.

"Once we get outta Claymore, that bounty pretty much makes me an ally in the other territories," he elaborated.

"So we're sticking to the plan and cutting through the Reach?" she asked.

"Aye," Henrick answered. "We'll break off the road after a spell, and sleep for the night. Wake up tomorrow, and keep the press on."

Serena looked up slightly to peek at the lonely Nielda in her waning crescent phase before saying, "With any luck, maybe tonight will be peaceful."

The next day, Henrick and Serena found themselves cutting across the rocky and rough grassland that was the Sword Reach. It would seem the splendor of the summer season would continue to bless them with a clear and sunny sky. A few clouds dotted the atmosphere above but nothing more than that.

Both of them managed to get some decent sleep as sleep might go while lying on the natural earth and a bedroll. The sleep was made possible without watches because of Sand as the feline was ever-alert, even while napping, and Henrick could not even fathom arguing against the sound logic portrayed by his traveling companion when she suggested it.

With the long road ahead, Serena thought this might be a good time to get to know the person she swore to follow, and after watching the symbol on

Henrick's back sway left and right for so many miles, the topic called to her.

"*Soooo*, how do you feel about the Twins?" Serena asked him while trailing behind.

"Huh?" The man's focus on the road kept him from hearing the question. Henrick slowed his pace a bit until he was able to walk side by side with Serena. He maintained a watchful eye ahead as the travelers weaved their way around large rocks and elevated outcroppings.

"The Twins. Nielda and Undine. How do you feel about them?" she asked again.

"To be honest, I'm not sure," Henrick explained. "I've never been one to rely on faith, or the beliefs that people try to impose on others. But that blue lady in cave gave me something tangible. Something that may yet prove their existence. Because of that, I have accepted that the Moons have a plan fer me."

"If I may. They are *quite* real. The Twins, as well as the other gods, live above us in the stars. There's more to it than that, but if you want, I could teach you about the Twins," Serena offered while looking his way.

"Aye. That's not a bad idea," Henrick agreed while meeting her eyes.

At that moment, as their eyes met, a sudden shudder struck their bloodstreams like the heat of a solar flare. Both of them felt a tightness in their chest, but they were reluctant to admit it. The strange and unfamiliar feeling brought upon an awkward silence that held for a few seconds but in reality, it felt like minutes. When the seconds were over, the two started to realize what was going on and it made Serena return her gaze to the landscape ahead.

Henrick narrowed his eyes a bit, taking a few more seconds to look her profile over before returning his eyes ahead as well.

"My mentor told me there was a sanctuary in Lumen. It's a tiny grove for moon-worshippers. Kind of how followers of Lumina pray inside of churches. When we get there, we should check it out," Serena suggested while keeping her eyes ahead.

"*Sanctuary*?" Henrick echoed.

Serena offered a smile and said, "Yep. And this is your first lesson: vassals of the Twins pray outside, and at night."

"At night, and outside. Got it," he repeated back.

Another moment of silence came between them, but it didn't last.

"Can I ask ye somethin'?" Henrick said.

This time her eyes met his, but her stare was enough to cue the warrior to go ahead.

"Have ye always lived out there in the wild, with yer cats?" he asked.

"Since I can remember," she answered with a hint of pride.

"Raised by tigers, but then who taught ye to speak so well?" Henrick asked.

"My mentor. He comes to see me sometimes," she replied.

"Will he visit while you're away?" Henrick asked another.

"It won't matter. He'll find me if he needs to," Serena answered plainly before looking up to the sky. In a way, her answer made her believe that her teacher was up above looking down, but alas, there was nothing.

Over the next several hours they found themselves climbing over rocks instead of going around them. The landscape had become craggy and jagged and there was no clear path through. The elevation would sometimes drop dramatically before slowly finding its way back up. With the absence of grass and bushes in this area, the heat of the sun was more profound as it radiated over the surface of stones.

They eventually climbed their way out of the vast rockiness as they continued west. The elevation began to climb a bit as an open grassland took over the horizon. The breeze rolling from the north did nothing to ease their burning skin, but as they took their final hop from the stone fields behind them, Henrick saw one last outcropping with a lot of shade underneath it. He knew it would be perfect for them to rest for a bit.

"Over here," Henrick said while pointing with his hand.

Henrick got underneath the shade before taking his backpack and equipment off for a moment. Once that was done, he sat down and instantly felt the relief and fatigue in his legs.

Serena and Sand followed suit.

"Oi! I *really* needed this," Henrick said through a heavy sigh. Henrick leaned back and rested his body against the stone. He closed his eyes and relaxed.

Serena held out a hand and felt the air weave through her fingers. She closed her eyes as well, but she did it to concentrate. In her concentration, she used her druidic magic to simply determine where she was in Claymoran lands. She had been out this way in the past, but didn't frequent it often. After reaching out into the wilderness with her empathic powers, she discovered a landmark in her search, and it was one that she had been to before.

"There's a pond directly west from here with trees. At the bottom of the Wall." she explained. "We could make it before nightfall."

Henrick didn't bother opening his eyes to look at Serena as he spoke, "That sounds good to me. Just gimme like twenty minutes."

Sand then looked at Serena from his lying position with a rather bland face. He swatted at the air in a playful manner before rolling on to his side completely.

Serena returned the glance with a shake of her head, "Twenty minutes, then."

After their break, they began crossing the tall bladed field of grass. Both of them looked upon their surroundings, constantly, for they knew the kind of dangers lurked out here beyond the rocks. Fortunately, they only saw the breeze ripple over the golden-green grass like waves at the beach. The smell of warm grass was prevalent in the air as the travelers stomped a path through.

Their short-term goal was to reach the wooded hills, and after some distance, the hills had come into view. They were only small blue humps on the horizon, but as they continued, a much larger piece of landscape began to rise up.

It was a tall and terribly long running cliff known as the *Hikaran Wall*. It served as a profound physical border between Claymore and the neighboring territory of Lumen. The 3,000-foot face had already begun to mask the horizon with shades of gray and brown.

As the growing landscape in front of them continued to grow in height, it was sometime after their halfway point through the field that the direction of the wind changed with it pushing against their backs.

Serena suddenly felt uneasy. Her emotions were not her own though, however, and she was actually feeling this sensation through her empathic link to Sand. It was more than unease, though. Serena sensed as she focused on the notion while trailing behind Henrick. She had sensed these feelings before through her link, and knew it only to be one thing.

"We're being followed," Serena said.

Henrick received the words, but without any physical reaction. "Do ye know where?"

"Directly behind us. Definitely more than one," she elaborated.

Henrick quickly milled about in his head and tried to think of the best strategy. Unfortunately, the vast grassy field held no real value or protection. They could probably crouch and crawl below the height of the grass, but Henrick figured that if the group behind them actually had some form of hunter with them, it would only delay the inevitable discovery.

If, by chance, the group following them were gnolls, their scent being carried with the breeze would nearly pinpoint their location. Henrick digressed to their current course of action.

"Let's keep going," Henrick started. "We'll have better odds in the hills."

A couple hours later, Henrick and Serena reached the base of the foothills, and on their approach, they found a beaten path leading up towards the nearest peak. The hills were cloaked by the Wall's shadow as the sun drifted into the afternoon.

After climbing the hillside for a spell, Henrick paused in his trek to regard the grassland below. Serena stopped as well because she knew the purpose of the moment. Far below them in the distant grasslands, they spotted a pack of humanoids following the path of stamped grass they had made through the field. Even from this distance, Henrick and Serena could count the five-person party.

"Outnumbered," Henrick's thought came out aloud.

Serena held her rebuttal to the notion for she knew that a group of warriors from Claymore would be no challenge for her, but she also did not want to alarm Henrick, as he was also from Claymore. Not to mention, his original mission was to hunt for her.

"We need to hide, then," she responded.

"Aye," Henrick agreed.

Before the two of them continued on their path, they witnessed the party below quicken their pace. Henrick and Serena followed suit as the knowledge of their pursuers sank in. Up the hillside they went, and at a couple points in the trail, it became so steep that they had to climb on all fours. The items in their backpacks clattered about as they went.

After a few minutes of their hurried pace, they crested the hill and saw the path leading forward into a dense thicket of trees. They took off in a sprint, and tried to take advantage of the small run of flat ground before going up the next hill.

On the next peak, they arrived at a large pond just as Serena had said. The location would have been a great place to camp for the night, but they would have to pass up the luxury given the circumstances. Henrick and Serena followed the path as it took them along the bank of the pond. The trees were about 300 yards away, and their pace did not let up. They had gotten out of sight from their opposition, and so it was the best time to avoid being spotted again.

Henrick spotted some animal tracks as he ran by. The tracks resembled that of a dog or wolf, but the large size of the track did not make Henrick feel any better about their situation.

"Is anythin'...else...followin' us?" Henrick asked between breaths.

Serena reached out with her empathic link to Sand, but the tiger was too much in a run to pay any attention to the scent that was in the air.

"Not...sure..." Serena replied.

200 yards away the trees stood, and it was at this point that the beaten path came to an end. Their trek took them through grass and bushes, and their pace had slowed a bit as they weaved through the knee-high branches and dodged the numerous rodent holes in the ground. Their current course began to take them away from the waterfront, and closer to the now-towering Hikaran Wall.

With the impending hunters on their trail, and Henrick's eyes at the front, Serena made the risky play of casting one of her druidic spells while they were in mid-flight.

Through the breaking wind on her face, and the panting of her breath, she whispered the notes of the spell, "*Gadael...dim...olion.*"

She could feel the enchantment spring forth, and the magic soon worked to remove the footprints of Henrick, Serena, and Sand. With their prints gone, it would surely be difficult to track them through sight, or so she hoped. As the prints disappeared, Serena was relieved that Henrick did not notice her action.

The trio continued their sprint towards the woods, and as soon as they got beyond the first set of trees, the elevation began to climb again. They did not stop running. When the pond and trail became difficult to see behind them, Henrick and Serena came to a stop and stepped behind the trees in order to rest a short bit, and catch their breath.

"*Henrick*!" the voice echoed across the landscape from a distance.

Henrick peered an eye around the tree he was hiding behind, and through a sliver of a break in the trees, he could see the bounty hunters down by the pond, and somehow, as he noticed, they had lost the trail.

"Seems they have lost our trail," Serena also assumed. "We should keep going."

"Aye," Henrick nodded in agreement.

The two of them stepped out from behind the trees and continued the climb up the wooded hills again. But just as they had taken a few steps forward, another sound echoed off the landscape. It was loud cackling and giggling, almost like a hyena, but not just one sound. There were several.

"Dammit," the bounty hunter leader muttered as the group of gnolls came over the rise on the other side of the pond.

"Gunner, what's our play?" one of the hunter's asked their leader.

"Form a line. Bertil, you're in the back with me," Gunner commanded.

Gunner, living by his name, cranked a bolt in his hefty crossbow, while the one beside him in the second rank, Bertil, began whispering words of arcane power until she had a spell of dark magic at the ready.

Gunner was a slim aerin man with short brown hair, and he wore leather armor under a dark green duster. Bertil was a huntari, a member of the feline race on Golterran, and a female with raven black fur and ragged-looking ears. Her hazelnut, almond-shaped eyes tracked the movement of all the gnolls coming into view.

"Damn, dogs," the huntari muttered.

The other three mercenaries, Hadrian, Duka, and Indra, took the front of the formation with shields and various single-handed weapons. Each of them were humans from Claymore. Hadrian was an aerin male of medium build, he had red curly hair in a crew cut, and an angular face. Duka was an odum male, bald head, and a thick curly beard. Indra was an odum female, she wore long dreadlocks and had light brown eyes.

Just as they had taken their defensive position, more gnolls stepped over the crown of the neighboring hill. In total there were 12 of the whimpering monsters. Each of them held spears in hand, and javelins upon their backs. The gnolls wore thick hides over their spotted fur.

Out of the 12, however, one of the gnolls seemed bigger in build, and held an impossibly large glaive in hand. The group of hunters already picked this one to be the pack lord. That one would be last to fight, and the first to feed.

"These dogs mean business," Hadrian said.

"Just stay focused, and watch for those darts," Indra said.

Just as Indra had finished her sentence, a javelin came soaring across the pond and struck true upon her shield. The jagged metal tip of the weapon tore a hole in her shield, and she had to work to get it loose.

The gnolls wasted no time, and with a raising of the pack lord's glaive, the rest of the giggling fiends began their charge.

"This is our chance, we can make a run for it," Serena said, already making a few steps up the hill.

Henrick did not move, and he stood there from behind a tree and watched as the gnolls barreled upon the hunters down below.

"We should help them," Henrick suggested without moving his eyes.

Serena stepped back down and placed a hand on his shoulder with a slight tug.

"Are you crazy? Those people are hunting us, hunting *you* for money," she retorted.

"Aye. But the gnolls *will* kill 'em," Henrick said with a grim tone. "And that doesn't sit right with me."

Serena turned to regard the fight down below. From what they could tell, one of the hunters was already down, and only one of the gnolls had been killed. The pack lord remained on the hilltop still.

She let out a sigh of relief. "Are you sure you want to do this?"

"Aye," he firmly answered.

Serena brought her eyes up to Henrick's after stepping down to get in front of him. "Then I have a confession to make."

Henrick looked at her quizzically but also blankly.

"I *am* the Witch of the Wilds," she stated. After that, she produced a small flame in her hand. A flame produced by magic.

Henrick was unflinching, but his mouth came open slightly as a sudden mystery about the woman became revealed. Back and forth he looked between the flames and her eyes.

Serena continued, "But I am actually a druid. A protector of nature, and not some witch."

He held his stare upon her intently as he said, "Ye know. Ye don't hafta be afraid to show this to me. I grew up with dwarves after all. I'm no stranger to magic."

His pragmatic response took her by surprise, and it pulled at a string in her heart as if that was the most unexpected answer she could have expected.

"Besides, what am I gonna do? Take yer head in the name of Claymore?" Henrick jested.

A resounding blast from a magic spell echoed off the trees, and it brought their attention to the moment at hand. Henrick took off in a sprint down the hill, bounding as fast as he could without rolling over.

Serena looked to her feline friend, "Suit up, Sand. Let's show 'em what you're made of."

Through raw strength, and mastery of his craft, Gunner cranked another bolt into his weighted crossbow with smooth motion. In no time at all, he set his sights upon another gnoll, and pulled the trigger. The audible clunk from his weapon was followed by the crunching sound of pierced bone at the bolt struck true.

His gnoll target fell to the ground, lifeless, but even with managing to get two of them down, the rest of his crew was having a more difficult time dealing out the damage.

Just a moment before, three of the beasts had pressured Duka, only to have a fourth toss their javelin which found meat and bone in the torso. The human lay there on the ground, beaten to a pulp as the gnolls did not relent after downing the man.

All of the bounty hunters knew that gnolls were bloodthirsty savages, but that knowledge did nothing to better the situation.

Streaks of green and red energy were relinquished through the clawed fingers of Bertil. The blasting noise would have been intimidating had they been fighting any other enemy, but the gnolls simply did not care about things like fear. Both of her spells had struck true on her targets, but the force that impacted the wild monsters were not enough to bring them down in a single shot.

Hadrian and Indra put forth all their energy and focus into their shield work. They fended off the attacks of several gnolls at once. The defense was steady at keeping the gnolls at bay, but it also made the humans stationary.

The gnolls then saw the situation for what it was. One of them peeled back from the melee and took up a javelin into a throwing stance. The creature giggled and cackled as it grew in confidence before coiling its arm and going for the throw.

The spear sailed through the air. Hadrian and Indra were expecting the weapon, but then it zoomed over their heads and found the shoulder of Bertil.

The huntari woman screamed and hissed in pain as the haft went a quarter way through. The huntari wobbled under the force and the weight of the weapon eventually brought her down to her tail. She reached up with her uninjured hand and tried to grasp the spear to get it out, but the increased pain of the movement wouldn't let her do it.

At this time, another gnoll broke away from the front line, and now the two gnolls rotated around the battlefield to flank the group to try to finish off the bounty hunter's mage. Gunner reared his crossbow up for another shot, but he too could now feel the pressure of the battle, and so his shot whistled by the quick-moving flankers.

One of the gnolls rushed ahead and let out a ravenous roar as the coming taste of flesh rang in its psychotic mind. Spear in hand, the gnoll coiled its hind legs, and leapt greatly through the air. Bertil closed her eyes and screamed as her demise came at the point of the diving spear. The remaining sunlight that glowed through Bertil's eyelids disappeared to shadow that was now over her.

But the end never came.

To her surprise, however, the shadow was not the gnoll. She looked at the ground before her, terror had already engulfed her demeanor, tears soiled the fur around her eyes. It was there at the ground before her that she noticed a pair of boots.

She hadn't seen it the moment before, but Henrick came running at full speed and caught the gnoll midair with a mighty bash of his shield. The weight of the beast managed to stop Henrick's momentum almost completely while the gnoll was knocked clean several feet away, and landed between Gunner and his two shield warriors.

Without a bolt in his string, the lead bounty hunter took his crossbow skyward, and brought the weighty butt of the stock down onto the face of the gnoll. The monster let out a whimper from getting its skull caved in.

There was no time to celebrate, Henrick turned his head to look for the pack lord, but he was not standing on the top of the hill. Henrick looked around, and could only wonder where the leader might have gone.

Henrick moved to join the other shield-bearers, but he had to stop himself suddenly. The act of trying to back pedal, while also trying to go forward, ended up putting him on his rump. He had to scramble to get out of the way as another monster ran by him to join the fray.

From what he could tell, it was a giant feline made completely of fire.

The bounty hunters on the front line found a reprieve from the fighting as all the gnolls had their attention directed at the new threat. Some of them braced for the imminent attack while others simply broke away and fled from the fire cat. As the fire cat engaged, the bounty hunters had to retreat as the sweltering heat from the elemental was too hot.

The fire cat pounced upon the first gnoll and with one bite, the creature's face became a mess of charred blisters and ash. The other gnolls who decided to stay and fight took to their new opponent and each of them stabbed at the cat with their spears. If their weapons did any damage to the elemental, there were no signs of success. It was like the elemental had no solid form as the spears went right through the cat and came back out smoking and blackened.

One of the gnolls then stepped in again, but it got too close and its fur ignited from the searing heat alone. In no time at all the giggling monster became engulfed in fire. It howled in terror, running around wildly while flailing its arms, and paid no attention to the body of water nearby. A crossbow bolt shot the thing in the back, bringing the creature down, and ending its screech.

The flaming spectacle destroyed the confidence of the gnolls' engagement. The rest of the gnolls that remained broke off in different directions before retreating. Their giggles became whimpering barks, and their noises in general faded into the distance.

The fire cat did not give chase. Instead, the Sand came about and took a sitting position between Henrick and the bounty hunters.

"Good boy," Serena came walking up afterwards. "Now change back."

The fire cat looked at her druid master as if understanding what she said. Before everyone's eyes, the flames lowered, the cat's body became darkened like a piece of animate coal, layers of blood, muscle, sinews, skin, and then hair reappeared as if being painted with pastels. When it was all complete, the tan fur and black stripes of a each bengal were present.

Henrick's eyes went wide from his sitting position, and he quickly turned his head to Serena while pointing his open hand at the feline. "Ye could've said somethin' bout yer *damn cat*!" he complained loudly.

"We were in the *heat* of the moment," she argued with a jesting tone.

As Serena finished, she had her eye on the huntari that was currently injured. The black fur glistened under the receding sunlight as the wound was still bleeding from a lodged spear. She kneeled down to take a look at the wound and the weapon.

Serena asked softly, "Does it still hurt?"

Bertil nodded as she responded with, "Yes."

"Good. Means there's no poison," Serena added.

Everyone else by this time had returned to their feet.

"Henrick, help me," Serena said.

"So, you *are* the fugitive," Gunner said.

Henrick did not regard the man as he joined Serena by Bertil's side.

"Hold her steady while I pull this free," Serena instructed.

Henrick came to his knees, and he held Bertil in place by her shoulders.

"Why'd you help us?" Gunner persisted.

"The same damn reason we're helpin' yer friend here," Henrick stated.

"*Argh!*" Bertil grimaced and gritted her teeth as Serena yanked the spear clean through the wound. Blood poured from the orifice, and the druid knew she had to work fast. Bertil fell unconscious from the shock, and Henrick let her down easy to her side.

"Okay, let me focus on her," Serena said.

Henrick stood up and faced Gunner.

"The world's runnin' out of decent folk," Henrick proclaimed. "All the way from the paupers to the King, himself."

Gunner scoffed at the words of Henrick, "Folk ain't decent when 5,000 dags are posted on someone's head." The bounty hunter waved a hand before pointing at Sand. "But since we're at an impasse...what'd you do anyway?"

"I tried to inform the King that Claymore was gonna to be invaded, and in return, I was exiled," Henrick explained.

"Invaded? By who?" the interest caused Indra to ask.

"They're called the shade," Henrick answered. "Dark people who worship Abyss."

Gunner raised an eyebrow while regarding Indra, his own interest had been pulled into the news as he was once a member of the Claymoran Army, and the man knew exile was not a common punishment, but he knew the laws well enough to know that doomsaying and indirect propaganda could be met with a non-fatal punishment.

"Exiled, you say?" Gunner asked.

"Before I could invoke the rite of combat," Henrick stated as the images of that memorable meeting in the throne room stormed his mind.

Gunner walked over to where Hadrian, the shield-bearing bounty hunter, leaned over checking on the broken body of Duka. The bounty hunter leader could only shake his head with a deep sigh at the quick devastation that had taken his compatriot.

"You and your companions *did* save us, so I suppose we can forgo any aggressive diplomacy," Gunner half jested.

"Aye," Henrick agreed.

By this time, Bertil had become conscious again after Serena placed a hefty healing spell to get the wound closed. The mage looked down at her shoulder, and she could not believe the miracle that had repaired her body. Complete strangers they were, but Bertil could not help reaching out for Serena and giving her a hug. Serena returned the sentiment.

Without a word from Bertil, Serena said, "Don't mention it."

After a minute, Gunner's crew regrouped around him. Likewise, Henrick, Serena, and Sand stood together.

"Let's take the gnoll heads at least," Gunner suggested to the others. "They're worth 20 dags a piece."

The bounty hunters went to each of the dead monsters, and used their carving knives to cut through the unwashed fur, skin, and bone of the gnolls.

"As for you," Gunner said, looking at Henrick. "Are you planning to return to Claymore?"

"Aye," Henrick said. "When the time is right. We're tryna find a way to stop the invasion."

"Stop in Solace again on your way in," Gunner suggested. "I'm curious to know what the rest of the kingdom thinks about an invasion. Might have some information for you when you get back. For a price, of course."

"Aye, I'll keep it in mind," Henrick said through a smirk.

The two groups gathered themselves and departed in opposite directions. Henrick and Serena were surprised by the outcome of the encounter as it would seem they had made an ally, but they also knew that four allies would not be enough. Perhaps out there in the world they had yet to explore, they would find more.

Back up the hill, and through the woods below the Wall, Henrick, Serena, and Sand continued their trek towards Lumen. There was still a little bit of daylight above them, and many more miles to go, but they had to put as much distance between them and the corpses. They knew the gnolls would return to eat them.

CHAPTER ELEVEN
THE LIBRARIAN

It had been three days since their encounter with the bounty hunters and the gnolls. The remaining journey through the hills below the Hikaran Wall remained uneventful save for the current day as the weather turned to dark clouds and rain.

The two days prior, the landscape continued to climb in elevation as they followed the Wall's base to the north. Once the northwest borders of the Sword Reach met with the starting point in which the Wall began, it was then a straight shot west to their next destination.

After a half-day's travel through soaked grassland and wet clothes, the City of Lumen came into view. Unlike Claymore, Lumen did not have giant stone walls that protected it, and instead, it had a simple wooden fence that traced the outside of the city.

There were, however, archways that marked the entrances into the city. Beyond the archways and the fences, it seemed as though the city grew in height, and near the center there were four large structures. Even from outside the city at a great distance, Henrick and Serena could see the banner of Lumen posted on the walls of the tall creations. It was a white flag with brassy-gold designs of an eight-sectioned circle, and the outline of the circle had small points to make it look like a sun or star.

With a pointed finger, Henrick revealed his curiosity and asked, "What're those big things there?"

"I'm not sure," Serena replied. "Perhaps we should head there *first*?"

"Aye," Henrick agreed to the idea.

As they got closer to the city from the field, they headed for the closest archway. More details came into view on their approach, and they could see the archways were ornately designed. They were made of stone, and the pillars were carved into the depictions of the deities. The east archway, the one in which Henrick and Serena were converging on, had the statuary of two mermaids as the pillars, and upon the face of the arch was a wooden sign with the name *Sister Street*.

"Nielda and Undine," Serena recognized aloud.

As soon as he was able to put a face to the goddesses that chose him, Henrick couldn't help but feel as though the Twins were waiting for his approach, as if they knew he would be walking through this portal into the city, and that this was some disturbing reminder that they were watching.

They weren't the only ones watching, though. There were several guards posted at the Twins' entrance, but each of the armored men paid no mind to Henrick, Serena, or even Sand. It seemed like they weren't enjoying the weather either, but they did end up shooting a seconds' glance at the travelers.

Based on the suggestion from his friend Melissa, Henrick should be looking for a library here in Lumen. He had never been this far west before nor to Lumen, and so he was not about to let these guards get away with their brief gander.

"S'cuse me, lads," Henrick said as he approached, hands on the straps of his backpack. "Which direction to the library?"

"Follow the road to the monuments at the center of the city, and look for a white dome," one of the guards explained with a pointing hand.

"Thank ye," Henrick said.

Through the mermaid archway they went. The street beyond it was laid with maroon-colored bricks that travel for a great distance until reaching the center of the city. The rain was pooled up in certain areas, but most of it was run off into nearby storm drains.

Even with the poor weather, there were still people milling about the avenues that broke off from the main street. Some of them that walked by wore necklaces, or amulets, or rings that all held different symbols from different deities. A couple of those symbols Henrick recognized while more of them he did not.

Of all the people that walked by, there was one in particular that stood out from the rest. It was a man dressed in white robes, trimmed in satin black, and upon the chest of the robes was a symbol of a black horizontal line, and from this line, three additional lines ran down vertically with the one in the middle being longer than the other two. Above the horizontal line, there was a green circle. The person's face was hidden by the cowl of the robes.

Serena noticed the bright colored robes as well, and voiced her own curiosity, "Wonder what faith that one belongs to?"

Henrick could only wonder the same thing in silence.

After a long moment of traveling on Sister Street, the trio had reached the center of the city in which they had seen the four monuments. However, passage to the center of the city would not be done without first passing through another archway similar to the one they had seen when they entered the city. Just as before, two stone mermaids held up the sign for Sister Street.

After passing through the archway, their sides were met with the towering four-story tall masonry monuments. Directly across the center of the city, they could see the other two monuments, and they took note of the statues of a feminine figure that were built into them.

"Those Lumina's are big," Henrick commented while identifying the depicted Goddess of Light.

As they took their first steps into the center of the city, they could spot the booths and merchant carts lined up along the inside of the circular road here, and unlike the street they had used, this place appeared to be where most of the population in town was. Heads bobbed in and out of view as the people of Lumen pounded their noisy footfalls about. The gibbering mash of a hundred conversations soiled the ears of the trio.

At the very center of this place, there was a fenced off patch of well-groomed grass. The small field held a gathering of large stone rocks, with the largest one in the center. Here, there were already people using the rocks as seats while a priest sat cross-legged on the larger one, giving guidance to his subjects.

"Is that the Sanctuary?" Henrick asked Serena.

"I don't think so," she answered. "Besides, it's still daytime, and there's no sight of the moons with all these clouds."

"Oh, right," Henrick muttered as he remembered his first lesson.

They weaved their way through the population of people. The many voices coming from the carts and booths were not just merchants. There were also vassals attempting to arouse interest in the deity they represented. It was not a moment later that they spotted a lavender robed youth trying to *sell* the religion of the Twins to those that walked by.

"For a mere one dag, you can learn all there is to know about the Goddesses of the Moons," the youth nearly shouted while holding up a pamphlet.

Serena's mind bubbled with turmoil as she passed by the booth. The druid could never understand why the civilized world would try to incentivize religion. She strongly believed that religion was something to be found or discovered, and that the discovery should forever change how a person lives their life.

"I suppose I should count meself lucky," Henrick thought aloud while also watching the advertisement.

"What makes you say that?" she asked.

"All these people are runnin' around, lost, lookin' for answers. Here I am. The Twins came lookin' for me," he explained.

Serena didn't respond, but her smirk was a sign that Henrick's humor allowed her emotions to remain calm.

Without saying a word, the two humans spotted the dome shaped structure on the southern end and then headed that way. They soon made their way onto Coffer Street.

This avenue was marked by an archway as well, but the columns for this one depicted a knight clad in armor and a salamander, a half-man, half-snake, holding a trident vertically.

Henrick knew right away from being a citizen in Claymore who the snake figure was, but he was unfamiliar with the armored figure.

"Sol and Gothic," the druid said as they passed under.

"*Gothic*?" Henrick questioned.

"Guardian of the Dead," she replied with Gothic's title. "He keeps the souls of the lost from falling into the hands of Nekratal."

As Serena filled Henrick's brain with more knowledge about the world, they came to stand before their destination at their right. The foundation of the dome-shaped library was rectangular, it stood above the ground by about 10 feet, and it was constructed of gray masonry brickwork. However, the library only used the back half of the foundations area, while the other half was used as a court before the entrance doors. The foundation as a whole was traced with rusty, blackened metal fencing.

The trio had to use a flight of steps that cut into the foundation before arriving at the surface above. From here, they got an even greater view of the structure before them. There were another 10 feet of bricks that rose up from the foundation to form the base before the large white dome began. Directly before them was a double-door entrance, and outward from the doors, there were windows every so often. Each window was stained and frosted white, and there was no possible way that anyone could peek inside the structure from the outside.

The white dome appeared to be made of large curved slabs of marble, and even against the contrast of dark clouds and rainy weather, the stark stone was able to maintain its brightness.

As the trio crossed the court to the entrance door, there were a couple of figures standing outside. They wore brown robes and stood underneath a short awning that was attached to the wall above. From what the travelers could see, the robed figures seemed pretty dry compared to the rest of the environment.

"Hold up right there," one of the robed persons said with a hand gesture to stop the visitors.

"What's the problem?" Henrick asked as they came to a stop before the awning.

"We are scribes for this library, and I'm afraid we can't let you in given that your clothing is soaked," the scribe explained.

Henrick and Serena could not argue with the reasoning as they exchanged looks to each other. However, their task was right before them.

"That's alright, we're only here fer information," Henrick explained.

"Of course, but I still cannot let you in," the scribe, without hesitation, dismissed any chance of dialogue that might dissuade them into letting the travelers inside.

Serena, in the midst of the conversation, looked back at Sand. She then made a series of clicking noises with her mouth, and then rolled her eyes in the direction of the two library guards. With her empathic link to her friend, she asked the large feline for a favor.

The tiger strolled out from behind his companion, and walked to stand between the guards, Henrick, and Serena. With a mighty and vigorous series of wiggling, the tiger shook loose all the moisture that his fur had been building up throughout the day.

Henrick, and the guards, held their hands up to protect their faces from the thousands of water droplets being flung everywhere while Serena stood there proudly, and embraced the cat's filthiness. Serena was overtaken by stifled laughter and the bouncing of her abdomen was proof.

"*Oh!*" the brown robed couple exclaimed in discomfort.

"What was *that* for?" Henrick asked Sand as if he thought the beast could understand him.

"Argh. Come on, let's go get clean robes," one scribe said to the other. Without a second thought falling on Henrick or Serena, the scribes went inside the library, and their robes were soaked from hood to toe.

The tiger took his rightful spot under the awning where he could avoid the rain for now, and he soon began to clean the rest of the water off his body with licks.

"Looks like we can go in now," Serena offered with a smile. "The *rules* have been broken."

Henrick only shot her a disappointed look before heading for the door.

Inside, and contrary to the exterior of the library, the inside was nearly covered in wood. The inside of the marble dome was being supported by a perplexing system of beams and rafters, and this system all met at the center where the largest support stood.

Henrick and Serena found themselves on a wide balcony, and on the left and right, there were stairs that descended down into the main section. Down below, it looked like a hundred shelves stood with countless volumes, tomes, and scrolls. The place smelled of old paper and pine oil. Due to the frosted windows and the already absent sunlight outside, the inside of the library was actually quite dark, but the many sconces around the library gave it a warm feeling that only complimented the similar temperature of the air.

Before they could take in the entire view of the library below, there was a small desk that sat between the two staircases, and it was being occupied by someone. The sound of dripping water caught the attention of the keen ears of the person behind the desk as she brought her eyes up from a book she was looking at.

"*You*...You cannot bring your soaked clothing in here," the person said while rising from her seat.

Henrick and Serena noted the gold eyes of the half-dryad that stood before them. She was also wearing brown robes.

"*We know*," Serena said with an exasperated tone.

Henrick followed up, "We're lookin' for information."

"What information?" she asked.

"We're lookin' for somethin' on creatures known as the shade, and it has to do with Claymore's first encounter with them," Henrick responded.

The person at the desk sat back down before relinquishing a large catalog from one of the drawers in the desk, and then she put it on top with a resounding thud. She was soon at work attempting to find a volume with such knowledge.

"What about them do you want to know?" came a voice from behind.

The voice startled Henrick and Serena, and they flinched and turned quickly to regard the voice that appeared behind them. The person at the desk brought her head up to notice the person behind the visitors.

"Headmaster," the half-dryad called him by his title.

Henrick and Serena felt shocked that the heavily clothed man was able to sneak up behind them as well as he did. He wore a thick, black tunic, and a long, dark brown trench coat over it. His hair was shoulder length, and gray. He also wore a pair of spectacles, and a gold necklace with a small, diamond-shaped ruby.

"Oh. Uh. We need to learn how Claymore defeated the shade," Henrick finally answered.

The headmaster narrowed his eyes in interest, and sized up Henrick and Serena.

"Follow me," the headmaster said.

The headmaster escorted Henrick and Serena down the stairs to the main floor of the library. The leather boots of the visitors made some dull squishing noises with every step, and all the people in the library could hear them.

Henrick's warrior instincts kicked in as he watched the headmaster. The gray-haired man stood nearly as tall as him with a similar build, but for all Henrick could tell, the headmaster made absolutely no sound with his movements. The peculiarities of it made him think that his senses were betraying him, and he was half-expecting to see the man become enveloped in dark mist or something.

But it never happened.

Henrick knew that he hadn't quite figured out how to use his *divine sense*, and even now he wasn't even sure it would work. As they tailed the headmaster, though, the man from Claymore sensed a coldness, like a draft that snuck its way into the library, but as he tried to tune his senses on the one with the trenchcoat, it was almost as if the man was empty inside.

At the bottom of the stairs, the headmaster led them through a door with the title of *Headmaster* posted on it. Inside, was a room that was directly located under the balcony between the two staircases.

The room was furnished with a couch off to the side, a couple of wooden chairs before a large, ornate, cherry wood desk. Upon the desk was a lighted oil lamp, a multitude of feathered pens, scraps of parchment, ink vials, and a stack of books. The chair on the other side of the desk was cushioned, and it was large enough for the large Headmaster to be seated comfortably. Beyond the area of the desk, the back wall was filled, floor to ceiling, with bookshelves that were near to capacity.

"Have a seat," the headmaster said as he took himself to his bookshelf. "And close the door."

Henrick took a seat while Serena closed the door before she sat as well.

After the headmaster pulled a book from the shelf, he sat down in his own chair and placed the book on the desk, but he did not open it.

"It's not every day that someone asks about the shade," the headmaster said after taking his round-frame glasses off. "The shade've returned...haven't they?"

Henrick and Serena looked at each other in wide-eyed surprise at the insightfulness of the headmaster.

"Aye," Henrick replied. "We don't know when, but they're plannin' to attack Claymore. I know of the stories. That the shade were defeated once, and I know, first hand, what they're capable of."

The headmaster's gaze focused on Henrick for a moment. "The shade *were* defeated once before, and I *do* know how it was done." the headmaster paused for a second. "Are you *really* from Claymore? I've never seen nor heard of a warrior with the Twins on their shield."

"Aye. I trained in House Darkbane," Henrick began. "And you probably won't believe this, but the Twins sent an envoy to enlist my help."

Simon sat upon and perched his arms on his desk as he leaned forward slightly. "An envoy? You're...their *champion*?" The headmaster's eyes narrowed a bit as he found himself muttering the conclusion he arrived at. In the beginning, the headmaster underestimated his visitors' purpose, but now that he was aware of their profound purpose in the matter, he suddenly decided that their trust could be valid.

The headmaster's last statement drew puzzled looks from the adventurers.

"This time, I don't expect you to believe me, but I was alive when that moment happened. When the shade were defeated," the headmaster explained while he looked down at the open palms of his hands. He returned his eyes upward to continue his story, "There were three Blade-Briar Brothers during the time that the shade fell. Samuel, Gannon, and me, Simon."

Henrick nearly sat up in his chair, but he used the arms to push himself back to remain composed. The man from Claymore was running through theories in his head on how someone could be sitting here from that time period which was nearly 700 years ago. Serena pondered the same thing but she remained more content on listening to the words of Simon.

The headmaster continued, "The shade were a very cunning adversary back in the day, and I doubt much has changed in their abilities over the centuries. It took me and my brothers to combine our abilities, our stations, and our armies to overthrow the shade.

"Samuel was the Chosen of Sol. The Champion to the God of Fire and War. It was an envoy from the

Salamander that tasked him with challenging the shade, and freeing the odum people from their enslavement. Gannon learned the powers of nature from the huntari, and he became as close as one could get to mastering the terran ways. And myself, as a priest of Lumina, I found very quickly how allergic those demons were to magical light.

"With that kind of intelligence in hand, I was able to suppress the supernatural abilities of the shade while my brothers tore apart their scouting patrols. As we took out their patrols, we drew them away from their castle, and after doing that for nearly a decade, we were ready to strike. But in order to force the shade from Umbre Castle, now Claymore, I had to figure out a way to summon more light than my spells could do."

Henrick and Serena leaned in on the edge of their chairs as Simon flipped open the book to a page with some dusty pages, and an image of a gold sphere.

"*The Esfera de Luz*," Simon called it. "First discovered by the Sancts on the eastern coast of the continent. The object is capable of emitting light as bright as a star. To the shade, it is a weapon of genocide."

After a moment of blankly staring at the page in which they could not read, Henrick had to ask, "Where's this artifact now?"

"Before I tell you that, I should warn you about using the Esfera de Luz," Simon's tone became more concerning. "The person that uses this object as a weapon *will* contract a terrible curse."

"What do you mean *curse*?" Serena asked.

"Do you know of Nekratal's Curse?" Simon asked the two in response.

"That's when dryads become undead sometime after they die," Serena answered.

"Exactly. When Nekratal's Curse happens, the dryads become undead that are feral and mindless, but the artifact turns the user into something completely different. A form of undead that is still half-alive, but deathly allergic to sunlight and just like the shade," Simon explained.

"You're the one that used it," Henrick managed to put some pieces together as Simon spoke. "That's why you feel empty inside, I can sense it somehow."

Simon nodded to Henrick's deductions. He said, "You are correct. Where I once required sleep and hunger; I now thirst for blood, and the allergic reaction to sunlight as the shade, is very ironic, if you ask me."

"A *thirst for blood*?" Henrick's nerves stood up at that notion.

"Do not alarm yourself. Animal blood is able to sustain me just fine," Simon assured them. "But as for your previous question, after I used the artifact to vanquish the shade, I had it delivered to the country of Harmon. That is the best lead I can give you."

Henrick sat back in his chair while Serena did not. Both of them took a moment to let the information sink in. Information that suggested that they were going to continue to travel east.

"One lead is better than nothin'. I thank ye fer your assistance," Henrick said. "The name's Henrick by the way."

"Serena," she followed the belayed introduction.

The three of them stood up as the end of their dialogue approached. Henrick offered his hand across the table, and Simon took the gesture of the hand shake.

"Well met, Henrick and Serena. If you truly have dealt with the shade before, then you know they can only operate in darkness," Simon began. "Keep that in mind. If you say they are going to attack Claymore, I can't even imagine what they have planned."

"Aye," Henrick agreed. "But this Esfera-thing is *our* best chance in stoppin' 'em."

"If time *is* of the essence, you should head southwest, cut through the wilds, head north once you are around the hills, and follow the base through the woods. Lionsgate will be on the other side," Simon advised.

After departing the library, Serena and Sand took the lead through town. She held out hope that the sanctuary was close to the center of town, but if it wasn't, she would still make the walk for it. She also hoped she wouldn't find any advertisers outside of it as well. She had never been to Lumen personally and only from the distant memory of her mentor did she know about it.

On the other side of the city center, the north side, they found themselves on an avenue called *Gold Street*. They passed under the archway, which had the stony images of Himokar and Aerith. A stone giant holding a shield atop its feet, and a faceless, humanoid, female figure, respectively. Shortly after this landmark, the druid found what she was looking for to her left.

The sanctuary took up the entire block in which it was plotted on. The walls of it were made of large slabs of stone that stood eight feet tall. The entrance to the place was an open and beaten pathway.

Serena wasted no time in going inside, and Henrick was not too far behind her. The inside of this place was filled with various trees, and there were so many trees that the light from the sky, even muddled by the dark clouds, was nearly kept out of this place. It was a very dark place considering it had no constructed roof. The visitors were not blind, though. Lamps holding candles hung from the lower branches of the trees to provide light.

Henrick had never seen something like this before, but it did have some kind of marvelous appeal to it. He felt comfortable, but he could not decide if it was because of the place, or if it was the fact that the rain was not getting through the trees. Even the pathway through the sanctuary seemed to be dry, and it actually felt warm in here.

The bushes that filled in the space between each trunk were all overgrown to the point that vines hung to the slab walls, and the trees alike. All the natural things in the sanctuary managed to block out a lot of the noise pollution from the streets, and the silence was enough that the crickets hiding in the weeds were singing.

After making their way through the trees, they came to a small clearing where a break in the boughs allowed the light, and the rain, from the sky to come in. Underneath the dull, bluish glow of the rainy day, a collection of sitting stones gathered around a hand-made, stone font of water at the center. The font had intricate designs on it depicting a wavy ocean under the phases of the moon. On the other side of this font stood a huntari male robed in a lavender gown.

"Greetings, and what a marvelous creature you have with you today," the priest said while rolling his R's and complementing Sand. "May I be of service?"

Serena's thoughts returned to that of the vassal making advertisements earlier, but she dismissed it as she did not want to start a debate about something in the civilized world. Instead, she focused her thoughts on the initial reason for coming here.

"Perhaps," Serena answered. "I am helping my friend here to learn more about the Twins."

Henrick was still in the midst of admiring the dark landscape of the sanctuary. The priest caught the image that was emblazoned on the shield before the warrior from Claymore turned around to regard the priest.

"Of course," the priest acknowledged. "Though I am intrigued. I've not met a warrior that carries the symbol of the moons."

"Heh, I've been hearin' that a lot," Henrick scoffed.

"And he sounds like...a dwarf," the priest proclaimed.

"Hehe," Henrick could only offer a small puff of laughter at the priest's words.

"Very well, my *intriguing* patron," the priest began. "If you believe in the Six, and the *Story of the Stars*, Undine and Nielda are the elemental goddesses of water and the moons. They were given life by Terra in order to protect our world when Lumina would rest.

"The Twins are benevolent deities, their foundation is built upon taking action, destroying evil by any means, and most importantly, making sure to always be kind. Whether it be your neighbor, or a beast. Let them decide their fate, and do not decide for them.

"The patrons of the Twins enjoy late evening seminars where we share our time to meditate under the light of the moons. Moonlight, in fact, is the balance of darkness and light. That balance is where the power of the Twins comes from. The best of both worlds to fight against the corruption of both worlds.

"Other than that, the Twins do not hold any type of scripture of beliefs like some of the other religions. So, there is no need to carry a book with you."

Serena found the priest's words to be concise, and could not disagree with the brief description that the huntari gave. She even felt refreshed to hear someone else speak about the Twins, even if it was in a place among the civilized world. She watched Henrick's face a couple of times to see if he had any sort of reaction to the information, but Henrick's warrior demeanor was unmoving until the end.

"Hmm. Perhaps the Twins are a good fit, eh?" Henrick thought aloud while regarding Serena.

She could only offer a smile and a nod before agreeing with, "Mhmm."

CHAPTER TWELVE
THE ROAD WEST

As Yobo traveled southwest, he followed the road as he had been advised, but instead of putting his feet on the beaten path, he remained on the outskirts of it. His purpose for doing so was privacy and practice. It was not long after his crossing of the Thunderbridge that he began to run through the concept of Suldo's Stand. Every so often he would attempt the Hesin's Cure and try to "mold" it in a way that would mimic what he saw from the other two monks in Telosa.

He tried over and over to get the technique to take shape, but it never would. During some attempts, the monk would get frustrated, and other times he chalked it up to the idea that he was missing some sort of component. This process, and the turmoil of failure, bothered him over the course of the next few days, and it was near the end of those few days that Yobo caught the first glimpses of his old hometown.

Crossroads.

Just as the name suggested, the town had a road that led in every direction, towards every other county in the Sword Kingdoms. The north road, the one heading to Telosa, and the one that Yobo had returned to with his feet, was absent of any other people save the monk that traveled it. He came to think about the scarcity of the north road, but just as he had thought about it, he dismissed the notion. Considering the presentation he got when he went to Telosa, he couldn't imagine anyone else really wanting to go there.

During his trek, he had made camp during the night, and although his days and nights had gone uneventful, the monk was fast running low on things to eat, and he had maybe a handful of dried berries and nuts left. When the cobblestone streets of the town ahead came into view, he silently reminded himself that he would need to find a way to restock himself for the next leg.

The sun was already high by the time the monk took his first step onto the streets of Crossroads. It was a typical summer day; the air was warm and the sky was clear. There were so many aromas floating in the gentle breeze that it actually thickened the air like a musk that smelled like everything and nothing at the same time.

Yobo knew he wanted to spend as little time here as possible. The source of his trauma came from this place, and with his first step into town, he could feel the lingering presence of his memories. The anger and the despair of those memories wanted to break free. They wanted to break loose.

He lumbered off to the side of the street and nearly crashed against a nearby wall of an unknown structure. He leaned against the wall for support, and his breathing was heavy as if the air was smothering him. His memories tried to show him the past, but he kept the images at bay.

He fought against his own mental anguish, and tried to discipline himself into focusing on his purpose for being here. *He was just passing through*, he told himself. He was here to continue his hunt. His hunt for the shade. The hunt for revenge.

The lingering presence then pushed harder. He fought to control his breathing while his adrenaline began to pump. His emotions reached a boiling point, and suddenly felt like he was about to punch a hole clean through the wall he was leaning against.

Yobo was determined to stay calm, though. He closed his eyes and continued to control his breathing. After a moment, he began to feel the sharp edge of his mental pain dull. At that point, he opened his eyes and began to scan the town for anything and everything to distract his mind.

The various buildings came in different sizes from what he could see. Yobo remembered that somewhere up ahead was *The Strip*, the main avenue that cut through town from the east to the west, and everything that sat behind the shops, the taverns, and the public services buildings was residential. That meant that he was in the northern residential section.

Each of the homes in this part of town were different sizes. Some big and some small, and if a person had or made enough money, they could afford to get a bigger home. For the most part, though, the homes all sat on foundations and because of the good weather in the *Gold Plains*, they were constructed with wooden framing and plaster. Of course, the plaster was painted different colors.

The environmental diversion allowed Yobo to get away from the wall and get back to walking. He continued to turn his head as he walked, and looked over the heads of the shorter people around him. Which was everyone, but in doing so, his eyes spotted another peculiarity. It was a person who had walked by him, and it was one in which he had never seen the likes of before.

The person appeared male, their skin was green like the skin of a pear, and his skin's texture seemed leathery with many small dark spots that were black in color. Then the monk noticed a pair of short obsidian horns protruding from atop the forehead, but not before shooting a full second's gaze into the dark eyeballs that sported green irises. Lastly, as the person came shoulder to shoulder with Yobo, he could spot a tail draping behind.

The monk was curious, but he had to agree with himself that a lot *has* changed since he was last here. Several minutes went by before Yobo reached the town square, and judging from the new signs posted above the avenue, the place was now called *Silver Square*.

Yobo stood there for a few seconds, staring at the sign, and almost scoffed at it in amusement as his memory replayed the image of this place from his childhood. The town square never had a fancy sign or a bunch of people roaming about so freely. As a young boy, he remembered it used to be quieter here, and not so bustling. Of course, he also knew that back in his day this town was run by a more *unscrupulous* organization, and that was when the town was still partly under construction.

He passed under the street sign, and noticed that the buildings in the square were decorated with colors of white, gray, and silver. The largest buildings here were taverns and inns while the small structures were the shops. He continued to scan across the square, and it brought his eyes to note that the color scheme traveled the length of the Strip.

The square, though, was filled with all manner of people: humans, dryad, dwarves, huntari, and a few more of the demon-like people. The place was literally packed with citizens and consumers alike, browsing in and out of the stores, but also taking a look at the goods offered by the many merchants who sold their product straight from a wagon or carriage.

The livelihood of the place brought a sentimental smile to Yobo's face, and even though he may have had a short history as a young padfoot, it was a welcome sight that Crossroads had become a town of splendor and commerce.

He walked deeper into the crowd, nimbly dodging people walking by him until he arrived at the most profound structure of the square, the sundial fountain. It was a wide circular basin that had a shallow sundial rising above the water's surface.

Running water shot out from tiny holes just under the surface of the sundial. The fountain used to be gray, dirty, and dingy, but now it stood in the square with pure white marble that was only complimented by the sunshine from above.

The sights were a wellspring of entertainment to Yobo. He spent the next few minutes standing there near the fountain, and he admired all the civilization that was around him. When he thought he had seen everything in the square, his mind arrived at one small dilemma.

He had no money to trade with.

His brain worked to develop a solution to his problem, and then, with the help of all the people swarming around him, he remembered the adventurers in the old days. They would come into his father's tavern to find work. It's been so long since he went into that tavern, he thought, and because of his time away from Crossroads he couldn't remember the name of the place. But Yobo knew that it was here at the town square. Immediately, his eyes began scanning the square again but this time in frantic anticipation.

The monk could remember, vividly, that the fountain was always visible from the front door. He narrowed his eyes on every building he studied, the images blurred as he went from one structure to the next. He paced around to the other side of the fountain to change his perspective, and once he did, his gaze focused on the shape of one of the taverns. From what the sign said, it was called *Oliver's Taphouse*.

Yobo's head tilted slightly as he could have sworn the place had a different name before, but he dismissed the notion as quickly as it came. He weaved between the busy people of the square once more, and took care not to bump into them as he knew his large frame would nearly run them over.

He reached for the door knob of the entrance when he arrived, but when he opened it, it was another door that came swinging open. All of a sudden, the town became swallowed in the darkness of his mind. For a moment, he saw the door to his old house where his parents were slaughtered by the giant shadow, and a whispered voice from his sister swept by his ear.

Help.

Yobo's heart thumped even harder in the moment as he was about to relive the nightmare again. His grip tightened, and he silently swore that he would rip the shadow apart if it stood behind the wooden portal.

Help.

His sister's voice rang again in his mind, as if it pulled the right strings that led to his inner demons. This time it was a shallow cry for help.

The metal of the door knob gave way to the raw, unbridled strength of the monk. The sudden shock of it shearing off was enough to bring the man back to reality. The door slowly swung open under its own weight with a few added creaks. The knob, however, was still in Yobo's hand.

The big man stepped inside the tavern as his nerves began to cool, but the place was completely empty at the moment. The air was thick with the smell of a distillery. The lobby had a collection of tables and chairs while the bar area was complimented with stools. Yobo took a few more steps inside, but before he could make it farther, a figure came out of the backroom from behind the bar.

"Hey!" the man called out. "We're closed."

The man was an aerin, heavy-set, and looked to be in his 50's. He was balding, and had a thick gray mustache.

Yobo held up the door knob in his hand. "I'm afraid I broke your door."

The aerin man came out from behind the bar and moved to stand before Yobo. He took the knob from the monk, and inspected it, and then looked over the large odum. After getting the measure of the monk, the man reared his head back a bit as he noticed Yobo's golden eyes, and then a sense of familiarity came over him.

"*No.* You couldn't be," the barkeep thought aloud in disbelief.

"What?" Yobo became confused at the moment.

While shaking his head, closing his eyes and wagging a finger towards the tall man, the barkeep continued, "Ya...Yu...Yo..."

"Yobo," the monk caught on and finished the barkeep's guessing.

"*Yobo!* You're ol' Marsuex's kid," the barkeep said with widened eyes. "My, you certainly *sprouted.*"

"You knew my father?" Yobo asked.

The barkeep moved to close the door to the tavern, and then he reached up to pull down a latch above the door to lock it once again.

"*Knew him?*" the barkeep scoffed. "I knew the whole Red Hand back in the day. But your old man, he was the only one to keep a dryad by his side, your mother she was. Still a tragedy what happened to the Hand?"

Yobo found the start of a story that could possibly shed light on something that has haunted him for years, and so he decided to see if there was more to it.

"What do you mean?" the monk asked.

The barkeep sensed the large man's innocence in the matter, and probably thought the man was too young during that time to understand what was going on. With so many years under the belt, he saw no harm in explaining a good piece of Crossroads history.

The barkeep began, "Ya see, the Red Hand was a thieves' guild. Both your parents were a part of the Hand. And if you have ever heard the saying '*don't get caught red handed*' that's where it comes from.

"But this town, and Compass, far to the east, was founded by a group of entrepreneurs known as the Silver Coats. The Coats are the ones runnin' these towns, and as time went on, they got tired of battling the Red Hand. The Hand loved to take their money, and give it to less fortunate people. That was their code. Fame over fortune. And not once did they kill or murder anyone.

"One day, though, the Coats had enough. Rich people don't like it when they start losing materials or wealth, and they have no moral compass once they do start losing those things. And so, they hired the Black Lotus to wipe them out. I'll tell you though. What the Coats 'ave done with this place is pretty impressive, but I have no doubt the Hand will return one day."

The name Black Lotus echoed in Yobo's mind as it was the next item he was searching for, but from what this man was saying, the Black Lotus sounded like an organization of assassins. He didn't know what to make of the information at the moment.

"I...had no idea about all of that," Yobo said. "I knew about the guild and my parents being in it, but I had no idea about the Silver Coats and their involvement. I appreciate you telling me all of this."

"Think nothing of it, Yobo, but tell me about yourself. Where have you been for the last decade or so?" the barkeep requested while he motioned a hand for them to sit at a table. He then went to the bar to grab a couple of pints of ale while he waited for his guest to say something.

Yobo took his equipment off his back and put it on the floor near the table before taking up a chair. He turned his head after sitting, as if looking off into the distance, before speaking, "It was the day after mom and dad were killed. I was moving through the streets, ducking into the alleys, but then I bumped into a strangely dressed dryad, wearing the same thing as I am now."

The memory of the day he had met Master Asulus, brought upon flashes of fear and anger from the most recent tragedy upon Skyreach. Yobo could feel his fists clenching as if he could choke the life out of the creatures he was looking for, but he remained calm.

The monk continued, "He took me in, and has been raising me since then. But now. I am on a journey to find the creatures that killed him."

At the end of the monk's words, the barkeep returned to the table and slapped the foaming mugs on the surface before taking a seat himself. He held up his own mug as if motioning for a toast.

"To lost but not forgotten friends," the barkeep said in a somber tone.

Yobo took his mug and clapped it against the barkeep's. The monk started with a small sip of the amber beverage to determine his likeness to it, and when he found the cool and crisp flavor agreeable, he took a bigger gulp.

After a big swig of his drink, the barkeep said, "The name's Oliver, by the way. I took this place over after your ol' man. What brings you back to town? Where ye headed?"

"Planesgate," Yobo answered.

"*Planesgate*? That's a six-day travel from here, but the road west will get you there," Oliver explained. "You got a horse? Or a wagon, perhaps?"

"I don't even have a dag to my name," Yobo revealed his lack of fortune.

Oliver suddenly chugged the rest of his drink before slamming the empty mug on the table. He then got up and walked back over to the bar. He reached under and produced a small but stuffed coin pouch. With a skillful toss across the lobby, the pouch landed inches from Yobo's mug.

"What's this for?" the monk asked.

"Your father's dues," Oliver explained. "People think that there's no honor among thieves. *Pfft*. What do they know? Your ol' man was a good one, though, and your mother."

Yobo felt truly thankful inside, but he lacked the words to express it.

"Plus, consider it a down payment," Oliver added.

"A down payment?" Yobo questioned.

"When ye get done chasing whatever it is you're chasing. Come back here to Crossroads. I know that robe you wear, and I could really use a good punch or two around here," Oliver explained with a smirk.

Yobo thought to almost look down at his saam, but in that second, he realized and remembered the power, reach, and knowledge of a master thief. After all, it was the things that his dad would try to teach him so many years ago.

"I'll consider it, but I'm willing to throw in a third punch if you got a room for the night," Yobo suggested.

Oliver only had one response for a statement like that, "You got a deal."

Over the next several hours, Yobo and Oliver shared their stories with each other while enjoying more ale. After finding a break in the conversation, the old barkeep gathered them a meal consisting of stew and biscuits. Ever since the monk went to live with the dryads, he had been living as a vegetarian. At first, he was unsure about eating the stew, but against his own opinion, and the fact that the food was free, he decided to stomach the meat and vegetable gruel anyway.

After the meal, Oliver gave Yobo a key to one of the rooms upstairs. The monk went to the room to drop off his gear. By the time he returned to the lobby, Oliver opened the tavern to the general public.

At first, patrons filtered in one, or two, at a time. The sunlight outside began to fade, and as the sky grew darker, more and more people flocked to the now glowing sconces. In no time at all, the tables became full, and groups of people started the first rounds of singing and dancing.

Yobo took up a seat at the bar and admired the camaraderie between all the different kinds of folk in attendance throughout the tavern. His cool and calm demeanor managed to break with laughter as he watched a drunken dwarf fall backwards off one of the tables because the legs finally broke under the constant pounding of boots.

The place was alive, and suddenly Yobo viewed his family history in another light. Was the removal of the Red Hand needed to bring this town to life? He couldn't help but bring the thought to the surface. He would never forget the time he had with his parents, but perhaps what happened was a necessary evil.

The thought disappeared just as quickly as it had come. The tall man's smile disappeared and turmoil began to twist his insides again. He had never known anyone from the Red Hand, nor his parents, to have concerning personalities. A lot of them he actually remembered to be kind people, and in Yobo's mind, at least stealing things did not result in death or murder.

In the time that he had spent learning about the Uireb Nen, and defining a way to walk the earth while respecting all forms of life, the big man could not help but wonder if there couldn't have been a better way to deal with the Red Hand. Yobo boiled his thoughts down into a single word. It was everything that he had seen since stepping into this town, and it explained everything in front him.

Money.

When he was still alive, the monk's late father had explained to him that money can make people act out of character, make them go crazy, do things they wouldn't normally do, and all those things could be amplified tenfold as soon as you forced it away from them.

It was late into the evening when Yobo arrived at his inner deliberations. He then got up from the bar and began his journey towards his room. Nearby, Oliver took note of the monk's scowl and decided to intercept him.

"Yobo. Ye alright?" he asked.

"Yeah. I think I understand my father's work now more than ever," he answered.

Oliver could only offer a smirk with a hand on Yobo's shoulder, "My friend, I'll be waiting for that third punch, but only when you're ready, otherwise it won't feel right."

"Don't worry. I'll find time to come back," Yobo said before departing for his room.

The next day, Yobo had awoken to a Crossroads covered by gray clouds. The ground shimmered with silvery spots of wetness from last night's rain, and the colors of the town became darkened with the day.

The monk was already out and about, and at least today he did not have to dodge the numerous people milling about the town. The streets were practically empty because of the rain. Puffs of smoke rose out from the numerous chimneys that stood above the roofs of the houses beyond the Strip. The people of this town sought to stay indoors, remain comfortable in their homes, and avoid the rain completely.

Yobo didn't think to hold anything against the people of Crossroads for the notion that passed through his mind, but as he looked at the town in this moment, he could only see flashes of his past. Flashes that reflected the kind of town he used to live in.

Still, however, he couldn't wrap his head around an entire town stopping business completely because of the rain. Something about it did not make sense, but he let the thought slip as it was not really important. His mind was more focused on following the road out of town. The road west to Planesgate.

As fortune would have it, he had some newly acquired coin and he was going to need it to restock his pack for the road. After a short distance from the Silver Square, Yobo turned his attention and entered a place with a sign that said *Gold Plains General Store* above the entrance.

Yobo stepped through the doorway with a sharp jingle from a small bell overhead. The place was quiet as there was no one else browsing the wares inside. The entrance was centered on a short narrow wall that was about 15 feet wide while the rest of the store was almost three times the length.

The wall to Yobo's right was organized, and covered completely by shelves and cubbies that were stuffed with various clothing items. Shirts, pants, hats, and shoes were scattered all throughout that area, and near the back of the store, jackets hung by wooden hangers.

The wall to the left was a blank pallet of gray painted plaster. An aisle traveled the length of this wall from the entrance to the shopkeeper's counter at the back of the store. This aisle passed by several other shelving units that filled the remaining space of the store.

Yobo began his first few steps down the aisle, and from this side of the shelving units he could spot that each one had a sign that briefly listed what was stored below. The monk's mind immediately began searching for a sign that would point him towards the non-perishable foods.

It was a few rows down that he managed to find one with a label that said *Rations*. Just as Yobo had stepped away from the main aisle, he felt the movement of air shudder across his ears, and he peeked over the furniture, which were much shorter than he was, and saw the shopkeeper step out from the room in the back of the store.

The two individuals immediately locked eyes, but the moment did not last when Yobo returned to his browsing. The shopkeeper was an average looking aerin man with black hair, a shaven face, and a pair of spectacles to aid his sight.

The monk recalled Oliver saying that the hike to Planesgate was a six-day journey, and based on the size of the ration packages, his pack was going to be full, and that meant he couldn't buy extras in case his pace became slow. The decision was already made up in his mind, and so he grabbed six of the rations, three in each of his large hands, and carried the items to the counter.

Yobo placed the items on the counter as gently as he could so as to not make too much crinkling noise. The shopkeeper did not say anything but he began picking up the rations one at a time and inspected the wrapping to make sure they were good.

"Six, huh? Where ye headed?" the shopkeeper asked.

"Planesgate," Yobo answered.

"You don't say," the shopkeeper's tone became that of interest as he took in the measure of the odum giant before him. "You're a big guy. Are you good at fighting?"

"I am," he answered.

The shopkeeper's face produced a genuine smirk before explaining, "I'll make ye a deal. I know a supplier that has a wagon going that way. He leaves in about an hour. You take these as a down payment from me, and you watch his back the whole way there. He might even pay you once you get there."

Yobo never considered mercenary work before, he felt as though the idea was meaningless. Risking life for money just wasn't a fair trade to him, but there were things more important than money at play, he instantly reminded himself. Things like revenge.

"The trip will get you there, *oh*, in about four days," the shopkeep added.

The final bit of information made the offer almost too good to pass up, or at least that was Yobo's train of thought, and the monk extended his hand to make the transaction legitimate.

"I accept your job," Yobo said.

The shopkeep shook the hand of the tall odum man, and with that, Yobo felt like he was another step closer to finding the shade.

CHAPTER THIRTEEN
THE PROMISE OF THE ROSE

"You know. I never mentioned this the whole way here, but you really are a big guy, even by odum standards," the merchant said about his new and favorite bodyguard.

Yobo could only offer a smile to the man, who he came to know as Duncan Ornival, but the merchant was busy driving the covered wagon, and so he never saw it. He then jested about an event from a day ago, "I'm pretty sure those highwaymen thought the same thing."

During their travel to the west, Yobo and the merchant were briefly paused by a group of brigands looking to collect a road tax. No tax was ever collected, though, for as soon as Yobo stepped out of the cart, his size, stature, and silent stare were enough for the bandits to admit their mistake.

As Yobo was still looking in the direction of the merchant, he saw something upon the horizon of the road, and used the many boxes that surrounded him in the covered wagon to heave himself to his feet before looking over the merchant's shoulder.

"Is that Planesgate?"

"It *is* my friend," Duncan confirmed. "Magic capital of the whole world."

Even from a great distance, Yobo could see a large, white tower, rectangular in shape, standing high above the rest of the city. Beyond the congregated mess of houses and shops below the tower, was the ocean, and it stretched out farther than the eye could see. The mostly clear and blue, sunny sky complimented the yet-to-be-known ambiance of the man's coastal destination.

Moments later, the wagon began strolling up one of the streets of the city. The big monk in the back continued to scan the environment that surrounded him. The street, which was laid with white bricks that appeared clean without a grain of dirt on them, and not one piece of trash could be spotted from Yobo's point of view.

The houses were constructed in similar fashion like the ones in Crossroads. The difference here was that many of them were painted sky blue or vanilla white. The similarities made Yobo's imagination wonder if the same person or people were responsible for the style. Unknown to him, though, he was correct. The wood framing and trim was made of a light-colored wood. All the homes had white bordered windows and a beige colored door.

"This would be a nice place to live," the monk thought aloud as the splendid environment continued to capture his eyes.

"I couldn't agree more," Duncan replied. "Now, this street is *Arcane Avenue*. This one is where all the merchant carts enter and park. Straight ahead is the academy, but at the end of the block on the corner is an inn called the *Soggy Periwinkle*. Most of these crates in the back are for them."

Yobo slightly nodded his head in understanding of the knowledge that Duncan was giving him, but he remained silent as the merchant spoke. He did acknowledge that the large white building with the tower at the end of the road was an academy of some sort.

"Which by the way," Duncan began while sifting through a pocket in his blue vest. The merchant produced a small pouch of coins, and he held it above his shoulder as an offering to Yobo. "It ain't much, but you caused me to avoid a lot of trouble on the road. It's the least I could do."

Yobo took the pouch of coins, and worked to put it in his backpack sitting on the floor of the wagon.

"*Whoa*, there," Duncan called out to the horses as he reared them, and the cart, to a stop.

Duncan and Yobo both gathered their belongings before stepping off the cart and meeting again at the side of it. Duncan offered a shake to Yobo which the monk gladly accepted.

"It's been a pleasure, big man," Duncan offered his words with a smile.

Before the two of them could part ways, Yobo thought about asking the man about the 'Black Lotus' that he was searching for, but he stayed his thoughts, and decided it might be better to ask someone from the city.

"Safe travels to you," Yobo said in return.

The monk deemed the location that Duncan mentioned might be a good place to start, and so, he continued up Arcane Avenue. After passing by some other merchant carts, he spotted the sign hanging above the inn's stoop that read "Soggy Periwinkle" with a purple flower below the name.

His large legs skipped the couple steps of the stoop, and went right to the top. While the building was rectangular in shape, the corner that met the corner of the block was built diagonally, and it was from this corner that the entrance was located.

He opened the door, and found himself in a small lobby room with a couple of benches. There was a staircase to the side that led to the second floor, and a hallway underneath the stairs that led deeper into the first. At the other end of the lobby, there was an odum man that sat behind a counter. The wall behind the clerk was littered with hanging keys, and each key hook had a number assigned to it.

"Greetings," the man said.

"Hello, my name is Yobo," Yobo introduced himself before continuing. "I am looking for something called a Black Lotus. Have you ever heard of such a thing?"

"Yes. The Archmage of the academy has a flower in his garden that goes by that name," the man explained.

"Thank you very much," Yobo said before he began to walk away.

"Hold on," the man paused the monk. "You won't be able to get into the school unless you are escorted."

"*Escorted*?" Yobo questioned.

"Indeed," the man confirmed. "You'll need a student to lead you in. Shouldn't be hard to find one after the school lets out. Look for the blue robes and the white hoods."

"Very well, thank you again," Yobo said before heading back outside.

Yobo plants his feet onto the bricks of the road. He tossed a glance to his left and right, and took note of the very wide street that traveled the length of the town from the southwest to the northeast, and according to the sign post that stood no more than a couple of feet from him, the road was called *Academy Way*.

Directly across Academy Way from him, was a tall, silvery fence, and gate, to *Planesgate Academy*. The silvery fence did not only run along the academy grounds, but it also continued to run the full length of Academy Way. The reason for this, from what Yobo could see, was that the northwest half of the city sat below a cliff.

Yobo could not spot any of the students in which the innkeeper mentioned, and because of their absence, his curiosity of the city's layout beckoned the monk's feet to follow Academy Way. He began by heading northeast. At the very end of Academy Way, he found that the road turned and traveled down a steady decline that led to the lower elevation.

Before he ventured down, he looked to his right, and noticed the entire block of houses and buildings at this end were in shambles. Some of the destroyed structures showed signs of scorching and other similar damage. Even though he had never seen something like this before, he could not help but feel a sense of eeriness about the ruins, even at this hour of day. The measure of interest became fleeting, however, and it was a moment later that Yobo began to travel down to the lower sections of town.

As he descended, he looked once or twice to his right side and noted the unguarded side of the declining road was also a cliff, but at the bottom of this cliff was the deep blue ocean.

Once he reached the bottom of the slope, he continued on the path forward. He made a few quick looks down the other roads to his left as he walked by them. In this part of the city, he saw citizens walking around or doing menial tasks along the streets.

Eventually, his eyes came forward again, and when they did it allowed him to notice the area on his right side. The cliffs that traced the edge of the water with the town road came to an end, and the Planesgate docks began.

Not all of the 13 piers had ships berthed, but there were still a handful moored. The ships all had different shapes and designs, and each of them held the colors of some country or kingdom that belonged to other parts of the world in which Yobo was not familiar with. The ships, at least to Yobo, were nonetheless impressive.

The dock area was full of people walking around, sailors going to and from the piers in which they were working, and all the clattering noises of civilization did nothing to dismiss the mewing of the seagulls flying overhead.

The sights and sounds of the place were in compliment to the scent of the sea. The salt in the air infiltrated the monk's nose, and that wasn't the only smell that assaulted him in his travels. He soon came to a part of the dock area where he observed several fisherman manning plainly built wooden kiosks, and at these kiosks, he saw fresh caught fish on display in a bed of ice. Some were big and some were small. Yobo couldn't describe his sensations at the moment, and he had no idea what types of fish those were, but the pungent spell seemed pleasant.

Yobo became unaware of the time that was passing during his tour of the lower city, but his attention was beckoned to the sound of a large bell ringing out across the town. His ears attempted to direct his eyes, but before he could connect to the location of the bell, he noticed the blue skies above were beginning to make a fade into the yellows of the afternoon. The tolling of the bell came again, and the big man's eyes were instantly drawn to the white tower above on the cliff. The only thing Yobo could think of was that the school was being let out.

Unfamiliar with the town, he doubled back, and took the same route he had traveled to get back up to the upper city. He did not run, but his pace was slightly quickened.

After a long moment, Yobo completed his journey back to the gates of the academy. There were an abundance of diverse looking people walking from the school, but all of them were wearing pale blue robes and white hoods. As he stood there before the opening of the gates, he actually found it hard to get the attention of the novice wizards as nearly all of them had their eyes covered.

He would half-reach out, and inhale in preparation to ask a question, but without eye contact he continued to get ignored. Patience, however, was something that Yobo learned from Master Asulus, and so he decided that perhaps if he waited for the herd to thin out that he may have better luck.

Yobo stood there for another moment, patient, hands behind his back, and he really couldn't believe that the school had so many students, but as he stood there and continued to watch the river of white hoods flow by, he did shoot a glance into the school grounds. Beyond the gate, there was a chiseled stone walkway that ran the length of the foreyard, and it was neighbored by a large flat lawn on each side. On one of those lawns, he could see some students with their hoods pulled down, and it looked like they were practicing some kind of martial art.

From what Yobo could see, their style was not anything he could recall from the Uireb Nen, but their activity, either way, piqued his interest.

A smirk sprouted on the big man's face as he arrived at a decision, and it wasn't long until he danced and tip-toed between the crowd of young mages. The contrast of his green saam against the blue did nothing to stop the flow of traffic, and it was like he was being ignored still. At the same time, though, that was what he expected.

Once he had made it beyond the line of the fence, he broke away from the crowd, and on to the lawn in which the group was sparring. There were three of them: an odum man, a dryad, and another person, similar to the green one he had seen in Crossroads, but this one had fiery red skin and appeared to be a woman. Each of them seemed pretty young in age.

The odum youth had a decent size afro and a goatee. He had silver earrings and a wide nose. He had a slim build, and his robes even looked a size too big.

The dryad had blonde hair that carried a greenish hue against the afternoon sun, it was combed back and down to his shoulders. His eyes were narrow and violet, and unlike his former companion, his robes seemed like they were excessively ironed.

The red woman had ruby-colored horns coming out from the top of her forehead, the trunks of which were hidden by her shoulder-length hair that was a dark shade of wine. Her eyes were rosy orbs with glowing burnt orange irises. She also had a pointed tail coming from the back of her blue robes.

At the moment, the odum and the dryad were trading tags on each other's body with open handed hits instead of with fists. As the two continued to go at it, Yobo could point out the mistakes both were making. The three of them paid Yobo no mind, especially since the woman had half her back towards the direction of the gate. However, when Yobo came to a stop, the woman heard the ruffling of the grass behind her, and turned to regard the large human behind her.

"Knock it off," the woman told the other two. "We have a visitor."

At the behest of the red woman, the other two paused their sparring.

"Greetings," Yobo said. "What is the name of your fighting style?"

The three of them looked to each other for an answer that they did not have.

The dryad said, "*It* does not have a name, but several of our instructors suggested learning to defend ourselves without the use of spells."

The human followed that, "Just in case, of course."

The red woman came in next but looked at her companions, "Which sounds ridiculous. We are mages. If we cannot use spells, then what purpose do we have."

Yobo said after smirking, "My name is Yobo. I am a monk from Skyreach. Can I offer you some help?"

Before the trio could muster an answer, Yobo walked over to stand behind the dryad. From this point of view, the three of them got a much closer measure of how tall the monk was. The dryad alone only came up to Yobo's biceps.

"Uh, sure," the dryad said.

Yobo bent his knees slightly and leaned over so that he could look over the dryad's shoulder and to the human standing before them. The monk kept eye contact with the human as he prepared instructions in his mind.

"A good punch is like pushing a box," Yobo began. "In order to move the box, you must use everything in your body to create force, but when you punch, you need to focus that force into a single arm. When you punch with your right, push your body weight into the momentum of the punch by pushing with your right foot, and swing your torso and shoulder into it as well."

"Sounds simple enough," the dryad proclaimed.

The dryad and the young human squared their shoulders in preparation to test their new advice. Yobo moved to the side to give the two of them space.

"Brace yourself," the dryad warned his partner.

The young man did indeed brace himself, planting his feet firmly in place, and widening his stance. The dryad closed the gap, and in using his imagination of the explanation that Yobo gave him, and the fact that the two males were friends, the dryad drove in with an open-palmed strike aimed at the man's chest. The dryad nearly pounced off the ground with his right foot as he lifted his coiling body. The dryad threw his shoulder into the strike so much that it nearly rested upon the cheek of his face.

Yobo felt a sense of accomplishment, and good will, as he witnessed the dryad push the human back several feet. The move caused the young human to lose his footing, and so, he fell backwards onto his butt.

Inexperienced in such a devastating strike, the dryad was left unbalanced to the point that the excess momentum caused him to stumble and eventually fell to the ground as well.

"Hmph," the red woman scoffed at the other two inside her mind, but even as she did, she could not deny the difference in power. Her intrigue was cut short, however, when a message rang inside her head. She starred in the direction of the academy and to the top of the tower as she knew that was the source.

Moira, escort your visitor to the Archmage, the telepathic message called her by name. She was unalarmed by the message, or its nature of delivery, as such things were commonplace in Planesgate.

"Yobo," Moira said. "The Archmage wants to see you."

Yobo glanced at the woman, "Very well." Yobo returned his eyes to the other two who were returning to their feet. "Keep practicing that punch, and try to learn to balance yourself."

"*The Archmage?*" The dryad stated as much as questioned, but it was not his place to say much more. He could only wonder what the Archmage wanted with the tall man.

The dryad and the younger odum watched as Moira led Yobo towards the Academy of Planesgate.

The young red-skinned mage led the monk on to the stone walkway that led to the academy doors. On their approach, Yobo took the next minute to look over the white building. The whole thing was constructed of sharp, sanded stone bricks. The stone was so sanded and polished that it appeared to be white in color from a distance. The building was in a horseshoe shape with the left and right wings extending towards the direction of the silver fence. As the brick-made walls came together to connect the different sections of the school, there were intricately chiseled columns that gave the place a more prestigious appeal.

With a wave of Moira's hands, and the shimmering spray of arcane sparks that followed, the large, intricately chiseled stone doors of the Academy came open. The door stood nearly 15-feet-tall, there were columns on either side. The outline of the door was also trimmed in gold.

Beyond the doors was a long hallway, about six people wide with brown granite floors that had a luster so perfectly waxed that it gave the illusion that the floor could have been covered in standing water. The hall traveled for 40-feet before branching into the wings.

At the intersection, and in front of Yobo and Moira, there was a small garden with different types of greenery and flowers. Each of the flowers appeared unique and not one of them was the same. Remembering his brief conversation from earlier in the day, the monk looked for the black lotus. He pretended to have an idea of what he was looking for because the water lotus was a common flower in the gardens in which he used to tend. However, he did not see such a flower.

On either side of this small garden, a set of stairs traveled upwards until coming to a landing, and then from the landings there was another set of stairs that connected to a single landing above that. This grand staircase, then sported one more flight of steps until the beginning of the second floor was right over the top of them.

As Yobo's eyes took in all the detail in front of him, he did manage to glance down each of the narrower hallways that toured the rest of the school. Through the branching hallways, Yobo could see several doors dotting the white walls of the school, and each of the doors was trimmed in gold, and the doors had a round top-edge like that of an elongated half-circle.

Moira paid no mind to the curiosity of the visitor, and she continued her escort by heading up the grand staircase. Yobo made sure he was not too far behind.

On the second floor, the monk came to see that it was almost a repeat of the floor below. However, the branching hallways were wider up here, and there were fewer doors from what he could see.

Moira led Yobo directly across the hall from the staircase, which was met with a much wider, but shallower, set of stairs. She continued to ascend and at the peak of the wide steps, there was another case of stairs but this next set spiraled along the squared walls as they ascended up into the tower.

Moira's demeanor changed a bit once she peaked the wide set of stairs. Her eyes looked upward through the open space of the tower for a moment as she received another telepathic message. Afterwards, she turned her gaze to Yobo.

"The Archmage is at the top of the tower," she stated plainly.

Once Yobo had made it to the top of the wide steps, Moira departed and went back downstairs. However, Yobo never saw her leave nor did he hear her words.

Before he could comprehend taking the stairs up the tower, his eyes fell upon another garden. This one was not like the other from the first floor. This one had a single flower, a black flower with a dark red core that shimmered with an unknown type of crimson magic. Everything else in the garden bed was wilted, decayed, and lifeless.

Yobo was not able to realize it, but he could not take his unblinking stare away from it. His feet shambled onward, his breath became shallow, and the blood in his heart began to ignite and get hot. The bloody thumps became the pendulum that banged against the walls of his mind.

All the anger and rage swelled inside of him, he began to vividly replay the events of his parents' death, the taking of his sister, the doubt of the other students when he first arrived at Skyreach, and then finally, when his master and the others were all butchered.

The environment around him, inside the Planesgate Academy, seemed to fade away until all around him was featureless landscape. His teeth began to chatter as he gritted them while the muscles in his face pulled his mouth into a snarl.

Suddenly, he was back, but when he turned his head to look around, he was in the home of his childhood, and not the academy. His head turned to the floor, and he expected to find the bodies of his parents. They were not there. The absent detail further pushed his mind to realize that nothing else was in the house as well. No people, and no furniture.

Yobo could see the front door from his position, it was the same position in which he watched over his dead parents. But no one ever came through. He became confused. His memories had never done this before, and he had to wonder what was going.

The rage and pain around the puzzling memory felt more explosive than ever, but the details of the memory never appeared. His thoughts were consumed by malice and all he wanted to do in that moment was kill someone, his sister's captor, or the shade he was hunting, it didn't matter to him in that moment.

Yobo 's eyes were then drawn to the wall to his left. From the solid wood, a red translucent figure walked out. It had no refined detail, but the monk could swear it was mimicking his shape. It said nothing to Yobo, but it extended a ghostly hand out to the half-dryad. Flashes, echoing words, and promises of power blinked through his mind in an instant.

The monk's anger and rage found the deal to be satiable, but as Yobo began to reach for the handshake of acceptance, he started to see the blue energy of a magic spell grow inside the red phantom's form.

"*Impressio Vi*," came the echoing words from the magic.

Before Yobo could realize it he was struck, violently, by a magic spell. The translucent waves of the spell crashed against him, taking him off his feet, and throwing away from the dark flowers allure. The monk slammed and slid across the floor until connecting with the wall not too far away.

The monk's eyes came to focus in the real world once again, and when he was coherent, he could see the figure of dryad at the base of the tower's steps. The dryad had shoulder-length gray hair, bushy brows, and green eyes. The robe he wore was dark purple and hung just an inch from the floor. His skin held an oak-like tone.

"In another plane of existence, the black lotus is known as the *Nessian Swamp Rose*. It is a dark and foreboding fauna created by Hemagorgon, the God of Power. The essence of dark blood magic is contained within, and it uses that magic to feed on mortal pain and suffering," the dryad explained.

Yobo remained silent as he listened.

"You are wearing my brother's uniform. But why? Who are you?" the dryad asked.

Yobo's eyes went wide as the notion struck him into a stupor. In that moment, he saw the uncanny resemblance between this dryad and his late Master Asulus. It was at this point that he picked himself up off the floor.

"My name is Yobo, I'm the last monk from Skyreach," he introduced himself.

"*The last*?" the dryad questioned with a discerning tone. "What happened to Asulus?"

Yobo explained, "Everyone was slaughtered. Lady Hinora, in Telosa, said some sort of creature called the shade was responsible. I am currently trying to find the shade to avenge Master Asulus and the others. He left me a list of things and places, to help me learn more about the Uireb Nen. One of those things was the black lotus."

The dryad narrowed his eyes at the monk as the story was told. Then he said, "You *spoke personally* to Lady Hinora? In Telosa?" The archmage's tone was almost disbelief, but the old dryad looked into the golden eyes of the monk with his years of insight. On top of that, the archmage was secretly, and silently, using magic to search for the truth, and when he found it, he could only smirk at what his older brother had been working on. "Very well, Yobo. Seems your story checks out. My name is Tigus, and I am the archmage of this school."

Tigus' eyes looked to the nessian rose before walking over to stand in front of it, and the archmage did not take his eyes off the dark flower as he continued, "The shade have not been seen in these parts for quite some time. For them to evade the divinations of the queen *is* troubling. So troubling, that it would seem that my brother wants you to know everything about the Uireb Nen. Even the dangerous topics."

"*Dangerous topics*?" Yobo asked.

Tigus held his smirk in place and relished at the opportunity of experimentation. He looked at Yobo, and said, "I may be the archmage, but my brother did teach me a few things about the Uireb Nen. You know how the magic works, I assume?"

"Yes," Yobo answered plainly.

"The dark magic within the rose is no different than the elemental magic of water," the Archmage explained. "However, the power within the rose will never bend to the needs or strength of will from a dryad, or in your case, one with a dryad bloodline. You have to have something that the flower wants in order to bargain for its abilities. From what we both have seen so far; it has already taken a particular interest in you."

Yobo, although cautiously, came to stand next to Tigus, and he also looked at the nessian rose in a moment of curiosity.

"What does it want from *me*?" Yobo asked aloud, but nearly directed the question to the fauna itself.

Tigus then explained in short, "That's the problem with blood magic. You never know the price until it is too late."

The monk could not help but feel a bit of hesitation and wrongness in using such a dark power. He had to wonder if that vision from a moment ago was the rose trying to bargain with him. In a small way, he felt guilty that he almost went blindly into a deal with it. The warning in his heart made it strange to comprehend that the Uireb Nen could even work with magic made of hatred and malice.

The warning notions passed, but not through any natural means or with a bit of time to reflect. Instead, he felt a quick and slight change in the air pressure around them. His ears twitched as he tried to focus on it.

Tigus saw the slight shift in Yobo's stance. The dryad narrowed his eyes as his superior hearing could not sense anything. "Yobo?"

"Someone's here. Hiding their ste-," the monk whispered almost silently, but he knew that the wizard could hear him, but the whispering came to a halt as a massive body, bigger than Yobo's, came crashing against him from behind with a wrecking ball of a shoulder. Yobo was sent flying across the large flower bed until he crashed against the stone wall on the other side. Yobo didn't move after his body came to rest.

A giant, dark-clothed, blue-skinned orc now stood where Yobo was.

Tigus repeated the somatic incantation from earlier, "Impressio Vi."

At close range the spell released massive pressure that threw both Tigus and the orc in opposite directions. The orc got tossed down the wide stairs but was able to land nimbly on his feet after performing a somersault. Tigus, on the other hand, also landed on his feet except now he stood with his feet planted on the wall as if gravity did not exist. The archmage has to look 'up' to lock his eyes on the orc.

"A bloodtooth? I didn't think your kind came down from Nix," Tigus said to the orc.

The archmage soon realized the orc was not alone as two more darkly dressed individuals came down the stairs from his tower. Tigus ran up the wall until he was upside down on the ceiling, but the pair of assassins managed to do the same thing. At that moment, Tigus realized the magically enchanted cloaks they were both wearing.

As the new assassins closed the gap with the archmage, Tigus masterfully conjured up a protective barrier. The shortswords that sought his throat were only met by a solid wall of purple energy.

The orc down below came back up the stairs, but without being able to walk on walls, he patiently waited for his team to knock down the piece of fruit he was so eagerly waiting for.

"Assassins from the Black Lotus, huh?" the wizard stated to himself. "Can't imagine who would want me dead."

Yobo slowly regained consciousness, and he writhed around on the ground a bit after taking such a massive blow. His eyes were blurry, and he used his arms and elbows to lift his torso and head up. He could see the purple barrier around Tigus, but it was still a fuzzy sight.

The monk then noticed some movement directly below. Beyond the dark rose that was not three feet from his face, a figure stood outside of the garden bed. His vision was still hazy, and the unknown assailant was just a dark silhouette. The silhouette seemed familiar, though.

The monk's breathing became heavy as he continued to stare at the comparison between the figure before him, and the dark one from his memory. The repressed despair and pain that held back the details became lifted, and Yobo's eyes went wide with terror. The veil of his trauma was clear, and it was like he could see his little sister on the shoulders of the orc that was before him.

Yobo's eyes began to weep as the anger and rage consumed him. His eyes were blurred no longer, but all he could see was red. The dark flower could feel the monk's growing emotional power; it offered the deal again, nearly begging this time, but the rage in his heart ignored the unspoken contract.

Yobo stood up slowly as he brooded over the death of his adversary.

"*YOU!*" Yobo growled at the top of his voice.

All the assassins, and Tigus, turned their attention to the source of the animal-like scream. The orc, in particular, recognized the issuance of challenge from the half-dryad, and could only smirk at the notion of the coming bloodshed.

Yobo threw off his pack and took his quarterstaff in hand. The monk's discipline was gone, and he closed the gap with the orc. Yobo neglected to measure the orc as he got closer, and failed to see that the blue assassin was bigger than he was, both in height and mass. The size difference didn't matter to the human.

At the edge of the flower bed, Yobo leapt into the air and brought the shaft of his staff to go for the overhead strike. The orc readied himself against the obvious attack, but this was part of Yobo's feint. In midair, the monk contorted his body into a twist, bringing the high overhead strike into a lower jab, and sent the blunt tip of his staff to the orc's face.

The orc was equally as fast in his movements as Yobo, and he managed to grasp the quarterstaff not two inches from his face. The orc stepped into the attack while Yobo was still in the air and thrust his meaty fist into the side of Yobo's torso.

Yobo was sent hurtling down the steps after losing his grip on his weapon. After the monk had crashed against the floor down below, the orc took the quarterstaff in both hands and snapped the wooden object in half over his thick knee before tossing the pieces carelessly to the side.

The orc assassin pulled his two shortswords out of their scabbards, one in each hand, and prepared himself. The orc could sense the recklessness in his opponent, and everything he felt about the human became true as Yobo came charging up the stairs immediately after getting to his feet.

"Bring it, mutt," the orc goaded with his toothy maw and a slur.

In a single bound, Yobo was back on top of the stairs. Tears continued to roll down his cheeks as he pressed the orc once more. Yobo stepped in, and threw a straight jab, but the orc remained quick and dodged the attack.

The orc took advantage of the basic attack, and aimed a blade at Yobo's ribs. The monk made sure not to put all his weight into his punch, however, and expected the orc to follow it up. When the orc did, Yobo lowered a hand to catch the forearm and stop the blade, and it was at that moment that time stopped.

When the moment passed, the orc found the forehead of Yobo smashing into his face. The blow connected, and a splash of blood erupted from the orc's nose. The assassin's eyes went black, but only for a second, and when the shock of the blow dissipated, the monk and the orc became suddenly locked in a flurry of dodged punches and missed cuts.

"Yes!" The Archmage cheered for Yobo when the headbutt hit.

Tigus' exclamation drew the attention of the other two assassins and brought them back to the task at hand. They attacked the magical barrier with their weapons, but to no effect, and without any disturbance to the archmage, he was free to deal with them.

He turned to one of them, and produced a blast of fire at close range using both his hands, but with no verbal component. The assassin's clothes instantly went ablaze, and it wasn't too long before the enchantment on the cloak was broken and the assassin fell to the floor.

After landing on its feet, the fallen assassin let the thought of the archmage slip away, and decided to attack the monk's back while he was busy with the orc. In the heat of the battle, however, the monk felt the presence behind him. Yobo suddenly stepped back from the orc, and quickly turned around to deal with the combatant, coiling his arms for a punch.

When the monk stood to face the assassin, the humanoid suddenly backed off and rolled away. Yobo was blind in his rage, and wasn't aware of the pickle he had entered into. The orc wasted no time, he dropped one of his swords, and used both of his mighty hands to drive down his blade into the back of the monk.

Steel met flesh, and Yobo could feel the chill of the metal going into his body. The strike was quick, and the orc pulled the blade free before sending a giant front kick to the monk's lower back to send him tumbling down the stairs once again.

Crumpled on the floor below, the monk gasped for air as he felt the steam of his life suddenly evaporating from the wound. His loss in strength was immediate, and he wasn't sure if he could get up on his own. Yobo's face was soaked from the crying rage, and it never stopped.

The archmage watched the spectacle happen below. He became stricken with awe as the assassins had gotten the better of his brother's former student. The mage then looked in the other direction, to the flower bed, and he realized the Nessian Rose would be the only means of survival. "The rose, Yobo! Bargain with it! Bargain for its power!" Tigus called out to the monk.

Even as the words left the mouth of the archmage, the presence of the dark flower tore him away from the plane of existence. Once more he entered into a dark, featureless landscape. This time, however, he would not be taken to the places from his memories. Before he could consider the idea of striking a deal with the nessian rose, the imagery of an altar appeared before him.

The altar looked like it was made from gory sinews, it was slick and moist with blood, and the flat rock wrapped in tendons at the top was inscribed with the orangish runes of a diabolical language. The monk stepped closer to inspect the altar and as he did, a floating scroll appeared above with a fiery, feather quill pen beside it.

A demonic voice echoed a message inside the monk's head. *Power is what I promise, and a promise is the price. The promise is over, when the light shines twice.*

Yobo heard the words of the voice, but in his current state he didn't care much about what the flower wanted. The monk wanted the orc dead. The monk wanted whatever he could have to get rid of his most haunting foe. The one from his nightmares. The blood magic gave Yobo a taste of what he was craving. Malice, hatred, pain, and violence.

The monk took up the pen and wrote his name on the line at the bottom of the infernal contract. As soon as the pen left the paper, Yobo was returned to the material plane. Something was wrong, though. He was still toppled over on the floor. The pain and gasping for air returned.

Did something go wrong? Was it just a harmless dream? A flash before his eyes? The monk could still feel the rage inside of his own heart as he lay dying. Yobo struggled against the throes of death and everything felt numb. He wasn't able to move under his own power. His whole body, including his uniform, was heavily soaked in blood. When the whimpering came to an end, the weight of the world pushed the final breath out of the monk and his eyes could only see darkness.

The orc returned his eyes to the archmage above and commanded the other assassins, "Break the shell and let's finish this."

"Wait, look," the assassin on the ceiling called out.

Yobo's body began to writhe again. Arcs of red electricity zipped across the skin of the dead monk. The open area of the monk's wound was alive with crimson lightning and it closed before the eyes of the assassins. The assassin atop the stairs, who had their cloak burned away, began to move for the monk, but the orc stomped his foot.

"*No!*" the orc commanded. "He will die by my hand lest you want me to wear your skin."

The assassin knew not to cross the demand of the homicidal orc.

Tigus, on the other hand, looked to the garden bed. In all his studies of the fauna, he had never known the flower to become inert, grayish, and lifeless after someone committed to a contract. The magician could only smirk at the unknown scientific results that were about to happen.

Life returned to the body of the monk but he stayed there on the ground as his heart and lungs got back to work. Where there was cold numbness, there was now heat and fireworks. A resounding thud echoed off the floor when Yobo placed his first hand in support himself in getting back to his feet. Red jolts continued to skitter across his skin as he slowly stood up, and through this process, he regained all of his strength.

The monk looked down at his hands and arms to witness the red magic upon him. His snarling face did not show the impressiveness flowing through his mind. But in his heart, he felt angry, enraged, and he wanted the orc, the killer of his parents, to be erased from existence. All those thoughts and emotions swirled together inside the core of his being, and he didn't know how to explain it, but he felt in control. Like the power was his.

The center of power for the Gunn Drambor is pain.

The phrase from his late master rang in the halls of his mind. Mastery of the shadows in his heart. That's what he needed to learn, but was this it? Or was the nessian rose merely opening the door to realize his potential? His imagination played with those ideas across a second's time, and at the end of it, he figured it out.

This anger and fear and rage inside him. It *was* his. Ever since he was a child, ever since his parents were killed, he had been hiding from his dark feelings. In this defining moment the nessian rose exposed him to the truth. These emotions were not a burden nor were they something to conquer in the passing time, and instead, they were means of strength. A resource by which he could tap into when he needed it.

In this realization, in the acceptance of his fears and pain, his mind felt clearer now than it had ever been. Now, he was going to focus that anger at the orc and its cohorts.

When Yobo felt his body was ready to fight again his mind didn't bother about trying to figure out how to perform Suldo's Stand. He just did it like it was natural. Before, he had practiced the technique, but all those times he had been holding himself back.

In the blink of an eye, Yobo took up the stance of Cova's Maw, he conjured the Hesin's Cure spell which took the form of a dark red magic orb, and before he knew it, the monk absorbed the magic of the red energy into his arms. The malicious power spread to the rest of his body, and the veins of blood near the surface of his skin glowed with a crimson intensity.

The darkness of the blood magic was invigorating, it was liberating, and it immediately felt addicting. With a clear mind, fueled by the nessian rose's influence, Yobo ignored the disciplines of the Uireb Nen. Life was no longer a thing to be respected, and when the energy tapped into Yobo's thirst for revenge, there was no turning back.

With conviction upon his face, Yobo warned the assassins, "None of you will leave here alive."

"Hahaha. Ye stupid mutt, there's only one way an orc leaves a battle. The victor...or not at all," the orc replied, blood still running from his nose.

"Good," Yobo said through a giant grin.

Yobo ran up the wide stairs once again, but there was renewed strength in his body that was backed by a conduit of dark magic. His steps were lightning quick, and upon the peak of the stairs, the monk charged at the assassin that set him up for the orc's blade. The monk drove in and suddenly danced to the side as the assassin's blade came forward. Yobo then slammed a full-power, iron-like fist to his target's stomach.

The assassin had no time to react or dodge the incoming blow. The monk's fist caused the assassin to keel over, nearly passing out from the shock. Yobo was not done, however, and against the hard floor beneath them, Yobo took his foot, and crushed the knee of the assassin. This time, the shock led to a world of unconsciousness, and now there was one less opponent to deal with.

The other assassin from above dropped down, and engaged Yobo with vengeance in his eyes, but Yobo leapt backwards, and in the midst of his air travel he conjured up a Hesin's Cure, and threw it at the assassin. The evil humanoid could not stop the full force of his momentum, and he was struck by the blast.

The magic reacted to its target, and exploded in a spectacle of red and black flames, and when the smoke cleared the assassin was already dead on the floor but in two different locations as the blast tore him in half.

Yobo, being consumed by the surge of power and his new abilities, didn't realize it but the Hesin's Cure did not remove the rage bounding inside his blood. If he had known he would have been thankful, because from opposite ends atop the stairs the monk and the orc squared each other down. The orc readied both his weapons for the suspense in the air to disappear.

In any other situation, Yobo might have waited for the orc to attack first, but the orc's life was forfeit. The craze for violence grew stronger and stronger. The monk made no more hesitation and closed the gap with the orc one more time.

As soon as Yobo came within range, he leapt into a dazzling spin and came out of it leading with a foot. The orc ducked, rolled to the side, and sprung up into a backflip that landed him at the bottom of the stairs. Yobo's foot continued to travel forward, and ultimately smashed a foot-sized hole in the stone wall.

The monk recovered quickly from the missed attack, and identified where the orc was. Yobo did not immediately pursue the orc because the big blue beast was waiting for the human to make his move on the stairs.

Yobo would remain relentless, however, and in a mere second, he summoned a small Hesin's Cure like he did with the assassin, and shot it at the orc. The remaining assassin dodged with unnatural reflex, but the orc's mentality kept its composure as he soon realized he needed to dodge another one, and third one right after that.

Each Hesin's Cure missed its mark but as the dark energy came into contact with the floor, it would explode and leave large pock marks behind. Fragments of the tile flooring dusted up the air.

"*Fulga Percentis*," came the words from the ceiling as the archmage let loose a spell of lightning that sought to strike the orc.

The orc was a master of his body, just as Yobo was. It was finely tuned to perform, and to kill, and avoid any other dangers to it. After dodging the third

Hesin's Cure, the orc had rolled backwards to end up on a knee. In this position, the orc raised up the blades of his knives into an 'X' formation.

The lightning crashed against the steel of his blades, but it also became apparent to the archmage that the weapons were absorbing the magic before completely nullifying it. This caused the archmage to stop his spell.

Just as the flashing brightness and crackling sound of the lightning dissipated, the orc could not have anticipated the large brown boulder of a knee that came smashing against his face. The sudden shock and momentum of Yobo's assault sent the orc reeling backwards on his feet until the orc was tripped up by the railing of the grand staircase. The orc fell down ten feet or so before colliding with the floor on the first level.

The orc was impossibly tough, and his thick-muscled body could endure much damage. The orc got back up to his feet and took a few steps forward just as he noticed that the monk was coming down the stairs in pursuit.

The orc then realized that he did not have his blades in his hand, or at his side anymore. That would not be a problem, however. The orc unleashed a blood curdling roar that echoed off the empty halls of the school.

As soon as Yobo came off the stairs, the orc rushed after him and led with a wild right cross. The monk leaned back to dodge but that was the intent of the obvious maneuver. The orc danced and brought the back of his foot behind Yobo's to trip and knock him prone.

Yobo almost went to the ground, but caught himself with his hands. However, it left him in an awkward position. The orc completed his spin and followed through with a meaty pile of knuckles. The punch sent Yobo rolling off to the side.

The connected hit sent the orc in a bloodthirsty frenzy, and he went flying into a scramble to catch the human rolling on the floor. Once the orc grabbed him, the orc mounted and pinned him into position before pounding at the monk's face. The devastating blows hit home several times and blood splashed up from the human's face. Yobo squirmed like a fish until he managed to get his arms free to block the following hits.

Both combatants still fumed with rage, and Yobo in particular was not about to let his own tantrum disappear. In a flash of movement, he threw an arm out to begin to conjure another Hesin's Cure. The intent was to blast the orc while he remained on top, but the orc saw it coming and just as quickly reached over to pin Yobo's arm down.

The two locked eyes, the bloody rage between them could have started a fire at that moment. The orc continued to hit Yobo with his other arm, and Yobo continued to block with his. All the while, Yobo held his concentration on the spell, and as he tried to maintain the spell, it began to grow in size.

In the midst of the orc's assault, Yobo moved his blocking arm to reach up and grab the orc by the collar of his darkened leather armor. At the same time, the monk used his legs to lock the orc in place. The strange tactic took the orc by surprise and it caused him to stop punching. It was only then that the giant blue humanoid realized what the monk's plan was.

Larger and larger the Hesin's Cure spell grew, but as it did, Yobo could feel the dark energies begin to leave his body. Fearful that he might lose the dark power altogether, the monk shot the dark red Hesin's Cure at the orc anyway, and with the orc unable to go anywhere, the spell connected.

The explosion reverberated in the air. The last ounces of power kept Yobo safe from the damaging effects of the spell. The same could not be said for his saam. Dark smoke filled the area where the blast took place. The monk could not see the orc, nor could he feel the collar of his leathers.

Yobo stayed on the ground as he was unsure about where the orc could be. For some reason, his gut told him the orc was still alive. When the smoke cleared, however, the orc was gone, and giant holes going through the stone walls of the adjacent room were now there. The hole led to the outside of the school and towards the cliff on the backside of the grounds.

Yobo mustered up his reserve strength to stand up and make his way out to the cliffs at the back of the school grounds. Pain shot through his body, he knew his ribs were broken in many places, and the lightning-like throbs told him that the dark energy was gone. Did the Hesin's Cure get rid of it? He had to wonder.

The monk stepped through the charred holes in the walls, and walked to the edge of the cliffs once he was outside. At the edge, he looked down below to the homes and structures, but the area was too busy to point out any small details, and Yobo could not see any holes in any of the roofs.

Yobo still felt as though the orc was still alive, but there was no way to prove it. For now, he was content in knowing that he had won this bout. Nevertheless, a part of him wanted to go down below to find and finish the orc off, but without the power of the nessian rose he decided that course of action to be unwise.

More of his wisdom came in the following thoughts, and it humbly revealed that he was only able to battle the orc because of the rose's abilities. He secretly and silently yearned to feel its exhilaration again, but if he was going to have any chance against the orc next time he would need to train and learn more about the Uireb Nen. More than he might have thought possible.

He wasn't sure about how he was going to go about that, but he already knew that there were still more items on the list from his late master. He was at least thankful that the experience with the nessian rose allowed him to bridge the knowledge gap on Suldo's Stand, and taught him to embrace the ghosts that haunt his memories.

Through all the self-deliberation, Yobo never gave the contract he signed another thought. Before returning to the school, all he could think of at the moment was that he couldn't wait to meet that orc again.

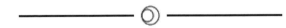

On the second floor of the academy, Archmage Tigus fended off the questions of the other teachers in the school, especially now that all the fighting and explosions had stopped. They were all gathered around him, and took notice of the damage around the halls.

"Now, now, everyone. I believe the attempt on my life is over," Tigus assured them.

"Members of the Black Lotus? *Here*?" one of the teachers questioned rhetorically to another.

Even as the words were spoken, a beaten and battered monk lumbered his way to the top of the stairs, but once he was there, he fell over and onto the floor.

"*Yobo!*" Tigus called out. The Archmage pushed his way through the other mages until he came to kneel by the monk's side.

"He's gone," Yobo shared before he fell unconscious from pain and exhaustion.

Tigus then looked over to the other teachers. "Don't just stand there, go get a healer."

As the other magicians spread out and cleared the area, Tigus had a clear glance of the nessian swamp rose flower sitting in the withered garden. The dark flower was still gray and inert, and the archmage could not sense that its sinister magic had returned. He could only surmise that Yobo's contract was still active. What did the human monk bargain with? What did the rose want in return? The archmage had to wonder.

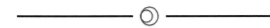

It was the next day when Yobo opened his eyes and found himself resting on a bed inside of a place he had not yet seen. The bed was comfortable and laden with clean smelling white sheets and covers.

He looked to the side and noticed a small table with a bundle of bloodied rags and a bowl of water. Beyond the small table, he could see several other beds, currently unused, and the walls were made of cobblestone bricks while the ceiling and rafters were made of wood and the floor was covered in beige tiles.

Light poured in through a window at the far end of the room, and directly outward from the foot of his bed was the only door into the room. Just as Yobo was looking at the door, he heard the knob and tumbler turn, and then the door came open.

Through the door, a priest dressed in a light blue robe walked in. It was a woman of half-dryad ethnicity, and Yobo could tell from her slightly pointed ears and golden eyes. Unlike himself, she had lighter skin, and dark hair.

As soon as the priest made eye contact with Yobo and realized that her patient was awake, she turned to face outside the room and called, "Archmage, he's awake."

A short moment after, Archmage Tigus appeared through the door, and Yobo noticed that he had a large book in his hand. He came to sit on an adjacent bed next to Yobo's.

"I can't thank you enough, Yobo. You saved my life," Tigus commended.

"You are welcome," Yobo said while trying to move and sit up.

Mentally, the pain from his injuries was still there, but as he finished his movement, he came to find out that his body had been completely healed. He placed a hand over his previously broken ribs, but the pressure gave him no discomfort. Yobo was astounded.

"Here," the priest came to his side and offered a cup of warm tea.

"Thank you," Yobo said as he took the cup.

"Now that we can talk about your reasoning for being in Planesgate," the Archmage began. "I have looked into the presence of the shade. I can only confirm what you have learned from Lady Hinora. The shade *have* hidden their agenda through means that not even I can comprehend. This means that one way or another, they are planning to strike against the people of Terra Sanguinar."

"Perhaps they have already started," Yobo suggested.

"Then we share the same sentiment in that regard," Tigus agreed. "My brother and the other monks, even against protest from Telosa, would have answered the challenge of the shade. It would be an educated guess that they are currently working to limit the resources available in this region before they attack."

Yobo could only agree, silently, with the notion. He then asked, "How can we stop them?"

Tigus made no hesitation in opening the tome that rested in his hands. He revealed a particular page he had placed a finger on. The page had a bunch of writing in the draconic language, but both of their eyes fell immediately upon the image of a yellow circle decorated with illustrated rays of light.

"It's called the *Esfera de Luz*," Tigus began. "The founders of the Kingdom of Claymore were the last ones to use the object, but it was specifically used to vanquish the shade seven centuries ago. It is a celestial artifact that is said to be created by Lumina, and it is capable of emitting terribly bright light. From what we do know of the shade, sunlight is capable of turning them to dust. In short, it is the perfect weapon against them."

"That is great news," Yobo exclaimed, a vague hint of vengeance in his tone. "Where is it located?"

The archmage chuckled for a bit before replying, "Hahaha. Fortunately, my friend, the shade can't hide that from my spells. It is being used as a source of light in a lighthouse. Far to the south. In a town called Aero."

CHAPTER FOURTEEN
THE LION'S DEN

Henrick, Serena, and Sand set out from Lumen the next day after their visit to the Library and the Sanctuary. Before they left, Henrick used some money to restock on dry rations and jerky as the trek to Harmon's capital was nearly seven days on foot. Cutting through the wilderness was a moot point between the two humans as they wanted to avoid any more would-be bounty hunters during their next leg.

They did not know much about Harmon, but the warrior did share with his companion that Harmon was not in a particularly friendly relationship with

Claymore. He elaborated to her that Claymore has had a long history of sticking its nose in the business of the other countries. Even with the Sword Treaty still active, the rulers of Claymore always seemed to have talent for trying to pick a fight. His hope was that because of the poor relationship that their presence would go unnoticed.

But there were still many miles to go until then, and the two of them were already in unfamiliar terrain. They could only guess what road block they would run into next.

After the first day on the trip, the bare and boring grasslands of the Golden Plains began to fade away, and it slowly transformed into a reddish, rocky expanse. It was a rocky desert that swallowed up most of the land between Lumen and the hills that protect Harmon.

With the early stages of summer still rampant across the continent, the cloudless sky found the travelers for every hour that the sun stubbornly remained above the horizon. It wasn't blistering hot, but it was still enough heat to make things uncomfortable.

By the third day, their faces were a mix of tan and red as their skin fought to adapt to the continuous warmth and sunlight. About halfway through the day, Henrick and Serena came to a stop in their travels as they happened upon the southern head of a massive canyon region known as *Siren's Scar*.

They took the moment to have a break. They drank from their skins, ate from their rations, and got off their feet for a moment.

During their break, they used some of that time to take in the sight of the Scar. The arid landscape faded into different colors as it ran deeper into the earth. Shades of white, then orange, white again, and then gray covered the bottom. In some areas, the gray was dark enough to where they could not tell if it was the canyon floor, or perhaps a deeper section in which the light could not reach, even with the sun as high as it was.

"I bet there's a whole bunch o' baddies down there," Henrick proclaimed.

"*Baddies?*" Serena questioned his vocabulary with a soft smirk. "You do realize I can't tell if you're human when you talk like that."

"What do ye mean?" Henrick questioned the strange statement.

"You've been living in Claymore for a bit now, and yet you still speak with the inflections of a dwarf," she judged.

Henrick could only scoff at her notion. "Hmph."

When the banter came to an end, they continued on their journey west, and it was by the end of the day that they came upon the southern base of the *Hunter Hills*. From here, the hills would stretch north for nearly a hundred miles, and somewhere on the northwest end was their destination.

They followed the base of the hills on the fourth day, their road trek through the wild turned north, and by this time, they had left the arid, red environment behind them. The travelers took their normal breaks throughout the day. In the early parts of the afternoon, Henrick and Serena spotted trees on the horizon. It was a few hours later that they came to the edge of a forest.

Where the trees met the hills, they found a beaten path where the trees had been cleared. There was a weathered signpost near the start of the path that said, "To Lionsgate." It was the first *real* sign that civilization was somewhere ahead of them. Henrick was glad to get confirmation that they were still heading in the right direction, but both of them were glad to take a break from the sunlight.

They pressed onward into the forest. After a few hours, evening twilight fell over the landscape, and with the summer's light having been suppressed by the leafy boughs during the day, it was no surprise that the forest was much cooler in temperature. To this end, Henrick and Serena both agreed to risk building a campfire tonight.

Another hour later, no more light could be noticed through the branches. The travelers were unable to see hardly anything in the darkness. Fortunately, Serena had the answer to their problem.

"*Éadrom*," she whispered the spell's incantation, and touched the tip of her quarterstaff.

The end of the staff began to magically radiate with a white light whose intensity was equal to that of a lighted torch.

"Neat trick," Henrick said after turning to notice the sudden source of light.

After another hour of trail through the forest, parts of the canopy opened up to reveal the full-point cycle of Undine in the sky. Nielda was not seen. The travelers took a moment in their walk to sit under the moonlight and take a breather.

Serena dismissed the spell on her staff. The light from the moon above was enough to see everything on the road. While Sand lay on the ground, the feline suddenly perked his head and ears up. The tiger stared off into the darkness to the northeast.

The druid felt the emotions from her companion, and with her eyes, she followed the stare into the shadows of the trees. She saw nothing. On seeing nothing, however, she noticed that the nocturnal insects of the night ceased their singing.

Noticing the concerned movements of his companions, Henrick asked, "What is it?

Serena stood up, followed by the other two. "I'm not sure, but we should get off the road. Come on, Sand."

The druid commanded with a wave of her hand. The three of them stepped off the beaten path towards the southwest direction. Their bodies and legs crashed against the shallow bushes with their hurried pace, and without the light of the moon or a spell, Henrick and Serena scanned through the invisible trees with outstretched hands.

The constant shuffling of leaves caused a noisy clatter, but after a moment they came to a halt. Behind them, they could only see the moonlit road.

"Serena," Henrick whispered in the dark while using a tree as cover.

No response came, and Henrick did not want to repeat himself. He looked back at the road, and just as his eyes fell upon it, a small humanoid shape appeared out of the darkness.

It stood nearly four-feet-tall, reddish skin, scraggly black hair with a couple of horns protruding from its head. It wore some kind of crude armor and had a spear in its hands. It wasn't a moment later that five more of the humanoids also appeared from the darkness of the forest.

Henrick recognized them from their descriptors, and knew them to be goblins. A vile and tainted race of blood magic worshippers. He also knew that where there is a pack of goblins, its hobgoblin commander was probably not too far away.

The warrior from Claymore decided that stealth was the best option here, and he knew that he could not move without risk of giving himself away. He figured the little demons must have seen the light from Serena's staff.

The thought made Henrick blindly scan the darkness in search of a sign for Serena, but it was no use. This moment reminded him of what Captain Spearfall had said. The thing about not getting sleep before a good fight. It was that memory that would drive Henrick to stay awake and stay alert to the invisible landscape that surrounded him.

He also came to accept the fact that there was not going to be a campfire tonight.

Morning came. The light of the sun was already a full hour above the horizon. Sometime after the goblins had walked away, Henrick sat down, perched himself against the tree he was hiding behind, and fell asleep.

When he finally awoke, he found his body aching, and his head pounded with a headache. After getting to his feet, he slowly brought his eyes around the tree and searched the road for any signs of the goblins.

But instead, he only saw Serena and Sand waiting.

After regrouping and continuing down the forest path, it was around the time that the sun was highest that they began their exit from the trees. Once they reached the end of their comforting shade, they could see their destination nestled into the hillside at the very edge of their visual limit.

It was a few more hours on the trail before they reached their destination. The beaten road from the forest continued through the grassy fields until ultimately leading to the entrance of Lionsgate, the capital city of Harmon.

The day was already reaching into the later hours of the afternoon, and the partly cloudy sky that had remained became large blots against the amber sky.

As they approached the entrance, Henrick and Serena spotted an open bench along the road. They immediately went for it while Sand went to lay down beside them.

"Looks like we made it," Serena said after a deep sigh.

"I could use a bed, and a drink after that hike," was all Henrick could say.

As they sat there on the side of the main road going into the city, each of them, including the tiger, could feel the road's ache at the bottom of their feet, and paws, respectively.

While they rested, their attention came upon the fair amount of traffic going to and from the city. For Henrick, it was a bit more than what he was used to compared to the gates of Claymore. People milled about while horses and mules pulled carts at the direction of their drivers.

The more interesting thing to Henrick and Serena, however, was the huntari. Some of them resembled humanoid versions of house cats while others appeared more like lions or tigers. Each of them had different fur patterns or colors, and there were more of them than anyone else.

"Oh. This is bad," Henrick muttered.

"What do you mean?" Serena had to ask.

"I'm allergic to cats," he explained but briefly.

Serena gasped in a facetious tone, "It makes sense now."

"Oh, does it?" Henrick stated as much as questioned.

"I've been wondering why you won't go near him," Serena replied in reference to Sand.

Henrick stood up and readjusted his backpack as he did not want to humor the sentiment of his suffering. But with all of that aside, he knew somewhere inside the city was their objective, and a comfy tavern bed. Serena and Sand followed close behind when the warrior began to take off.

As they approached the front of the city, the whole scope and layout of the place was in their view. The 12-foot walls in front had a gate to the left and right, both gates had large ivory-colored statues of a lion, and there was one statue on each side of each gate. The city as a whole was nestled at the base of, and between, two foothills. Sections of the hills, higher in elevation, had been excavated and leveled so that more homes and structures could be built. At the opposite end of the city, and at the very top of the hill, there was a large building that they imagined would have a view of the entire city.

Their eyes came back down to the walls in front of them. Standing between the two gates, and pressed against the city walls, was a wooden building with a sign facing the main road that said, "Gate Passes." The side of the building that faced the road had kiosk-style booths in which a patron simply walked up to receive service from one of the many workers.

From what they could see, there was only one booth open, but fortunately, there was no line for them to wait in.

Henrick and Serena approached the booth. The clerk at the desk was a female huntari. The best way to tell the genders apart on a huntari was the shape of their eyes, and the females had almond shapes while the males were more round. Aside from that, this one's furry body was mostly black with white patches here and there, and an especially profound patch around her right eye. Her eyes glistened with the light of the setting sun.

"Good afternoon," the clerk said with a rolling tongue on the "R."

"Hi," Henrick offered in short. "We're new here, and, uh…"

"We're traveling historians," Serena finished his thought with a bit of adjusted honesty.

"Ahhh. Adventurers," the clerk suggested. "Not to worry. If I can just get your names, this won't take long."

"Henrick Skullbright," he replied.

"Serena Rendria," she followed.

The clerk's feather pen and ink went to work, and in a matter of minutes, the huntari produced two gate passes for the city. The passes were small wooden cards that had their respective names and the occupation of *adventurer* on them.

Eager to get in, Henrick began to walk off, but he was only able to get a few steps in before coming to a stop as he heard Serena start another dialogue with the clerk.

"Would your town happen to have a place of historical records? We like to look at old legends and the like," Serena asked.

The clerk turned her head at the setting sun, and then back to Serena, "The historical archives are on the College Rise, straight into the city using either the north gate or the south gate, and on the first landing going up the hill. They would be closed about now. Best to catch them in the morning."

"Thanks," Serena said before joining Henrick's side.

With the gate to the left, the north gate, being closer to them, they decided to head that way. They passed by the giant lion statues before the gate guards checked their passes. With no issues, they entered the city.

As soon as they were through the gate, Henrick spotted a garrison on the left side of the road. No doubt to keep the gate well manned at all times. However, it was the next building that really caught his attention, but it wasn't his eyes that took the note first, it was his nose. The smell of fried potatoes and beer wafted out from the door and windows of the tavern.

They looked above to read the sign. *The Lion's Den*.

"We're stayin' here fer the night," the man decided on the spot with a nod of his head. Henrick already began walking for the entrance.

Serena looked down to her companion. "Come on, Sand. You're sleeping in luxury tonight."

Although Serena never really cared for the comforts of society and civilization, it was hard to argue with laying on a bed after traveling such a great distance. She also doubted her feline would argue the point either.

The druid and her animal companion followed Henrick inside, but as Sand entered the domicile, the lobby full of people, humans and huntari, suddenly sobered up and came quiet. The place wasn't terribly loud to begin with, but the sudden silence was felt no less.

The druid stopped in her tracks, and took a measure of everyone in the room, in which they all looked at the tiger at that moment. Her, nor Henrick, could figure out what was going on.

The barkeep, at the other end of the room, broke the silence, "Hey! Y'all gonna stare?"

One of the huntari patrons suddenly got out of his seat, and placed his own plate of food on the floor before Sand. The plate had a sizable piece of rare steak on it.

It was like a form of entertainment for the patrons, because as soon as Sand took ahold of the steak in his giant maw, the tavern patrons offered a cheer of, "*Huzzah!*" before continuing their side conversations.

Henrick and Serena went straight back to where the bar was. The barkeep was a large and muscular huntari male who had a silvery tiger coat. He had green eyes and his ears were pierced with bare steel loops.

"May I ask what that was about?" Serena was curious.

"New faces in town, eh? If it couldn't be more obvious, wild cats like your friend over there, are considered sacred to our people," the barkeep answered.

"Hmm. Interesting," Serena said while turning her narrowed gaze on Henrick.

But the man was already starting to rub one of his eyes from sudden dryness. "You might have to take the lead on this one, Serena."

"We need rooms for the night, and some food to settle us in," Serena requested to the barkeep.

"Of course, it's on the house," the barkeep said. "Take a seat, and I'll get it going."

Henrick and Serena went to the closest open table and sat down. Once there, the throb of the road was felt again. It was no time at all, the barkeep brought them a pitcher of beer and a couple of tankards to share it.

Henrick's allergies were in full throttle inside the tavern, but in his mind, beer was an acceptable solution to his misery. He filled his tankard, and took the whole thing down in one run.

"*Oh!* That's cold," Henrick blissfully complained.

Henrick slunk down in his seat a bit while sipping on his second mug. Serena managed to give the beer a try, although she didn't care much for the taste, or the allure of the beverage.

With the weariness of their travels, and the distraction of comfort with good food and drink; none of these things were enough to take the soldier out of Henrick, and it was his attention to his own alertness that picked up on the conversation at the next table.

"What about Aero?" An aerin man asked softly to his comrade who had come in the door just a minute ago.

"That round object at the lighthouse down there. I heard a rumor that ol' Fenri tried to take the damn thing," another man answered.

"He tried to take it? They kill 'im?"

"Nah, they caught him. He's holed up in Aero right now. Wanted for questioning apparently."

Henrick sat up in his chair all of a sudden, and stared into Serena's eyes with all seriousness, and whispered to her. "A lighthouse. That's where it is."

CHAPTER FIFTEEN
FATE

Henrick and Serena made little hesitation in the morning following their overnight stay in Lionsgate, and with Sand in tow, they were back on the road towards their new destination. After a full day of heading southwest, they arrived at a small pitstop kind-of-place that sat off to their right side.

From what they could see, there were no houses of any sort, and seemed like the only thing that existed here was taverns and shops. Before they had taken the short side road that led to the center of this pseudo-hamlet, there was a sign that identified the place as *Talibis*.

During their stay here, Henrick rented a room, but Serena was more reluctant about staying in a smelly establishment for more than one night in a row. With that sort of preference, she and Sand decided to stay out under the starry sky.

On her way out into the darkness of the wild night, she had seen all sorts of people come and go from Talibis. Since they were strangers to this land, there was no way of knowing what kind of unscrupulous people were around, and Serena wanted to avoid any kind of negative attention. She really wasn't worried about her personal security, especially since she had Sand at her side, but she still wanted to keep a low profile as much as possible.

When the next day came, the trio were back on the road. After a half day of traveling, the sun was well into the early afternoon hours by the time Aero popped up on the horizon. The cloudless sky was a mix of blues and yellows, and when the travelers got closer to the town, they began to see that several of its structures towered over the rest.

Eventually, they arrived at their destination, and the road they had been following led them straight into the merchant's square on the edge of town. The square was mostly in a circular shape, and the shops lined the borders of it.

Along the southern end of the square, there was a place that towered over everything else, to include the rest of Aero. It was a five-story-tall tavern called *The Siren's Song*, and the building was a chaotic mess of windows and balconies. Up and down the structure, whether it was through the windows, on the balconies, or on the roof, people were seen enjoying their drinks, dancing, or sharing stories.

Just like the tavern, the merchant's square was heavily crowded with people from all walks of life, and every member from every race on Golterran could be spotted here. The airways were noisy from the hundreds of conversations happening all at once. It was a giant gaggle of mumbling and banter, and to top it off, there were merchants screaming about the goods they were advertising.

The sight and sound of everything before Henrick and Serena was overwhelming, and the druid more than the warrior felt disgusted.

The rest of Aero stretched onward beyond the square and also to the north and south. Somewhere further to the west, the masts of ships could be seen standing above the roofs, and because they saw the ships in the distance, they figured their lighthouse would be in that direction.

"Maybe we should *go around*?" Serena suggested to Henrick.

"Aye," he agreed. "This place is makin' me head hurt."

At the advice of Archmage Tigus, Yobo had taken on some fresh supplies for the new leg of his journey. Additionally, the archmage had made arrangements for the school's ship to take him south to Aero. Since his destination was more than 400 miles away, he could not argue the chance to have a less arduous trip.

The small blue schooner known as the *Bolt of Knowledge* was set to turn his 12-day hike into a smooth 6-day sail. While onboard, Yobo enjoyed hot bean soup, a bunk, and all the stargazing he could handle when night would fall.

When he found himself in his bunk, he would at times remove his tattered green saam from his backpack. The robe was in complete disarray; the chest had a large area that was burned away and the backside had a clean slice that was caked from dried blood.

If it had been anyone else, the saam might have been garbage, but to him, it was a reminder. A reminder of his quest, his late Master Asulus, and of the blue orc he patiently waited to reunite with.

For now, he wore the blue and white robes of Planesgate Academy with his enchanted red sash on the outside.

During his voyage, Yobo got some opportunities to assist the crew of the ship with the sails, the dropping and pulling of the anchor, and he was able to gain knowledge on some of the more basic maritime routines. The crew was glad to use the monk's size and strength for the activities that were planned for the days at sea.

There were a couple of times where the sea state had changed as the Bolt followed the shoreline that sat on the horizon to the east. During these moments, the lively waters of the ocean pushed the small ship into near-uncomfortable lists, and it made Yobo hold on to something for fear of being tossed overboard. The monk had no sea legs, and when it happened the first time, the crew could not help but enjoy the sight of the tall man being defeated by the gentle forces of nature.

When Yobo came up to the main deck on the sixth day of the voyage, he was greeted by the bright sunny sky, and that light illuminated the Bolt's approach to the port town of Aero. The destination was nearly 10 miles away, but its presence among their ocean environment was nonetheless a beacon of civilization.

Just like in Planesgate, there were many different types of ships that were docked here. On the north end of the docks, the monk could see the lighthouse next to a pier that had a large blue and white ship next to it.

As the Bolt of Knowledge passed by, Yobo was unable to determine if he could see the Esfera de Luz inside the glass room at the top. The sight of the lighthouse pulled on an anxious string in his heart. He felt as though he could dive in the water and swim the rest of the way. Instead, he remained composed and told himself that he would be there soon enough.

The schooner from Planesgate was soon into its docking procedures. The crew made the lines ready; the small boats were lowered so that the boatswains could be ready on the pier, and long oars were put in the water to maintain the ships correctness as it berthed.

Yobo got out of the crew's way as they moved about the decks, and eventually he found himself looking over the starboard side railing at the stern. About 300 yards away, he spotted a long black and white ship with two masts that was anchored out. There were no sails lowered, and no colors hoisted.

His attention on the lonely ship was short-lived when he returned to focus on the crew of the Bolt again. The mooring evolution took nearly an hour, but once the ship was in place, there was a series of whistles to notify everyone that the ship was secured. The crew then worked to set the gangways up, and after Yobo said his goodbyes to the crew, he went ashore.

The pier must have been 100 yards long, and once the wooden planks turned into the streets of Aero, Yobo's first instinct was to turn left and head straight for the lighthouse. Instead, though, his eyes were forward, and right in front of him was a tailor shop called *Laya's Tailoring*. It didn't take much consideration for the monk to decide that he needed to get his saam repaired, or if it was even possible.

Yobo entered the shop only to have the door strike a bell hanging from above. The chime was quite audible, and it alerted the absent clerk of the monk's arrival.

"*Just a moment!*" came the call of a female voice from the back room.

Yobo glanced in all directions as he waited for the shopkeeper to appear. There was, of course, the shop's main counter before him that was an easy couple of paces away. To his left, there was a loom, and to his right, there was an assortment of different fabrics organized and neatly folded inside of cubbies that went from the floor to the ceiling.

The woman then came out from the back room while brushing off some debris from her clothing. Once she brought her head up and had Yobo in her sights, she flinched as she became completely startled by the size of the man.

She was five-and-a-half-feet-tall. She had locks of straight black hair which she tucked behind her sharp dryad ears, but she also wore a brass hairband around the back to keep her hair even more neatly gathered. Her eyes were just as dark, and her skin held a tawny, pine wood hue. Her clothing was like a travel-style dress, it was royal purple in color, and she wore a brown apron over it.

"C-can I help you?" the woman mustered as she recovered her composure.

Their eyes met in a moment that seemed to last minutes, and it left Yobo equally stammered. In that split second, and for reasons unknown, the presence of this dryad made his chest ache in a way that he had never felt before. He was suddenly and profoundly interested in the tailor. After a few seconds, his presence of mind came back to him and he managed to get himself out of his stupor.

"Is that *your* name on the sign outside?" Yobo asked her.

"It is. I'm Laya," she responded before offering her hand for a shake.

Yobo accepted the shake, and his massive hand nearly swallowed hers whole. In the honest gesture, he could feel the warmth in her soft and delicate hand. The small dose of her charm was taking over his ability to remain aware of his surroundings. The feeling was so alien to him, but he had no way to with it other than to ride its blissful course.

"I am Yobo," he managed. He then pulled his backpack onto the counter and revealed the broken, green robes to her. "Do you think you could repair this?"

She took the item and pulled it out from the wad that it was currently in. After spreading the robes across the counter, she noticed the more-than-obvious damage.

"There's...quite a bit of material missing, singed areas around here, and the back is really stained. What caused all of this?" she asked after making her assessment.

"I am afraid that is a long story," was his response.

Laya's eyes then pointed to a piece of furniture by the counter. "You're welcome to take up the stool," she offered. "It will take about an hour to fix this, but how about you tell me your story while I work. If it's a good story, maybe I can give you a discount."

She displayed a smile that took away Yobo's ability to decide, turning him into a poor sap, and he soon found his rear on the stool. He then asked, "How far back in my story do you want me to go?"

"How about where you come from?" she suggested.

As requested, Yobo regaled Laya over the next hour with his own personal history starting from when he was a small boy in Crossroads. He reminisced about how he used to live with his parents, how he was learning to be a pickpocket, but then he ultimately led that bit to where his parents were murdered by an assassin.

He continued by explaining that he was struggling a lot after that loss, but then he met Master Asulus after trying to steal from him. Instead of being punished or ridiculed by the old dryad, he was instead taken to go live with the dryads, and while he lived with them on top of the Skyreach, he was able to learn the martial art known as the Uireb Nen.

His tone became slightly darker when he lamented on how his family of dryads were killed while he nearly blew himself off the side of the mountain. The monk explained how his master left behind a note with a list of things for him to find and discover. He told her how he has been to Telosa, Planesgate, and now in Aero in search of answers for a creature known as the shade. He also added that his visit in Planesgate was where his robe was damaged as he had to fend off some assassins.

While Yobo told his story, Laya made repairs to the green martial arts uniform, but she did not make handmade repairs. Instead, she used a couple of different magic spells to animate some sewing needles and to conjure replica material to match that of the robe.

In the beginning of the repairs, Laya had some stitching thread tucked underneath the counter that she fed through the needle first, but when the spools were running low, she held out a hand as if reaching for something in midair. Her eyes went beyond her hand and to a shelf that was a couple of yards away. Before Yobo realized it, a fresh spool of thread floated by his face and went straight to her hand.

The action caused Yobo to pause during his storytelling. In his mind, he had to wonder how she did that, because when the motion was complete, he noticed that he did not sense the tingling of arcane energy in the air that was normal when magic was used.

"How did you do that?" he had to ask with a raised eyebrow.

"Uh. I had a customer from a long time ago that called it telekinesis," she explained. "It's something

307

that I was born with, I think. I grew up in an orphanage so I wasn't really able to ask my parents about it, or anything like that."

"Hmm. It's interesting," the monk said. "Now, where was I..."

As Yobo got through the rest of his storytelling, he was completely oblivious to how open he had become since walking into the shop. He was unaware that his anger and despair never surfaced when he brought up the misfortune of his two families. Somehow, perhaps subconsciously, he knew that he could trust Laya with his secrets.

When the life story of the golden-eyed monk from Skyreach came to end, Laya produced a near-new saam for Yobo to wear. He wasted no time in taking the item from her and putting it on, but not before taking the other one off.

Laya looked Yobo up and down, and considering everything she had just learned from the half-dryad, he had a certain air about him. She thought of him as innocent and determined in the midst of his own suffering. Even without him revealing those emotions, she could sense them, and because of that she could see his resolve. Yobo was by far the most interesting customer she had ever had, and she toyed with the idea that she felt admiration for him.

"It looks like the day I got it," Yobo complimented the work.

She offered him a smile, and a, "Mhmm."

"What do I owe you?" he asked as if willing to pay any amount.

Laya lowered her eyes towards the floor in a fit of bashfulness, "I'll let it go for a trade."

Yobo narrowed his eyes on her, but when both eyes came open again, she lifted her head. Their two stares met, and at that moment, they could sense the other's interest.

"When you're done with your quest, you should come back and tell me about it," she suggested through almost trembling words. "That's the trade."

Yobo offered a smile in return, and suddenly he could not remember the last time something made him smile like he was right now. He then replied, "Of course." At the notion of his continuing mission, his mind came spinning back to the task at hand. "Before I leave, though, would you happen to know anything about the lighthouse?"

Henrick, Serena, and Sand weaved their way through the entire town to avoid the overcrowded streets as they headed for the shoreline. They arrived in the area of the docks near the southern end, and when they did, they turned to the northwest when they did not find their lighthouse. Just as they put their eyes forward, though, they could see the top of it peeking over the lineup of ships in port.

The trio felt a little thankful that the street going through this part of town was wide, but the place was no less busy. The diverse collection of ships was parked to their left while warehouses, offices, and some shops fill the side of the avenue on their right.

The sound of the crowded street was dulled by the echoing calls of dockworkers, sailors, and seagulls. The air carried a salty tang, but once or twice, Henrick and Serena would catch a whiff of brackish sewage that made them reared their heads back in revulsion.

As they traveled farther along the docks, the denseness of the crowd lightened, and on their final approach to the pier that led to the lighthouse, the crowd had completely dissipated. Henrick, more than Serena, could see why that was.

Several guardsmen, dressed in the blue and white naval uniform of Harmon's Navy, stood watch in order to quarantine the final pier, and the lighthouse, from the public. This visual indication made Henrick hold out a hand to stop Serena and Sand from going any further. As they stood there in suspense for a few seconds, they glanced at the large ship next to the lighthouse, and the name *Sea's Lion* on the back of it.

"What's the matter?" the druid asked.

But Henrick was already trying to consider their next move in silence. He could feel the end of their 600-mile journey at the other end of those wooden planks. He knew that he was not about to give up on reaching his goal. Not when they were so close. He turned to regard Serena, hoping an idea would pop out from her presence, but then his eyes fell down to her feline friend.

"Hmm. Let's see if they like cats, too," Henrick said.

The man then continued towards the lighthouse's direction. Henrick went straight for one of the guards, and as he got closer the guard stepped forward to challenge the approach.

"Hold, citizen," the guard said with a raised hand. "This area is off limits with the ship in port."

"*Oh?*" Henrick exclaimed, but in reality, he almost expected this sort of assertiveness. "We were just hopin' to see the lighthouse up close."

"Unfortunately, we cannot let anyone proceed by order of the admiral. Please, go about your day," the guard instructed politely.

"Aye. Thanks," Henrick said in return.

The three travelers turned to walk away, and it was a short moment after that when Henrick spied a bench off to the side with its back against one of the many warehouses. They walked over and sat down. Henrick slouched over a bit, placing his elbows on his thighs, and shot his eyes back towards the direction of the lighthouse.

"Oi. We're *so* close," Henrick said with a hint of anxiety in his voice. For the moment he was at a loss for how to proceed other than waiting for the ship to leave, but there was no telling when that might be.

"I could...sneak by them," Serena suggested.

"Nah. Ye'd get caught," he shot the notion down.

"No. I won't," she retorted.

The sheer confidence in her words drew Henrick's eyes to her, and he was suddenly interested in how she was going to accomplish the task. Serena's face then changed to one that showed perplexity as she was trying to determine his train of thought, and then it popped in her head.

"Wait! You mean you don't..." she exclaimed while cracking a smirk at the man.

"*Don't* what?" he asked in a non-mocking tone.

"The brown cat you saw on the day when we met...*that was me*," she admitted.

Serena's words hit him like he was getting hit by a brick. He instantly shot his confused visage towards the ground in disbelief, and his eyes rolled back and forth as he drank in the implication of what she just said.

"*What the shite?*" was all he could say.

"Hahaha," the druid laughed at his lack of understanding.

Henrick returned his gaze upon the woman. "You're telling me you change into-" his question was then cut short when Serena placed a hand over his mouth to silence him.

"Yes, I can. However, there are still those in this world that view it as witchcraft," the druid explained. She then removed her hand before getting up from the bench, and headed towards the nearest alleyway between the warehouses. "Keep an eye on Sand for me."

As she disappeared, Henrick and the tiger exchanged unamused glances to each other.

Serena made a couple of turns until she found herself in an alley that was hidden from the sunlight. When she was gone from the public's eye, the druid stood there in the cool air and began to concentrate. In her mind, she had to silence the sounds and smells of civilization in order to get the information she needed.

This was part of the process that druids needed to be able to transform into animals. She reached outward, beyond the dark alleys and the warehouses, with her empathic abilities. She reached outward to find the animal that she had in mind. In this case, it was a seagull.

She found her task to be easy as there were many seagulls near the docks, and the constant mewing that came from the birds allowed her senses to lock onto them.

Once she had the information she needed, it was in no time at all that she summoned her druidic powers to fruition. Her body magically changed shape. She shrank to stand a mere foot-and-a-half, white and gray feathers sprouted from her figure, her arms turned into wings, her feet turned into webbed claws, and a yellow beak grew out from where her mouth was.

The act of changing shape always gave her a feeling of tightening discomfort, but as the magic did all the work, the process was relatively painless.

But when the process was complete, Serena filled her air bladder with as much air as possible before pushing off the ground with her flapping wings. She was quickly in flight and took her altitude above the roofs of the warehouses. Free from the cool shade below, she made a banking turn and headed towards the lighthouse.

Overhead, the druid circled the tall white structure, and from what she could see with her avian eyes, there was no golden sphere that might have resembled the object that they were looking for. She made a couple more passes and looked through the glass again and again.

On her third circuit, she turned to fly directly at the lighthouse to land atop the balcony. She remained a seagull in order to maintain her stealthy task and waddled towards the glass door that was cracked open. Once there, she stuck her beak into the gap and wriggled her until the door came open enough for her to walk in.

She peered into the glass room at the top of the lighthouse. There was a metallic frame made of brass that was shaped to hold a large round object, but the object was absent.

Henrick and Sand remained at the bench. The feline was rolled over on its side and found himself inside of a quick nap under the warmth of the day. Henrick, however, was busy watching the sparse people milling about. Of all the individuals that he glanced at, his eyes became stuck on a large odum man wearing a green robe and a red sash.

The peculiar individual was not more than 20-feet-away, and just like Henrick did a moment ago, this stranger came to a stop and gazed in the direction of the lighthouse. It was like the warrior from Claymore was looking at an echo.

Henrick's attention then snapped to the side as he noticed Serena stepping out from the alleyway.

"The Esfera de Luz is not up there," the druid explained.

"*What!*" Henrick questioned with disbelief.

Just as the warrior made his remark, his eyes then snapped on the man with the green robes who was now approaching the trio. Henrick surmised that the stranger overheard the exchange of words, and was probably lured by the name that was audibly revealed. The presence of the stranger also caused Sand to perk his head up.

"Greetings," the large odum said on his approach. "Are you looking for the Esfera de Luz as well?"

"*Aye*," Henrick confirmed with a raised eyebrow, and his puzzled tone made him sit up straight.

Serena regarded the stranger with an equal amount of interest. Her mind was blown away that someone else was looking for this thing at the same time as them.

The large man then offered a friendly hand to Henrick before introducing himself, "My name is Yobo, and I am afraid the artifact we seek was taken by pirates."

Henrick immediately thought back to the conversation he overheard in Lionsgate, and he begrudgingly and silently cursed at the discovery that the rumor from those people was true. Regardless of how he felt at that moment, Henrick still managed to stand up and accept the gesture offered to him.

"I'm Henrick," he started before waving a hand to the others. "This is Serena, and that's Sand."

Sand remained silent and unmoving as he watched everyone. Serena offered a shallow smile and a nod at the mention of her name.

"Do ye know anymore?" Henrick asked. "We've come six 'undred miles to find this thing."

"I have been on my own journey as well," Yobo said. "The pirates that stole it are being held prisoner in the dungeon of the navy base." The monk shared his information while pointing his eyes towards the walled off section of the city to the far northwest beyond the docks. "They are led by a man who calls himself Captain Fenri. He too, is a prisoner."

While Henrick and Yobo looked to the north, Serena kept her eyes on the stranger before them. She didn't do it out of caution or suspicion, but rather she was interested in the implication of this chance meeting.

"Yobo. Why do you seek the artifact?" the druid asked.

The monk then lowered his head and his eyes. He held in place for a short moment as his history played out in response to that question. It was like a lightning strike, though. The flashing images were gone as soon as they had come. After a small sigh, he answered with, "There are these creatures known as the shade. That artifact is supposed to destroy them."

The tone of his words resonated with Henrick and Serena, and it was becoming more apparent, to some extent, that they were all on the same wavelength.

"The shade kill some o' yer people, too?" the warrior asked the monk.

Yobo quickly brought his eyes up to meet Henrick's. The look in the man's golden eyes was confirmation that did not need words of expression to answer the question.

"Our meeting is not a coincidence," Serena stated. "The Twins have *pushed us* together, Henrick."

At the sounds of her words, Henrick could only think back to the water nymph in the cave, and the image upon the shield on his back was clear in his mind. He could not argue with the reasoning at hand, but he also had to wonder who else out there has been adversely affected by the shade. Even with the Esfera de Luz out of reach, Henrick, in a small way, felt better about their mission and hoped that more allies would come to reveal themselves.

Yobo was also moved by the druid's opinion. He knew of the Twins, but he never would have considered a religious approach to the destined meeting with the trio in front of him. His memory went back to that fateful night. Both of the moons were full and only now did his imagination take on the idea that the goddesses *were* watching him that day. Perhaps they tried to send him a message and he just didn't understand it, yet.

Everyone was lost in their thoughts, and the silence eventually drew their attention to the navy base once again. Individually, each of them attempted to think of a way to go about their next step.

"So, we need to get the information from that pirate?" Yobo asked rhetorically.

Henrick, being the soldier that he was, knew the Harmon Navy would not let strangers near the pirates without arousing suspicion. The guards from earlier wouldn't even let them near the lighthouse which only led him to assume that he wouldn't get within 10 feet of that dungeon or the base.

If there was an option on the table of his mind that seemed feasibly successful, it was probably going to have to involve the pirates. Little bits of his imagination were starting to fill in the blanks to the rest of their dilemma, but Henrick shook them away in moral defeat.

"I need a drink," the warrior digressed before turning to walk away.

Yobo, Serena, and Sand fell in behind Henrick. The warrior from Claymore figured they could worry about all the pirate stuff tomorrow. For now, he led the troupe south through the docks. During their earlier trip through town, he could have sworn he saw another tavern somewhere. He already knew he didn't want to stay at that noisy place in the square, and so he held out hope that his eyes didn't deceive him.

At the edge of town on the southside, Henrick found himself before a small location called *The Drowning Cat*. He immediately grew a devilish grin on his face. In his head, he knew that Serena would *love* this place and its name, but even though he was going to have a bit of fun with it, he thought the place was appropriately named considering the huntari that lived in Harmon.

"If you think we are staying at a place with a name like *that*-" Serena started to retort but then stopped when Henrick cut in.

"These people're cats. Cats gotta drink, too."

"I've been meaning to ask," Yobo whispered to Serena. "Why does your friend talk the way he does?"

"He was raised by dwarves," she shrugged with hands held up in defeat.

"Hmm. That's very peculiar," the monk stated.

Henrick was the first one inside, and he beamed by the tables and other furniture until he got to the bar. The lighting inside was low, and the glowing candle sconces complimented the dark wood that framed the inside. The plastered walls were painted blue which allowed the place to be warm and keep the chilly sea breeze out. As was the norm, the aroma of beer and ale filled the air.

There were a few tables being occupied by other patrons, but compared to the other locales in town, this place felt empty. Most importantly, it was quiet.

When the door closed behind Serena and Sand, the barkeep appeared from the back room. He was a large and muscular huntari with the mane of a golden lion, iron rings that pierced his ears, and he wore a dark leather apron over a beer-stained shirt.

"Welcome, folks. What can I get you?" the barkeep asked.

"Beer and lodgin' for the three of us," Henrick stated.

"All together?" the lion said.

"Aye."

"Hmm. I'll do twenty dag for the lot of you," the barkeep offered. "That will cover meals, rooms, and ale."

After Henrick made the exchange with the huntari, they headed for an open table and waited to be served. During this time, and after they got nourishment as well, Henrick and Serena shared their stories with Yobo, and in return he shared his.

In conclusion, at least for Yobo, he deemed the meeting with the warrior and the druid to be a good sign, and he was definitely not deaf when Henrick brought up the notion of the shade invading the Sword Kingdoms. At that point, the monk's search for vengeance would most assuredly become complete if he destroyed an entire army of shade. In his mind, the shade were the only problem in the universe, and genocide was definitely a suitable answer.

Sometime later, after they had finished their meals and drinks, nightfall fell over the western coast of Golterran. Henrick managed to take himself to his room to sleep off the heavy buzz that he had been working towards. Before Serena and Yobo went to their rooms, the monk sought to get the druid's opinion on their situation.

"What are your thoughts on the pirates?" Yobo asked her.

She paused for a moment to consider the question, and then she answered, "I'm not sure, to be honest. I don't know what to expect from them, but just so you know, I'm going to go talk to them tonight."

Yobo ran the idea through his head, but he hadn't the slightest clue about how she was going to accomplish that. His curiosity then became voiced, "You are? But how?"

"I'll tell you later. We can meet in the morning about it," Serena said.

"I have just met you people, but I believe that I trust you already," the monk admitted. "In the morning then."

And with that, Yobo and Serena went to their rooms.

As Serena had mentioned, she would not be getting to sleep any time soon. When she entered the room, Sand suddenly trotted in front of her in order to get on the bed first.

"Pfft. You're pathetic," she scoffed.

Serena walked across the room and opened the window on the other side. The room had a good view of the ocean and the last pier of the docks area. The dim glow of the Twins in the sky made it possible to see the horizon in the distance. The moonlight begged her attention, and when she looked up, she found Nielda was performing her waxing gibbous while Undine conducted the waning gibbous.

"Please let this night be a success," she whispered to the celestials. After a pausing moment of silent prayer, she turned to her feline and said, "I'll be right back."

The tiger pointed his eyes towards the druid, but he made no efforts to lift his head from the soft mattress.

Serena kneeled down to get on all four hands and knees before she began to concentrate. Once her mind and heart were centered, she transformed into a small chocolate brown tabby. It was in no time at all that she leapt onto the window sill, and charted a path down from the second story to the ground.

She traveled along the short overhang of the roof to the backside of the tavern, and from there she was able to use the stacks of boxes, crates, and barrels to get down. As soon as her paws were on the earth, she took off into a sprint.

The sudden rush, speed, and adrenaline of being a cat was liberating, and if there was ever a feeling of pure freedom, this was it. She was able to run faster than she could as a human, she could jump just as high, and the wind that ran through her fur was close to therapeutic.

When she got to the north end of the docks, she laughed inside her feline skull when the guards had no idea what had just flown by them. Or perhaps they did know. Perhaps they did see her run by. It didn't matter, because not one of them turned to give chase or intercept.

The brown cat kept going until she arrived at the base of the wall that surrounded the Harmon navy base. Serena zipped to and from the shadows that loomed between the lampposts along the nearby street. Eventually, she found the entrance into the base, and with her lighting-like speed, she ran right by the guards, and they were not aware of the feline presence.

Inside the walls of the navy base, Serena looked around at the various buildings so that she could try and figure out which one held the dungeon. Unfortunately, they all looked the same: wooden structures with white walls, blue roofs, long, and rectangular in shape. Some of them were two stories, and she assumed it probably was not one of those.

She clung to the shadows and prowled deeper into the base. After a bit, maybe three-quarters-of-the-way in, she noted one of the buildings on the did not have a standard wooden door like the rest, and instead, it had a door made of steel bars. Furthermore, it was the only structure she had seen so far that had four guards posted on the outside.

As she crept closer to that building, she became aware that her cat form would be able to fit through the bars. Her padded paws made no sound as she circled around to approach the building from behind the guards outside. Her small legs increased in pace as the moment was at hand, and then she slipped inside as soon as she was able.

However, she came to a scratching stop once inside the building and had to quickly bolt off to the side to hide under a table. At the other end of the room, from the entrance, was a solid wooden door that led further and elsewhere, but that wasn't what she was hiding from.

Opposite from her table shelter, there was a desk and two more guards. One of the guards was sitting down, and the jingle of a keyring sounded off everytime he shifted in his seat. The other guard was hunched over the desk and was writing something inside of a large ledger with a feather pen.

Once the ledger was properly filled out, both of the guards motioned for the solid wood door. The one produced the keys from his waist, unlocked the door, and opened it so that the other one could walk inside.

Serena saw her opportunity and streaked across the floorboards with every ounce of speed she could muster from the feline figure. She flew into the dark gap of the open door just before it closed again. In her flight, she grazed against the boots of the guard going in.

"*Mangy cat*," the guard cursed.

Serena was already jogging down the stairs she found inside, and when she reached the bottom, she estimated the place to be about 30-feet below the surface. The place down here was built with cobblestones that were either covered by mold or moss. The places smelled of salt and urine, and the aromatic sensations were amplified tenfold through the nostrils of a cat.

But she continued through the dungeon anyway, and after traversing a long, slow-curving hallway she arrived at a chamber with many jail cells on both sides of her. This area was lighted with hanging lamps, and the light revealed that each cell was constructed using thick iron bars that were bolted into the floor and ceiling. She could see the pirates in each cell, each side of the dungeon had five cells, and looked like there were 10 of them in each one. There were 100 pirates holed up in this place, she deduced. It was a small army, for sure.

Every so often, the druid would look behind to keep tabs on the guard who was making his way through the complex, and although she couldn't see him yet, his noisy feet echoed off the walls.

The druid kept going and softly trotted to the end of the dungeon. The pirates didn't even look at her as she snuck by. At the back of the dungeon, she discovered an unfinished wall where the bricklaying had come to a halt. She investigated the dark areas behind and discovered a shallow pool of water, bare earth with thick roots draping in the damp air, and a bucket with rope attached floating on the surface of the water.

The brown cat looked up and noticed a cylinder of bricks built into the earth with more iron bars installed over the top. Beyond the iron bars, she spotted Nielda looking down upon her.

A well? She thought in her mind.

When Serena was done inspecting the darkness of the wall, she looked back and noted that the guard was already walking back out of the dungeon. She remained hidden in her cat form until she heard the echo of lock's tumbler.

When the sound came, she reverted to her human form and stepped out from the darkness behind the unfinished wall. Her figure was noted by a couple of the pirates. They began to whisper among themselves until most of them were standing up and staring at her. That was when she decided to break the ice.

"Which one of you is Fenri?" Serena asked aloud. Her voice softly echoed off the walls.

Suspense washed over the dungeon. All the pirates muttered to themselves, conversing with each other in whispers. They were curious about the "witch" as they called her, and they wondered what she wanted from their captain.

From the middle cell on her left, a voice echoed back to her, "That's *Captain* Fenri to the likes of you, lass."

Serena moved to stand before Fenri's cell, but she remained in the center of the passageway.

When the captain finally came to stand before the bars, he continued, "Pretty *darin'* of you to come down here, witch. What do ye want from me?"

"Myself, and a few others, have come here looking for the round artifact that you stole," she explained. "Where is it?"

"Bahahaha," Fenri busted out in a fit of laughter. He then tried to imitate Serena's voice for his follow-on mockery, "Oh look. Another do-good tryin' ta twist me arm. Hahaha."

The rest of his crew joined in with their own laughter.

Without words or somatic components, she sparked to life a small flame in the palm of her bare hand. The minor feat of magic was enough to make an impact on the pirates for they all immediately fell silent.

"Who are ye?" the captain asked with narrowed eyes.

"I'm a *witch*. Said so yourself," she answered with her own mocking tone. She dismissed her flame when she continued, "But if you must know, the Sword Kingdoms is going to be invaded, and the Esfera de Luz is the key to stopping the war that is coming.

Fenri rubbed his chin through his black beard as he considered her words. Deep inside is his heart, he felt the call of destiny. It was the only reason he and his crew sailed back out to meet the Harmon Navy.

Fenri's boss wanted the Wailing Wolf to get captured so that one day, he could provide passage to his liberators. Or at least, that was what he was told.

The Captain of the Wailing Wolf was a man of opportunity, chaos, and ferocity, and the man knew himself well enough that he would never pass up the chance to prove that for no matter of reason, would it be a good idea to break his pirates out of prison.

"Hahahaha," Fenri exploded with laughter once more, but this time it was from the insane imagination that swelled his brain. For the last month, he had to hear the echoes of non-stop celebration coming from the town since his capture. And if the town of Aero wanted a party, he was going to give it to them.

His crew all smirked for they already knew their leader had something devious planned.

When Fenri composed himself back to normal, he said, "I won't be tellin' ya where the orb is. Sworn to secrecy, ye see. Hah. If you want the damn thing, me and the boys'll hafta take ye there."

Serena looked around at all the cells, and then back to Fenri. She stepped a little closer to his cell, and narrowed an eye on him. "A *jailbreak?* That's what you want?"

"Breakin' us out of here is the first of many things, but without these prison bars, we'll handle the rest," the captain declared with a confident grin.

The pirate crew whispered and snickered at the underlying words of the negotiation.

Fenri then continued, "My ship is anchored out beyond the docks. All you have to do is make sure you're onboard when we leave."

Serena pondered on the words of the pirate leader. She wasn't sure about the whole idea of a jailbreak. She had no idea how these pirates might behave once they've been let loose upon the town. She was concerned with people getting hurt, but she also had to consult with the others before making a decision. In the midst of her thinking, she had unknowingly swayed toward Fenri's cell by an inch, and it was at that precise moment when the pirate reached out and grabbed the druid by the collar of her leathers. He forcibly pulled her close until she came clashing with the iron bars and her face rubbed against them.

She instinctively tried to wrestle herself away, but there was nothing she could do against the captain's inhuman strength. She found herself face-to-face with the man.

His breath reeked like bad pickles as he spoke through yellowed teeth, "Me and my crew have been rotting in here. Awaiting the arrival of someone like you. Now, I don't know if you're that someone, but right now, ye are. On me life, and the name of my late mother, you'll have your treasure. But only *if* we get out."

The captain then released his grip, and Serena stumbled backwards a bit. The short ordeal that Fenri just performed irritated the druid. That irritation was unlike anything she had ever felt before, and it grew emotional and angry. In the heat of her sudden shock and adrenaline, her mind had already made the decision.

"*Fine*. Tomorrow night. Your *boys* better be ready," she accepted the accord.

The druid departed the light of the lamps, and used the shape of a small bird to escape the dungeon through the well. Once in the sky, she could see that the well was located in the merchant's square, and from this point, she headed back to the tavern.

Back down in the dungeon, and across from Fenri's cell was Constance, his first mate. He heard the whole exchange between his captain and the witch. "Do ye think she'll be back, Cap?" he asked.

"She'll be back," he proclaimed. Fenri then spoke so that all of his crew could hear him clearly, "Listen up, maggots. Our time has come. We're gonna take the navy by the balls tomorrow night. Are ye with me?"

A round of "aye" reverberated in the dungeon.

"If a man or beast should stand in your way, take it down. The goal is the Wolf. Be on there, or be left behind. It's time to go home and see our families."

His speech ushered in another round of "aye" in the smelly air.

CHAPTER SIXTEEN
ALPHA

"They want us to *what*?" came the protest from Henrick.

It was already the next morning, and one by one, Serena had pulled the others into her room to discuss the matters of the night prior with her visit to the pirates. The druid explained to them what was said, what the terms of the conversation was, and ultimately, that the pirates needed to be broken out of their prison.

"We cannot break them out of their prison," Henrick added to his retort.

"The captain of those pirates said he would take us right to it. To the Esfera," Serena argued in return.

Yobo had been sitting there, listening to the story, and was beginning to realize he might have to be the voice that swung this decision. Yobo, like the other two, was wanting to reach the fruition of their quest, but he wasn't convinced that unleashing a riot upon the people of this town was right.

They were pirates and criminals. There was no way to trust their words, or actions upon being set free. While those facts did permeate in his mind, it reminded Yobo about his youth as a padfoot. Even among the Red Hand, before their demise, there was a form or code of unspoken honor among them. Perhaps the pirates had a similar code, but there was no way to be sure.

The monk thought some more on the matter. Even if they could trust the bargain with pirates, their actions would be unpredictable during the escape. Many people's safety would be in jeopardy. With respect to all the life that was around him, Yobo came to his opinion.

"The words of the pirates, if I may, are not in question," Yobo chimed in. "It is their chaotic nature, which endangers a lot of people, that makes this option too risky."

"*Risk?*" Serena echoed the word aloud, a tone of irritation in her voice. "We have an army at our disposal. In that dungeon. If the pirates-."

Serena got cut off from finishing her argument when Henrick suddenly stood up, and voiced his decision over hers, "We're not doin' it!"

Sand picked his head up off the pillow and bared his razor-sharp teeth at Henrick. Henrick remained standing, however, and wouldn't let the threat of the tiger sway his judgment.

Serena, on the other hand, felt like she was pushed back into the corner, and the feeling was similar from when Captain Fenri grabbed her. Henrick's words stung her from underneath her skin. The two of them had been traveling for such a distance, and she felt herself growing on the warrior from Claymore, but in her mind, at that moment, it would seem the sentiment was not both directions, and that made her emotional state even worse.

It would seem that Henrick and Yobo were dead set on stagnating as a law-abiding citizen in the face of completing their journey. In a very small way, she had to respect their character, but there was something greater, and more important to her than any law.

She was a druid of the Ember Grove. The petty rules and organization of civilization had no place in her heart or mind. This belief was especially solidified when her thoughts dug deeper into the subject, and the idea was that civilization usually took the resources and bounties from nature, and rarely did those things get returned.

She then thought of the shade, the children of Abyss. The dark creatures were attempting to gain a foothold in the Sword Kingdoms, and although it seemed they were going to target Claymore, a civilized city, she could not ignore the threat they posed to the rest of the land should they be victorious.

In the grand scheme of civilization, however, there was but one rule that also could be found out in the wildernesses of the world. That was survival of the fittest, and this was one of those defining moments. It was success, or failure; kill, or be killed.

Serena stood up to meet Henrick's eyes. She spoke with a cold tone, "If you think I have traveled all this way, at your *side* no less, to be stopped by this notion, then you are sorely mistaken, Henrick. The shade are going to invade Claymore. They will kill everyone. Everything. Do you think morals will weigh heavy on their minds?"

Henrick and Yobo remained silent.

"Tonight. I am letting those pirates loose on this town. If you want to find the Esfera, make sure you are on their ship when it's ready to leave. It's the only one anchored out."

The two men did not have a rebuttal at that moment, but Henrick then turned to Yobo.

"Come on, lad," Henrick said, knowing that her mind was set in stone. "Let's leave her be."

Sometime later, Henrick and Yobo found themselves walking the docks of Aero. They followed the main avenue to the north at a slow pace.

"Has your friend ever been irrational before?" Yobo asked Henrick.

"Not that I recall, but we've not come to a squabble like this before," Henrick explained. "But she is a woman. She'll act on her emotions."

"So, you believe her to go through with this plan?" the monk asked.

"Aye," Henrick replied. "And she has a point, I suppose. We do risk it all by not doin' anythin'."

Yobo did find sound reasoning in Henrick's words as they continued their walk.

Henrick had noticed something about Yobo that he hadn't brought up before, but after having a life in Claymore, he had to ask.

"I noticed you don't carry any weapons?" the warrior asked.

"I had a staff before, but an orc broke it," Yobo explained.

"An orc?" Henrick asked, trying to get more details.

"Yes," Yobo simply answered.

A silence fell over Yobo at that moment. The memory of the recent encounter with the killer of his parents distracted his mind from the conversation, and it made him pause, but just for a second. Henrick caught the shift in the air around the monk, but the moment was fleeting, and Yobo returned the initial question.

"Yesterday, when we shared our stories, I had mentioned that I was taught martial arts by the dryads," the monk explained. "The Uireb Nen is what it's called, and through it, my hands are my weapons. I have a few other tricks, but I'd rather not display them in public."

"Interestin'," Henrick said. "In Claymore, House Odoko teaches their warriors martial arts, but it's more wrestlin' than punchin'."

Yobo had no idea about this House Okoko, but he could not help feeling a tug of interest inside his mind. Perhaps that could be an opportunity to expand his knowledge in the future.

About halfway up the street, they turned their route onto one of the piers, and they continued along the wooden planks until they reached the end. They had passed a couple of ships during their walk, but now they looked out across the ocean. Sure enough, there was a ship anchored. Yobo had seen that ship when he arrived in town.

"What should we do in the meantime?" Yobo asked.

"We should walk around some more," Henrick said looking at the ship that was anchored out. "We can try to locate a small boat so we can get to the ship when the time comes."

"Take someone else's boat?" Yobo questioned the idea. "Would that not make *us* pirates?"

Henrick scoffed at the notion. He could only offer a confirmation, "Aye."

Eventually, night had fallen over the coastal town of Aero. Neither of the moons had yet to rise to take their place among the sky. Without the soft glow of moonlight, the night seemed especially darker, and even the docks seemed more quiet than normal. Of course, that could be because all the sailors were partying at the Siren.

Once more, Serena found herself emerging from the shadows in the dungeon that held the pirate prisoners. All the salty dogs became aware of her presence, even though she silently walked by as she headed for the stairs to go retrieve the keys.

"I knew ye would come, lass," Fenri said as she walked by.

"Be ready," she said back to him.

She climbed the stairs at the other end of the hall, and eventually came to the door that she knew was locked. She knew that she needed the keys off the jail-guard that was on the other side, and that she needed them to come to her.

She decided to simply knock on the door.

Knock. Knock. Knock.

"What the?" came the shallow voice of the guard.

The jingle of keys, the scrapping of chair legs on the floor, and heavy footfalls soon followed a short pause. The sounds got louder as the guard approached the door. The tumbler of the lock turned.

At that precise moment, Serena grabbed the door handle, and yanked the door open. The jail-guard was still holding the key while it was inserted into the door, and the sudden momentum startled him and pulled him in like a vacuum. The unusual clatter alerted the other guards standing outside the building, and Serena's adrenaline kicked in as she realized she had to act fast.

She grabbed the key out of the door, slammed the door shut, and locked it from the inside. She turned to find the jail-guard standing on the tips of his toes as they tried not to fall down the stairs.

Serena would not let the guard succeed, and so she delivered a swift kick to his backside. The guard was sent rolling down the long flight of stairs, ultimately crashing at the bottom, and getting knocked out.

The cheering pirates echoed in the dungeon halls. Their freedom was on the brink of realization, and it was a short moment before Serena got to the bottom to retrieve the keys.

The metal instruments clanked against one another as Serena sprinted to the cell that Captain Fenri was in. She put the key in, and let the door fly open.

But the captain stood there and did not make a move. After a few long seconds, he then made a casual stroll from his cell completely. He made some chewing noises with his mouth as if tasting the sweet air of freedom on the other side of his black beard. He continued by nonchalantly rubbing his chin through the thick hair.

"Are you going?" Serena asked with a questioning tone.

"Bahahaha," Captain Fenri scoffed at her. "Ye got no style, lass."

The captain then took his steps to stand in the middle of the dungeon so that as many of his crew could see him. The excitement in his men was about to burst with glee.

With an upraised fist, the captain yelled, "To the Wolf!"

"To the Wolf!" his crew repeated.

CHAPTER SEVENTEEN
THE WOLF AND THE LION PART TWO

Side by side, Captain Samuel Fenri, and First Mate Constance, stood at the head of an army of pirates waiting to bust through the door that was just up the stairs. The echoing thuds upon the door suggested that the alerted guards were attempting to break the door open, but it wouldn't budge. From the sounds of the voiced commands on the other side, there had to be a handful of armed military personnel trying to get in. The key to the door rattled as it was left in the deadbolt.

In a brief moment between the thuds, Captain Fenri nonchalantly knocked on the door. There was no banging afterwards. The pirates could hear the command to "*draw swords*" coming from inside the jail office. Without a care for caution, Captain Fenri looked down at the key and unlocked the door, but he did not open it.

The pirates crew brimmed with excitement and anticipation for the door to come open, but nothing happened.

Captain Fenri furled his brows with disappointment, and knocked on the door again. This time his keen hearing picked up the muffled steps of a guard approaching the door. The captain coiled his body, ready to spring upon the unsuspecting person. The rest of the pirates read his body language as the signal, and they, too, readied themselves.

Fenri's nostrils flared in the moment, and without turning to his crew, or his First Mate, he whispered, "There be twelve men."

Fenri did not dare to take his eyes off the door, but the nearby pirates nodded in acknowledgement.

The door finally came open, and as soon as the crack revealed the light inside the office, Fenri grabbed the edge of the door, and used his unnatural strength to force it open. The captain charged the guard, and lifted him off his feet. He carried the man through the office, clearing a path through the other soldiers, and to the outside of the building where he tossed the man 10 feet away.

Half the guards followed the captain in pursuit, while the other half remained in the office. Unfortunately, the ones in the office were left to be victim to a dogpile of pirates that erupted from the dungeon. There was nothing they could do against the swarm of salty sea dogs. The Harmon guards were pummeled, forced to the ground, pummeled again, and disarmed as the pirates went.

Some of the pirates, under the direction of the First Mate, found the evidence chest tucked in a corner, and they immediately went to town, kicking and beating the chest, trying to get it to open, and when that wasn't working, they hoisted the chest up, and slammed it against the ground until it did. Boards and iron rivets gave way, and inside the chest was their captain's tricorne, and his coat. The First Mate gathered the items, and put them on before joining the rest of the crew in the fray.

Down by the docks, Henrick and Yobo could hear the ringing of a large bell in the distance. They saw every soldier on the docks at that moment sprinting towards the navy base with their cutlasses drawn. Earlier in the day, the two had spotted a small paddle boat, and with the threat of the pirates underway, it would seem that there would be no one to stop the two of them from taking it.

"I guess it is now or never," Yobo said.

"Aye, let's get to their ship," Henrick agreed.

Henrick and Yobo ran off in the direction of the small boat. It was on the beach at the far south end of the docks. The navy base was to the north. Both of the men each took a side of the boat and pushed it into the water before hopping in. They quickly put the oars in the water, and started to paddle their way out. After getting a short distance in the water, the monk took note of the exceptionally calm water, and the absence of any breeze.

"I wonder how the pirates plan to get away without the wind?" Yobo wondered aloud.

The statement allowed Henrick to notice what the monk was referring to.

"A good question," Henrick offered. "One I hope the pirates can answer."

Henrick's mind didn't pay much attention to the thoughts of wind like the monk, and instead he was focused on the moving lamps aboard the pirate's ship, but he did notice that whoever was holding the lamps was near the stern. No doubt they were looking towards the sound of the bell at the navy base.

"There're guards on the ship," Henrick said.

Yobo moved the thought of the guards to the front of his mind, and was already thinking on how to deal with them as best as possible. He said to Henrick, "I have an idea. Follow my lead when we get there."

As they got closer, they took note that the ship was nowhere close in size to that of the giant galleon that was in port, but it was similar in size to some of the other ships. Without knowing the secrets of the pirates, they did have to wonder how a shallow ship could stand against any others.

Once the splashing of the oars came within reach of the ears of the guards, one of them turned to notice the duo paddling a small boat. The guard then alerted the other three that were standing next to him.

"Ahoy!" Yobo shouted up to the guards. "The pirates have escaped prison!"

The guards looked at each other, and each of them had a look of grim confirmation upon their face.

"It can't be," one of the huntari guards said to the others.

"What are we going to do?" another huntari said.

"Aero needs you! Take this boat!" Yobo used his words to pull at the strings of duty in the hearts of the guards.

The guards then muttered amongst themselves. One by one they nodded with a notion of agreement. They came down from the quarterdeck in a hurried walk, and threw down a rope ladder.

"Come on," one of the human guards said. "Stay here until someone returns."

Henrick and Yobo climbed onto the main deck of the ship, and when they were aboard, the guards then climbed down, and they immediately began paddling away.

"Good idea," Henrick complimented. "Playin' with their sense of devotion like that."

Just as Henrick ended his words, he looked around at the deck of the ship. Crates, barrels, ropes, and other various equipment were completely strewn about. The visual chaos nearly overwhelmed Henrick. Claymore was a landlocked kingdom, and so it wasn't known for having ships, or any sort of nautical knowledge. Henrick had no idea where to even begin.

Yobo on the other hand, had learned much in his short time aboard the Bolt of Knowledge, but without the complement of a full crew they were limited on what they could accomplish. Still, there was one thing they could do by themselves.

"We have to get the anchor up," Yobo offered.

The Harmon Navy Base was in full alert. Every military sailor was on the base grounds, any of them that had been sleeping in the barracks were woken up, and the constant ringing of the bell attracted all of the guards that were out on patrol through town.

It was in no time at all that the base had exploded into a giant battleground. Swords, spears, maces, axes, and furniture legs were held by the pirates and sailors, alike. Clanging steel alongside the shouting of fervor. Smoke had begun to rise over the walls of the navy base as some of the buildings, to include the dungeon office, were set ablaze early in the riot. Bodies littered the street of the base, some dead and some still living, but not one of them was a pirate.

In the midst of the melee, Captain Fenri could see that his bloodthirsty crew was getting distracted by all the fighting. "*Connie!*" the captain shouted at the top of his lungs.

"Oi, Cap?" came the loud response from directly behind.

"Can we get a move on?" the captain asked as much as stated.

"To the Wolf!" Connie screamed.

"*To the Wolf!*" came the echoing and reinvigorating chant. The cheer was also a command, and it rechanneled the pirates to stay focused.

The east end of the navy base was where the entrance was that led to the rest of the town, and at the west end was a pier that was solely for Harmon ships to dock. The dock had more direct access to the water, but with two ships docked, and loaded with powder and cannons, the pirates chose to take their chances out in town.

The pirates continued their push through the navy base, but as the pirates closed the gap on the entrance, the gate to the base suddenly came closed, trapping the pirates inside the walls. Some of the pirates charged the gate in an attempt to force it open, but it had already been barred from the outside.

Captain Fenri and Constance turned to look to the west to see that some of the sailors were preparing ground cannons to fire upon the group of pirates. With the distance between the pirates and the cannons, Fenri knew they couldn't reach the cannons quick enough before they shot.

The captain was not about to let his men get slaughtered like trapped rodents. He focused on his inhuman abilities, and with his gritted teeth he ran at the cannons like a wild rabid animal. His speed was unlike anything the sailors, and some of the pirates, had seen before. It was a secret that the captain usually kept to himself, but the moment gave him no choice.

In the distance, he could see the spark of the fuse. It got shorter and shorter. He was closing in on the cannons, but even with his speed, the fuse was burning faster than his feet were moving.

"*No!*" Fenri muttered through his teeth as the fuse light sank into the barrel of the cannons.

Fenri then stopped in his tracks as he heard the echoing incantation of a spell.

"*Siorahd Delun.*"

The earth tore away beneath the feet of the sailors and their cannons like a tidal wave of dirt, washing the weapons off to the side.

BUM! BUM!

The cannons fired, but they were no longer aimed directly at the pirates, and instead, they fired into the burning structures of the navy base.

As Fenri came to his sliding stop, he looked ahead of himself, and he noticed Serena standing behind where the sailors were. He shot her a nod of acknowledgement before returning his gaze to his crew and the barred gate. Fenri moved to rejoin his men who were beginning to create human ladders in order to get over the wall.

Serena took her small bird form, and returned to the sky. She landed outside of the base, and next to the well where Sand was waiting for her. She retook her human form.

"Come on, buddy. Time to go show off," Serena said to the tiger.

Sand offered a roar of approval. The druid and her companion raced off towards the entrance of the navy base. When they got around the corner, she saw what she had seen from above, but the horde of sailors and city guards did not worry her.

"Now, Sand," she commanded.

The tiger growled angrily in concentration. The cat's skin and fur blistered and boiled, flickered and seethed until it was all burned away. All that was left was a giant tiger made completely of elemental fire. Like a wild animal frolicking in the wilderness, Sand charged out into the large gathering of soldiers, roaring and growling as he did. The first sightings of the firecat were so terrifying that the fear spread among all the others like a contagion.

"*Demon!*" some of the soldiers yelled.

Others would scream, "*Get it away!*" or "*Run!*"

The adrenaline of the hunt fueled the tiger's instincts, and Sand started to run after everyone that chose to turn their back to him. The intense heat from the cat started to ignite some of the residential buildings as Sand chased the soldiers through town.

The actions of Sand cleared the way for Serena, and it was in no time at all that she was able to slide the bar on the entrance gate to get one side open. With the door open, the pirates flooded into the streets of Aero.

"*To the Wolf!*" The cry echoed through town as the pirates stormed off for the docks.

Captain Fenri and Constance were side by side behind their men.

"Get them to the ship," Fenri demanded during the run.

"Aye, Cap," the First Mate acknowledged before seeing his captain break off from the main group.

Captain Fenri did not have all of his belongings, and Constance knew this. Fenri, by himself, sprinted down the pier in which the Sea's Lion was docked. Through all the fighting that had been going on, the captain refused to pick up a weapon that wasn't Betty. Fortunately, he had a sneaking suspicion that Betty was still in hiding onboard the Wailing Wolf.

To that end, Fenri was worried about the Wolf's most coveted secret, and if he knew the Admiral's level of self-comfort, then the thing he was looking for was onboard the galleon.

Half-way down the pier, the captain noticed that not all of the sailors were called to battle the prison riot, and he saw two of them moving to meet his charge. The sailor on the left started with an overhead swing with their cutlass.

The captain pivoted to let the obvious attack miss, the captain then grabbed the sailor by his white wool shirt and used the momentum of the attack to flip him over onto his back. The toss knocked the wind out of the sailor.

The captain twirled around, and bent over backwards to dodge the swinging of the second sailor's cutlass. In his own style and fashion, the pirate captain stepped into the sailor's space, and pushed him up and out. The sailor flew several feet away, rolling off the edge of the pier, and into the water below.

The captain was not in the mood to play around like he usually was. He was on a mission, and he was not going to let the galleon or any of its crew get in his way anymore. He had been dreaming about this day, and he knew that this was probably the only opportunity he was ever going to have to get rid of this damn ship.

He hopped up the wooden brow and the captain did not find any more resistance from Harmon sailors. He took a moment to let his surroundings sink into his mind. He was aboard his nemesis ship, and this time he wasn't in chains. The four masted ship was a beacon of power and security upon the seas and Fenri could feel it in that moment. It was because of this ship that the Wolf usually steered clear of Harmon waters when possible.

When the moment passed, Fenri sprinted for the double doors leading into the Admiral's quarters, located under the quarterdeck. Beyond the double doors, there was a short passageway with five doors: two on the left, two on the right, and one in the back.

The passageway was made with fine wood, stained and shined to a bright and reflective surface. The edges and corners of the doors and walls were trimmed with gold.

Fenri went to the door in the back, and opened it. It was then, that he realized that the Admiral had not come back from Lionsgate, and he remembered while in prison, the Admiral had stopped by to see Fenri, and told the captain that, he, the admiral, was going to meet with Harmon's government on how to best deal with the crew of the Wolf.

The Captain of the Wailing Wolf grew a smirk on his bearded face as he kept the memory on the side. Standing in the doorway, the captain could see what he was looking for on the admiral's desk. He walked in slowly, and reached for the golden chain that sat among map scrolls and other nautical navigation items. He pulled the chain up, and connected to the chain was a large, uncut yellow gemstone.

The captain put the necklace around his neck, and fidgeted with it each time it tried to get caught on his hair or beard. He turned a blind eye to the rest of the furnishings in the room, and exited. Going back through the short passageway, he moved to gather a lamp that was hanging on the wall.

Like a preacher walking down the aisle of a church, Captain Fenri walked across the main deck with the lamp held out in front of him, and a grim look upon his face. He found the ladder to the lower decks, and began his descent. One deck after another, he continued to find his way from one ladder to the next until he was near the bottom of this ship, and in the holds.

Down below, he found gunpowder barrels, but not just enough to outfit the galleon, he also found barrels of powder with his pirate's symbol on it. The same powder that was on *his* ship. The Harmon Navy confiscated every ounce of it. This was the long game that Fenri played, and the one he was patiently hoping to see come to fruition over the last month.

Without any profound words to say at the moment, Fenri took the lamp in his hand and tossed it as far as he could into the hold. The sound of shattering glass was music to his ears. When he saw the flames lick the wood of the barrels and start to catch, he immediately started to run up the ladders. He used his hands and feet in unison as he climbed up. The man was on the brink of giggling as the ecstasy of chaos filled his demeanor.

The pirate leader was under the moonless night once more, but as he climbed the ladder up to the quarterdeck, the first rumblings of explosion shook the ship so much that he tripped over his own feet.

"Shit," Fenri cursed after falling to his stomach.

Onboard the Wailing Wolf, Henrick and Yobo assisted the pirates getting on their ship as they all swam out to meet it. Even Serena and Sand, no longer a flaming cat, swam out to the ship, but some of the crew had to use rope ladders to pull the tiger up, and onto the deck.

BOOM!!!

A deafening cacophony roared across the night sky, and a fireball shot fifty feet into the air above the deck of the Sea's Lion. The blast completely engulfed the ship in flames, shredding it into flaming splinter shrapnel, and cracked it in half like an egg. The shockwave sent deep ripples across the surface of the otherwise calm ocean waters.

As soon as the roar of the explosion ended, the next sound the pirates heard filled their hearts with astonishment. Their visitors, however, had to wonder.

"*WOOAAHHOOO!!*" came the joyful screaming voice of a burning person flying over the ship, and barely missing between its two masts before crash landing into the water on the other side.

"What the hell was that?" Henrick said aloud.

Everyone on the ship had watched the flaming comet sail by, but the pirates already knew who it was.

"That was the Cap'n," a man standing nearby said through a smile. He offered his hand, "Name's Connie. Saw ye helpin' the blokes. Who are ye?"

"Henrick, and this is Yobo," Henrick introduced himself and the monk.

"Henrick?" Serena said as she came to greet him with a hug.

The sentiment to Henrick was almost surprising considering how he had spoken to her earlier, but he could not deny her embrace in the moment, and so he met her hug with his own.

"Oi, a friend o' the witch?" Constance asked as much as stated.

"I thought you might not come," Serena admitted while paying her attention only to Henrick.

Henrick then held her by her shoulders, and eased out of the hug so that they could look in each other's eyes.

"What can I say? I didn't want to do it like this, but you were right, this was the only way," Henrick admitted.

The moment that Henrick and Serena were sharing at this point caused an unusual thump in their hearts. They could both feel that there was something to explore, but they knew this was not the time or place for it.

Meanwhile, Connie turned his attention to the crew of the ship. He commanded, "Oi, avast ye maggots, get the ship ready."

The pirate crew scattered in all directions. Through the organized chaos, it became apparent that the pirates knew their positions well and they assumed them with haste. They were all excited to get out of that prison, and more than that, they wanted to get back out to sea where they belonged, and get back home to their families. The sails on the two-masted ships were dropped, and pirates climbed up to the crow's nests, and of all the things that needed to be ready, the infamous colors of the ship were flown: a white flag with a spread crow.

"Connie," Yobo began to get the First Mate's attention. "How will we leave without the winds?"

"Once the Cap'n's onboard, he will get us out of here," the man responded.

Just as the First Mate spoke of his devilish captain, Fenri came climbing over the starboard rails of the ship, crashing upon the wooden deck with body before rolling onto his back. His clothes were sopping wet, of course, but they were nearly burned away as well. The pirate leader took a quick moment to breathe and not move. His head was reeling and buzzing from adrenaline and his ears rang from deafness.

One of the crew came over to the captain, and handed him a bottle that was half-filled with rum. Fenri immediately lurched his head upward to take a big swig of the drink, and after a few seconds the captain sat up.

"Connie...man...the helm," Fenri ordered through deep panting.

Captain Fenri supported his sitting posture by holding himself up with an arm behind him. With the other arm, he closed his eyes, and he reached out into the air. He tried to concentrate in that moment, trying to push beyond the ringing sound, the aching body of getting blasted away, and now, with the rum in his system.

Henrick, Yobo, and Serena looked at the captain with speculation, but they also noticed that the rest of the pirates were going on as if everything was normal.

After about a minute of Fenri maintaining his position, the yellow gem upon his necklace began to glow, and it was a second later that a strong breeze revealed itself. With the sails catching the winds, the Wailing Wolf was soon on its way, and into the darkness of the open seas.

CHAPTER EIGHTEEN
THE BLACK WIND PIRATES

It was on the following day that the sails of the pirate ship found natural, favorable winds, and these winds brought the seas to life as the Wailing Wolf headed east. The wind brought on a cool breeze that blew over the deck of the ship, carrying the spray of moisture with it. The sudden chilly effect was a direct response to the heated rays of the summer sun.

The watery blue environment was dotted with patches of white foam. Five-foot swells rolled over the surface of the ocean, and they exploded into salt spray when the cutting wind would leave its wake across the crest. The ship listed mildly as it moved through the ocean. It slid down on the waters everytime it found a trough only to get pushed back up by the following wave.

The state of the sea was nothing that the pirates couldn't handle, though, and because of their experience, there was only a skeleton crew of about 15 or so pirates up on deck, to include the captain and the first mate. The bulk of the crew was somewhere below deck resting in their hammocks, and due to the excitement of the previous night, the captain demanded a holiday at sea. Those that remained up top were merely there to hoist or set the sails, but they were also there to keep watch on the horizon.

Even with their mindful attention on the west, they knew there would be no sign of any other ships in the bay for the next couple of days. The pirates had dealt the Harmon Navy a serious blow with the complete destruction of the Sea's Lion, and once the story had spread of what the pirates had done to the large naval vessel, the pirates' reputation would now make them the most feared company on the open seas.

For the time being, though, the pirates' cove was something that was on everyone's mind. The crew wanted to get back to their families, and the guests aboard the Wolf wanted to get there as well, even if they didn't realize it yet, but in truth, Captain Fenri thought about the cove more than anyone else at this time.

As he stood there with a relaxed hold on the helm, he remembered why he and his crew went to get captured in the first place. It was only a few months ago when he had been instructed by their *boss* to steal the Esfera de Luz from the lighthouse. But the events that took place afterwards: his capture, the strangers showing up to look for the artifact, and then those same strangers fought to free the pirates. Everything happened exactly how it was explained to him. Of course, Fenri smirked and laughed to himself as his train of thought skipped to the part where he took it upon himself to ignite all that gunpowder.

First Mate Constance noticed his captain's shoulders vibrating from the withheld laughter. Even though his captain wasn't looking, nor did he say anything, he knew his captain was still feeling giddy after last night's events.

Fenri's laughter soon ended as his thoughts returned to the cove, and his boss. The foretelling of the future didn't really bother him all that much. It was more that he and his *royal* bloodline of pirate captains held the secret of his master's existence. No one in all of Golterran is supposed to know the existence of his boss. Fenri, and his father, were the only two living people in all of Terra that knew the secret truth behind the pirates.

With all that in mind, Fenri knew the Esfera de Luz would be right at his master's side, and he had to wonder if his boss was intending on revealing himself to their guests. As his thoughts dwelled on the visitors on his ship, Fenri figured it was probably time to get to know who these people were. He could see the tall green-robed man standing at the bow of the ship while the other two leaned over the rail on the starboard side.

"Wha'd'ye make of them?" Fenri asked Constance, but without looking at the man.

"I don' be thinkin' them enemies," Constance said. "O' course, they helped us out've that shite dungeon. That's enough for me."

The first mate's words held some simple reasoning, Fenri thought. He rubbed his chin through his thick, black beard as began to agree with his friend.

"Aye," he said before he paused. "But I don't like havin' that cat on board."

The eyes from both pirates lingered off to stare at the large tiger who was sitting at the side of his druid companion. They both remembered, vividly, of that flaming cat running amok in town. The whole damn crew on the ship probably has the same feeling.

Fenri looked to the stern of the quarterdeck where another pirate of his crew stood. The man's gaze was upon the horizon aft of the ship.

"Eddie," Fenri called to the skinny, bald, aerin pirate.

The pirate came to stand next to the captain and first mate. He asked in a deep, salty voice, "Aye, Cap'n?"

"Tell our freeloaders that I wish to speak with them," Fenri ordered.

"Aye," the pirate turned after his response and made his way across the main deck.

Eddie, as was his name, went to Henrick and Serena first, gave them the captain's request, and then proceeded to the ship's bow to do the same thing with Yobo. Eddie then took the port side of the ship to return to his post on the quarterdeck once again.

Henrick and Serena were the first ones to step up on to the quarterdeck. Yobo was not too far behind.

Once there, everyone waited for the captain to start his dialogue.

"Since we be havin' a holiday on board, I thought it would be fittin' if I could...get to know what kinda cargo I'm carryin'. Who are ye people?" the captain asked before looking at Henrick. "You first."

"Oh, well," Henrick replied in short, lowering his eyes a bit as if searching for the right starting place. "The name's Henrick. I'm from Claymore.

"Serena, also from Claymore, and I'm a druid, not a witch," she answered as Fenri's questioning eyes fell on her next. Serena's eye held a glint of angst at the notion of being called a *seawitch* by the pirates.

Fenri then turned his head to the opposite side to look at the large man in the green robes.

"My name is Yobo. I am from the Skyreach near Telosa," the monk introduced himself.

"Very well. Me name's Fenri. Samuel Fenri, and this is me First Mate Connie," Fenri returned the sentiment and followed it with a pointing wave of a hand to Constance. "This ship is the Wailing Wolf, and the band of misfits, criminals, gamblers, and degenerates onboard are known as the Black Wind Pirates." After a moment's pause to let the profoundness of the names sink in, Fenri continued, "To break the saltiest of dogs out of prison shows ye want that damn orb pretty bad, but why, I wonder?"

Yobo spoke first. "Of all the mountains in the Sword Kingdoms, I lived on top of the tallest one. Up there on the mountain, I lived in isolation with the dryads for a decade, and during that time, they taught me martial arts. But one night, these creatures called the shade, attacked our home and slaughtered everyone. I survived, and later I learned of the shade, and of an artifact that would destroy them."

The Yobo could sense his emotions swelling up inside of him like it always did. His mind took him away, and in the matter of a second, he could see the carnage on the Skyreach all over again. The flash showed amber blood everywhere, but when he looked again the flash was already over, and he was back aboard the pirate ship.

Henrick felt the heat from Yobo in that flash of a memory. He wasn't sure if it was his divine sense kicking in or not, but his warrior senses made the hair on the back of his neck stand up. The feeling was only there for a brief amount of time, perhaps not even a second before it was gone. In a small way, Henrick was astonished by the experience while noticing the others felt absolutely nothing.

"Revenge, eh? Not what I was expectin' from you lot, but I like it," Fenri said. He glanced over in Serena's direction. "Ye got a story, *seawitch*?"

Serena noted the mockery but she spoke anyway, "I've lived in Claymore for most of my life. As I came of age, my mentor taught me the ways of druidic magic. I'm charged with protecting the wild lands of Claymore. On the far eastern side of the Sword Kingdoms is the Kadavar Wastes, and from there, I have witnessed the shade encroach beyond their desert. I don't know what their *ultimate* goal is, but I managed to follow one of their trails. That's where I found this one...." She brought her eyes upon Henrick to finish her meaning.

Henrick continued from that point, "The shade're plannin' to invade Claymore. After that, who knows where else they'll turn their white-eyes. After meetin' Yobo in Aero, it would seem that the shade're interested in more than just gettin' Claymore back. As he stated, the artifact is gonna be how we fight back."

Captain Fenri wrestled a hand on his chin through his beard after hearing all the tales. "Hmm. Dire straits indeed." He spoke with a half-interested tone, but then he began to fancy a silent guess about his boss's intentions.

"What about you?" Henrick asked the captain. "What's yer story? How did a bunch of pirates manage to leave that town without losin' a single man?"

It was an extremely valid question, Fenri thought, considering that the pirates started with no weapons, they took the town by storm, they fought hard with what they had, they destroyed the Harmon flagship, and at the end of it all, every single person *was* accounted for. In fact, none of them had any serious injury. Cuts and bruises for sure, but Henrick, Serena, and Yobo had to wonder.

"Bahahaha!" Fenri unleashed a hearty laughter soiled by chaos that floated in his brain. He laughed so hard that it forced him to bend over, holding himself up upon his knees, and letting go of the helm.

The visitors flinched as if to grab the helm themselves, but they didn't move, nor did the first mate, who showed a proud and confident smirk. Fenri stood back up, and composed himself to man the helm again, and prepare for the answer.

"How best to explain?" He returned his focus to steering the ship as he spoke through a devilish grin. "The sandari live on the south side of the bay, but their capital city lies deep in the desert. They have a sacred form of lifestyle called bushido. But only the sultan's royal guards are taught how to apply their virtues to combat, and no one outside the sultan's palace, or anywhere else on the face of Terra, is permitted to know the forms, or how it is taught."

"You're saying your crew knows this fighting style?" Yobo asked.

"Aye." The short answer came.

At the mention of the sandari, and their unique form of fighting style, Henrick pulled the sandari water blade from the sheathe on his back. Fenri, out of the corner of his eye, caught the shimmer of the blade that was revealed, but the captain did not look at it, for he already identified the weapon being carried around early on. Henrick looked at the blade resting in his hand as held it up.

"That is one of their blades ye hold in yer hand," Fenri added.

"How did ye manage to learn this *bushido*?" Henrick asked as he imagined learning the secrets himself.

"Sorry, lads, but that be one thing we be takin' to our graves," Samuel said. "Now about your first question, Henrick. The ship be somethin' of a family heirloom. Passed through the generations of my family, and each Fenri that is born is destined to be the captain. The rest of the crew, you'll find that most of 'em do this business, because it is the family business.

"We live free to do what we want, when we want, to steal whatever we want, and from whoever we want. That is how Aerith would have wanted us to live. Without borders or chains. Without anyone trying to tell us how to live a *good* life."

The sentiment of unbridled freedom in the words of Fenri struck a wholesome string in the heart of Serena, however, Henrick could only feel the sentiment of chaos from the pirate leader. Yobo, though, found the pirate leader to be intriguing, because the man claimed to be an agent of freedom, who was free of borders, but he could tell how trained, and more so, how disciplined his crew really was.

"And speakin' of good life. Ye should enjoy the rest of the trip. We'll be home soo enough," Fenri led on.

"Where's home?" Serena asked.

Fenri felt that since they were going to be there, there was no harm in just telling them one secret. "Lost Flame."

Later that day as the onset of the afternoon came, the sunlight from the west highlighted the sharp points that crested over the horizon, and the place known as Lost Flame came into view. The jagged and rocky landscape that surrounded the inert volcano made it impossible for any water-bound craft to get near it.

Henrick, Yobo, and Serena watched the towering earth rise up into the sky as the ship sailed closer. Each of them darted their eyes to the lonely peak and everywhere along its base. None of the pirates' guests could see or point out anything that might have looked like a pier or a hidden cove.

From the port railing of the pirate ship, the three of them, along with most of the crew, watched to the north. The violence of the ocean crashed hard against the volcanic rock reefs that rose out of the water like shark teeth. The entirety of the landscape above the water was a scorched-rock scenery of stone and obsidian. The orange and red light from the sun did nothing to make the place less ominous. To everyone on board, with their imaginations, it almost seemed like the place was on fire, burning, or red hot.

Dark storm clouds loomed over the volcano and even those inexperienced in the ways of sailing could tell the storm was heading their way. To Captain Fenri, though, this was the sign that the Wolf was ready to get lined up, and the helm passed on to the First Mate.

"Connie, take the wheel," Fenri said as they made the exchange.

The call to Constance drew the attention of Henrick, Yobo, and Serena. They looked back to see the captain stepping down from the quarterdeck, and as this was going on, Connie spun the helm to point the ship north, and directly at the jagged landscape.

The storm was then upon them, and it moved quicker than any storm could have possibly moved, or so the visitors thought. To the rest of the crew, however, this was the price of coming home. As the first drops of water fell upon the decks, Sand went into hiding below.

"Ye better be holdin' on," Fenri warned his guests as he walked by.

The ship creaked as it angrily listed against the choppy waters. 10-foot swells jumped up to burst into clouds of salt spray, and they slammed into the side attempting to capsize the Wolf. The battering ocean was deflected against the hull, shooting water 20-feet in the air, and drenching the decks when it came back down.

Henrick, Yobo, and Serena held on to ropes and the railing to keep themselves from going overboard, but as they struggled, they watched Captain Fenri and his superb sea legs traverse the deck until he stood on the bow of the ship. That's when they looked beyond the ship, and into the distance, there was "V" shape in the crags in which the ship was aimed for.

Captain Samuel Fenri began to concentrate on the power inside the yellow gem around his neck. Just as he did in their escape from Aero. The sails tightened and buckled against the magical source of wind. The speed of the Wailing Wolf picked up without regard to the winds of the storm. The ship, still contending with the force of the oceans, was off in a desperate race to return home.

With the onslaught of the storm, the afternoon sunlight was all but gone by this point. Cracks of lightning introduced themselves, thunder shuttered through the air with deafening roars, and bolts of electricity struck near the top of Lost Flame.

The moment was close at hand. The brigantine crashed against the rebelling waves, and the heaving of the ship was nearly bringing the entire bow into the shallows. Still, Captain Fenri stood his ground, embracing the storm as the focal point of his concentration. Brighter and brighter, the gem's glow grew with intensity, and it got so bright that even with his back turned, everyone else could see it.

Constance watched ahead, using the light of the yellow gem to aim the ship. The first mate could see the imminent collision with the crags ahead, but he had full faith in the captain's abilities, and based on what he heard next, he knew the captain was making progress.

"*Oohahaha!*" the pirate captain screamed his laughter into the face of the storm.

No one else could see, but Fenri's eyes had turned to solid orbs of glowing lavender magic. A power that was deep inside his body, but a necessary power required to push the abilities of the yellow gem to its heights. He raised his arms off to his side, and his hands and fingers were taut with blissful rage.

"*Raawwwhhhh!*" the captain let out a primal yell as he conjured the ancient magic.

"Batten down, ye blokes!" The first mate yelled across the deck to the crew and the visitors.

The wild spectacle made the visitors wonder about the beast-of-a-man they were on board with. The captain seemed like he was nothing but fearless and feral.

Next, giant blasts of wind barraged the sides of the ship. The visitors looked over the railing to see the primal winds pushing the water down, and away from the ship. However, the visitors did not realize how wrong they were in their observation.

Instead, the winds were in fact picking the ship up and out of the water completely. The listing and creaking of the ship came to a halt. The storm and the rain remained a rebellious force, but now there was no stopping the Wailing Wolf from sailing smoothly through the air.

"This is unbelievable," Henrick remarked with wide eyes.

The three visitors looked over the railing as the ship floated through the air and over the jagged rocks and spikes that were directly below them. Each of them was equally astonished.

"We're flying." Yobo added to the previous statement.

"We're not done, ye fools," Constance yelled at the visitors in warning. "Hold on."

At the behest of the first mate, the visitors returned to their positions that they had before. They held their ropes in preparation for the next part, to which they returned their gaze forward.

There was a pirate at the bow, who was watching the underside of the ship, and once the ship was clear of the jagged rocks, he yelled, "Clear!"

And after a short moment, a pirate near the stern of the ship, gave the same call, "Clear!"

Not a moment later, Fenri relinquished himself from the concentration of the wind spell. The momentum continued to carry the ship forward, but now a majority of that momentum was forced to go another direction.

Down.

The ship fell from its hovering state and crashed into the channel of water below. Walls of salt water splashed in all directions, covering the obsidian beaches in fizzing foam. The ship's bow dove into the waters, but the buoyancy of the ship was insistent on keeping it on the surface. More ocean water poured over the decks and down the ladder wells.

By the time everyone realized they could stand comfortably aboard the ship, they noticed that the storm had completely dissipated. It almost felt like the storm was there just for them, and they probably weren't wrong. The sky became clear and the afternoon sunlight had returned, but the walls of the channel blocked it from touching the ship directly.

When it was all said and done, Fenri turned to make his way back to the quarterdeck. The crew worked hastily to hoist up the sails to prevent any wind, or breeze, from moving the ship. For now, it would be accuracy, and not speed, that would get them home.

"Don't tell me ye do that *every* time?" Henrick asked as the pirate passed by.

"Aye. Every time, and every time there be a storm to challenge us. The Flame likes to be makin' sure we are practiced," Fenri answered.

Henrick, Yobo, and Serena followed Fenri up to the quarterdeck, and during this time, the whole of the pirate crew was up on the main deck, anxiously awaiting their return to home port.

"That gem has incredible power, doesn't it?" Serena asked as much as stated.

"The Wind Stone of Anaroc. That be its name," Fenri explained. "As the legend goes, each of the ancient titans placed an ounce of their god-like powers into artifacts such as this one. So far, this is the only one that has ever been found, but it serves to prove that they do exist."

The three visitors found themselves looking at the set piece of the golden necklace at that moment. They silently accepted the presence of such an item, and they all had to wonder if the *Esfera de Luz* contained similar powers.

Of course, Henrick and Serena had a small idea of its power after meeting Simon in Lumen's library, but to see such power first hand made them feel a bit unnerved at what they could possibly be attempting to unfold in the world.

"We should be reachin' the cove in due time," Fenri said. "I suggest takin' this moment to relax, and let the breeze dry you off."

They all looked ahead as Constance smoothly and slowly guided the ship through the narrow channel that slithered through the crags. By this time, Sand made his return to the main deck.

"Does this place always feel like..." Yobo spoke, but then paused to try and find the right words.

Instead, Fenri finished the sentiment, "Like the mountain is watchin' us? It certainly does."

Going through the channel, the three visitors nearly looked straight up at the towering peak of Lost Flame. The presence of slumbering, fiery devastation kept their silent minds humbled. They felt as though they were in the presence of an ominous, deific force. They each had to wonder what trials and tribulations might await them at this pirate cove.

He couldn't explain it, but unseen eyes upon them and the ship only made Henrick feel confident that this was it. He was going to bring an end to his quest for the artifact in which they were all looking for. The Esfera de Luz.

The Wailing Wolf departed the narrow channel sometime later, and entered into a lagoon that was hidden away from the rest of the world. The crystal-clear body of water was large enough for the ship to do circles in. Tall cliffs outlined the edges of the lagoon, and on the north end, there was a large waterfall. To the right of the waterfall was a large ship-sized cave, and the twinkle of hanging lamps sparkled from inside the sheltering earth. To the left of the waterfall, there was another narrow channel.

Every pirate on board the crusty ship was up on the main deck to take in the sight of their home, and it was a sight that Henrick, Serena, and Yobo took in as well.

"Sound the horn!" Constance called out.

A pirate on the bow, held up a signaling horn, and blew once, twice, and thrice. After a brief pause, another horn blow came, mimicking the series from before, but this time it was from inside the cave. The pirates onboard dispersed. Some went below deck to man the oars. Some pirates jumped off the side of the ship with mooring lines around their bodies before they began swimming to the cave. It was all a part of their mooring routine.

As the ship got into position to be moored, the descending sunlight pierced straight through the narrow channel at the other end. The pirates' guests took note of the channel, and the otherwise straight line that led out to the open sea.

"How come we didn't come that way?" Henrick asked Fenri with a pointed finger.

"Ha. Now where's the fun in that," Fenri scoffed, but after a short pause, he elaborated. "But since ye be wantin' to know. There be a giant tunnel at the bottom of the lagoon here. It carries a very strong current that shoots out that way. We can leave through there, but we can't come in."

The rear of the ship was then lined up with the cave, the oars came in, and the pirates from below came up to assist with the heaving of the lines. There were four lines in total, and each line had a gang of pirates ready to pull on command.

First Mate Constance stood at the stern of the ship, and once the signal came from the pier inside the cave, he gave the first of many, "*Heave!*"

In unison, the pirates repeated the command, "*Heave!*"

Sometimes Constance would call out, "Avast port," or, "Avast starboard," depending on how he needed the ship to move into the cove. The crew would repeat every command as it was called. The process was slow and steady, but it was necessary to keep the ship from bumping into the pier.

As soon as the ship was where it needed to be inside the cove and the U-shape dock, another horn blow was made on the pier, only to be answered by the horn on the ship. This signaled the pirates on the ship to tie off the mooring lines to the stanchions, setting the ship in place.

During the ship's berth, Henrick, Yobo, and Serena took in the sight of the pirates' cove. Beyond the dock at the stern, families and children were lined up, and awaited the return of their loved ones. Behind them, was a giant slope of stone and lava rock that had a long and winding wooden ramp that nearly reached the ceiling of the cove as it traveled to the peak. Upon this peak at the very back of the cove, was some sort of stone structure wedged between the natural earth.

On the sides of the cave, were the homes of the pirates and their families. The homes were dug into the cavernous walls. Each of the homes had a wooden balcony that acted as an entryway before going in the door. From each balcony, the homes were connected by wooden gangways that traveled all the way to the ramp at the back of the cove. There were five levels of these homes on each side.

The visitors then brought their attention back to the pirates as a heavy thud resounded when the brow came down upon the wooden planks of the pier.

"Take yer leave, gents!" the captain called out.

On command, the pirate crew disembarked the Wailing Wolf to reunite with their families, and those without families went to reunite with their own private stash of booze. Henrick, Yobo, and Serena, with Sand in tow, waited for the crew to all leave, but as they watched the crew go ashore, they spotted an older man standing on the pier. The man had an unmistakable resemblance to Fenri, save for about a 20- or 30-year difference. When the crew was all gone, they stepped off the ship and Fenri was right behind them.

"How'd it go, son?" the older pirate said just before the two embraced each other in a short and hearty hug. His voice was deep, and raspy.

"Ha," the pirate captain scoffed. "We won't be seein' the Lion for a long time."

"What did you *do*?" Fenri's father asked through his equally thick black beard.

"I *blew it up*," was his response.

A nonchalant stare suddenly locked on to Fenri from his father. The stare made Fenri freeze up with concern as he returned the glare. Then the two pirates could not hold it in any longer. "Bahahaha!" the two pirates burst out laughing. After a short bit, they both ended their fit of laughter with a heavy sigh.

Fenri's father then turned his eyes over to their guests. He walked over, and offered a hand to each of them, "The name's Jack Fenri."

The visitors each introduced themselves.

"Henrick."

"Serena."

"Yobo."

"These're the ones-," Captain Fenri began, but his father cut him off.

"I know, son," Jack said as he looked at his son. "*He* summoned me while you were gone. Said he wanted to speak to this one, specifically."

"*Me?*" Henrick questioned while standing at the end of a pointed finger. He placed his own hand on his chest as he said it.

"Aye," Jack confirmed.

Samuel Fenri rubbed his chin through his black beard. "So, he's intendin' on revealin' himself to these strangers?"

"Aye, son," Jack answered. "We'd be wise not to deny him."

Henrick looked at Serena and Yobo with puzzled looks, and with no explanation as to what was going on, and so they remained silent.

"But. That'll be tomorrow. Tonight, you shall rest. You'll have your prize soon enough," Jack said with cryptic tones. He pointed with a finger to a large wooden structure at the end of the dock and before the ramp. "Ye'll find bunks at our tavern *there*. It ain't much as we don't get many visitors."

The pirates that did not have families to entertain were already hanging outside the tavern at the moment. The crew had pints of beer in hand, many of them either sat or stood on the tables, both inside and outside. Cheering and slobbering singing filled the air. The scene was truly incredible considering the pirates had only been off the ship for no more than five minutes or so.

"Now, if ye'll excuse us, me and the boy have some catchin' up to do," Jack said before him and Samuel walked away.

Samuel, and his father, found themselves at their home on the fourth tier of the cove on the north side. The two pirates sat in chairs on their balcony overlooking the cove, and the ship below. Between the chairs was a small stool with a bottle of rum and two small brown glasses on top. Samuel grasped the bottle, and pulled the cork out with his teeth. After spitting the cork off the side of the balcony, he poured some of the strong beverage in each glass. The two began to drink, and swig the alcohol down.

"Glad to have ye back, son," Jack said.

It was then that they tapped their glasses together in a quiet toast. Both of them never made eye contact, and instead they kept their gaze downward upon the Wailing Wolf as she sat silent in the hidden port. The cove and all of its lamp light gave a cozy feeling against the nightly atmosphere just outside.

As the hours grew long, the crew and their families had all retired to their homes. The cove was relatively quiet, save for the sound of vague salt water washing on the cavernous walls below.

Samuel and Jack continued to drink in the silence of the night as they filled their glasses, repeatedly. Drink after drink, they remained silent in each other's company. Eventually the bottle ran dry, and Samuel's mind fell on the recent events.

"To be honest, pop, I wasn't expectin' them to show up, and bust the crew out," Samuel admitted.

"Aye, son. It's unnervin' how much the beast knows. Especially, when it hasn't happened yet," Jack

371

added to the sentiment. "But don't ye be forgettin' why *He* smothered the flames of the mountain last year."

"I haven't," Samuel said.

Samuel and Jack, both, sat in silence with the weight of the words from their boss. On numerous occasions, from before the collapse of Mount Magnus, and leading up to this night, their boss had given them insight on the suffering in which the planet was enduring. *He* had told them that Nielda had set things in motion, but their boss would not reveal any details. Instead, he gave the pirates a quest, here and there, to guide events in the right direction.

Samuel and Jack never really were ones to dwell on a thought for long, even if the thoughts had profound notions.

"Another bottle?" Jack asked his son to break up the silence.

"Aye, pop," Samuel answered.

As the night grew longer, the father and son pirates continued to sit there and finished off the second bottle of rum. It was at that time both of them managed to fall asleep in their chairs.

The next morning, a dwarf man by the name of Belgarun, returned to his tavern after getting some sleep. Upon his return, he found the tavern grounds, both inside and outside, littered with empty tankards, trash, and unconscious pirates.

The dwarven barkeep was not upset by any means, though. In fact, this was his favorite part of the day.

"Ohohoho!" Belgarun fiendishly laughed through a whisper as he weaved his way across the maze of bodies. Eventually, he made it through the tavern and to the back room.

The inside of the tavern was one big room, save for the small cleaning closet in the back where the bar was. There was also a nook on the left side that had bunks that were three beds high, six in total.

From inside the cleaning closet, Belgarun pulled out a wooden pole with a hook on the end and a bucket. With the items in hand, he snuck his way back out of the tavern, and used the items to pull a bucket of water out from underneath the pier.

Belgarun rolled up his sleeves before unhooking the bucket from the pole. His demeanor became overjoyed with adrenaline that was complemented by the devious smirk hiding under his blonde beard. He hoisted the bucket up into his hands and with a honed toss of water that had been refined over the years of cleaning pirates up off the floor, he managed to splash every salty dog sleeping outside.

Every single one of those pirates got an icy dash of salt wash that instantaneously brought them back from the dead. Satisfied with his work, the dwarf repeated the process, and tossed a second bucket on the pirates who were sleeping inside. A symphony of groans and moans roared to life from the hungover pirates which assured Belgarun that his life had meaning.

Off to the side and in their bunks, Yobo and Serena watched the debacle take place, and they couldn't help but join Belgarun in laughing. The two of them looked around and noticed that Henrick was not among the waking pirates, nor was he in one of the bunks.

"Where's Henrick?" Serena whispered aloud.

Henrick had already been woken up by Samuel and Jack, and he was now following the two pirates to the stone structure at the back of the cove. Upon reaching the top, they stopped before an ornate frame that was centered on the wall of burnt stone masonry. This frame looked like it could have been the right size for a door, but there was no door.

The frame was intricately chiseled, top to bottom, to have the shape and design of flames, the top corners were curved inward, and centered at the top where the flames met, was a circle. Inside the circle was the impression of an eight-toothed gear.

Henrick didn't know what to make of the strange construction, but he had to count on the pirates that they knew what they were doing. Just as the thoughts had crossed Henrick's mind, Samuel leaned up against the wall inside of the frame. The pirate squared his shoulder and braced himself. With one good push, using his supernatural strength, Samuel caused the wall inside the frame to make a clicking noise. A second later, the stone wall revealed a secret door as it slid inward along a track.

"Come on," Jack said plainly to Henrick.

The three of them walked into the hidden chamber. Samuel used a lever on the wall to get the secret door to close once again, but after it was closed, he hoisted two iron bars and placed them on the back of the secret door.

"Ha. Barrin' a secret door? Is that necessary?" Henrick scoffed.

"It's to keep the crew out while the other door is open," Samuel replied. "The boss ate the last one that got curious."

"*Ate?*" came the concerning retort from Henrick.

From where they had entered the secret chamber, there was another chamber to the left through a doorless opening. They entered the other chamber, and on the far wall was another chiseled frame much like the one from before, and just like before, this frame had no visible door. The three of them stood there in silence, and Henrick looked between Samuel and his father, but they were both looking at the doorway.

"What, now?" Henrick asked.

Enter, came the dark voice from inside his head.

Henrick immediately returned his eyes to the frame ahead of him, and to his surprise, the frame was now open, and the wall that was once there was completely gone. Through it, he could see a glimpse of a dark cave. The smell of sulfur and burning metal filled the chamber, and it complimented the intense heat that followed it.

"The boss calls," Samuel answered the question grimly.

Henrick had to wonder what exactly he was getting himself into at this point. *The last curious pirate was eaten?* The thought echoed in his brain. What did that mean? He grew a concerned look as he prepared his mind to go forward. He thought that maybe his adrenaline would kick in, or his heart would beat out of his chest. Instead, he was strangely calm, and he was aware of it. He had come this far, and whatever was waiting for him on the other side, he would handle it as best he could. The thought of his home being ruined by the shade and a false king got his legs moving until he stepped through.

The cool, stale air from the stone room evaporated instantly, and the heat that flowed through the air completely surrounded him as his form was unknowingly transported through nearly a thousand feet of solid rock. When he stepped into the dark cave, Henrick turned to look at Samuel and Jack one last time, but they were there. There was only a matching frame of flames with a gear on top, and there was no way back.

Henrick's eyes returned to the only direction he had: forward. He was in a narrow cavern that was dimly lit by an unknown light source, but several yards in front of him the cavern made a turn to the right. Orangish-red light peaked its way from around the bend.

When he turned the corner, the narrow cavern immediately expanded into an enormous chamber that was directly connected to the main vent of the dormant volcano. The light of bubbling hot magma allowed Henrick to see everything in the vent chamber. The most astounding feature was the giant piles of treasure that lined the cavernous walls on his left and right.

Gold coins, gemstones, trinkets. The piles stood twice Henrick's height. However, in between the two piles of treasure, near the standing pool of lava on the other side of the chamber, was a stone pedestal with a dimly glowing, golden orb sitting atop its surface. He had never seen the object before, but he knew it was what he had been looking for this whole time.

It was the Esfera de Luz.

He almost thought to rush over and remove the object from the pedestal, but he knew the intense heat from the lava would cook him alive. Something other than the heat, however, made him pause at that moment.

Henrick could sense it, whatever it was, and it was perhaps the most malevolent aura he had experienced since gaining his new abilities. The darkness he felt radiated outward from the pool of molten metal ahead. To his disbelief, though, it also felt like the darkness could sense him as well, and with that connection in his heart, Henrick drew out his sword.

"*HAHAHAHA!*" came the thunderous laughter that reverberated off the cavern walls.

The source of the darkness then emerged. First, its giant, multi-horned, multi-spiked head rose up from the lava with a long serpentine neck. Molten metal dripped from its scales as it climbed out. The first leg met the stone floor with a tremor that Henrick could feel in his feet, and when the second leg came up, the giant beast pulled the rest of its massive body out. Lava continued to splash on the floor as it left the pool. Once free of the heavy, blazing liquid, it spread its large, sinewy wings, and the beast had a long, spined tail that was thicker than any tree Henrick had ever seen.

Its thick scales were black as charcoal, and they glistened with a dark red against the light of the magma. Its eyes were solid orange orbs that served as evidence of the beast's sinister and fiery nature. Its body billowed with smoke and steam as the temperature rapidly fell. The giant winged reptile stood over the pedestal in challenge to Henrick's presence.

As the beast made its grand appearance, Henrick never took his eyes off of it, he met the creature's eyes when he was able to, and he had instinctively donned his shield. In the midst of it all, Henrick felt that he was ready for anything.

"By the gods, what are ye?" Henrick whispered under his breath.

"Yes, what am I?" the giant beast repeated Henrick's question by speaking the common tongue of mortals. Even the creature's voice sounded like fire. "What ever could I be, *morsel*?"

Henrick was surprised that the creature heard his whisper, but he refrained from showing it. He was too focused on watching the creature's every move.

"You should feel prized to know that I exist, little worm," the beast said through razor sharp teeth. "To know that a god lives among the mortals. To know that I can burn the world to ash should the fancy strike my desire. But. To put it simply for your *feeble* mind. *I am A DRAGON!*"

Every syllable sent echoing tremors along the walls; tremors so strong that Henrick struggled to remain steady on his feet. The dragon made sure that his voice carried the immense power buried beneath its scales. A power that made the pool of magma bubble and flare.

"And I am known as Drextramlcrosis," the dragon added.

Henrick was unsure of how to carry on a conversation with such a being, and when the human did not produce any words, the dragon decided to prod.

"Don't tell me you've lost your nerve, *paladin*," the dragon said.

"*Paladin*?" Henrick repeated the word due to its unknown significance.

"Rahahahaha," The dragon offered a devilish laughter. "You truly are underwhelming." The dragon lowered its head with its serpentine neck so that Henrick would be no more than a few yards away and could take a closer look at its enormous maw. "That is what you are, and what you are becoming," the dragon explained. "That's why your divine sense can detect *darkness* in others, why you are free of dread in my presence, and why you have never been afflicted by sickness or disease."

Henrick fought off the thumping convulsions to cough when he caught a whiff of the hot and smoky breath of the dragon's, and beyond the shadow of those six-foot fangs, the human could see the glowing of fire inside the creature's throat.

The words of the dragon danced around in Henrick's head for a moment. How could this creature possibly know so much about him, and not a moment before, he hadn't a clue that such a monster existed in the world? What else did this dragon know? He had to wonder. From what the human could tell, based on how it was talking, the dragon had a massive superiority complex, and figured that with a small amount of bearing, perhaps he could use that to his advantage.

"Tell me, *great dragon*, is all of that due to me appointment to the Twins?" Henrick asked.

"*Nielda* has chosen you, not the Twins," the dragon corrected him while bringing its head back up. "Perhaps that little detail was something the nymph left out in the tiger cave. Undine has her own paladin. Just as each of the gods do. Even the dark ones. But to answer your question, yes."

Henrick kept his gaze on Drextramlcrosis, but he could not help himself in making a quick glance at the artifact. The gaze was not unnoticed by the watchful eyes of the dragon.

"Ah, yes. The orb. That *is* why you're here," the dragon said.

The dragon took a few steps back, his giant claws quaking the ground as he moved. The dragon pinched the tiny Esfera de Luz between two fingers, and then dropped the orb just several feet in front of Henrick.

"What will you do with Lumina's Seventh Star?" the dragon asked.

"With yer vast knowledge, ye must know the shade have their eye on Claymore," Henrick stated more than asked, and he assumed the dragon already knew. "I want to use it to defeat them."

There was a slight hint of reservation in the human's words, and the dragon's infinitely superior insight picked up on it.

"Hmm. But you don't want to end up like the life-stealer?" the dragon said, referring to Simon Blade-Briar.

Henrick was astounded once more on the dragon's knowledge of recent history.

The dragon lowered its head once again as a means of teasing, and said, "Let your yellow-eyed friend use it?"

"And let him sacrifice his life instead of mine? I think not, dragon," Henrick argued. He knew the creature was referring to Yobo.

"Hahaha," the dragon laughed, bringing his head up again. "You misunderstand, worm. Your friend has the means of circumventing the curse that the orb afflicts. Not even he realizes it, but he will."

"What do you mean?" Henrick had to ask.

"Your friend knows the old art of the dryashu. The gray dryads," the dragon explained. "He carries a darkness inside himself as well. You must have sensed it."

"Aye," the human confirmed.

"Let him use it when the time comes," the dragon advised. If the dragon was able to wear an even more devious grin on its face, it did so at that moment.

It was then that Henrick moved to pick up the orb. It appeared to be made of solid, gold-stained glass. Glittering colors of yellow, white, and gold shimmered over the surface of the orb as it emitted the dim glow. The object was about a foot in diameter.

"How does it work?" Henrick asked.

"Hahaha," the dragon offered only laughter. "I have faith you will figure it out."

Henrick took a minute to place the orb in his backpack. When he finished, he looked upon the dragon again. Something about the dragon had been itching Henrick's mind since walking into the creature's lair.

"I've been wondering, dragon. Why the pirates?" he asked.

"How curious of you, little one. But I suppose there is no harm," the dragon began. "My existence is unknown from the world for a reason. Should I reveal myself, it would beckon the challenge of others. Many of my kin have made that mistake and paid the price. The pirates bring me treasure, and they are my agents in the world. Speaking of which, I want you to take the young captain with you to Claymore. He will be of great value in the battle of yours."

"Too bad ye couldn't come yerself, I'd love to see ye in action," Henrick offered.

"Hahahahaha," the dragon laughed maniacally. "The gesture *is* tempting, and I've not tasted the lust for war in ages." The dragon paused as if considering its next words while looking to the collapsed vent above. "The shade have hidden their intentions from the flow of time." The dragon then paused to return its eyes to Henrick. "I will be watching, paladin. Should the shade invoke the purpose for which I exist in this world...well, that will be up to them."

Henrick could only wonder what the dragon was talking about, but with the possibility that Drextramlcrosis could aid in the coming war, he was content with how the conversation went. He had the Esfera de Luz, and ultimately, that was the reason for him being here. Now his quest was done, and it was time to get back home.

"I thank ye, dragon, for yer...*perceptions*," Henrick said as he began to motion for the exit.

"Remember, morsel. I do not exist," the dragon warned. "Not to your friends, not to anyone. Betray my trust, and I will eat you."

It was some time ago when Henrick disappeared with Samuel and Jack. Serena had been waiting for their return by sitting at the end of the pier on the north side. Sand sat next to her. Both of them watched the calm waters of the lagoon while relaxing to the sound of the waterfall.

Every so often, Serena would vigorously scratch the top of Sand's head. The tiger would rear his head up when she did, showing that he was enjoying the massage. The feline purred loudly, and when she would give her arm a rest, he would nudge her with his big nose until she resumed.

The tiger's attention was soon taken by the movement of a rather large object sailing through the air. The object was a large bird, and the cat's eyes followed the creature's movement until it came to rest on the very end of the bowsprit on the Wailing Wolf.

"What's up, buddy?" she asked Sand.

The feline shifted with excitement and licked his lips with anticipation. He secretly wished he could chase the bird down. Serena followed the tiger's gaze, and after a few seconds, she spotted the bird in which Sand was staring at.

It was indeed a large bird that had come flying into the cove, but it wasn't a seagull or some other type of coastal avian that swooped in. It was an eagle, and more specifically, it was a blood eagle. Its body was covered in dark brown feathers, but the downs and tail feathers had bright red hues.

Serena knew that the blood eagle placed its habitat in the northeast regions of the continent, and when she recalled that information, it drew her to the next logical explanation. The bird wasn't actually a bird in the first place, and the last time she saw a blood eagle was when she saw her mentor transform into one. That conclusion made her stand up.

As Serena and the eagle locked eyes, the bird took flight and departed the ship-sized cave. It descended in altitude slightly, and finally came swooping around the earthen corner near Serena.

Serena watched the bird make its maneuvers, and in following it with her eyes, she saw a narrow rocky path that led out of the cave from beneath the docks. She hopped down and followed the path around to a slightly larger surface. It was here that she found a familiar face.

It was an aerin man. He wore a cloak of brown eagle feathers that draped from his broad shoulders to the ground. His jet-black hair was short and slicked back. His face had a profound jawline that was showing signs of stubble. He was about Serena's height, but maybe a couple inches taller. As Serena came around the bend, she met the gaze from his light brown eyes.

"*Kormanth*," Serena said with a smile.

"Hello, Serena," the man replied. "Sorry I haven't stopped by in a while."

"I was beginning to wonder, honestly," Serena admitted.

"I've been trying to track down a necromancer for the archdruid," Kormanth explained. "That's also why I've been searching all over for you. How come you left Claymore?"

"*How come*? Has the grove not seen what's coming?" Serena began. "The shade from Kadavar. They are going to invade. I'm here with some others, and we're getting an artifact that will stop them."

"*The shade*?" he said as he folded his arms and stared at the ground to ponder a bit. "Either way. The archdruid is summoning the entire grove."

Kormanth then looked at Serena again. "You and I will be the last to arrive. If your information is true, you should present this to the grove."

"*You* have to believe me on this," Serena nearly pleaded.

"Like I said, the rest of the grove will need to hear that," the man suggested. "If the shade are deemed a more dire threat, then we can look into fighting them, but for now, we need to go."

"I...I need to tell the others that I am going, then," Serena said with hesitation. After traveling for so long with Henrick, she had come to respect his company, even with his ignorance for the larger world outside of Claymore. But she still couldn't leave him, or Yobo, without letting them know.

"Of course, but be quick," Kormanth said.

"I will," Serena nodded.

Without another word, Serena returned to the cove. Sand was the first to meet her as he hadn't moved from his previous spot. She scratched the tiger's chin when she came to stand beside the giant feline.

"I have to send you back to Kor Magnus for a bit, buddy," Serena said.

The tiger grunted in disappointment before lowering his head for the inevitable defeat.

"Hey," the druid told her companion while kneeling before the tiger. "I'll bring you back as soon as I can."

She stood back up and placed a hand on top of the tiger's head. With a flash of flame and smoke, the tiger vanished into the air. Back to its home plane of existence.

Serena continued down the pier until she was where the ramp and the tavern met. As she approached, she saw Henrick, Yobo, Samuel, and Jack standing there, and in Henrick's hands was the Esfera de Luz.

"You *got* it?" Serena said.

Henrick hoisted the orb up to his eye level so that they could all get a better look at it. "Aye, and now it's time to head home."

"I'm afraid I will have to meet you there," the druid's words brought on the curious and concerned gaze of her companions.

"What are you talking about?" Yobo asked first.

"I am being summoned by the head of my grove," she replied.

Henrick, more than anyone else standing there, knew the price of duty and commitment, and understood that she had to leave. However, Henrick found his tactical mind coming back into play as the quest was over. He thought of all places in Claymore, villages and the like, from which they could lay low and make a plan to get back into Claymore. They would need a place in which Serena could rendezvous with them, and so he decided to pick the last village they were in together.

"We will wait for you in Solace," Henrick finally said. "Be safe out there."

"Okay, you too," she said with a nod. Serena returned to the north end of the docks and followed the rocky pathway out of the cave once again. She did not return.

CHAPTER NINETEEN
THE FALL OF THE BLACK LOTUS

"Bar the door!" the succubus screamed at her subordinates with her fiendish voice.

Three of her assassins rushed out of their line formation at the other end of the room. They slammed the iron door shut, fighting against the charging invaders from the other side. The iron bar hanging on the wall nearby came down to seal the door shut. However, they knew from the initial skirmish that it would not stop the dark creatures for long.

The opposing force had taken the fortress grounds above, killing nearly all of the troops that were defending it, and they were quickly attempting to break the footing that the few remaining assassins had inside their own hideout.

The succubus, and the assassins with her, stood in a hallway made of old greenish stone bricks, but the color didn't matter because the place was completely dark. The presence of the aggressors had extinguished all sources of light from the torches and lamps.

The succubus used her innate, demonic nature to conjure magic in the form of bright red energy in her hands, and this energy provided light to the ones that could not see. The light revealed her pale blue skin, streaks of demonic scales ran down the outside of her arms, legs and all over her torso. Her eyes were dark orbs with glowing yellow-orange irises. Her hair was reddish-orange like the color of fire, and she wore a glossy black leather dress that allowed her to show off her feminine features. She held a sword and a whip in her hands.

The largest of the succubus' minions was a blue-skinned orc, and he was the first to step away from the barred door. "These beasts are formidable," the orc admitted through his long-toothed maw.

"They move through the shadows like we do," another one of the assassins said. This one was a green-skinned male ru-era. He had short and pointy black horns protruding from his forehead. He wore a satin, dark blue robe, but he did not carry any weapons.

"Martaak, Ferio, shut your mouth," the succubus demanded, calling the orc and ru-era by their names.

"Gather your breath and *stop* wasting it. We need to get to the portal chamber before they do."

"Yeah, Martaak. We wouldn't want you to fail another mission, now, would we?" another assassin, a female odum, teased him. But the human wasn't just an odum, she was half-dryad as well, her golden eyes were evidence. The woman had a pair of enchanted daggers at her belt.

"Hmpf," the orc, Martaak, simply scoffed at the words.

"Come," the succubus bade them.

Just as the assassins began their retreat through the hallway, dark mist began to seep through the tiny openings around the door. The assassins and their demonic leader passed by several nooks in the hallway that had stone statues that have been worn by the passing of time. They ran through an intersection that took the hallway to their left and right, but they ignored those directions, knowing that they would be dead ends.

After several more nooks, they passed through a door and into the barracks of the hideout. There were countless bunks, tables and footlockers in the room.

Martaak was the last one through the door, and he immediately turned around to throw down another iron bar across the back of it. The first of the invaders was already down the hallway leading with its jagged sword, and before the door would close all the way, the blade made it through. The orc slammed the door closed anyway, pinching the weapon in place, and putting his body weight against the vertical surface to prevent the advancement of the invader.

The succubus turned around, the deepest feelings of malice for the invaders swelled inside her already dark heart. *"Now!"* she commanded the orc.

Martaak opened the door, revealing an ever-growing line-up of the shade warriors. The demonic energy in her hands flared with power and rage in an instant. She aimed her magic down the hallway, and the spell released with a deafening blast before a large red beam cut a path with unbelievable speed. The dark creatures had nowhere to go, and it didn't matter if they were in mist form or not. They all exploded into cinders and glowing red sparks.

As soon as the spell concluded, the orc slammed the door and sealed it. The assassins were back on the move, and through another door. They repeated this process as they passed through several more chambers. Eventually, they ran out of doors.

And It was through the final door that they arrived in a much larger chamber. It was octagonal in shape, the ceiling was flat and about 25 feet high, and the room was nearly 80 feet in diameter. At the opposite end of this place, there was a raised portion of the floor that acted as a stage. There was a stone pedestal at the head of this stage, and on the wall behind it, there was an enormous, pale green gem.

The giant crystal formation was approximately 12 feet in height and eight feet in width. It was smooth and mostly round, and it protruded from a natural stone wall that cut into the chamber. The gem glowed with an equally pale green light that illuminated the whole chamber.

"I'm going down below to open a portal. Kamala, *you're* the Speaker, do what you need to," the succubus commanded.

"Of course, Lady Severin," the half-dryad, Kamala, said.

The succubus, Severin, descended a flight of stone stairs to the right of the stage. Kamala crossed the chamber, stepped onto the stage, and came to stand within a few feet of the giant green crystal. Martaak and Ferio stood before the stage, and anticipated the next arrival of the invaders. All of them knew it would only be a matter of time before they came banging against the door.

The orc took the two shortswords off his back and readied a fighting stance. The ru-era held out both of his hands and conjured the magic of a spell between all of his fingers. The arcs of electricity were like webs between his digits and a white and blue ball of lightning sparked to life.

Then, as if on cue, the dark mist began to slip around the edges of the door. One by one, the shade retook their humanoid forms as the light of the giant crystal forced them. Martaak closed the gap as soon as the first one stepped forward, and if any of the other shade tried to come at the orc from the side or behind, Ferio was there to blast them with a flash of lightning.

Kamala placed a hand on the large green gem as the fighting had started. She could see the swirling of magic inside, and the warmth from that magic began to transfer to her hand. She closed her eyes as she felt the dark energies invade her body. She concentrated further, trying to search for her deity's guidance.

"Belladonna. *My* Belladonna," Kamala whispered to glowing light. "The children of Abyss have come. I want your boon so that I can slay them all."

The Goddess of Poison, Lust, and Sin remained silent in Kamala's mind, but she could feel her goddess' warmth inside her core as more energy continued to transfer through her hand. It was a very intimate and hot sensation that caused most of her body to start throbbing with pleasurable reverberations. Her breathing became heavy as she struggled to concentrate.

This was not the first time she communicated with Belladonna, and every time before this moment when Kamala had done so, the deity always challenged the fortitude of her *motivational salience*. There was never a day when the half-dryad didn't yearn for the sensation, and each time, she prayed that it would not be the last.

The pulsing, orgasmic vibrations turned into convulsions, and that's when Kamala collapsed to the floor. Her body and mind was ravenous and drunk as the dopamine shot off inside her brain like a pile of gunpowder.

Martaak and Ferio continued to battle the shade, but they were getting pushed back. They were moments away from backstepping into the stage. The orc fought wildly with his blades: stabbing, slashing, and parrying incoming swords. The ru-era shot lightning in all directions, and when the lightning would connect with one of the dark creatures, it would arc and strike another, and another. This was allowing the two assassins to stay alive, but it would not be long until they were truly overwhelmed.

The shade filled up half of the chamber, but the light from the large gem was keeping their transformation abilities at bay. This made the fight for the assassins manageable, but it was far from easier.

Feeling returned to Kamala's body and she slowly struggled her way back to her feet with legs that felt like jelly. Her eyes shined with the same pale green light as the large crystal. Belladonna's warm embrace was there inside her body, and she swelled with power and malice as the boon started to take hold.

As she stood there staring out into the dimly lit arena, everything stood still, suspended in time, but she was free to move around. She pulled her enchanted daggers from her belt, and as soon as her hands came upon the hilts, the steel shimmered with a dim green light.

Kamala. My Kamala, My fang, came the echoing voice inside her mind. *You have enjoyed my caress for many mortal years. You have been vigilant, violent, and faithful. You will be deserving until someone else takes your head.* The voice paused for a moment. *The shade. Destroy them. All of them.*

The animalistic energy in her body sent her into a murderous flight. She ran at full speed and weaved a wild pattern between all the shade. She used their glowing white eyes as a focal point and made sure that her daggers plunged into every single one. When she found no direct path to a pair of eyes, *she* would transform into a splash of dark mist, like the shade, and would teleport to her next target. To the members of the Black Lotus, this was known as *shadow-stepping*.

Destroy them.

The voice of Belladonna echoed in her mind again, commanding her once more. The Speaker of the

Poison God pounced around the arena, stabbing all the white eyes she could find. There were so many of them, she thought, and so she went back for round two. Making sure she didn't miss any of them.

The rush of the kill carried her onward and onward. The feeling was that of euphoria, lust, and love as she was a whirlwind of steel, and death. Her body was drenched in sweat from the burning heat inside her body.

Eventually her path brought her to the entrance of the large chamber, and it was here that she found the end of the shade horde. Satisfied with her work, she parked her feet before the sealed door, and standing directly behind her was the last dark creature that her blades had found.

As Martaak and Ferio continued to defend themselves against the pushing offensive of the shade, they couldn't help but notice the darting green light that found its way through the ranks of the dark humanoids.

In an instant, all of the shade fell over and evaporated into nothingness, and for Kamala, time returned to its normal course but her eyes remained illuminated with green energy.

"*Ruh*? What the hell happened?" Martaak grumbled.

"Our speaker did her job," Ferio answered the question.

Once the evaporative cloud of the dying shade dissipated, the other two saw Kamala standing before them. She did not say anything, nor did she move at that moment. She only observed more dark mist bleeding from around the edges. The orc and the ru-era saw it as well.

"Come on, let's get out of here," Ferio suggested.

The three assassins sprinted for the stairs that descended deeper into the earth. Down the stairs, Ferio smashed his fist against the handle of a lever, sending it downward. Following that, the grinding sound of metal on metal enveloped the air as a large slab of stone moved to seal off the stairs from the chamber above.

At the bottom of the steps, the assassins entered a small room. In a circular fashion around this chamber, there were seven nooks, and each nook had a chalked oval on the back wall. At the center of the room, there was a brass stand that held a solid blue object in the shape of a diamond, and the stranger artifact was inscribed all over with demonic runes.

At the moment, Severin was channeling her dark magic into the object. The runes glowed with fiery energy, and the assassins could see that a few of the nooks had portals open.

"We have lost," the succubus proclaimed in a very angry tone. "We are all that remains of the Black Lotus, and thus I relinquish your blood vows."

Ferio read into the hidden marks of the succubus's words. He asked, "You mean to stay *here*?"

"Yes," Severin answered. "I must destroy the runestone, once you three leave."

"How *noble*. But also very smart, milady," Ferio complimented.

"What do you mean?" the orc asked since he didn't understand.

"If she stays behind, and the shade strike her down, she will merely get transported back to Aphro Turnus," the ru-era explained.

"Belladonna's home," Kamala added.

At the end of the conversation, the mist forms of the shade floated into the room, and encircled the assassins and their leader. They did not take their humanoid form, however, but the assassins were out of time. The three minions split in different directions, running towards different portals.

As her loyal servants came within a few feet of their respective portals, Severin raised her hands up into a hammer. She charged up her entire body with more demonic power before smashing the runestone into pieces with her fists. As the portals failed and began to close, some of the mist-form shade slipped through to chase down their prey.

Severin was then the only one that remained in the portal room. The only one left in the Black Lotus hideout. The rage of a cornered mother boiled in her blood. She was a demonic force made to make her last stand. She vowed that she would not be defeated, and if things were going to end, she would make sure none remained alive.

She conjured and pushed her magical power to its peak. The scales upon her skin seethed with fire as her strength became amplified.

With sword and whip in hand, she screamed across the echoing walls, "*Come on, dryasaltu! Face me!*"

CHAPTER TWENTY
THE EMBERS IN THE DARK

Night had come by the time Serena and Kormanth neared their destination. They spent the last few days in their avian forms. Serena was a seagull, and Kormanth was a blood eagle. They had rested when they needed to, but they were in a hurry to get to their secret grove.

Serena could sense a familiarity with the landscape below, and she was certain it was the southern end of the Hunter Hills, the natural barrier to the country of Harmon. It was the same area that she and Henrick traveled while on their way to Lionsgate.

The rushing air of the night sky was calm and cool. The two moons were out, but Nielda wouldn't be there for much longer as she was setting. Nielda was in the process of reaching her third quarter while Undine was exiting her waxing crescent. The world below was covered in a pale light, a couple of campfires could be seen in the distance, but other than that, it was dark.

For Serena, this was going to be her first time at the hidden enclave, and her first time meeting the other druids, save for Kormanth. She was excited and concerned. When she was growing up, her mentor had always talked about the other druids, and what their specialties were. However, on a number of occasions Kormanth had always cited that if the druids ever had to meet, like they were about to, then there was something terrible going on.

Part of her concern drew from her short conversation with Kormanth a few days ago. At the mention of the shade, it seemed like Kormanth did not know anything about them, and perhaps the rest of the grove did not know as well. If that was so, then what else could be out there in the world that begged the attention of all the druids in Terra Sanguinar. Who was this necromancer that Kormanth spoke of? She figured that her answers would be gained at the meeting.

Once the two flying druids were over a portion of the hills covered in forest, the blood eagle began to dive. Serena followed suit. Within a few feet of the tree tops, Kormanth cut upward in a sharp swoop and let the wind beneath his wings carry him. Serena was right behind him. When the blood eagle made a banking turn to circle around, the seagull caught the sight of a clearing below.

Once the circle was complete, Kormanth dove down again. When he came to be inches off the ground, he swooped upward, and as he came to pull up, he changed into his human form to come to his feet after a small slide across the dirt.

Serena, however, floated down, and fluttered her wings to slow her speed and descent. Once she put her webbed feet on the ground, she, too, reverted back to her human form.

Serena took in her surroundings once she had gotten her bearings in the right order. The clearing was surrounded by the spruce trees that covered the Hunter Hills, but at one side in the clearing there was a cave. The entrance was surrounded by large boulders, top to bottom, and lying outside of the cave was a large grizzly bear.

"We have arrived," he said. Kormanth began to walk towards the cave once Serena was finished taking human form.

Serena trotted to catch up to him. "Is he or she going to let us in?" Serena asked, referring to the bear in their path.

But Kormanth continued to walk and didn't reply to Serena's question. Instead, he called out ahead, "Dehlan!"

The bear got up from its laying position and stood on all fours. Kormanth and Serena could see a painted blue stripe upon the bear's snout. The blue stripe seemed peculiar to Serena, but then the form of the bear began to twist and wither until it became another creature altogether.

It was a female orc. Her hair was dark, long, and braided. Her skin was a light brown, and one of the tusks protruding from her mouth was pierced with a small ring. She was wrapped in bear skins and leathers.

"Kormanth. We have been looking for your arrival," Dahlen said in a deep, rocky female voice.

When the orc finished her statement, the large stones around the cave entrance began to rumble and shutter. Serena was caught off-guard by the sudden ruckus, however, Kormanth was not. The rocks and stones rolled around until they met at a point near the mouth of the cave. As the boulders came to their meeting place, dirt rose up from the ground and created an earthy mixture. Soon this mixture took the form of a giant earth elemental.

In an instant, the elemental exploded into a cloud of dirt and dust. The smell of fresh soil filled the air all around them instantly. When the mess had dissipated there was a female dwarf standing before them.

"Kadrah," Kormanth acknowledged, then paused for a quick moment. "You're looking quite...*heavy*."

Kadrah had a light skin tone, blonde hair that was braided down to her butt, and wore simple clothing that was covered and stained with dirt. She stood over half of Serena's height. Kadrah looked younger compared to Serena, but they all knew that the dwarf had many years on even Kormanth. The dwarves of Undertrone were long-lived people.

It was a sight to see in Serena's eyes, but she couldn't help but feel unnerved by the spectacles of Dahlen and Kadrah. For years, she had been using her animal forms to sneak by or to get what she wanted or needed. But at this moment, she realized the naiveness in herself as she did not suspect the bear, or the nearby rocks, to also be druids like her.

"Is that anyway to be greetin' a lady, Kormanth?" the dwarf woman asked with a light dwarven accent.

"Of course, I was referring to how *large* your elemental form was," Kormanth elaborated with a tone of jest. "Are the others waiting for us?"

"Yes, they are," Dehlan said.

"Very good. Come on, Serena," Kormanth said.

Without another word from any of them, the four druids walked into the cave with Kadrah leading the way. After a short distance inside, the cave took a mild bend to the right and this is when the natural stone walls held burning torches. The bend then straightened out and the light from the torches in the chamber ahead illuminated the rest of their path.

The four of them entered the cavernous meeting room. The walls were covered with roots from the trees above, and at the center of this room, there was a large stone table that was carved out of the ground itself. Large rocks had been placed around this table to serve as seats for the druids that were meeting here.

Serena was the last one to enter the chamber, and as soon as she did, she drew the eyes of the eight other druids standing in attendance.

Directly across the table was a rather tall and muscular dryad, but this one also showed signs of age. Serena could only wonder how old he really was. His straight, silver hair draped down to his shoulders, and his eyes were a hazelnut brown. He wore a thick, brown leather mantle on top of his fur clothing.

"Young lady," the tall dryad addressed Serena. "I am Arch-Druid Levinar." The dryad took a bow in the midst of his introduction. "I believe this is the first time you have been in the company of our complete circle."

"Yes. It is," Serena answered.

"Then I bid you welcome," Levinar offered. He pointed with an open hand to each of the druids at the table as he introduced them. "This is Loria, Lamans, Ti'or, Reeth, Jan, and Ryusa." Each of the druids either nodded a head or waved with a hand as their names were called. "You've already met Kadrah and Dehlan."

Loria was a dryad. Her hair was a dark green bob, and her eyes were violet in color. Her facial profile was angular like many dryads, and she had patches of freckles across her cheeks. She was very petite, and wore simple clothing of a seafoam green shirt and brown pants. Her skin tone was light but it had a viridescent hint.

Lamans was a male gnome, and of all the many things that Kormanth taught Serena when she was younger, she remembered that gnomes were not of this world, and those that did live on Terra were very few and far between. Otherwise, the gnome's skin tone was light. His hair, bushy eyebrows, and full beard was yellow-blonde, and he couldn't have stood higher than Kadrah.

Ti'or was a male huntari. His fur was white as snow, save for a single orange patch around his left eye. He wore padded leather pants, but nothing on his torso.

Reeth was another brown-skinned orc but male. He was similarly dressed like Ti'or, but comparatively, the orc was a giant of thick muscle. He had an ugly face and a toothy mouth. He was bald, but had a short-length beard.

Jan was a sanct, a human from the east. He had straight black hair that came down to his shoulders. He wore a headdress of red and blue feathers, a sleeveless leather jacket without a shirt underneath, and some dark brown pants. Unlike some of the other druids, he wore a pair of leather shoes.

Lastly, there was Ryusa. She was a dryad. Her skin was dark as the spruce trees outside the cave. Her eyes were green but they resembled the eyes of a serpent. Her features were less angular than Loria's. She had white tribal-like paint across her face and torso. Her clothing was made from the skins of large reptiles.

"Nice to meet you all, finally. I'm Serena," she said while taking a slight bow.

She met the eyes of the other druids, but more than once her gaze fell upon the empty seat. There were 12 seats at the table, but only 11 druids were assembled in this cave tonight. The arch-druid caught her curiosity.

"There is one druid who is not here. A hermit named Sorin. He watches over the lands of Ravenlock." The arch-druid let his own eyes fall upon the missing druid's spot during his speech. "Now, to the matter at hand. *Baron Tal.*"

With the end of the introductions and the topic of the meeting presented, the druids sat down.

Kormanth made no hesitation in divulging his report, "To put it plainly, I have not been around to see everyone regularly because I have been keeping tabs on the Baron. He has abandoned his lair and started a trek to the north. I followed him into the Cobalt Mountains, but somewhere along the way, he disappeared." He paused to let his words sink in. "When I lost his track, I turned around to investigate his tower in the Sangmere. Deep in his lair, there was a journal of his laying open in a laboratory. In short, he has abandoned his home in pursuit of something called the Chalice of Souls. Seems he had been locked away in his tower for months studying different books on the matter. Whatever this chalice may be, it can't be good."

The rest of the druids remained silent as Kormanth finished his report and digested the findings.

Then Kormanth continued, "However, there may be another threat that beckons our attention. Serena?"

Serena's eyes went wide, but only for a brief second as she didn't expect her part of the conversation to come so quickly. The rest of the druids looked at her with skepticism as none of them had the measure of their youngest member, yet.

"Does anyone here know of the shade?" she asked them.

The druids looked to each in question, but Levinar was the only one that kept his narrowed eyes on the woman.

"The shade have not been seen for nearly 700 years," the archdruid said with a hint of disbelief. "They saw their defeat at the hands of the founders of Claymore. On what basis do you bring this topic to the table?"

Serena elaborated, "The shade are going to invade Claymore, soon. They have already begun targeting their patrols, and they already slaughtered all of the dryads living atop the Skyreach."

"*Skyreach*?" Loria blurted out.

Some of the druids looked at Loria with a quick glance in response to her sudden emotional outbreak.

"Unfortunately, I do not know who else they might have attacked by now," Serena added.

"My brother was a *monk* on that mountain. If he is gone, I will find these bastards," Loria proclaimed.

The dryad drew in the looks from the others again. It was unknown to Serena, but Loria was a hot-tempered creature. Of course, the young druid was starting to see it.

It was then that the archdruid stood up from his seat. The other druids looked at him and expected him to say something about the topic at hand, but no words came. Instead, he stared down the tunnel of their cavern with a concerned look. The other druids then turned to look the same direction.

A sense of dread crept its way into the druids' hidden enclave as the first couple of torches on the wall suddenly lost their light. The other druids remained silent as the spectacle continued and the next set of torches went out.

"What is happening?" Ti'or questioned aloud.

"It's the shade," the archdruid announced. "Magical fire and light. That is their weakness. Kadrah, clear a path."

Under the command of the archdruid, Kadrah was the first one down the hallway, and as she went, she transformed back into an earth elemental. Like a giant boulder, she barreled down the cavernous tunnel. She felt the contact of something against her stony form, but there was nothing solid.

Serena didn't hesitate once Kadrah disappeared into the dark, and she let loose two bolts of fire down the hallway. The flames did not strike any targets, but it did force the black mist hanging in the air to change into humanoid shapes. The effect only lasted for a few seconds, and when that time was over, the creatures returned to mist.

Reeth noticed the supernatural ability of the invaders, and so he was next to enter the hallway. As he charged forward while his body blistered and boiled until flames shot out from the cracks. When the rest of his skin was shed, he was an orc-shaped fire elemental. He made his body ignite, covering the entire hallway from floor to ceiling like he was a wall of flame. The flames caught the dark mist and turned them into cinders.

Without a word from anyone else, the other druids ran out of the cave following Kadrah and Reeth. Once outside, the assembled Ember Grove came to realize that they were vastly outnumbered.

Nielda had set from the sky, but Undine remained. With the faint glow of the blue moon, the druids could see that there had to have been 100 of these dark humanoids. The druids stood in a semi-circle outside the entrance of the cave as they looked onward to their enemies. Strangely, however, the shade remained at bay.

"Are they *waiting* for us?" Serena muttered as she stood next to Kormanth.

"They are staying out of the light," Reeth noted.

"These are the creatures you spoke of?" Kormanth asked rhetorically.

"Yes," she answered plainly.

All the other druids heard Serena's confirmation as they stared at the army before them. The creatures looked like a cloud of smoke with their glowing white eyes dotting about, and it almost seemed like the battle had come to a stalemate just as it began.

"Without the shadows, they cannot hope to defeat us," Levinar proclaimed.

As the druids remained stationary, the shade in the back ranks moved to the left and right until the druids were surrounded on all sides. Reeth flared his flames, increasing the light he was emitting, and pushing the shade back, but only slightly.

"Perhaps the bastards didn't think this through," Loria said. "We can stay like this until the sun comes up."

Just as Loria finished with her mocking of the shade, a streak of black lightning shot across the group of druids, and took one off their feet when the spell had struck from behind. It was Ryusa. The dryad flopped upon the ground like a limp doll.

"Death magic. Fan out," the archdruid called.

"But stay close!" Reeth added with a call of warning. Reeth ignited his body even further. His flames burned hot and bright, and at this level of magic, the orc knew he would not be able to help fight much, otherwise he would risk burning out.

The nearby shadows of the night disappeared, and the misty forms of the shade were forced to revert into their darkened humanoid forms. The druids could also see the sharp armor that hid behind the smoldering veils.

Levinar transformed into an earth elemental, the aspect of nature for which he was most attuned. He took his place next to Kadrah, and together, they looked like a couple of earth-molded tanks. They stood near the front by Reeth, and began to swat at the shade. Clacks and crunches filled the air.

Jan transformed into a giant, gray dire wolf. His fangs formed a mean snarl in his maw, and his body was riddled with razor sharp spikes. He drove into the shade ranks, and came in behind the massive clubs that were the fists of the earth elementals.

In a similar fashion, Lamans grew, and morphed into a 16-foot silverback gorilla. When his transformation was complete, he jumped and thrashed wildly, crashing his boulder-size fists into the ground as an act of intimidation. The shade weren't so easily shaken, and so the gorilla-druid pounced in the fray.

Ti'or took the form of an air elemental. He was almost completely transparent, and his body was nothing more than swirling air. His near-invisible form picked up dirt and dust from the forest floor, but his action came in the form of a funnel, and he used that funnel to fan the flames from Reeth's body, directing the flames at the imposing army.

Dehlan returned to her bear form, but this time it was a bear meant for battle. Like Jan, her body became a dire form of her aspect of nature. Thick brown fur hid the iron strong body underneath, but it couldn't hide the spikes that rose from it. The orc druid's mouth was so large in this form that it was possible for her to bite a creature in half, and she didn't waste any time in making a few examples.

"If it's annihilation they want, then I suppose a little cheating won't hurt," Kormanth said. As he finished his proclamation, he performed his most unique animal form that he knew. His feathery mantle turned into a cloak of fiery feathers, flames reached out of his eyeballs, and his arms turned into wings that shared the same look of his cloak. After a short moment, all the morphing effects became a single creature of legend: a phoenix.

Serena stared at her mentor in amazement, and a majority of that amazement was from the fact that druids could only transform into animals that they came into contact with. She had to wonder where such a beautiful creature existed, and for Kormanth to know the form meant that one lived somewhere in the world.

Loria had a different set of affinities among the Ember Grove. Unlike the others who held animal or elemental forms, her aspect was the art of druidic magic, and because of that, she remained as a dryad. She immediately fell into her spellcasting, and began using a spell she called *Gossamer Glow*. The spell shot out globs of sticky, spider-like webbing, and her intended group of targets became covered in gluey silk that restrained their movement and illuminated them with magical, pale blue light.

Serena was awe-struck by all the druids in her circle. She felt pride to be among them as they all stood there sharing the same peril before the shade. Her admiration was soon fading as her mind fell on a distant memory. A memory that began this journey, and the whole reason she went looking for Henrick. While she thought of these images, her eyes fell upon the lifeless form of Ryusa. Anger began boiling in her blood as the battle came into a full swing.

Her memory then went back a little further. To a time when she had a conversation with the water nymph in her cave. A time before these recent events. The water nymph, the envoy of the Twins, had told her that the time of the druid groves was waning. That all the enclaves had a part to play in the coming struggles, and that once she was on her mission, many of her druid-kin would perish. Including the ones before her.

Her anger became mixed with fear of the shade, fear for her fellow druids, and of the lands she swore to protect. She didn't want to believe the words of the envoy, and so she held onto that sense of pride, whether it was foolish or not. She was going to hold on to it by being here with the rest of her druids.

Serena's heart pounded as her spirit fought to reach a new height. Her fear, her anger, and her love for the world all came crashing together. All the emotions swirled and mixed, and in the pot of her core, she found something else.

Unbridled courage.

Through instinct alone, she reached down into her mind and her heart. She listened to the fond memories of her animal companion, Sand. Her feline friend was the answer to her quest for power. She spent nearly every waking moment with the animal, and she had all the information she needed from her friend, both as a tiger *and* an elemental. The ferocity swelled inside of her.

Serena's fair skin boiled and cracked; blistered and charred. She fell down on to all fours as she drank in the fury of such a form, and it wasn't long before she let loose the flames that sat beneath. Serena had taken the gift that perhaps her tiger had been trying to teach her all this time. At the end of the transformation, the young druid became a blistering fire cat.

"Looks like the young one is more grown up than we thought," Loria stated.

Reeth turned to regard his fellow druid who had also chosen a fire form. "Hahaha. Time for some fun, little one."

With all the transformations complete, the shade met the charge of battle from the druids. The roaring flames from Reeth continued to prevent them from taking their misty forms, and allowing the druids to kill them.

Levinar and Kadrah stood their ground and focused on protecting their grove members from zealous attackers. They continued to swat across the front ranks of the dark humanoids. But without any warning, Kadrah dove head first into the ground, smashing into a group of the shade before melding with the earth.

Underground, the dwarf-druid glided through dirt and stone as if she was swimming through water. Above, she could sense the chomping of boots from the shade, and she homed in a particularly noisy section of the ground. From that section, the elemental emerged from the earth, exploding the land into an enormous cloud of dirt and stone shrapnel. The sudden force sent many of the dark warriors flying off their feet.

Jan and Dehlan rushed headlong into the Children of Abyss, smashing and thrashing as they went. The shade in the front ranks were powerless to stop the pressure from the giant beasts, and so handfuls of them were defeated in rapid succession.

The dark warriors that managed to get out of the way quickly turned and led with their swords. They swung at the thick hides, but most of them missed the fast-paced animals or they simply did little to no damage.

Behind the right flank, the spruce trees came to life as Loria worked her magic. The trees sprouted legs and arms, and then uprooted themselves before engaging the shade. The walking trees waddled their way forward, and attempted to stomp on any who were unsuspecting. The presence of the new combatants drew attention away from the druids.

Kormanth, from a high altitude, dove down at amazing speed like a star falling to the earth with the flames from his feathers trailing behind. He cut a sharp, banking turn as he came within a foot off the ground and raked across the enemy with obsidian talons. He tore a cauterizing line through the abyssal creatures before returning to the sky, but while he was up there, his superior avian eyes caught a glimpse of cold truth that only he could see.

Down the hill, there was a second black mass, and the trees that covered the foothills hid their appearance from the others. There were hundreds more of the sinister monsters lurking below, and suddenly the flying druid was beginning to feel uneasy about their chance of victory.

Kormanth sought to warn his fellow druids but as he came about, he spotted another peculiar concern. Standing above the entrance to the druids' cave, he could see a small gathering of the dark humanoids. The phoenix had to wonder what the smaller group of them was waiting for as they were not participating in the battle, but rather, they were watching it.

Down below, Lamans bounced around in a fit of rage as he carried his large form through the dark humanoids before his feet. He crushed the shade under his knuckles and smashed them with the back of his battering hands. He would then pound the ground with his knuckles at every chance he got as the frenzy went on.

But then Lamans felt the cold, numbing shutters of death strike him square in the back as a bolt of black lightning shot across the air. Half the druids turned to look behind them to find out that they had enemy sorcerers in the distance.

Suddenly, the idea of complete victory was becoming a grim notion of uncertainty.

Another of the dark sorcerers let loose another dark spell but this one was aimed at Reeth, the source of the shade's stalemate. The spell never got to him, though. Instead, the necrotic magic struck against a barrier of moonlight. Black and lavender sparks of magic popped and sizzled as the protective spell repelled the sinister energy, and in the end, the barrier held. Loria stood her ground at the back of the druids' line and defended their position. She threw a glance towards Lamans, but the ape's form had disappeared. She knew the gnome was gone from this world.

Kadrah, Levinar, Jan and Dehlan continued their assault on the main force of the shade while Serena turned to bolster their backside with Loria. Kormanth, from the sky, also turned his attention to the sorcerers.

Serena broke through the sea of dark warriors without much trouble as the shade did not want to mess with living fire. The firecat was already barreling towards the position of the shade casters, and without the mass of an army before her, she could see that there were five.

From atop the cave entrance, a bolt of black lightning streaked by her flaming whiskers, but Serena was a cat, and she was too swift. Missed attack was a fatal mistake that allowed the druid to gain significant ground in her pursuit.

While one sorcerer was focused on the ground assault, the other sorcerers had their focus on the druid in the sky. Two of them gathered their energy for another spell while the remaining two completed the components to their spells. This time two jolts of black lightning shot up into the night sky, but the aerial target was blazing fast with an even quicker reaction time.

As the set of spells missed him, it was the opening that Kormanth needed to begin his descent. He dove down like a meteor, his speed was incredible speed, and it was enough to make the next two death spells zip by him harmlessly. From a short distance away, the druid swooped upward before hitting the ground, and sailed towards the small group of shade before spinning into a spiral.

The shade sorcerers were prepared, though, and they collected their nerve against the encroaching phoenix. They sent another wave of black lightning. Four separate spells shot forth at the flying druid, but the druid anticipated the attack and performed a barrel roll to dodge all four of the spells.

The sorcerer who had been focused on keeping Serena at bay was not happy with his subordinates' failure at that moment. He took his focus off the ground and let loose his own Finger of Death spell at the phoenix-druid. With precision and mastery of his craft, the fifth and unexpected spell, followed right after the missed attacks and struck Kormanth in the head.

Kormanth's phoenix body turned black and charred, but the spiraling momentum of flight still carried him forward. The hardened shell of the phoenix hit the ground, tumbled and rolled. The dead avian of legend came to rest near the group of the shade sorcerers, the burnt-out husk began to crack in various spots, and from these cracks, flames licked their way into the air.

BOOM!!!

The dead body of the phoenix exploded, wiping out the group of shade sorcerers. The blasting sound echoed for miles, and caught the attention of everyone engaged in the main battle. A giant pile of ash was all that remained of the aftermath.

As the sound of the blast subsided, Serena could feel the loss of her mentor in that moment, but she would have to pay her respects later. She turned back around and rejoined the main conflict. Serena couldn't believe her eyes when she saw how much larger the size of the shade army had grown. How many could there have been, she thought. With this many, her mind rolled onto the idea that the shade had been planning this for a while.

On her sprint back, Serena silently watched for the others to account for them. Sadly, she was unable to see the dire bear that had been rampaging through the ranks of the shade. Dehlan was nowhere to be seen, and she had to wonder how the orc had been defeated.

The next thing that she and the druids saw was the shade throwing out thick ropes and nets to catch the wild wolf that continued to berate their front line. But the ropes didn't slow down Jan at all. The dark warriors put more focus on the wolf and attempted to weigh the druid down by putting as many of the dark humanoids on the nets as possible.

Jan suddenly found resistance in his movements, but he was caught up in the moment. He had remained in his animalistic rage for so long that he was unable to pull himself from his wild thrashing. The shade jumped up and dogpiled the ropes and nets, and this forced Jan to be stationary.

In between the openings of the ropes and nets, the dark humanoids produced impossibly large crossbows, and with these weapons, they launched thick, barbed bolts from close range. The heavy shots found the flesh of the wolf and pierced deep to get the blood flowing.

The shade that were nearby began hacking and stabbing at the wolf. The pain of the jagged blades and deadly force of the crossbow bolts quickly took its toll. There was a primal howl, and then there was silence as the dire wolf disappeared underneath the blackness of the dark creatures.

Reeth saw his druid friends perish, but he *had* to focus so that the others could keep going. They continued to fight the shade, but he was soon beginning to realize that they were going to be overwhelmed. Three of his comrades were gone, and even though he would give his own life to protect the lands of Golterran, he had to consider the preservation of the grove.

The flaming orc called out to his leader, "Levinar, we will not survive if we keep this up." The other druids heard the words as well, but they dared not pause from the fighting.

Levinar, in his earth elemental form, leaped into the air only to perform a belly flop on the shade underneath. His form crashed into the ground before it disappeared into the earth, and after swimming through the dirt below, the arch-druid reappeared from the ground just behind Reeth as his dryad self.

"Perhaps you are correct," Levinar said in a cool tone. "But look around. They won't even get near you. The light harms them, and as long as you burn bright, we have a-"

The arch-druid's words were cut short. The flames of the orc's body flickered as a crossbow bolt sliced across Reeth's shoulder. The bolt might have killed the orc had he not turned to regard the arch-druid, and instead the bolt found the neck of Levinar. Reeth gazed in horror as the bolt sunk into the dryad's flesh.

The dryad's glistening amber blood poured from the wound, and Levinar found that he was unable to breath while his blood began to slip down into his lungs. In mere seconds, the dryad collapsed. However, as the arch-druid fell limp, Reeth was there to catch him before he could hit the ground.

Several more bolts flew at the group of the druids. Ti'or, in his air elemental form, turned on the defensive after seeing the arch-druid go down, and formed a protective tornado around the druids. The violent air tossed any incoming bolts harmlessly away.

For now, between Reeth's light and Ti'or's tornado, the druids were a fortress that could not be penetrated. They chose this moment to take a brief respite. When Kadrah noticed what her friends were doing, she dove into the ground again, but not before smashing a few shade along the way. Back in her natural dwarf form, she pulled herself up out of the ground, and inside the tornado.

The druids kept watch as the shade remained at bay. They sought to avenge their fallen companions, but even the shade proved to a fierce adversary. They all knew that they needed to get out of this situation if they were going to survive.

Reeth was on his knees while he cradled Levinar's head. Still in his fire elemental form, he used his empathic abilities to sense the last flickering light of Levinar's life. The orc felt a firm grasp on his forearm as the dryad tried to hold onto his last ounce of strength. His eyes never came open, and soon, he was truly gone. The grasping hand then fell limp.

Reeth then embraced the deceased arch-druid, allowing his flames to burn the body, and turn it into ash. The other druids knew that Reeth was second-in-command among the Ember Grove, and as the funerary rite came to a completion, he was now the arch-druid.

For a moment, it seemed as though the presence of the battle disappeared, and the orc fell into a bit of grief as the ashes of his master were carried off by the winds of the tornado. He then stood up, and looked around to his other druids.

"How are we going to get out of this?" Loria wondered, as did they all.

"We could try to escape, but I don't think they will let us," Reeth admitted.

Serena relinquished her fire cat form, and returned to being a human. She then suggested, "I know this is probably the worst time, but what do you think a *daylight* spell will do to these things?"

"*Daylight*?" Kadrah repeated.

"Levinar *said* these things hated the light," Serena said.

"Let's find out," Loria replied, continuing the notion. The dryad then leaned over to pick up a rock from the ground, she then incanted the words for the spell, "*Solas en lae.*"

The hand-size rock suddenly became imbued with light that was almost unbearable to look at. The druids even had to look away, but as they did, they could see that the shade began to back up a bit further. In that moment, the otherwise harmless spell might have become their best tool in fighting the dark creatures.

"Ti'or," Reeth called out.

On command, the tornado fell away, and as soon as it did, Loria threw the light-imbued-rock into the crowd of the shade that seemed most dense. The intense light pushed away the dark mist surrounding the shade, and the ones closest to the source instantly turned into a cloud of ash.

Without another word from anyone, the other druids returned to their humanoid forms, and began casting the Daylight spell as more rocks were found. The dark humanoids suddenly found themselves scrambling over one another to get away from their one true weakness. Reeth remained in his fire form to protect his companions as they continued their assault.

"Oi, we need a *bigger* rock," Kadrah nearly screamed with excitement.

She retook her earth elemental form and pounded her chest with resounding thuds. Loria knew where the dwarf was going with this idea, and followed up by imbuing the elemental form with the Daylight spell.

The next thing that the shade realized was that they were now being chased by a light-imbued boulder. Kadrah's form rumbled through the forest as she flipped her way to sudden victory. Puffs of ash flew everywhere as she caught up to the retreating warriors who were unable to get away.

Loosely following Kadrah's path of destruction, the other druids fanned out with light-imbued objects. The shade were in full retreat, and after about another hour or so, the dark humanoids' presence was gone from the hills. When it was all over, the druids regrouped at the mouth of their cave.

When the druids returned, they found a young aerin man sitting patiently outside the cave entrance. It was Kormanth but it was like he had aged about 30 years younger. It was to the point that Kormanth was more or less a teenager.

"Hahaha," a small fit of laughter was all the orc could offer the man.

"Spare me your humor, Reeth," the young druid said while sporting a playful grin. His voice even sounded younger.

"*Kormanth?*" Serena guessed after hearing the boy's voice.

The boy was now the center of attention for all the eyes in attendance.

"Alright, before I get asked a million questions," Kormanth began. "When a phoenix dies, it is reborn inside of its own ashes, and it continues its life from an earlier point. I did have a bit of misfortune up on the hill, and this is the result."

"I think he looks adorable," Kadrah chimed in.

When Kormanth gave them a scornful look, the other druids simply laughed at his positive misfortune. When the moment was over, the druids fell silent in contemplation over the ones that they had lost during the night. They even managed to look across the battlefield and to the bodies of the fallen.

"What now, Reeth?" Ti'or asked.

"Let's tend to our friends, return them to the earth, and then we will discuss what to do next," the orc replied.

The druids spent the next several hours giving their fallen comrades a proper burial. Near the top of the hillside, the druids had a clearing marked for their fallen. It was here that they used their druidic magic to open the earth, place the unclothed bodies of the dead deep into the dirt, and then closed the fissures. Through this rite, the druids gave the resources of their bodies back to the planet in which they lived on.

When this was all said and done, the light of the morning sun began to illuminate the sky. The druids meditated in sitting positions until the sun was fully above the horizon. The yellow-orange rays of sunlight warmed their skin from the departing night.

Reeth was the first one to break the silence as he stood up. It was not a common thing for druids to

421

have a sense of vengeance or to disturb the balance of the world, but Reeth was an orc. All the tribes of the orcs believe that they were made by Sol, the God of War and Flame, and war was something that all orcs had in their blood. It was in every fiber of their being.

"Alright, my druids. We are going to Claymore," Reeth said.

CHAPTER TWENTY-ONE
THE RUINS OF ROTOR

It was shortly after Serena left that Henrick, Yobo, and Samuel began to discuss their next step with Jack in attendance as well. At the behest of Drextramlcrosis, Henrick shared that Samuel Fenri would accompany the two travelers on their return to Claymore. The captain did not *outright* protest but the younger Fenri saw no need to rush headlong into another fateful encounter. He told them that he would take care of the planning, and that the remainder of the day should be used for rest and reflection, but in actuality, he just wanted one more day to sip on rum.

The next day came, and according to the calendar inside the tavern, it was the 1st of Smoldethar, the second summer month. The light of the late morning sun poured into the silent pirate cove, and the heat and humidity already began to fill the air. Henrick and Yobo met Samuel and his father at the edge of the docks that faced the lagoon. The two pirates had just finished with their departing, one-arm hug.

"...just make sure that when push comes to shove, ye don't hold back," Jack finished saying as Henrick and Yobo walked up.

As they approached the pirates, Henrick and Yobo couldn't help but notice that the crew of the Wailing Wolf was absent, and both of them silently exchanged looks in search of an answer, but nothing clicked in their minds.

"You two ready?" Samuel asked them.

"*Ready*?" Yobo repeated. He made a quick glance at the ship again before saying, "Are we not taking your ship?"

"Bahahahaha," the two Fenris laughed at the same time.

"The boys've been stuck in prison for the last month. Now what kinda captain do ye believe me to be?" Samuel asked rhetorically. "No. We're gonna walk on the wind today."

Jack stepped away to make sure that he was not a part of the ritual that was about to take place.

"Get over here, and grab a hold of the harness," Samuel instructed as he turned to face the lagoon and the narrow exit channel.

Without much understanding of what was about to happen, Henrick and Yobo walked up to the man from behind. They noticed he was wearing some sort of leather harness that was strapped across his chest, back, over her shoulders, and over his coat. The presence of the harness did nothing to shed light on the situation, but regardless of that, they grabbed ahold of the leather straps.

It was then that small winds began to pick up around them and encircle them as a group. The wind stone began to glow with warm magic. The winds gathered in strength. The dust upon the docks whipped up to make the magical, dancing air visible to all who could see. Stronger and stronger the winds reached the peak of their power. There was then a vibrating, high pitch tone as the magic climbed towards its point of release.

"So, what exactly is go-," Henrick attempted to ask through a yell but was cut short by the release of the magic.

The winds exploded and charged out of the pirate cove like a supersonic bullet. The releasing pressure caused the Wailing Wolf to rock and list inside of its cavernous port. Rum bottles and other trash got sucked out of the cove in a spiraling whirlwind of natural raw power. The sound was that of a loud pop but it was not deafening. The waters of the lagoon and the exit channel split apart on the surface as the winds headed out.

In the aftermath of the spell, Jack was still standing on the docks, and the other three had vanished.

Henrick and Yobo looked around, but everything seemed like a blur to them. They were more or less standing still, but from what they could tell, they were traveling above the surface of the open seas at an impossible speed.

"It's called windwalkin'," the pirate answered Henrick's unfinished question. "The greatest of gifts that the wind titan can bestow upon a mortal."

"This is incredible," Yobo said. "We should be in Claymore, quickly."

"Not quite," Fenri disagreed. "We can't be travelin' across land like this."

Samuel didn't feel like explaining the finer details of his statement, but secretly, he knew that traveling on land in this state was highly dangerous, especially since he knew that the stone, more than likely, hasn't recharged completely from its last use. He had to hope that there was enough power to get them to the shore, at least.

"So, where're we headin'?" Henrick asked.

"The ruins of Rotor," the pirate answered.

Henrick knew about the ruins of Rotor, although he had never been there. It used to be an ancient odum city, but that time period was deep in the past. In a time before the shade initially struck a footing in Terra Sanguinar. However, he did know it was directly west from Claymore City, and a three-day hike to the town of Solace.

Henrick could hardly believe that he was heading home. It's been a month since the shade had ambushed him and his comrades at Wastewatch. It was also a month ago that he was exiled from his home in front of all the royal houses of Claymore, and since then, he traveled to a few places he had only read about in books, places he had never been to before, and he had come into the company of other criminals. He silently scoffed at the idea that he was a criminal of two holds, but he knew it was all so that he could stop an invasion.

He had traveled more than 600 miles on foot to find the ancient artifact. During his journey, he believed that he had found some new friends, and each of them shared some despair at the expense of the dark creatures who sought to destroy his home.

Henrick's mind then changed course and his thoughts fell back to the meeting with the beast in the volcano. He had to wonder if the dragon, with its superiority complex, had actually been showing him a small amount of bearing? But why would it do that? It was a random thought that he quickly dismissed as he moved on the footnotes of the conversation.

Henrick thought about the mantle that he wore. The title of paladin. He couldn't stop thinking of the word and what it meant. He did feel a little satisfied that he had a single word answer to describe what he has been through, and the things that he was able to see and *sense.*

It's what you are, and what you are becoming, the words of the dragon echoed in Henrick's mind.

Furthermore, the Paladin of Nielda did not skip the part where he was not the paladin of the Twins, and apparently, he was not the only paladin in the world. He wondered where the other paladins might be, and if it was possible that they might show up to aid in the coming battle. The thought carried him on until he was truly puzzled.

The contradiction between the stories of the dragon and the water nymph bothered him the most. If the dragon was right, then where was the Paladin of Undine? Henrick's thoughts came to a halt when he heard the voice of his companion.

"You look lost in thought," Yobo asked Henrick.

"I'm just glad to be headin' home," Henrick deflected. "But me mind is heavy on the road that is still before us."

Yobo nodded to his friend. "Indeed. I can't wait to fight these creatures. Between us, and that orb, their reckoning is coming."

An hour had passed by the time the shoreline came into view on the horizon. The morning sun was still upon the cloudless day, and even with their expeditious travel, they could feel the warmth of the bright rays upon them.

The rocketing winds then came to a halt as soon as the black sand of the beach was under their feet. The inertia of the sudden stop was never felt by the windwalkers, but that didn't stop the sand from being flung in every direction. The spell ended as soon as the flying particles came to rest. The feet of the travelers softly came down upon the solid but damp ground. At that moment, Henrick and Yobo released their grip on the harness, and Captain Fenri took it off before throwing it to the side.

"Welcome to the Ruins of Rotor," Samuel said with a wave of his hand.

The landscape beyond the beach was littered with stone pillars, structures, and collapsed buildings. Several feet ahead of them, there was a wide street made of square stone tiles traveling from the beach and on to the main avenue through the lost city.

The design of the stone structures was rather plain, but everything seemed to have a block or rectangular shape to it. Some of the faces to these shapes were chiseled or engraved with symbols that no longer had meaning in the world, and the place was silent like the ghost town that it was.

Henrick took the point as they moved through the ruins, he did have a shield after all.

They walked up the beach and onto the main road. For as far as they could see, smaller pathways branched off into the rest of the city. Some of these other routes were blocked off due to fallen structures while others were nothing more than shaded nooks.

The ruins were interesting to look at, and for Henrick and Yobo, they could only wonder what splendors the city had in ancient times, or perhaps what mysteries lay beneath the rubble. It was also the vast destruction which held many places to hide. Dark corners where monsters could lurk.

After a short jaunt, Captain Fenri's nostrils flared at the scent of something nearby. "Wait. We're not alone," the pirate whispered aloud while pulling Betty from his belt.

The other two turned to regard the pirate, and saw that the man was pointing at a small monument ahead. Standing in the middle of the street, there was a small altar of some kind, and as they got closer, it became apparent that the altar was a sundial. On the other side of the ancient device, on the ground, they could see the clothing of someone, or something.

Henrick signaled Yobo and Fenri to fan out to the sides while he walked straight ahead to the sundial. Together they approached, and as they crept forward, the captain was able to identify the familiar smell. It was the metallic scent of blood.

The scent drove Fenri to rush ahead in order to get a better look. He made a sharp cut in his path until he literally pounced and landed square on the sundial. From his point of view, there was indeed a person, but they were unconscious in a pool of blood that was all over the ground. The pirate noted an empty vial near the still hands of the unknown person. The captain then hopped over the person, and after landing on the other side, he came down to a kneel before them.

Henrick and Yobo joined the pirate at his side. The monk looked down upon this person, and the dark leather armor that held on to their torn cloak. The uniform was too similar to mistake it for anything else, and with that, he knew this to be a member of the Black Lotus.

"It's an assassin," Yobo warned.

As the word came out, a look of prejudice fell upon the figure. Then the three companions saw two daggers lying inside the folds of the cloak, solid evidence that perhaps Yobo's words were true. Fenri collected the two weapons, and put them on his belt.

"A fellow criminal," Fenri offered. The pirate reached over to slightly lift the cowl covering her face. It was the face of a beautiful odum female.

"We should leave them here," Yobo said.

"Agreed," said Henrick. He also knew a good deal about the dark neighbors of Claymore. "The Black Lotus is infamous all over the Sword Kingdoms. This one would sooner slit our throats than accept aid."

Fenri paid no attention to the words of the others. He carefully and quietly put his ax on the ground before reaching into a pocket hidden inside his coat. He produced a small vial of red liquid, and then he tilted the assassin's head back. Henrick and Yobo put narrowed eyes on the captain as he popped the cork off the vial with his teeth before spitting away. He then poured the liquid down her throat, and then stood back up with his ax in hand.

"Now where's the fun in that?" the pirate finally replied, but as he stood there waiting for the potion to take effect, he held Betty at the ready.

After a long moment, the assassin began to make slight movements as she was regaining consciousness. Her fingers and hands twitched. She produced low moaning sounds as she grimaced the pain away. She squirmed uncomfortably as if her large cloak was trying to swallow her, but it was all a good sign that the healing properties were working in her bloodstream. The sensation was like having a bunch of itching under the skin, but it was merely momentary, and the effect was gone almost as soon as it started.

The bright sun of the sky was blinding to her eyes. She reached for her cowl and pulled it over her head more tightly. When she realized that she was still alive, her mind went into a shallow panic. She looked side to side, and grabbed at her waist, but her weapons were gone. She couldn't comprehend what had happened because she thought for sure that she was dead.

Henrick and Yobo readied themselves for anything to happen. Fenri, on the other hand, casually stood there and waited for the assassin to consider that three individuals stood no farther than five feet from her.

The woman lifted her head slightly, and forced her eyes to peer through the dazzling sunlight. She could see the shadows that surrounded her, but whoever these beings were, they were not who she was expecting.

"Ye don't worry. We ain't gonna harm ye," came the unfamiliar voice in the woman's ears. "Not yet."

The assassin then placed a palm upon her belly, the point in which she had been stabbed by a sword. The wound was gone, and so was the pain. It didn't take much for her to understand that whoever these people were, they must have healed her.

She couldn't see their faces against the daylight, but she did see an outstretched hand waiting for her own. She refused to take it, though. She was alive, and that meant these strangers had outlived their usefulness, and to put it simply, she just couldn't trust them. She thought about it more, though, and for the moment, perhaps, she would at least play along until she can fully recover and find her weapons. Her own stubbornness wouldn't go away, though, and she decided to use the support of the sundial to stand up.

"Who are you?" the woman said in a demanding tone. She used a hand to block the sunlight from her eyes, but it did nothing to stop the blinding effect. "You tell us what happened first?"

She couldn't decide if she should make something up, but she also knew that she could not say anything about the Black Lotus and how the guild of assassins was pretty much extinct. If she did that, it meant the word would spread to unknown lengths, and the ever-ominous fear of the Black Lotus would disappear.

She did not underestimate the unknown persons and their intelligence, and since the one in front of her held a weapon, she could guess that they had already surmised her profession.

The assassin then decided that *some* of the truth might be more manageable. She answered with, "I was attacked by a group of shade."

"*The shade*?" Henrick and Yobo said simultaneously.

The woman shot narrow eyes out from under the darkness of her cowl when the two repeated her, and from what she could tell, they knew what she was talking about.

"Who *are* you people?" the assassin asked.

"The name's Samuel Fenri, a pirate of the bay, and Captain of the Wailing Wolf," the captain introduced himself with a bow and his tricorne over his chest.

"I'm Henrick, I'm a soldier from Claymore, and we're actually out here to put a stop to the shade."

"I am Yobo, the last monk of Skyreach."

Something strange fluttered in the mind of the assassin just then. She felt a string being pulled in her heart as her distant memories flew backwards in time. She wanted to throw back the cowl to know that what she just heard wasn't a jest of some kind, but the sunlight was still just too much for her.

"I had a brother named Yobo once, but not from Skyreach," she said.

Yobo was taken off guard by the assassin's statement. His facial expression was a sign of sheer confusion, and he was at a loss for words. His mouth hung open as he tried to comprehend that, perhaps, after all these years, his sister was still alive.

Yobo's heart pounded and struggled at that moment. All his anger, pain, and suffering were from the sight of his parent's death and his sister being carried away by the giant orc. How could this all be happening? How could his sister be a member of the

Black Lotus?   It seemed impossible.   It was impossible, he thought.

The name slipped out of his mouth with a tone of disbelief, "*Kamala*?"

The assassin then turned her head to look at the tall man. Her hood blocked the light from this angle and she could see that he had golden eyes, just like she did. The two of them looked each other in the eyes even though the monk couldn't really see inside the cowl. There was an air of confirmation.

"Yes. That *is* my name," she answered.

"Bahahaha," Fenri busted out laughing at the reunion of the brother and sister, but it wasn't towards the sentiment of it all. It was something else, "Ye see boys, this is the reward fer takin' risks. Hahahaha. You were 'bout to leave 'er fer dead."

The other three then shot the crusty pirate a discerning look.

Henrick thought about the implications of finding this assassin. Was it another fateful meeting? Was she another ally that was ushered into their path to fight the shade? He wasn't sure how to digest this one.   For now, he wouldn't bring himself to judge Yobo and Kamala on whether or not they truly were brother and sister, but he also couldn't ignore the idea of having a member of the Black Lotus in league with them.

The warrior from Claymore then thought about the information that had been laid out. If she was here, injured, and she got attacked by shade, then what does that mean? Did the shade attack the Black Lotus? If so, to what end would that matter? Surely, the Black Lotus wouldn't have stood against them in a war, or at least, that was his thought.

Henrick's eyes became fixated on Kamala as his thoughts dwelled on a missing piece of the puzzle. "The shade that attacked you. Did ye kill 'em?" Henrick asked.

It was then that the rest of them looked at her for an answer.

"There were four of them. I killed one, but another managed to stab me before the sun was up," she explained. "The other three are around here somewhere. I'm sure of it."

All four of them couldn't help but feel a sense of paranoia as the dark creatures could be hiding anywhere. They all looked around at the dark corners and nooks of the ruins, but nothing was alarming.

It was in the brief moment of frantic observance that Henrick decided that this would be a perfect opportunity to try and hone the first ability that came to him. It was the only ability that both the water nymph and the dragon would confirm. The ability to sense darkness in other creatures. As a measure of asking for assistance, he took his shield and put it on the ground with the face of it towards the sky. He kneeled down, and placed his hands on the face. He closed his eyes, and concentrated on what he was trying to do. Although, he had no idea if this was how these sorts of dealings worked.

"Henrick? What is it?" Yobo asked.

The others watched Henrick as well.

"I'm gonna try and find these shade, and then we're gonna take 'em out," Henrick explained.

His eyeballs nearly rolled into his head as he used his mind and heart to search the ruins. Somewhere within the cold, dark, and dry air of the shadows of the ruins, there was an echo. It was the same sensation that overwhelmed that day he mustered before the keep, and it felt just like the shade he fought at Wastewatch. The warning signs of danger buzzed across his skin, and made his hair stand up. He focused on the vibration for a second before opening his eyes. He pointed face to the largest building on the main road to his left.

"They're in that one," Henrick proclaimed.

Yobo began walking towards the building, but Kamala came to stand in his way.

"Wait. You cannot fight them in the dark," the assassin warned.

"We won't have to," Yobo assured her, and after that he looked back at Henrick who was pulling the Esfera de Luz out of his pack.

As soon as Henrick pulled it out of his bag, though, he suddenly realized he hadn't had a chance to try and get the thing to work. He stood there looking at the object for a few seconds before Fenri figured out what was going on, and considering his own experience with magic items, the captain knew exactly how to explain it.

"Just tell the thing what ye want it to do," Fenri said. "I'm sure the *boss* told ye not to play rough with it. So, just tell it to shine like a campfire, or a torch."

In the midst of the captain explaining it, the images of the words popped into Henrick's mind, and the artifact took those images as the commands to come. It was then that the orb lit up with a brightness that could even be seen against the morning sunlight.

"There we go," Henrick said.

With that, the four of them walked towards the building in question. From what they could see, the building was remarkably sound. The structure still had two wooden doors, although they were barely hanging on to their rusted hinges.

Fenri moved up ahead, like he did before, and crept up to the door. He peered inside through the gaps in the wood. Thin beams of sunlight filtered its way to the dark inside from the weathered wood ceiling above. The captain wasn't there to observe with his eyes only, though, he also sniffed the air that flowed from inside. The sound from his nostrils was quite loud.

But then something happened. The captain's eyes began to water, and he instantly swatted a hand to cover his nose as the acute senses of his nostrils rose to their heights. He held himself up against the wall of the building with his free hand, but his nostrils were already out of control, and he fell down into a squat. He tried to not cry, but his face became flushed against his resistance. He rose to his feet once more, feeling the rush reaching its peak.

Yobo asked in a concerned manner, "What's wrong?"

The captain faced away from the others, and made one large inhale before, "*Aachhooo!*"

"A sneeze?" Henrick mocked the pirate.

Fenri used his nose to inhale a bit, but all he found was the sound of flapping mucus. He used the sleeve of his coat to wipe the wetness that ran from his snout. He answered Henrick's inquiry with a congested voice, "It be dusty in there. I can't smell a thing, now."

Henrick scoffed at the pirate before returning his eyes to the still closed doors. Yobo stood at the opposite side of the door from Fenri. Kamala was right behind him.

"I don't see anything in there," Yobo said as he, too, peaked through the door. "There is light, though, and another door in the back."

"That must be where they are," Henrick guessed.

Yobo tried the rusty door handle, but it neglected to turn. By the time that the monk took his hand off, Fenri had recovered from his sneezing, and saw that the door was not cooperating. The pirate rubbed his bearded chin and pondered at the jammed knob.

"Allow me," Samuel said. He took a position before the door, and without a word of what he was going to do, he gave it a bashing with the bottom of his boot. After a few kicks against the aged wood, though, the door just fell apart into pieces. The clattering of planks resounded against the stone walls. "Aye. There we go."

"Yobo," Henrick said to get the tall man's attention before handing the orb to him.

Being the one with the shield, Henrick went in first with his shield up in front of him. Fenri followed just behind him with his ax ready. Yobo and Kamala were behind them.

Once they were out of the direct sunlight, their eyes were able to adjust and see the room in its entirety. Between that and the light from outside, the ancient interior seemed like it was a living room or a lobby of some kind. Ruined furniture lined the walls while a table sat in the middle. Scraps of moldy cloth were scattered across the floor as if a rug or carpet used to cover the stone floor. There was another wooden door at the far end, like Yobo said, which no doubt led further into the building. The ceiling was nearly 15 feet high, and there was no second story of any kind.

With the sunlight gone, Kamala had removed her cowl to reveal her straight black hair, and her eyes, but they were not gold like Yobo's. Instead, the assassin's irises carried a vibrant pale green light.

Everything, so far, appeared to be safe inside the structure. The paladin could still feel the dark presence he had honed in on, but against those feelings, Henrick caught something in his eyes that none of them noticed before.

Henrick pointed to Fenri's belt, and said, "Fenri, look."

The captain looked down to his waist to see the pair of daggers that he had swiped from Kamala. The silvery, short blades had a dim green glow upon the metal.

"Ah, enchanted," the pirate remarked.

The siblings also looked, and Kamala immediately darted her eyes upon her weapons.

Fenri smirked at the assassin, but it was more out of male desire than anything else. Other than that, however, he did manage to catch her eyes on his waist, and the daggers. Without another thought, he returned the weapons to her hands.

"Don't ye be losin' these, lass," the pirate said to her.

She took the daggers back, but without any acknowledgement to his demeanor.

After that, Henrick and Samuel began moving towards the door at the far end of the large room. If the shade were still around, Henrick was almost sure that they would be waiting for them in the next room.

"So, what do these shady things do?" Fenri asked.

"They're creatures of Abyss. They can teleport quickly, they show no mercy, and they have no honor," Henrick explained in brief.

The pirate then gave the ancient furnishings in their current room a glance, and he was curious about a detail that Henrick had yet to bring up. Fenri then asked, "Do they smell like ash?" Even as he asked the question, he took into account that none of the old furniture had signs of burning of any kind.

"I can't say fer sure," Henrick replied.

"You *don't* say?" the pirate spoke in a rather cocky tone which drew a puzzled look from Henrick. The pirate spoke while keeping his gaze on the furniture, but after another second, his eyes fell straight down to the floor as he wrestled a finger and thumb on his hairy chin. Then the wrestling stopped suddenly, as if the pirate caught a very slight noise at the very edges of his keen hearing. "Hahahaha," the pirate started laughing loudly through a fiendish smile. "They're *definitely* in there."

"I'll open the door, roll that thing inside," Henrick whispered to Yobo.

Yobo offered a nod, and held the orb as if he was going to bowl with it. Henrick reached for the door knob with a tight grip. As the air in the room suddenly grew serious, Fenri brought up his ax, Betty, and Kamala readied her daggers.

Henrick then opened the door with a single, fluid motion, but the wooden portal was old and rotted, and the door knob was the string holding the door together. When that string finally got pulled, the boards of the door flew apart in a billow of dust. Yobo didn't wait for the cloud to settle, and he threw the orb inside the room.

"*Ksssss!*" came the hissing noise from inside.

Yobo spoke as quickly as he could when he heard the noise, "What was *that*?"

Just before the plume of dirt and dust evaporated, a dark, elongated limb reached out from the now lighted room. The sinister claw grappled and sank into Henrick's chest as though he did not wear armor before pulling the warrior into the room. The momentum and sudden shock forced the paladin to drop his sword and shield, but then he grabbed at the limb with both of his hands. He tried to pull the claw off of him, but there was no use. Henrick then felt waves of cold numbness pulsing throughout his body like his life energy was being sucked away.

Fenri, being the closest to Henrick, swatted with Betty, and made a heaving overhead strike at the limb that grabbed the warrior. The blade of the ax never found its mark, and instead, the chopping head was intercepted by the jagged blade of the dark creature that walked out from the doorway.

"Hahaha," the captain laughed as the blades clanged and locked against each other. That wasn't what made the pirate blurt out though. It was his own unpredictability and thrill of chaos.

Fenri completely let go of his ax, and then grabbed the shade with his bare hands. The pirate didn't care how much dark mist surrounded the creature; he snatched the thing from around the collar, and proceeded to hip toss it into the table at the center of the room. The shade crashed into the wood before it exploded into planks and splinters. The pirate recovered Betty and chased after his target that was struggling to get back up.

441

Yobo and Kamala stepped forward to meet the second, and third, adversaries that walked through the door. The siblings engaged the new shade targets.

Henrick continued to struggle to get the dark creature's claw out of his body, and with every passing second, he could feel himself losing strength. With the light of the Esfera de Luz in the room, he could see that this creature was not a shade, and whatever it was, it felt far more malevolent than the shade. Henrick gritted his teeth as the pain continued to surge through his body like a poison.

The shadow demon, for that's what it was, cackled at Henrick as if mocking him; as if letting him know that there was nowhere to go. As the demon drew the life force from Henrick, its own power was growing, and it knew that the human could sense it. The demon wanted to drink in the fear and despair of its victim, but from this mortal, he sensed none of those things.

Henrick's arms were losing feeling, and his breath was getting heavier and deeper. He needed this thing to let up for just a moment. However, it was becoming apparent that the time would never come, and his own time was running out.

Through all of it, though, his will did not waiver. He continued to struggle and fight even though it was useless. Henrick grimaced and gritted his teeth, and it was then that something from his subconscious began to step forward as the images from his eyes grew dark.

It was his divine sense. It was this extraordinary ability that sparked him along his fateful journey from Claymore. It allowed him to sense the darkness around the King of Claymore, and since then, he had been able to sense the darkness of the shade, a watery envoy of the Twins, and a dragon. But in all that time, there was one thing he hadn't sensed. There was one direction that hadn't occurred to him.

The darkness within himself.

The idea never became a thought. Why would it? There was no explanation or evidence that the divine sense could be used to find something inside the soul. As Henrick teetered on edge of death in this moment, the evidence was revealing itself. His spirit was hesitant on taking this path, but he knew he had to do something, or he was going to be this demon's next meal.

Even though the images were dark, Henrick forced his eyes shut before searching within himself. He searched his soul and his heart as tools to dig deep. He reached inward with his feelings like a shovel. The leeching claw from the demon begged his attention, but he could not afford to listen to it. After what seemed like a long moment, he went into a trance that seemed to carry his spirit away from the world.

It was then that Henrick found himself standing on the surface of an endless body of water. The waters were calm, they were dark blue against the darkness. Up above, and all across the sky of this strange place were the thousands of stars that dotted the nightly sky.

The claw of the demon was absent. No longer buried in his body. He wondered what just happened, and that led him to a possible conclusion. Did he die?

"Hello," Henrick called out, his voice echoing off into nowhere.

There was no answer in return. Not immediately, but then Henrick felt the presence of another. A darkness. When he turned around, he saw a small orb floating above the watery surface that shimmered with lavender moonlight.

The paladin approached the magical orb, and just as he began to, a figure revealed itself. It was the ghost of a woman that stood on the other side of the floating sphere. She was devoid of any finer details, but her translucent silhouette glowed with a shade of light blue.

"Henrick," the woman called him, her voice echoing in the void of the strange dimension. *"I'm so proud of you."*

Henrick couldn't explain how he felt at that moment. Her voice was unknown to him, but it had a warming familiarity to it. He found that he was unable to formulate a thought or response to the ghost, but he nonetheless had to wonder who she was.

"You have made it this far," the ghost continued. *"And it is time for you to know more about Nielda. She is the Goddess of the Moons, yes, but it is her job, and also yours, to fight the forces of darkness, with darkness. In the absence of light, there is darkness. Nielda, with the help of her mother, Lumina, has learned to use the light, and the darkness, to create moonlight.*

"There is nothing else in this universe of ours, that Abyss fears most, then to have his own element turned against him." She then pointed with a hand to the floating orb. *"This is the moonlight that resides in you.*

The power that has been entrusted to you. Remember this saying: 'Embrace the night, and from the moons, call forth the light'."

The ghost then waved her hand as if to fling the flickering magic orb straight into Henrick's chest. As soon as the magic contacted him, he was sent spiraling back to where he was. At the claw of the shadow demon.

Deep inside the core of his being, he felt himself pushing back the foul energy drain of the abyssal creature. He sensed that which was buried deep inside him. The lavender light of the moon shone with the radiance of Nielda in his mind's eye.

Henrick's eyes finally opened, his vision was no longer blackened, and he brought his gaze down upon his hands. They quivered as they renewed the fight against the buried claw of the demon.

Embrace the night, and from the moons, call forth the light, the phrase rang in his head. And that was when Henrick manifested the divine energy to the surface, covering his body in a veil of moonlight. Pulsating thumps of magic worked through his body, and it began to restore his strength. The moonlight seared the claw of the shadow demon, but Henrick could feel the vile creature resisting.

The Paladin of Nielda drew all the moonlight to his hands. He raised an arm into a coiled fist before smashing down on the stretched limb of the shadow demon like a divine hammer. The demon's arm shattered like it was made of glass. It released a hissing howl of pain and hatred. Henrick fell to a knee as the demon's hold on him was gone, and then he was left with just one problem.

He was *furious.*

Without hesitation, he charged headlong into the demon and pinned it against the wall with a giant thud. The demon did not flinch against the damage, and it lurched over with its elongated neck to bite at Henrick's face, tearing off flesh from his jawline. Blood exploded all over his face.

"*Raahh!*" Henrick unleashed a roar of bestial wrath.

The paladin resummoned the moonlight to his fists before he began to beat the face of the demon. This time, it was the demon that had nowhere to run. Henrick held the demon in place by the throat and delivered punch after punch. The demon took massive damage at the hands of Henrick's knuckles, chunks of its head crumbling apart against the divine pressure. After a while, the paladin could sense the darkness fading from the creature with each hit, and just as the darkness was getting ready to bottom out, he reared back before delivering a fatal uppercut.

A shriek of pain and horror came from the shadow demon as it went through the throes of death. The demonic creature then went silent, then limp, and then it began to dissolve into nothingness as its dark spirit returned to its home plane.

In the other room, Yobo held the stance of Cova's Maw as he stood toe to toe with his foe. This had been his first encounter with the creatures that he vowed to hunt down and destroy. The monk relished the moment while he focused on dodging each attack, watching every angle the jagged sword came from, and this was all in an attempt to learn how the creature maneuvered.

However, the shade had been doing the same thing, and in the midst of the missing attacks, the dark warrior changed its movement patterns mid-swing, and doubled back with its sword. The feint was enough to play at Yobo's confidence and throw the monk off-guard. The wicked blade came across at the large man, and the tip of the blade managed to tear a shallow cut across his pectorals in the opening of his saam.

Yobo did not grimace in pain nor did he flinch. Instead, the monk took the split-second opportunity as the shade recovered by stepping forward and launching a heavy haymaker at the shade's face. The connection resounded with a crunch as if the dark creature's helmet had been slammed with a pile of bricks.

The shade reeled backwards from the sheer force, and it had no presence of mind to consider how surprised it was that the monk was capable of such physical power. It tried to recover quickly, but the half-dryad was already upon him.

The tree trunks for legs that the monk had coiled and whipped at the shade with all the man's weight behind it. Yobo struck with a flurry of three kicks, and he made sure he led with the ball of his heel. The shade sensed the peril before it as it hissed in defiance.

Yobo's opponent sought to meld with the shadows in the room, and shadowstep out of the way. Or at least, it would have wanted to. The light that poured into the building from outside, and through the ceiling, prevented it from transforming into mist. Suddenly, it was too late for the shade to move. The dark creature cursed at the monk in its vile language.

The monk finished his combo with a flying side kick that connected at the chest. The cracking of armor plates and ribs sealed its fate. The force of the kick sent the shade flying back into the rear chamber where Henrick was pulled into just a second before. As he watched his adversary crash against the floor its body began to evaporate.

In the reflection of his small victory, Yobo didn't look to acknowledge the small wound that he had sustained. There was also no need to, because the sensation of the superficial injury had disappeared when it healed itself.

In the end, though, the success of the skirmish was all that mattered, and by the time Henrick and Yobo were finished with their respective opponents, Kamala and Captain Fenri had finished with theirs.

"Is everyone good?" Fenri asked as he came to join Yobo and Kamala.

No sound came from Henrick, however.

The three of them walked to the back room with their weapons drawn, but they quickly put them away when they saw the man standing over some of the furniture in this room. The chamber resembled an old bedroom or perhaps a barracks. There were a number of collapsed beds, broken cabinets, footlockers covered in white mold, and weathered nightstands. The bed in which Henrick stood over silently was still in one piece.

As the companions regrouped by Henrick, he spoke, "I've seen this in a dream."

Upon the bed was a skeleton. It had weathered bones, cobwebs, and a layer of dirt and dust. Henrick's attention was focused on the skeleton and it was because of what the skeleton wore. It was an intricate suit of chainmail that was made of lavender-dyed metal links, and there was a design up and down the center of the torso that looked like a spout of silver waves. There was also a matching helmet on the floor to the side.

"Ye had a dream of the bed, or the skeleton?" the pirate jested.

Henrick didn't seem to pay Fenri any mind. Instead, he began to remove the skeletal remains, and the grime from the armor as he gave it a closer look. The armor had no signs of fatigue or tarnish, and the leather sheets on the inside holding it all together seemed to be in good condition as well. The paladin had to wonder how long this had been here.

"Give me a few minutes to put this on," Henrick requested from the others.

Henrick removed his breastplate, which had holes and rust in many places. Once it was off, he tossed it upon the ground. It didn't seem to matter to him anymore, especially if this other armor was in better condition.

The dream in which he had seen this armor before seemed to compel him in the moment. First, the shield, and now, this armor. What was the purpose of his dream? What was it trying to tell him, or show him before? Was all of this *really* preordained in some mystical timeline? Or was it merely a preparation for what was to come?

Most puzzling of all, as the memory was fresh in his mind, was the ghost that had just spoken to him. He made the connection, and immediately suspected the woman-spirit to be the same one from the vision. However, he still didn't know who she was.

Then the other half of the dream showed up. The part where Claymore was burning, and the shade invading. He had to wonder if that would come to pass as well. Would all of this be for nothing? For as far as he had come, would it all end badly? The thoughts plagued his mind as he took a few minutes to don the new armor.

When he was done, he gathered the Esfera de Luz and replaced it in his backpack. He walked out of the room, and regrouped with the others outside. The armor glistened under the sunlight, and Henrick was surprised at how well-fitted the armor was as he moved around in it. When put the helmet on, he was equally impressed at how the thin T-shaped visor did not impede his vision by a whole lot.

When he was done fawning over the armor, this was when he noticed there was still plenty of time left in the day, but at the same time, they were losing precious time.

Henrick said, "Alright, let's go. We must get to Solace."

CHAPTER TWENTY-TWO
WHISPERS IN THE KEEP PART THREE

"Insuno vox transitum, Umbra Hadara," Anima Scarm spoke the incantation.

The dark orb that sat on the pedestal came to life with magic just as it did so many times before when the shade attempted to contact his commander. The lightless chamber that was hidden in Claymore Keep's dungeon hummed with the arcane energies that made the connection to the homeland of the shade.

"Anima?" came the familiar voice from inside the dark purple orb.

"Umbra Hadara, I've come to make my report," the shade said. "The warband took heavy losses at the hands of the druids, but the troops reported them as scattered and broken. The Black Lotus has been completely wiped out as well."

"This is good news, for once," the umbra said. "What of the portal stone?"

"Their demon leader destroyed the stone before we could capture it," Scarm explained.

There was a moment of silence from Hadara, an air of irritation that Scarm knew all too well. "Then perhaps I spoke too soon."

The facial expressions from both of the shade leaders could not be shared, but Scarm scowled at his commander. In fact, he was furious. He could not wait for the umbra to arrive in Claymore. The moment he would lay eyes on Hadara, he would strike him dead, and take full control of the armies of Lacus Perdia. He would return to the homeland as a hero after Claymore's fall.

"But no matter," Hadara changed his tune quickly, and it caught Scarm off-guard. "You were not there."

Umbra Hadara *almost* sounded sympathetic for Scarm's position in the dealings of the Sword Kingdoms, but the shade in the dungeon dismissed that thought. More than likely his commander was attempting to be patient as the day of the coming battle was growing near.

"With the portal stone destroyed, we will have to march to Claymore. In this case, we have three generators that we will be escorting through the wasteland," the commander said. "In 20 days, the humans will find their demise on the horizon, and then we will begin the assault immediately. We will be leaving Lacus Perdia today."

"How much of the legion will be arriving in Claymore?" the Anima asked.

Hadara let the question hang in suspense, and then he answered, "There will be nine of the ten divisions arriving. Plus, we have a surprise for the blood bags."

The connection in the orb was then severed. The room grew quiet once more as the magic energy in the room dissipated. Scarm stood by the pedestal as the information sank in. The coming invasion was going to be glorious, and soon he would no longer have to deal with the humans. He gathered himself, and left the chamber. He closed the hidden door, and departed the dungeon.

Inside the hidden chamber, the air became disturbed by a low clatter. The cabinet in the corner of the room had gone untouched by the shade, but now, the dark humanoid was gone. The stirring in the tall piece of furniture slowly pushed the doors of the cabinet open. With just a crack, the creature inside had enough space to see outside of it. To the hidden person, it seemed to be clear, but the situation was still highly dangerous.

When the hidden creature decided that it was safe to come out – he did.

The half-dryad ranger, Sirus the Hood, slipped out of the cabinet. He softly came to his feet before closing the cabinet doors behind him. Once out, he performed some quick stretching exercises as he had been cooped up in that cabinet for nearly six hours waiting for his target to show up.

The mission was a success, though, and now he had proof that not only did the ancient enemy of Claymore lurk about in the darkness of the Keep's dungeon, it was also communicating to someone else, and soon, he would report this information to Lady Darkbane, the person who gave him this assignment. First, though, he would take care of the object in the room.

From his belt, Sirus unhooked the light mace he had brought for this mission. Previously, he had hid himself in a cell the last time the shade came for a visit, and before the dark humanoid was done using the crystal ball, he had exited the dungeon.

Now, he stood before the communication device and glared down upon it. Without letting another second of hesitation or reflection get the better of him, he brought up the mace, high above his head, and swung it downward with the weight of his shoulder and torso. The blunt head of the weapon crashed into the glass-like surface.

The orb shattered into a thousand pieces. The magic contained inside puffed out as if gas was being released from the pressure. Streaks of dark blue magic energy arced out from the destruction like tiny lightning bolts. After a few seconds, the magic dissipated.

The shade now had no way of coming back here to contact whoever it was on the other side. However, that meant that the shade would soon find out about this, unless some action was taken.

Sirus, with his job completed, came before the hidden door and activated the secret button on the inside wall. The scrapping of stone was loud, but he was certain that the shade was gone. Once the door was fully open, he looked out beyond the cell door. The coast was clear. He activated the secret button inside the cell to close the door. After that, he snuck through the remainder of the dungeon and made his way out.

CHAPTER TWENTY-THREE
A BIT OF SOLACE

The last few days had been uneventful, and fortune remained on the side of the companions who had left the Ruins of Rotor three days ago. They were able to camp and sleep each night without any disturbance. Unless you count the grumbling of a sober pirate who neglected to ration the rum hidden inside his coat.

They had already begun their start on the present day, and it was noon by the time the morning clouds had burned away. It was upon this hour that the heat of the summer set in and the first signs of their next destination showed up on the horizon.

Fields of tall crops, like corn and wheat, covered most of the landscape as it began to flatten out from the otherwise rocky grassland, and as the borders of the wilderness fell behind them, a light breeze, carrying the scent of livestock, greeted them.

"Where are we?" Yobo asked. "I've never seen anything like this."

"This is the outskirts of Solace," Henrick answered. "It's a farmin' village. These're the corn fields."

As Henrick explained this to the others, they approached the fields and came on to a beaten road. Between the corn stalks and the endless avenue ahead of them, it felt more like they were walking down a hallway. Yobo and Fenri felt as though it would continue for miles and would never end. Henrick, as well as Kamala, knew that that was not the case.

"When we get to this village, what is our plan?" Kamala asked with slight agitation in her voice. She continued to feel uncomfortable under the sunlight. Furthermore, it felt like the eyes of the unknowing were watching her. Whereas, at night, she could be invisible, and her eyes could see better. For now, she had to keep the cowl over her head, and keep it low.

"There's a bounty hunter who I'm hopin' is still in town. If he's there, I'm gonna call in a favor," he answered. "If he's not there, we'll have to get a messenger from the local guards, which I would like to avoid."

"Can we trust this bounty hunter?" Yobo asked.

"With the price on my head, I'm sure of it," Henrick elaborated, which drew in a surprising look from Captain Fenri.

"Hahaha," the captain busted out in laughter. "Now ye be speakin' me language."

Henrick offered a smirk at the pirate's humor, but he didn't turn around to show it. He then added, "After that's done, I'm gonna see if he can get one of the house leaders to come out, and escort us into the kingdom."

A short time after the dialogue, the four of them passed by a couple of flag posts that held the red and black banner of Claymore. Even with the heat of the day, it was the reminder of those banners that prompted Henrick to put his new helmet on. He thought that if his face was hidden, perhaps no one would recognize him from the wanted posters that might still be up. Of course, he hadn't shaved since he left, and now, he had a nasty scar on his jawline from a monster bite.

Eventually, the corn fields fell away to smaller fields with smaller crops. On one side, there was a field of bushes that had purple flowers, and on the other side, there was a field of growing melons, and from the looks of it, they were cantaloupes.

The companions scanned the open air of the changing environment, and it was by this time that the village of Solace came into the far reaches of view. As they got closer, the beaten road became one covered in packed gravel and small rocks.

Henrick led the way with his helmet still on. At first, he felt a bit worried as his mind quickly revisited the idea of being recognized, but he soon countered his own thoughts with a variety of opposing factors.

The first one was his thoughts falling on one of his companions, more specifically Yobo's sister, Kamala. She still wore her dark uniform, and although nothing on the outside screamed that she was a member of the Black Lotus, the Claymoran Army was still trained to identify them. Not to mention, she would still be the more suspicious looking of the group. Henrick also thought, as a side note, that it was weird that the two had just been reunited, but while on the road, they hardly said anything to each other.

Then Henrick thought about Samuel, and he could only laugh inside his own head as the pirate would look *completely* out of place in the village, and in the city. He thought, perhaps, that someone might mistake him for a bard or a jester. He silently swore to himself that he would fall over and laugh hysterically at the man should that happen.

By the time Henrick got to the end of his thoughts, the sides of the road became traced with simple wooden fencing as the group entered into the village proper. Small homes came to neighbor each other on both sides of the road. However, the density of the structures had almost hidden the guard shack that was directly ahead of them.

One of the guards up ahead took note of the approaching visitors, and that drew them to alert the other three guards. In no time at all, the four guards stood up from their bench inside the shaded structure. Their eyes beamed at the reflection of light on the shiny armor that was coming their way. However, the light did not blind them to the fact that

459

each of the companions was uniquely dressed from the others.

"Hold up, travelers," one of the guards called out. "Who are you?"

Henrick could see that this one was a sergeant, just like he was, but the paladin hesitated for a second as he did not want to give his name. There was still a small chance that, even after a month, the whole Claymoran Army was on the lookout for him, but he struggled inside himself at that moment as he did not want to lie.

The hesitation would go unnoticed, however, as Fenri stepped forward in his casual, nonchalant manner. He walked right up to the sergeant, stopped, and then swung his hands out wide as if all purpose in life was fleeting.

"By the gods, man, tell me ye got alcohol here?" Fenri asked the guard. The pirate's words soon took on a delirious tone, but no one else could tell if it was an act or if he was for real. "We've...been on the road since...since Harmon. I need a *drink*."

"Oh. You're adventurers," the sergeant established. The lead guard turned to look inward at the village, and pointed in the direction he knew that the tavern was in. "You can find the Three Moos right over there."

Without another moment wasted, Captain Fenri led the walk into the village. The other three followed closely behind as the guards returned to their lackluster job. With Henrick's shallow level of paranoia, he was actually impressed that the captain's dialogue got the soldiers to stand down, and with that, his thoughts returned to the path ahead.

A few minutes later, the group arrived at the Three Moos, and they had the place all to themselves as no other customers had come in, yet. Henrick knew that it was the middle of the week, and the calendar on the wall only confirmed it. This meant that the farmers, especially given the hour, were out tending to their fields and homes.

Fenri wasted no time and engaged the barkeep. As the barkeep worked on getting a pitcher of ale, the pirate couldn't help but notice the wanted poster on the wall nearby. He also saw the price tag on Henrick's head, and then begrudgingly threw a silent curse at the dragon who had sent him on this path. However, based on the sketch, he did notice that since the hanging of the poster, Henrick's hair was longer and he had a short beard now. The captain then smirked as the opportunity shined in his devilish mind.

The barkeep handed over the large drink, and Fenri tossed the required coin on the surface of the bar. The pirate turned to rejoin his traveling companions, and sat down at the table they had picked out.

"Tell me, Henrick," the pirate began while speaking aloud. "What'll it take to *not* turn in the bounty over there?"

The mention drew the eyes of the others to the poster on the wall. Then, they all looked at Henrick, who was still wearing his helmet. However, in the interest of Fenri's challenging words, he took the thing off and set it on the table. He narrowed his eyes at the pirate who couldn't take his focus away from the ale he had already started drinking. The pirate knew he was being looked at.

"Me boss told me to come with you," Fenri recalled as he prepared to lay out the *finer details* of the undocumented contract. The pirate then rubbed his chin through his black beard. "He never said in what manner I had to follow you, nor did he suggest I go back empty-handed. Hahaha." Fenri's laughter was proof that he thoroughly entertained himself, but also that he may be serious.

If there had been a spark of tension in the air at that moment, it would never come to fruition as the four companions had their attention drawn to the individuals walking through the door of the tavern. Yobo, Fenri, and Kamala had no idea who the armed strangers were, but Henrick knew.

"I knew I smelled money when I saw that shiny armor walking through town," Gunner said as he walked through the door.

Behind the bounty hunter, his own companions, Bertil and Indra followed him inside. It was Bertil, the black fur huntari, who looked around at the table, and noticed that someone was not with their mark.

"Where's the girl that was with you?" Bertil asked, referring to Serena.

"She had to go, but hopefully she'll be here soon," Henrick answered.

"*Really!* That means no one to get in the way of collecting that bounty," Indra suggested to the other bounty hunters.

"Hahaha," Fenri began with a laugh. "Get in line, lass. If anyone is collectin' that money, it's me. I have him under my custody as we speak."

"I think *you* should get in line," Gunner retorted. "If it wasn't for his friend's firecat, we wouldn't be having this negotiation."

462

"*Oh?* We're negotiatin' now," Fenri said with high eyebrows.

"Well, I figure 5,000 dags is still pretty decent to split four ways," Gunner suggested. "That's still more than six months' worth of pay 'round here."

Henrick buried his face in his palms as he listened to the prattling of those talking about the bounty on his head which forced him to let out a deep sigh. At the end of his exhale, though, he opened his eyes, and peered through the gaps in his fingers as the thought had just popped into his head. Henrick stood up suddenly, and everyone fell silent.

"*Yes*," Henrick announced. "That's a pretty good idea." He then turned to look at Gunner, and said, "I'm gonna need ye to go to Claymore and get Lady Darkbane. Tell her, and only her, that I am in custody in Solace."

Everyone eyed him curiously.

Gunner then rolled his eyes around in thought as he saw the direction of the idea. He asked, "And you think this will get us paid?"

Henrick only held his confident look at Gunner in confirmation.

"Very well," Gunner added before looking at his two accomplices. "I'll go. You two stay here and make sure our prize goes *unmolested*. I should be back tomorrow." He finished his statement with a quick, shooting glare at the unknown pirate captain at the table.

"I appreciate yer honor," Henrick offered to Gunner.

"Don't bother with your thanks," the bounty hunter said. "I can't ignore what you did for us. From one Claymoran to another."

At the end of his statement, Gunner left the tavern. He walked down the road a bit, heading east as he did, and it wasn't long before he was gone from sight.

Just as one was leaving, it would seem that another was arriving. Through the windows of the tavern, Bertil's keen eyes noticed some new movement on the road heading west. There was a group of six diverse individuals, but as the eyes of the black-furred sorcerer continued to scan the party, she noticed a familiar face within their ranks.

"There she is," the huntari exclaimed while bumping a hand on Henrick's shoulders.

It prompted Henrick and the others to look out the window as well.

"Who is she with?" Yobo asked aloud, and rhetorically, as no one else could have possibly known that answer.

"I guess we'll find out," Henrick replied. He moved to the door and stuck his head and arm out of the doorframe. He waved at Serena, and her group, before calling out, "Serena! In here!"

The call beckoned the stares from the druids by her side.

A short distance away, the obvious question came from the druids' leader, Reeth, "Is that the one you spoke of?"

"It is," Serena answered.

On their journey to Solace, the druids had asked Serena many questions about the coming conflict. They wanted to know who else was involved, what led her to hike across the region in search of a fabled artifact, and why they were heading into a hornet's nest that despised the use of magic. She filled them in and elaborated to them on what she knew, but she made it a point to explain that this person, Henrick, was someone of high interest to the Twins.

Given the recent tragedies at the hands of the shade, Serena could not help but feel a little bit of relief in seeing her friend's face. She then felt a swelling inside her chest, but just as the feelings came on, she had to push them down.

It was her station as a druid that forbade her from any personal interests that she might have in development. The druids of the Ember Grove were meant to stay focused on preserving balance in the world, and distractions would most certainly take away from those important duties. With her druid kin by her side, she did not want to alarm them to any feelings that she may have towards Henrick, but at the same time, she also did not know how intricate her feelings might be. For now, she thought, she could at least remain on positive, friendly ground.

After the initial wave down, Henrick went back inside, and waited for Serena's group to enter the establishment. The giant orc of brown skin was the first to walk in, he was followed by Serena, Loria, Ti'or, Kadrah, and Kormanth.

At the sight of Reeth, Yobo found small hints of prejudice seeping into his mind as his memory thought back to his encounter at Planesgate. Of course, that orc had blue skin, and this one was clearly different. The monk could not, however, dismiss his own imaginations that this orc could quite possibly be just as savage. Yobo also noticed that this orc did not carry any weapons, and because of that, he had to wonder what the orc was capable of.

Serena came into the tavern and came to stand before Henrick. Her eyes immediately noticed the scar on his jawline before she managed to see his new armor. She then leaned in to give him a one-armed hug over his shoulder

Henrick could sense her conservative demeanor, but he decided not to pry, and so he returned the firm embrace. Otherwise, he was equally relieved to see her again.

"I see you found something new," Serena said as she looked upon the shiny armor.

"Aye," Henrick replied. "Found it after we had a run in with a group of shade."

"So, you *fought* with them, too?" Serena said.

"*Too*?" Henrick questioned, and as he did, his eyes wandered on to the other druids in her company.

"The shade sent hundreds upon us," Reeth responded. "They took five of our kin before we could defeat them."

"Then you have seen better luck than I," Kamala chimed in. At this point, on hearing that the shade were attacking other groups, she suddenly felt this meeting in the Three Moos was no longer coincidence and that she could now probably trust everyone in the room. Due to this revelation, and her comment, the eyes of everyone else was upon her as she continued, "The Black Lotus has been completely wiped out by these wraiths. They, too, sent hundreds after us. For all I know, I could be the only one left."

An air of unfamiliarity came over Serena at that moment, and Yobo was the first one to catch the peculiar glare during Kamala's statements.

"Serena," Yobo said to get her attention. With a wave of his hand, the monk introduced his sibling and said, "This is my sister, Kamala."

Serena regarded the two siblings, while also looking into those glowing green eyes, "You have a *sister*?"

Suddenly, Henrick made note of his own rudeness and shifted the dialogue. He said to all in attendance, "Oh. Where're me manners? The name's Henrick."

"I'm Bertil."

"Indra."

"My name is Reeth," the orc introduced himself before pointing his hand at his druid companions. "This is Loria, Ti'or, Kadrah, and Kormanth."

"I am Yobo of Skyreach," the monk followed up.

At the mention of Skyreach, the flared ears of Loria twitched in that moment as the emotions bubbled inside of her. She said, "*Skyreach*? Was there a dryad there named Adare? And what happened up there?"

"The shade *butchered* the dryads," the monk answered, a hint of angst in his words. "And yes, there was a monk named Adare."

The dryad druid silently brooded with Yobo; the want of revenge could be felt in the room. The sentiments would soon become short lived as the last person, who purposefully withheld his introduction until the end, suddenly stood up with his empty pitcher raised high.

"Captain Samuel Fenri at yer service," the pirate stated loudly. After a second's pause, "Now, if we're all gonna stand around, and toy around, and fool around," Fenri finished his statement with a wink to Serena. "We're gonna need more drinks."

It was obvious that the pirate was suffering from a slight buzz, but that didn't stop the pirate from going back to the bar to get another pitcher.

"It's not a bad idea," Henrick offered with a shrug.

"I'll second that," Kadrah added.

After a long moment, the Three Moos suddenly became a busy place. Everyone was ordering a drink while some of them ordered food. Everyone was divided amongst the tables in the tavern, but at one of the larger tables, Henrick, Yobo, Reeth, Serena, Kamala, and Fenri sat.

During this time, several citizens of the village came through the tavern, but none of them seemed to stay for very long. The sight of so many strangers gave an uneasy feeling. The barkeep did not complain, though. The visitors were actually bringing him more coin than he was used to during the middle of the week.

As the last villager departed, Henrick looked around the room, and at everyone that had come together for this moment. He felt hopeful. He had wondered if he would find more allies, and with the help of his new friends, there was more than he was expecting.

"So many of us have been affected by the shade," Henrick let the thought slip aloud before taking a sip of his ale.

The others looked at him after being pulled away from their own drinks and meals. Most of them shared the sentiment.

"Hahahaha," Fenri cackled at Henrick's notions. He had his chair leaned back, and boots propped on the edge of the table as he took swigs of his drink.

Everyone in the room turned to regard the pirate. Some of them had to wonder if the man was demented or something, but they were curious if he was laughing at Henrick's statement or maybe just some other wild idea.

"What's so funny?" Serena asked the pirate. There was a hint of annoyance as she assumed his mockery. "We are all here because of what the shade have done."

Fenri then let the front of his chair slam down upon the wooden floor, and he used the momentum to sit straight up on the edge of it. The pirate retorted, "Oh, but it is funny. Don't 'cha see the bigger picture, lass? These shady creatures have been roamin' the lands in a quest to knock off all the secluded power groups in the Swords." He paused to allow the words to sink in a bit before continuing. "They be tryin' to secure the success of their invasion. They don't want anyone else gettin' involved. Luckily for them, though, Claymore has already done most of the work for them. No other country, in all of Golterran, would even think to come to the aid of Claymore. Pretty darn smart if ye ask me."

Fenri could feel the sting of his words on the others as he sang praise to the shade's strategy. The historical implications of the pirate's dialogue was lost to everyone but Henrick, and the paladin was well aware of Claymore's bloody past.

Everyone threw their eyes on the captain, but Fenri didn't have to look to know they were there. Nevertheless, he replied to the glares, "Now, don't tell me ye didn't figure that part out? His tone was almost mocking. "Perhaps, I gave y'all too much credit."

Henrick lost the sound of Fenri's voice as the cold logic rang inside his head. The realization of his naivety struck him until he was frozen in place. He didn't know how to process the info and it began to tear down his hope that more allies would join their cause.

The pirate practically called everyone stupid, and Yobo, more than anyone, didn't like that. In fact, his buried anger pushed him to hate the captain at that moment. Silently, the monk wished that Fenri hadn't spoken at all, and the tall man especially didn't like the notion that his family on Skyreach was nothing more than a stepping stone for the shade's grand scheme.

Kamala, on the other hand, felt no such remorse for the loss of her fellow assassins. In her mind, they should have fought harder. However, she could not deny that with the Black Lotus gone, she was lost to the world at large. After being reunited with her brother, she had to wonder if there was a new path for her to follow. She was not one who believed in coincidence or chance, but she did believe that there was some unknown significance behind her meeting with Yobo.

As she sat there inside the tavern, she could still feel the warm presence of her goddess, Belladonna. Somehow, the boon did not subside, and she was still the Speaker. Perhaps the Lady of Sin still had an agenda for her favorite assassin. She didn't want the invigorating heat inside her body to go away, and so, she sent a silent prayer that she would do anything for *Her*.

For the remainder of the day, everyone tried to enjoy their meals and drinks in quiet contemplation before splitting off to go for a walk, or to get a room for the night. The salty captain, though, carried a smirk until the sky became dark and he never stopped his drinking.

"They're all idiots, boss," he muttered as if the dragon could hear his words. "Every single one of 'em."

CHAPTER TWENTY-FOUR
A BIT OF SOLACE PART TWO

Morning had come. The early hours of the following day, even for summer, were premature for the sun to rise, but there was a soggy yellow glow upon the horizon that suggested that sunrise *was* coming. There was a breeze in the air that carried the scent of rain, but it never fell. From what little light there was in the sky, low hanging clouds could be seen.

Following Captain Fenri's statements from the day before, Yobo couldn't bring himself to stay in the tavern. He needed time away from the pirate. He found himself joining the druids as they set up a camp on the western outskirts of town, and his sister stayed there as well.

They sat upon a fallen log that had been positioned around their campfire. Every once in a while, Yobo would look at his sister, and her eyes, and could only wonder where her golden irises could be. The subtle glances were not unnoticed by the assassin, and so she asked, "What is it, brother?"

"Why are your eyes green, sister?" Yobo observed. He wanted to know more about his sister, but he wasn't sure how else to break the silence. Where has she been all this time? Why did she become an assassin? How many people has she killed? It was these very questions that halted any sort of happy reunion and why he hadn't said much until now.

Kamala wanted to avoid or dodge any deep dialogue with her brother, but at the same time, she knew that if she did not entertain him, there was no telling when or how many times he would ask the questions that she could see on his face. It was at that realization that she let her eyes meet Yobo's.

She answered him, "My eyes are a warning. A sign that I am the highest-ranking member of the Black Lotus. To hold such a station means that I am also the guild's divine Speaker to Belladonna."

"The Goddess of *Sin*?" Yobo questioned with a small measure of judgment in his voice. "How did you come to be a patron to *Her*?"

"You were there, brother," Kamala said. "Our parents. The giant orc that carried me away. That's how the Black Lotus recruits its members. They kidnap children and train them to be killers."

Even as Kamala spoke, Yobo could see the horrific memory being recalled to his mind's eye. His parent's bodies crumpled on the floor. Blood everywhere. The thought paralyzed him with fear, both in the past and present.

He couldn't understand how Kamala could talk about it so openly. No matter what he seemed to do, and no matter how much energy he put into his discipline and martial arts, the pain still resided within him. It continually tried to pull him apart, or at least, that's how he felt about it. Yobo's eyebrows lowered as he looked at the ground while Kamala spoke. She saw her brother's turmoil, but that didn't stop her from moving on. Emotion was not her strong suit.

"I survived my training," Kamala continued. "I took initiative where I needed to in order to survive the ambitions of my guildmates. When the time came, I proved myself by killing the guild's speaker, and in doing so, I became the speaker. I am Belladonna's champion. From where I am today, I am grateful that the Black Lotus took me in."

Yobo heard every word from his sister, but at the same he was unable to be content with the idea that his sister had been thriving this whole time while post-traumatic stress had plagued him for more than a decade. His buried anger found contention between the pirate and his sister.

The monk felt his demeanor spiraling out of control inside. He turned his palms upward and stared at the emptiness of his hands. Something felt familiar about the sensation as his heart sank his mind into the darkest depths of his being. Yobo then saw the flash of red beneath the skin of his palms.

It was the dark energy from the Nessian Swamp Rose.

He could sense that it wanted something from his sister like a nagging animal gnawing at his soul. The monk's growing snarl was evident that the desires of the rose were becoming his own, and it was then that he wanted to have a taste of what the chosen of Belladonna was made of.

Yobo stood up and began walking away from the camp, and as he did, he spoke in a brooding tone, "Come, sister. Let me see what your *profession* has taught you, and I will show what I have learned over the years."

They walked a few hundred feet from the camp, and once they found a clear spot, Yobo faced his sister and took up the stance of Cova's Maw. Kamala, of course, could see what his brother was after, and she relished at the thought of doing something more practical to get to know her brother.

"You want to *spar*?" she asked, but she already knew the answer.

"Let us see what Belladonna has given you." Yobo answered. Even as he spoke, the veins in his muscles surged with beads of dim crimson light. The monk took off his saam, and threw it to the side.

Kamala smirked at her brother as she pulled her daggers from her waist. The assassin could see Yobo's glowing blood from her short distance away, and she felt proud of her brother knowing that he pursued an art of fighting like she did. She widened her stance and raised her daggers in preparation for the match to unfold. When her mind and body were ready, the light in her eyes flared with bright intensity.

The assassin wasted no time, her confidence pushed her to make the first move, and she rushed towards her brother. Her steps were quick like lightning. The heat and lustful sensation from Belladonna's boon prodded her into a blurring speed. As she closed the gap, she coiled her arms in preparation for the thrusting stab.

The shallow sting of the short blade across his shoulder instantly kicked Yobo's instincts into high gear as the image of his sister disappeared. The glow of the enchanted daggers seemed like a wisp of light streaking across the clearing, and everytime the wisp got close, the monk found himself leaping backwards. In the midst of one of those leaps, he charged up the Hesin's Cure and launched the red spell at the coming attack.

Kamala paused while performing her confusing dance around her brother, and came to regard the glowing red sphere that he summoned. She stood next to the spell as it, and everything else, was suspended in animation. Yobo was capable of magic, and from the looks of it, blood magic. She wondered how else her brother might surprise her.

But suddenly Kamala had to do a cartwheel to get away from the red Hesin's Cure as its time returned to normal. The spell struck the ground before exploding, destroying the ground, and withering everything else nearby. The assassin didn't understand what had just happened. Was it another of her brother's? Either way, once she recovered from her nimble movement, she rebounded back into her violent flight, but just as she had taken off, she saw Yobo's feet return to the ground.

It was at this point that the monk could see his sister again. It was at this point that the power of the rose calibrated its combatant to match the challenger.

Kamala paused once again, but it was because she realized what was going on. Time did not return to normal; her brother was merely catching up to her speed, but that didn't stop her for very long.

The monk was prepared to go on the defensive, but he found that his sister was still very quick. She snaked her arms through her brother's deflecting hands, and forced him to feel the stinging slice of razors, not once, but twice across the flesh above his waist. The sensation caused the monk to swing outwardly with his fists only to find his target missing, and there was only a cloud of dust left in the wake.

The assassin did not stop her attack with just a couple of bites, though. She came back around as her brother recovered from his wild jab. Her daggers found flesh again and again. The meat on the side of his torso screamed as it became more tender with each cut. The monk's shirt became soaked in blood. The thrill of her successful violence fueled her lust for battle.

But the ecstasy from her brother's pain made her blind to the fact that even though she was finding her mark on Yobo's body, the monk's wounds were regenerating and closing.

The wounds did more than drip blood, though. Yobo had been silently keeping tabs on each strike that was made against him. He timed the strikes. He measured the angle of every slice and cut, and soon he began to make educated guesses on where the next one would come from. At the end of his painful studying, he became aware of his sister's pattern.

When the next cut was due to arrive, Yobo swung his giant arm outwards and backwards. He felt his sister's form, and her chin, as his elbow caught her in a devastating clothesline. Kamala found her brother's quick elbow jab to be unexpected, and when she was struck, her flight abruptly ended and she crashed onto the ground in a series of tumbling flips.

The monk did not hesitate, and he took the opportunity to conjure another Hesin's Cure. The dark red orb of magical light came to life in Yobo's hands before he performed Suldo's Stand. He came to hold the vicious energy between both hands, he forced the sphere in half, and spread the dark magic across his forearms. His entire body came to shimmer with a crimson veil.

Kamala returned to her feet and wiped the blood from her bottom lip. Across the clearing, she witnessed her brother warp his magic. She continued to hold a smirk at her brother's power, and she almost wished that he could have been a part of the Black Lotus with her. They would have made an unstoppable team.

The assassin's smile quickly became a snarl when Yobo came barreling down upon her position. Kamala readied herself again in an instant, and before either of them knew it, arms and blades became locked into an endless struggle. She found that her brother was keeping up with her.

Yobo effortlessly dodged the blades of Kamala, and sometimes he would simply push on her wrists to parry or deflect the attacks. Likewise, Kamala ducked and weaved between the heavy hammers that were her brother's fists.

After only a few mere seconds of the melee, Kamala changed up her tactics, and threw out a feint with her attacks. Yobo went for the deflection, but soon realized that the blade was not there. The monk grunted as the glowing dagger sliced across his abdomen.

The small victory was short lived, and by the time the steel blade completed its swing, Yobo swatted at his sister. His knuckles found the cheeks on her face. The force of the punch was unbelievable, and it stunned Kamala to the point that she stumbled backwards. She tip-toed as she tried to recenter her balance, but ultimately, she failed and fell down.

Survival instincts kicked in and she scrambled around on all fours to get some distance from her brother. When she came to a stop, she remained on the ground, and stared up at Yobo, but he did not pursue her. She took a measure of what had just happened, and came to understand that her feint was actually his feint. She realized that her brother was willing to take damage in order to deliver it back, and tenfold from the way her face felt at the moment.

She had never faced an opponent like this before, and she wondered what she could do to stop that sort of strategy. As an assassin, she was well-trained in combat, sword play, and stealth, but she relied on her targets to break under the inevitability of death. She came to the comprehension that whatever her brother had been getting into all these years, it was turning him into something that she could not contend with.

She felt humbled at the hands of her brother, and because of that, her otherwise cold demeanor suffered a crack.

"I went back to look for *you*," Kamala shared loudly.

Her words came just as she noticed Yobo's feet move, but the monk came to a stop just as quickly. Yobo remained silent while the green glow fell away from the eyes of the assassin, and they were once again a bright golden hue. She could feel Belladonna's boon leaving, but she didn't know if her time had run out or if it was taken away.

"I wanted to see you again," Kamala continued. She came to stand up at this point. "But it seems you have been doing well."

The monk froze as he wrestled for control of his mind and body. Since Planesgate, he had no idea the dark magic of the Nessian Rose was still lingering inside him. It still wanted to fight, and Yobo silently felt the same way, but he had no desire to destroy his sister. She was literally the last ounce of family he had in the world, and it was upon this topic that he and the rose came to a disagreement. It was then that Yobo decided that he needed to get rid of it, put the demonic spirit back to sleep, and there was only one way that he knew of that could do it.

He forced himself to turn around and face the open wilderness. The dark red energy in his body resisted, it attempted to electrify Yobo from the inside out.

But the center of power for the Gunn Drambor was pain.

The stinging shocks made him fuming mad, and it only aided him in his quest for salvation. The anger gave him focus. He looked within himself, he looked at the images of his childhood, he looked at the aftermath from the slaughter on top of Skyreach, and he brought the rage from those traumatic experiences to the front of his mind's eye until his fury pushed him into an unbreakable meditative-like trance.

Just as the light of Lumina came over the horizon, he began to force the dark elements out of his body. It was just as he had done on that fateful night when he forced the clouds from the sky, and he put everything his heart had into the Hesin's Cure.

The magical orb of glowing red energy came forth, clouds of shimmering crimson siphoned out from all around him, and he began to wonder how much more was buried deep inside. He reached in with his feelings, searching the corners of his mind, his heart, and his spirit. Bigger and bigger the spell grew, and the concentration of power was so immense that streaks of red lightning shot out across the ground, digging up the singed dirt in its wake. The sound of roaring thunder accompanied the morning sunlight.

In the distance, the glowing magical power could be seen and heard by the now-alerted druids. The disturbance traveled farther, and in no time at all, most of Solace was aware of it. The villagers could see the top of the dark red star and the air hummed and cracked with violent magic.

You can't get rid of me, the demonic voice warned Yobo from inside his head. *We had a deal. A promise for a promise.*

The monk ignored the voice as rage had sealed his mind from any sort of distraction.

It then came to an end. Yobo was done searching, and he had found every last piece and scrap of the dark presence in his body. It was all collected in probably the biggest Hesin's Cure that he had summoned to date. The malice and hatred were gone. He felt as though he could breathe again, but at the same time, he was still in his angry meditation.

With the spell coming to its completion, he could see what he needed to do in his mind's eye, but he had to wonder if he was capable of pulling it off. Notions of doubt seeped into his brain, but he quickly pushed them aside. He had to. He was the last of the Gunn Drambor, he *was* the master, and he told himself that failure was not an option.

Just like Master Tresa and Purall, Yobo squeezed the giant spell into a smaller, compact form before launching the giant red sun of magic power into the air. Yobo followed up by spinning back into the Cova's Maw again and again. He completed the somatic components of his spell casting quickly and masterfully. He brought forth the powers of wind and earth, and with these elements in hand, he shot a boulder-size bullet into the red orb.

BOOM!!!

The blast echoed for miles and after a second, the clouds above gave way to the sudden change in pressure. Yobo stood his ground defiantly against the blast while Kamala held on to her daggers, which were deep into the ground. As the last shuddering vibrations departed, the red cloud of smoke dissipated. The dark energy was no more, and Yobo looked upon his empty hands for good measure.

When Yobo turned to look upon his sister, he found that she was not the only one there. Serena, and the other druids, came up running to the clearing. Looking out farther, it looked like the whole village had been summoned to spectate. Dogs could be heard barking in the distance. He could even see the militiamen, and the other adventurers, racing through town.

"Yobo?" Serena called out. "What *was* that?"

The monk took a small moment to consider the accomplishment of overcoming the influence of the Nessian Rose, but also to consider how best to respond. He answered with, "Something I had to get out of my system."

"My brother would always talk of the things he was capable of," Loria exclaimed. "I never imagined those monks were capable of *that*, though. Incredible."

"Ha. We'll see if the shade feel the same way," Reeth added.

Yobo gathered his saam before he walked over to his sister. By this time, she had returned to her feet. Her golden eyes met with her brother's, and she returned the smirk that he was on his face, however, they didn't say anything at that moment.

When the rest of the party showed up at the clearing, the town's guards were also there, and they had their weapons drawn.

"All of you. Stop whatever you are doing, and come quietly," the sergeant demanded.

When everyone turned around to regard the men, they also noticed several other people approaching from behind on horseback, and of everyone gathered in the clearing, Henrick was the one that knew every single one of the riders.

"Stand down!" The call came from one of the riders. It was none other than Marc Blade-Briar II.

483

The guards turned to regard the command, but when they realized who it was, they were completely flabbergasted. Likewise, Henrick was also concerned about the arrival of this house leader.

"Go on. *Return* to your post," the next command came with a stern look and a tone that warned the guards to not challenge him.

It brought the four guardsmen out of their silent stupor, and they ushered themselves back to town. As they departed, the riders dismounted. The other riders were Melissa Darkbane, Gunner, and to Henrick's surprise, the fourth rider was Sirus, someone who Henrick assumed was lost to the shade.

"Oh my god," Henrick said as he came to meet Sirus with a handshake and a smile.

"Henrick. It's been a while," the ranger shared the sentiment.

"*Henrick*?" the blonde woman cut in. She sized up Henrick while looking over the new suit of armor. Her eyes then came upon his facial scar, and she used a hand to forcibly turn his head to get a better look. "You certainly didn't have that when you left. It'll have to do I guess."

She extended a hand for a shake and when Henrick accepted it, Melissa pulled him in for a hug. Off to the side, Serena watched over their exchanges. The druid recognized her as the woman who said goodbye to him when they left Claymore. She became washed over with a wave of concern, but she did not understand the nature of her feelings at the moment. Luckily, her confusing emotions became interrupted by the voice of another.

"Can we *get on* with it?" came the voice of Marc Blade-Briar II, and instantly, the others could sense that he carried an air of impatience around him.

Henrick then looked around, and from what he could tell, everyone was here. Himself, Serena, Yobo, Samuel Fenri, Sirus the Hood, Melissa Darkbane, Marc Blade-Briar II, Gunner, Indra, Bertil, Reeth, Loria, Ti'or, Kadrah, and Kormanth. To the paladin, the clearing was as good a place as any to have a private and concise conversation.

Henrick became the center of attention as he stepped forward, and then he began, "Alright, suppose everyone's 'ere. Let's get down to business." After the commencement statement, all the others moved about to form a circle, and after that he took it upon himself to break the ice, and he pointed his eyes at the respective parties as he spoke. "To most of us here, the shade've made their presence known. Druids, people from Skyreach, myself and Sirus, and even the Black Lotus. They have already started their invasion." He then shot a glare at Fenri. "They have pre-emptively attacked those who they deemed worthy of a response to their plans. As we all stand here, it is clear that their plans *are* worthy of a response."

Sirus then cut into the conversation, "I've already told Leaders Darkbane and Blade-Briar, but there is a shade roaming the keep in Claymore. It has been using the dungeon to secretly communicate information, mostly to the shade home in the wastes. It is a sorcerer of some kind, but unfortunately, whatever it is capable of, we do not know. It does, however, have some sort of hold on our King."

"If it's anything like the shade that we encountered, it will most likely wield death magic," Reeth added.

"But we have learned that our magic is effective against them," Loria also added.

"That's right. Magical fire and daylight destroys the shade completely," Reeth confirmed.

As if he was cued, Henrick suddenly set his backpack on the ground, and produced the artifact inside. Everyone's eyes fell on him at that moment, and the item in his hands, the Esfera de Luz.

"Light won't be a problem," Henrick proclaimed.

"What is *that*?" Indra asked.

"*Great Goddess*, is that the Esfera de Luz?" Melissa asked. Melissa's profound reaction only grew the curiosity of the others who had yet to see the thing.

"Yes," Henrick answered.

"This will help us fight the shade," Yobo added while pointing at it.

"However…there is one important thing about this," Henrick began while holding a hand up. "We cannot use it as a means of destruction, elsewise the artifact bestows a terrible curse on the user."

"*What*?" Marc retorted in disbelief. "How are we supposed to kill them, then?"

Henrick explained, "As we found out, we *can* use it to suppress the abilities of the shade. It can keep them from turning into mist, and at that point, they can be fought with swords."

Everyone there soaked in the knowledge presented so far by those that had spoken. Some of them nodded in acknowledgement, and some did nothing.

"So, what about the King, Henrick, and the shade that is controlling him?" Gunner asked.

As the question came out, everyone looked to him for the answer. Marc Blade-Briar II, especially, wanted to hear that one.

"I would like to formulate a more thorough plan, but tomorrow," Henrick began. His brows lowered as the determination boiled inside his soul. "I'm gonna to do what I hesitated to do the first time. I'm gonna to do things the Claymore way. I'm gonna invoke the First Law and drag that shade out from wherever it is hidin'."

"The First Law? What's that?" Kadrah asked.

"The First Law of Claymore is war," Melissa answered.

Marc II then recited the famous proverb of the First Law, "War is combat. Combat is honorable. The honorable seek the truth. And the truth solves everything."

CHAPTER TWENTY-FIVE
THE FIRST LAW

Henrick stopped on the road astride a chestnut mare as the whole of the city came into view. Being able to physically see the untouched capital was a feeling of relief, but as he stared at his home from the outside, he knew what was waiting for him on the inside.

Melissa, Marc Blade Briar II, and Sirus also came to a stop. Judging from their silence, they understood the purpose for which he paused.

The early morning sun had just begun to peak over the distance horizon to the east. The shadows cast by the walls made it seem like the outer city before them was trying to hide from the sunlight. The grassy fields on either side of the road looked like a blanket of green with the sparkling of dew drops twinkling with the reflection of light. The air was crisp and fresh, and the breeze worked to dissuade the coming warmth of the day.

Henrick then looked south, and all across that horizon was the deep blue body of water known as Starfall Lake. Small boats, more than likely fishers, could be seen paddling out into the waters. All around the castle-city, the rocky grassland was dappled with dark shadows and dots of gray and white. The entirety of the scene was like a painting. .

"You know. It's only been a month," Melissa mocked. In reality, though, she was keeping Marc II from blurting out.

"Closer to a month-and-a-half," Henrick argued with the same mocking tone.

Henrick and the other three riders continued to trot down the road.

After the gathering yesterday, all of the companions of Henrick, Serena, and Yobo hashed out a more formal plan. They all agreed that it would be best to not draw any unwanted attention before the big event, and so the plan was to have the group split up and enter the city at different times. Everyone else was supposed to have gone through the west gate before sunrise. For now, the riders just needed to hold out hope that everyone was already waiting inside.

Before they could find out, the clean wisps of air were soon replaced by the smell of livestock and burning metal. The clanging of a smith's hammer

489

could be heard echoing from an unknown direction. The road led them through the smattering of small wooden houses and structures that made up the west outer city, and just like the outer city on the east side, this place was also littered by a population of transients who had lost their way, or were taxed out of their homes.

Henrick, more than the other three at the moment, found it all morally disgusting. The current King of Claymore had been bleeding these people dry for some time now. At least, he hoped, that this was all due to the fact that an agent of the shade was behind all of this. If there was even a slight chance that this had been going on before the shade showed up, he might enjoy fighting the king either way. Deep down, though, he wanted to solve all the problems that Claymore was suffering. Exile or not.

The paladin watched the citizens as they gathered on the sides of the street. They whispered amongst each other and their words could be heard floating about incoherently.

In the outer cities, it was considered rare to see the house leaders travel through town. Some of the more disgruntled citizens thought it even more rare to see one outside the confines of Claymore's inner walls, but to see two of them side by side? The common folk that were in the middle of the road moved aside as Lady Darkbane and Master Blade-Briar II led Henrick and Sirus through town. The muttering continued to swirl in the air as they tried to guess or make sense of the brightly armored warrior.

"Hmm. They're really lookin' at you, Henrick," Sirus mocked.

"And why wouldn't they?" he questioned in response before adding a last bit. "Ye can see this armor from a mile away."

"Haha," Sirus could only offer a laugh in return.

"Rest assured that our enemy isn't going to take their eye off of you," Melissa chimed in while half-turning in her saddle.

A few minutes later, the riders passed through the western gate. It was the gate that Henrick used when he departed as an exile, and it was the same gate when he rode out with Thor Spearfall. Beyond the gate, the group entered the Grim Ward. The section of the city was another large residential area but the entire north-end of it was the designated home for the graves of the honorable.

Unlike the rest of the city, this was the only section of town where the streets were lined with short iron fences. The fences provided a small measure of protection to the many mausoleums that stood above the mossy ground. Furthermore, as the name suggested, the homes and buildings in the part of the city had gray roof tiles.

Inside the Grim Ward, were the bounty hunters Gunner, Bertil, and Indra waited for them at an intersection. The bounty hunters also had six hounds with them. Yobo and Kamala stood nearby on one of the corners of the split road. As everyone moved to meet in the middle, they all noticed that someone was not with them.

"Where's Samuel?" Henrick asked aloud.

"He walked off. Said he wanted to take in the sights," Yobo replied.

Henrick could only keep his unsurprising disappointment inside and shook his head at the

491

consistency of the pirate. He had to wonder what the *real reason* was for the dragon wanting him to come here. Perhaps, the dragon was amused by the captain's unpredictable behavior.

"No matter. We move on without him," Melissa said. Her words prompted everyone else to move forward.

The intersection had three roads. One led to the west gate, one led south through the rest of the district, and one led east to the Grim Gate and inner city. The inner city is where they headed.

The guards at the inner-city gate became curious at the large party that approached, but when they noticed who was leading them, they came to an erect military stance.

"At ease," Marc II commanded.

Without the need to explain their situation, the guards obeyed and allowed everyone to pass. With Melissa and Marc II to guide them, there was no need for Henrick or anyone else to provide credentials. To that effect, the path to the keep was going to be a simple trot for them, and as they approached the doors to the keep, the leaders of the other two houses appeared at their flanks.

"Such a bulky collection you have with you, Darkbane," Tyr Vicidian said with narrowed eyes and a tone of suspicion. He then pointed his gaze at the brightly armored, and helmeted, warrior. "Who is that?"

The Vicidian Leader's question went unanswered, but as was finishing his words, the riders dismounted from the horses. The weasel-of-a-man scanned over the rest of the party and took note of the bounty hunters and their dogs. Suddenly, the pieces were starting to fall into place, but Tyr kept his narrow view and remained silent.

Everyone there then began to walk towards the large doors of the keep.

"Are you sure you want to stay out here, Marc?" Melissa asked the Blade-Briar Leader as they walked side-by-side.

"No, but I don't want to be up there, either," he answered honestly. "If what you have told me is true. I trust you will get things done."

"I will," Melissa simply offered while her tone was serious. In the years that she had known Marc II, the man had never shown fear. Even now he didn't show it, but she could sense it in his words. She then looked ahead to the guards outside of the keep, and voiced her command, "Open the doors!"

As the guards opened the doors to the keep, everyone looked inside. There were more guards, army officers, serfs, and other such officials roaming about the entry-lobby, or sitting in furniture. There were tables, chairs, couches, and the largest Claymoran flag pinned upon the wall on the far side.

The large group came into the lobby, and with so many foreigners inside, the citizens began to leave due to their *social discomfort*. Once inside, they stood in a circle as their plan was about to unfurl.

"The bounty hunters and the dogs will remain down here with Marc," Melissa explained. "The rest of us will be upstairs in the throne room. We do not want to be disturbed, and that is for the safety of those that should not be involved."

Some of them nodded in acknowledgement while others did not.

"We do not know what is about to unfold," she added, and she would have continued had it not been for the words of another.

"*Unfold*?" Tyr piped in, drawing in the eyes of everyone.

"What is the matter, Tyr?" Roland, the Odoku House Leader, asked the man, but nearly rhetorically. "Is it not obvious?" The odum man then smiled. "Tradition is about to unfold. As it should have last month." He then looked at the armored Henrick. "The path of cowards has no place in Claymore."

The skinny man curled his nose and brows at the words of Roland.

After a moment's pause, Melissa could only agree, "Well said, Roland. If there is nothing else, let's go."

Lady Darkbane led her half of the party in single-file formation to the first door on the left from the entrance. After this door, they took a slight left, and then a right as they went through a hallway. They went through another door, and beyond it was a simple chamber that housed the stairs leading to the second floor. The stairs traveled straight up at a decent incline, and once they were at the top, a small hallway trailed into the second floor of the keep. They did not stop on the second floor, though, and instead, they continued to walk ahead. They went through a doorless frame, and into another chamber that had the stairs leading to the third floor.

At the top, the stairs placed them in a hallway. It was wide enough that the group could walk two-abreast. After a couple of right turns, and then a left, the group came around the corner to find four guards standing outside the throne room doors. Each party took note of the other.

Melissa, without saying a word to the guards, took her strides to the ironbound wooden double doors of the throne room. She, as well as everyone else, could hear two men having a heated discussion inside.

"Wait out here," she said while looking at Henrick, Yobo, and Kamala. She then looked to Roland before continuing, "Let's go inside."

Melissa opened the doors. Her, Roland, and Tyr entered the throne room, and because of the arguments going on, the two shouting men did not even hear, or see, the visitors arrive.

"...The kingdom is in unrest, and the turmoil is beginning to show our weakness," General Hormac argued to the King of Claymore. "Even the troops are growing weary."

"Then go have a discussion with the houses about it. But it doesn't matter, we are at a time of peace in these lands. There is no one to fight. It is expected to have some complacency in our forces," the King shot back.

"It's not complacency," Melissa called across the throne room.

Once inside the throne room, Roland turned around, and he closed the doors. The king and the general put their eyes on Darkbane.

Melissa continued, "Our citizens have been asking about the tax money and where it is going. A question I wish someone would share with the rest of the top leadership here." She shot a glance at Tyr before returning her eyes to the king. "Furthermore, our commanders and lieutenants are starting to question the strength of our leadership."

"*Darkbane*, where have you been?" the King questioned through gritted teeth.

"Touring the countryside. We *do* have outposts, your majesty. Our weakness has already bled from these walls and our villages are beginning to worry. An unseen adversary has been taking advantage of our *growing debilitation*."

The facial expression of the King was one of skepticism, but in reality, he did not pay attention to anything that she was saying. As his discerning look scanned the entryway of the throne room, and that's when he noticed someone was not there.

"Where is my son?" the King asked.

Melissa did not answer the king's question, and instead, she continued to press her concerning thoughts, "I have been personally investigating these issues to make sure an attack was not upon us yet. But I have come to the conclusion that someone, perhaps the dryads, or one of the other countries, might try to attack the kingdom soon." Melissa then swallowed the lump in her throat as she summoned the statement that needed to be heard. "I hope sitting on that throne hasn't made you forget that we have enemies out there. Peaceful times or not."

The words stung the superior ego of the man in the throne. Fittingly, the king rose from the throne in a quickened manner. The crimson-tinted chainmail glistened from the sunlight pouring in from the stained-glass windows as the brooding monarch moved forward, but the large flamberge remained strapped to his back.

Melissa did not flinch, nor did she make any indication that she was going to reach for her weapon or shield. She saw the kind of man or creature that was before her from the last time, and she knew it was a coward. However, she couldn't comprehend whether or not it was the actual king, or the master controlling the puppet. But it didn't matter. She played her bet that the king was not going to take a swing on her.

"You will watch your tongue when you speak to me," the King demanded with a pointing finger, spitting as he spoke.

"Are you going to exile me, too, sire?" Melissa shot back. She made sure that her eyes told the king that she was ready to fight.

Hormac stood off to the side, and up until now he had remained silent. He scoffed, "Hmpf. If that is the course action, I would have to strike him down myself."

The King's furious face turned to gaze upon the confident mask that the General of Claymore wore. The General could see through the bluster as clearly as Melissa could, and knew that no strike would come.

The confidence was misplaced and the underestimation was laid in stone. Those were the last moments of General Donovan Hormac as the large wavy-blade of the King came screaming through the air in an unreal show of aggression. With one fluid motion, the flamberge came off the king's back, smashed through the bridge of the General's nose, and glided through the rest of his head in one clean cut. The greatsword splashed the ground with blood and brain matter. The rest of the body fell limp in an instant.

The King panted heavily as he recovered from the devastating attack. When the King turned to regard Darkbane, she still had not drawn her weapon. Roland moved back a bit in anticipation for another assault. Tyr stepped off to the side as well, but he secretly applauded the death of the general.

"Does that look like weakness to you?" the king said with a tyrannical voice, nearly screaming through his teeth.

It was not a second later, at the end of the king's challenge, that the throne room doors came open again. Two guards from outside rushed in to investigate the loud popping sound and the clanging of metal against the stone floor.

"The general was not armed. It was not an honorable kill," Roland warned.

From the entrance of the room, they were able to see the aftermath of the king's attack. Everyone else outside could see it as well.

"The general?" Henrick voiced in a loud whisper. The paladin could feel it, then. The darkness inside the throne room. It circled around the king. It was strong, but this time, thankfully, the power of the darkness did not overwhelm his bearing.

"The king has slayed the general," Melissa announced to everyone while holding a hand backwards to stop the guards from approaching further.

Everyone else remained unmoving, but Henrick walked in to stand beside Melissa, and he never took his eyes off the king as he took his backpack off, drew the sandari water blade, and took hold of his moon-bearing shield. The bright colors upon Henrick's armor drew the king's eyes immediately, and they became fixed on the paladin. The king sized up the unfamiliar soldier in his presence, but when the king saw the shield, he realized who it was.

"The exile," the King said. "You should have died out there on the Shelf."

It was at this moment that Henrick felt his journey reach its tipping point. He traveled so far to get to this point. Nothing was going to stop him now. He solidified the mantle of paladin in his heart. The Twins. No. Nielda sent him on this path. This was his mission. The moon goddess was a direct opponent to the forces of darkness, and he was going to make sure that the dark creature before him was going to feel it. He was going to fulfill his destiny, and end the disorder that had been plaguing Claymore for years.

"My name is Henrick. A paladin in service to Nielda. I am here to challenge the throne of Claymore under the First Law," he declared in a strong, loud voice. "I know what you are, shade, and you owe me this fight."

As the words echoing off the walls came to an end, the room fell silent. The issuance of the First Law against the throne has not been done for countless years. Some of those who watched the declaration of the coming fight exchanged unblinking looks between the king and the paladin. The others, especially the house leaders, held serious looks on their faces, but not once did they take their eyes off the king who had yet to respond.

Yobo, who was outside the throne room, stepped in to get a better look at the king. His rage was already building inside, and his face held the visage of brooding vengeance. He said through a snarl of teeth, "Your kind will pay for what you have done."

The King's demeanor then relaxed completely. "Hahahahahahahahaha," the beastly, old man with the crown laughed and cackled at the sudden turn of events. He regained his composure with a sinister smirk. "Good. That means this little farce is *over!*" The voice of the King had a hint of joy, and grew in volume as his sentence came out.

The king held out a hand with contorted fingers as he summoned the dark magic within his body. When the spell came to life, the doors to the throne room came closed, pushing the two guards out with it, and then it became sealed with a magic lock.

Everyone else flinched and had to take a look at the unexpected movement at the door, but Henrick and Yobo never took their eyes off the king. With no other notion or words, the king charged across the throne room floor. Henrick readied himself for the first attack.

The house leaders made no movement to interfere, but they shifted their position to the sides of the room in order to give the combatants room. To them, and the people of Claymore, this was a sacred ritual, and it didn't matter what the king was or was not.

At first, Yobo flinched as if to get involved with the bout, but Roland was already upon him. He reached out with his arm to stop the monk, and pulled him to the side.

"Let your friend do this," Roland said in Yobo's ear. "By law, we cannot interfere."

King Blade-Briar began the encounter against Henrick with an uppercut. The flamberge arced and sparked as the tip grinded across the stone floor. The paladin took note of the power being applied to the two-handed sword and dared not to put his shield before it.

Henrick back-peddled and let the blade go wide. In the heat of the first moment, the paladin almost thought to dive in and start his own swordplay but he hesitated. The others in the room saw the perfect opportunity for the challenger to strike, but for reasons unknown to them, Henrick did not take it.

As Melissa watched, she began critiquing Henrick's movements. She was the one that taught Henrick how to use a shield and how to battle against every type of weapon. Because of this, she could understand the angle that would soon take shape.

The king followed up his first attack. He spun and came around to side-slash at Henrick's neck. The sword found steel as the shield deflected the blade's momentum up and away. This time, the paladin took the opportunity. He brought his curved sword up in a stabbing motion and went for the king's chest.

The older man was ready though. He removed a hand from his flamberge to reach past the blade, and grabbed a hold of Henrick's forearm. While holding the paladin's swordarm, King Blade-Briar brought up his right knee and front kicked the torso of the paladin. The crashing muscle was something of legend. Henrick felt the force of the blow reverberate through the armor, and his body alike. But the paladin did not waiver, though, and he used that grip on his arm to hold himself in place.

The king was persistent, and he kicked again and again. The bashing foot continued, but the paladin managed to get his shield in between as the second blow came. When the kicking didn't seem to work anymore, the king released his grip. He held the greatsword firmly in both hands once more before bringing it down into a chop. When Henrick noticed the attack, he quickly brought up his shield to block, but the king's face produced a snarl at the successful feint, and the next devastating kick finally took the paladin off his feet.

The force of the blow was enough for Henrick to drop his sword before flying backward. The king grinned at Henrick as the paladin managed to stay on his feet, but he was back on the charge. The younger warrior before him was disarmed which gave the older warrior the advantage.

Audible whooshes tore through the air when the flamberge went searching for flesh. Henrick dodged the blade, blocked when he needed to, and a couple times he threw his shield forward into a bash and met the force of the swing with his own. When the paladin followed through with another of his bashes, the timing was perfect, and the metal rang as the two objects came to meet. At this particular meeting, the vibrations shook the flamberge so violently that the king felt like there was electricity in his hands.

Off to the side, Melissa smirked when she heard the defining tone bouncing off the face of the shield.

The warrior-king was forced to stall until the vibrations stopped, and that was when Henrick drove forward with the symbol of the Twins, and pushed Marc Blade-Briar backwards several feet. When the paladin pulled himself from his charge, there was now a couple yards between the combatants.

The two warriors came to a few seconds of pause. Henrick sized up the king, but also made a glance at his fallen sword. When the king caught the glimpse, he used his foot to kick the blade even farther away. Shade or not, the paladin fought a tenacious foe, and he was beginning to realize that. In his mind, though, the paladin couldn't understand why the creature was not just flinging magic everywhere.

Unless, he theorized, that this *was* just the king that he was fighting, but something about that just didn't make sense. Nevertheless, he would take his opponent as they came. He liked it that way. No handicaps.

With nothing but a shield in hand, Henrick stood his ground with no sign of hindrance in his confidence. The paladin did the only other thing he could think of with his empty hand. He made a "*come on*" hand gesture at the king, and said, "*Bring it.*"

The king snorted before coming in with a heavy overhead smash, but Henrick didn't step back or to the side. Instead, he pounced forward and rolled across the floor as the blade came to meet the stone floor. The paladin raced over to get his sword back at the other end of the room, but his opponent was upon him in an instant.

There was another downward arc from the flamberge. Henrick timed the block, and stopped the blade completely against the face of his shield. The paladin could feel the shockwave of the forceful attack in his forearm. Henrick was a creature of martial combat, just like everyone else in the room, and he knew the king must have felt the returning reverberations in his hands.

The king was forced to stall again from the shocking sword hilt, but this time the paladin had his weapon, and Henrick made a slice across the abdomen of the king. The foreign blade cut right through the red armor. The giant man grimaced and grunted as the sudden pain worked to fuel his battle rage. Henrick did not let up, though. Once more, he drove his shield into the torso of the king, and pushed the old man until they were squared up in the center of the room again.

This time the king began to realize that his foe was formidable, but physical combat was not its profession, and so the puppet master decided that the game was over. The cover had already been blown. So, why should the king play with the humans any longer? The king reached out with an arm and aimed his contorting fingers at Henrick. He summoned the power of death, and before anyone else could realize it, the king shot black lightning at Henrick.

The paladin brought his sword and shield up in an attempt to block the spell, but he had no way of knowing if it would do any good. In truth, he wasn't sure he was ever really prepared for such an assault. In the flashing moments before him, it was like he was paralyzed in place, unable to respond to his unforeseen defeat.

When the dark magic struck, it sizzled and burned, crackled and snapped.

But Henrick realized he was still standing.

He brought his eyes forward again. The king was still channeling his spell, but it was Henrick, who realized first, that the magic became attracted by the metal of his sword, like lightning to a lightning rod. The paladin smirked in that moment, and he lowered his shield, revealing to all what was going on. The spell then ended.

"You've come prepared," the king said, a small hint of disappointment in his voice.

"And you're weak," Henrick taunted.

Weak? The single word of the paladin echoed in his dark mind. He was not weak, he told himself. He was the best there ever was. It was why he was chosen to sit and rule the humans. It was because of him that his people would regain their land in the coming invasion.

But the insults of Umbra Hadara snuck their way in. The anger, anxiety, and rage boiled inside the king at that moment. He was losing his composure. His breathing became heavy and then quick. The king's eye refocused on the paladin and he knew exactly what to do next.

He charged the paladin, closing the gap, and brought his flamberge up high once more. Henrick readied himself, but the paladin found the attack to be *too* obvious. It was so obvious that it was almost deliberate. The blade could go in any direction should the paladin choose to move, but he remained stationary.

In House Darkbane, the shield was the true weapon of the house. The sword was merely a distraction that caught the eyes of the oncoming threats. This situation would be no different, and when the king was upon Henrick, the paladin jutted the top edge of his shield at the downward hands of the king. The simple maneuver was accurate and precise, and judging from the crunch that followed there were probably a few broken fingers as well.

The flamberge lost most of its downward momentum and clattered away some feet behind Henrick. The hands of the king could no longer hold the weapon.

The king flew into a fit of rage as the primal scream was unbridled and near-deafening. The sound of pain-stricken fury was backed by another source of power. The shade that lurked inside. The windows in the throne room cracked, and the cry of anger could be heard all through the keep and inner city.

Afterwards, those who were in the throne room began to remove their hands from their ears. Each of them had an awe-struck look about their faces. Even Henrick had stumbled backwards a few paces due to the noisy load that was before him.

The paladin looked upon the king's sweat-beaded face. The black, misty aura that enveloped the king was more prevalent than before. The king fell to his knees, and grasped his head with his broken hands. Marc Blade-Briar couldn't muster the strength to lift his head enough, but he managed to scream out, "Kill me!"

Henrick and the others remained silent. What was that voice?

"Kill me!" came the strangled scream again.

"Lumina's Light. The shade has him possessed!" Melissa called out to her friend.

There was little time to think at this moment. Somehow, the breaking of bones allowed the king, the *real* King of Claymore, to snap out of his apparent possession. The paladin saw it for what it was as soon as the words left Darkbane's mouth.

Henrick nearly tripped over himself as he rushed for the flamberge that laid just a few feet behind him. Within a second, he was upon the weapon, and got the blade into his hands shortly after dropping his shield and sword. The paladin seemed to move in slow motion in this critical moment, but he managed to get beside the fallen King. He raised up the blade, and curled his arms in anticipation for the fateful

506

swing. The heavy weapon came down, and crashed into the spine of the King of Claymore at the back of his neck. The greatsword carved its path halfway through the muscled neck. Only trickles of blood splashed on the floor, but the king was now dead.

The body of the monarch remained in its kneeling position, and Henrick stood very still in that moment as time paused throughout the whole universe. Everyone inside witnessed the defeat of the king. Possessed or not, it was a defining moment that would live forever in the records of Claymore's history.

Henrick still held the blade's hilt as it rested upon the human meat. He stared at the vorpal blow as suspense overtook him. He could still sense the darkness in the body.

And that was when the king exploded with dark energy. The body remained intact, but from the late king, the throne room became enveloped by the black shroud that could be nothing more than the presence of a shade shadowmancer in action.

The sunlight that came in through the windows was snuffed out, and the room was covered in a smoky, dark brown light.

Outside the throne room, the doors suddenly became covered in a magical, smoky darkness. The four guards stood there with Kamala and Sirus. After a few more seconds of staring at the doors with anticipation, the shadow expanded more and more until it spread throughout the whole of the keep.

"Sounds like the boss is finally done hiding," one of the guards outside the throne room said.

Kamala and Sirus reared their heads at the words of the guard. They weren't sure what the guard meant, but they narrowed their eyes on them.

"Perhaps Claymore will finally be ours again," another one said.

"What are you on about?" Sirus questioned them, barely able to see their figure in the darkness.

The guards turned their attention to the ranger and the assassin. They exchanged looks with each other, and then suddenly, they drew their swords.

Kamala had been watching them in those short moments, and she already held her daggers in hand. She let the first guard come at her, but she calmly stepped to the side. Her dagger found the neck of the guard, and as quickly as the combat began, the first one was down. The cold-blooded demeanor of the assassin returned the green glow of her eyes.

Belladonna's boon was back.

She found herself staring through the magical darkness as if the air was clear. Kamala pressed forward. She would not allow these fools to gain a single second of advantage against her. She danced, blinking in and out of the shadows that enveloped her, and used her enemy's environment against them.

The guards were not prepared to have such a forceful reaction from the half-dryad.

Her precise attack and execution brought down the guards quickly and swiftly. Each time, she went for her favorite spot: the soft tissue of the jugular. Blood splashed all over her and the floor. The sudden rush felt like the fix she needed. Her hands trembled as she tried to remain composed against the lovely heat in her core.

To Sirus, it seemed like the woman disappeared into the shadows, and before he could realize it, the opposition was splayed across the stone floor.

Kamala went for the throne room doors, but when she reached for the handles, the spell of warding zapped her hands, prohibiting her from interacting with them. The door was sealed, and there was no way for her to assist her brother. She placed a hand on the nearby wall, and silently thanked her goddess for not abandoning her.

"Let's go," she suggested to the ranger before heading downstairs.

During the flight, they both had to wonder: why were humans siding with the enemy?

Outside the keep, everyone in the inner city witnessed the dark shroud that fell over the keep. Within minutes, the barracks, the Claymoran Army, and everyone that could have been rallied, was rallied. Thousands of troops stormed in the direction of the keep's doors.

"Oh, shit," Gunner said as he witnessed the mass of warriors closing in.

Gunner, Bertil, and Indra readied themselves, but they did so knowing that there was going to be nothing they could do to stop the soldiers of Claymore. Even with the Blade-Briar House Leader standing at their side, it would not be enough to dissuade them from their actions.

It was then that the six hounds returned to their humanoid forms. It was an orc, a dryad, two humans, a dwarf, and a huntari that now stood before the entrance to the keep.

The Claymoran Army as a whole kicked up a storm of dust in their wake as they approached, their screaming battle cries only made them seem more menacing. All of them had weapons drawn.

It was then that Loria responded with a protection spell, and when she completed her incantation, a magical barrier formed. It was the same spell she used during the battle with the shade. The dome-like veil of violet light that came forth kept the soldiers from entering the keep, but it also kept them from harming those who stood watch over the entrance.

The soldiers rushed at the magical wall and swung their weapons at it. There was no effect, and it angered the troops even more.

"Stop!" Reeth screamed at the army, but his voice was nothing compared to the shouting mob before them.

"Your throne has been usurped by an imposter. Your leaders are acting to thwart this...sorcerer," Serena tried next, but again, no one heard her voice.

Marc II then saw what the druids were trying to do. The use of their magic disgusted him. It was against Claymoran Law after all, but he could not deny its use for right now. He also thought: how could he possibly expect his soldiers to listen when he was obviously letting the laws of Claymore go to the side. Nevertheless, he found their ambient rioting equally annoying. It was all of this that drew him out to the front.

As he stood there, inches from the first warrior, they continued to shout, and it was only pissing him off even more. When he couldn't take it anymore, he made his presence known.

"*SHUT UP!!!*" the angry house leader shouted.

The volume of his voice was greater than the mobs, and the shuddering of the air he caused nearly stunned the warriors in front him. Lost in the stupor, the mob soon grew quiet.

Samuel Fenri came walking out from the second story hallway as Kamala and Sirus descended the stairs from the third floor. Their eyes met in passing and Sirus stopped while Kamala continued to head down to the first floor.

"Who turned out the lights?" Fenri asked the ranger.

"You're the one Henrick was looking for." Sirus stated more than questioned.

"The situation clearly isn't about me so..." Fenri tried to deflect. "What's going on?"

"Henrick and the others are fighting the king right now," Sirus said. "And it would seem that some of the guards around here are not on our side."

It was just then that the pirate's nostrils flared up. The smell of sweat and poor hygiene assaulted his sense of smell. The bearded man turned to look at the three newly arrived guards behind him. Even in the darkness, Fenri could see their bodies shuttering.

"Get out of here, lad," Fenri advised. "I'll deal with these."

For the first time, in a very *long* time, Fenri found his voice taking on a more serious tone. In his mind, and the events taking place in the keep, it would seem he would have to take a break from his demeanor of entertainment.

"Go, now," Fenri said again when he smelled that the ranger was still there.

This time, the ranger did leave, and he headed downstairs.

Through the shadows, the pirate could see the black mist leaving the bodies of the guards only to form into the shape of the possessors. The guards collapsed to the ground as the mist took its corporeal form. The reformed shade took the weapons from the guards and then stabbed them in the back, making sure they would not get up.

The four combatants stood there at the precipice of the coming melee, but in reality, the shade were stalling. Coming down the stairs, and out from doors deeper in the hallways, more shade revealed themselves. Now, there were 11 of them in total.

"Hahahaha," Fenri screamed with laughter, and his eyes became solid orbs of lavender. He showed his teeth through a sinister, snarling grin.

The shade did not care about the human's laughter at the situation, nor did it matter that some of the pirate's teeth began to grow longer and sharper.

In the throne room, the swirling winds of the shade's shadow magic flowed in a clockwise circle. Henrick and Yobo now stood back-to-back in the center of the shrouded chamber. They both realized that whatever this shade was, it was vastly different from the others that they encountered.

To Henrick, the presence of the shade's darkness was literally everywhere, and he couldn't pinpoint where it was. Every once in a while, the paladin and the monk would spot a dark, featureless face floating around with the sinister white eyes of the shade. Just as soon as they would see it, though, it would disappear.

Henrick did not have any weapons in his hand. When the shadows came to life, he had let go of the flamberge, and he wasn't able to retrieve his sword and shield. Instead, he had conjured the power of Nielda, just like he did in Rotor, and he held that power upon his glowing armor in defiance of the shadowmancer's form.

The dim brown light made it hard for Yobo to see, but what he couldn't see, he tried to find in the movement of the air around him. Unfortunately, all he could sense was the constant swirling of the wind.

Their thoughts fell upon the others in the room, but neither could see where they were at.

"Who are ye?" Henrick shouted at the swirling darkness.

There was nothing but the sound of moving air.

"If it will not speak, let us make it," Yobo suggested.

"The Esfera?" Henrick asked.

"Yes."

"It's in me bag. In front of ye somewhere," Henrick explained.

Yobo did not respond, but he tried to focus on what he could not see. He knew the direction of where Henrick's bag was, and when he took a small step in that direction, Henrick moved with him. Inch-by-inch, the two warriors moved until finally Yobo felt the bag with his foot. He reached down to grab it and produced the Esfera de Luz. The monk told the orb to glow with his mind, and sure enough, it obeyed.

As the orb's magic came to life, Yobo felt a tingling sense in his mind. He could feel the magic as if the thing was made of an elemental essence. His eyes narrowed as he thought about the theory. Last time, it was Henrick that activated the orb, and the monk thought that, perhaps, that was why the presence of elemental magic had escaped him.

"We can't use it to destroy, right?" Yobo asked Henrick for confirmation.

"Aye, but there's somethin' else," Henrick began. "This is the worst time to talk about it, but Samuel's boss said you had the ability to avoid the curse. I just wasn't sure how to bring it up before."

The admission from Henrick was the confirmation that Yobo needed to turn his theory into a probability. Instead of explaining everything, the monk stated, "I'm going to take it into my body."

"Wait, *what?*" the paladin replied.

"Protect me," the monk said.

Henrick maintained the glowing moonlight that shimmered over him, and he kept his eyes on the shadowy form that floated around them.

Yobo took the stance of Cova's Maw. He concentrated and began to channel Hesin's Cure. The monk still wasn't sure how he was going to make this work. He thought back on how the Nessian Rose bargained with him, but as he searched inside with his mind, the orb did not want anything from the monk. No matter what Yobo put on the table, the elements did not budge. When that didn't work, he took the standard approach, and simply tried to draw out the elemental light inside. Again, the elements did not budge.

Yobo then began to mentally stress himself out as the failure seeped into his demeanor. He concentrated on what was in the orb. He could definitely sense the power inside, but something was missing. There was something preventing him from claiming the light.

The monk then narrowed his eyes, and thought about the orb from a different angle.

What if the orb *was* a Hesin's Cure spell?

The possibilities flipped around in his head. There was just no way that that could be possible. *Right?* Yobo then stared blankly at the shadows surrounding them at the moment. This was where he was supposed to be. He could feel it. This is where he needed to be. Standing against this wicked foe.

He played the strings of his own heart. He was the last Gunn Drambor. He was the master of his art. His center of power was pain. The pain he had for his parents, and his late Master Asulus. It was more than just pain and memories. It was what defined him as a person.

One shade was not going to get in his way, but if this one was so powerful, how devastating its defeat would be for the ranks of those beasts. Yobo could feel the fury building inside of him, but he remained in control. Perhaps the latest encounter with the spirit of the rose taught him to be the master of his own pain. He welcomed the wounds that haunted him, and he would use them as strength.

Before Yobo could even muster the end of his thoughts, his instincts over the ebb and flow of the Uireb Nen took over. He warped the Esfera de Luz into Suldo's Stand. The golden magic shimmered over him, and tiny sparkles of light dusted across the monk's body.

Henrick never turned his eyes away from the swirling darkness as Yobo completed his ritual.

"Go for your weapon," Yobo told him with a confident smirk.

In the anticipation of the coming confrontation, the paladin left his partner behind, and rushed headlong into the dark void. Yobo spun around, facing the direction that the paladin went, and as his feet became planted, he shot a light-infused Hesin's Cure at the darkness.

From his aiming hand, Yobo came to launch a beam of light with the intensity of the noon-hour sun. The beam bolted for the black cloudy form and the shimmering energy struck home. It vaporized the mist instantly. Henrick retrieved his weapon and shield just as he was able to see it. When he came back up and Yobo's spell harmlessly struck against the stone wall, the black swirls replaced itself and the throne room was dark once again.

Out from one of the dark corners of the room, a streak of black lightning came rushing out, and struck Yobo directly in the back. The monk fell into a roll on the ground in response to the lethal spell. Yobo survived the blast, but he felt it split his robe and his skin open. The toll was heavy but the monk was still breathing.

The winds of the shadow magic returned, and the sorcerer disappeared once again. Through the giant hole in his saam, Henrick could see the terrible blackened injury the monk sustained. As Yobo returned to his feet, Henrick was glad to see the monk was still good for the fight. The two returned to their back-to-back formation.

Another streak of black lightning cracked across the throne room, but this time it came from another location inside the darkness. Henrick and Yobo were more alert now, and they caught the spark of the spell flickering to life.

The monk was quicker and he dropped to the floor to avoid the attack. "*Here!*" he screamed to Henrick.

The paladin spun around and brought up the water blade to diffuse the magic that threatened them, but when the spell ended, they lost the presence of the sorcerer once again.

Henrick found Yobo's back once again, and then asked, "Think ye can do that beam thing again?"

"Yes," Yobo answered.

Yobo took his Cova's Maw stance again, and quickly conjured the magic of Hesin's Cure. Henrick continued to keep a lookout as his normal means of detection were not working on their enemy. The cracking of thunder reverberated off the throne room walls, but the spell never came at the two.

"*No!*" came the sound of Melissa's voice.

Henrick and Yobo managed to turn their heads, but they could not see anything in the darkness. The paladin and the monk grimly realized the sorcerer was now focused on the others in the room.

"*Melissa?*" Henrick called out.

"The bastard got Tyr. I don't know about Roland," she said.

Based on the following silence, they knew the answer.

For the third time, the crack of black energy shot out from the darkness. Henrick and Yobo dodged the coming spell, but the sandaran blade fed on the fourth one that followed it. Yobo took his Hesin's Cure and blasted the spell in the direction of origin.

But the dark storm was resiliently intact.

"At this rate, the shade's gonna keep tryin' until it hits us," Henrick said.

"My thoughts exactly," Yobo added.

"Aye, we could use a miracle about now," Henrick added.

Bang!

"What was that?" Henrick said.

"The doors to the throne room?" Yobo replied.

Bang! Bang! BANG!

After a few more loud clatters of something large bashing against the throne room doors, the magic seal eventually gave way to a much greater force, and the force carried onward until it shattered the doors into a million splinters. The dust and broken wood got caught up in the swirling wind of the dark magic.

Henrick did not turn around, but Yobo could only stare with wide eyes at the beast that made large strides into the center of the throne room. It stood nearly eight-feet-tall, and was completely covered in jet black fur. Its face sported a maw of razor-sharp teeth, and it had solid lavender orbs for eyes. From what the monk could tell it was some sort of half-man, half-wolf.

Henrick could feel the monk pushing against him at that moment.

"What is it?" Henrick asked.

The creature had an ax hooked on its belt, it wore a captain's coat, and around its neck was a glowing yellow stone hanging from a necklace. To top things off, it wore a tricorne.

"Is that...the pirate?" Yobo questioned with a tone that was part confusion, part terror.

"Hahahaha," the guttural laughter of the werewolf came forth. "Started the party without me, I see."

The response forced Henrick's curiosity, even in the midst of the situation, and the paladin turned to look.

The transformed Samuel Fenri sniffed around in the air as if catching the scent of the shade, but the werewolf pirate was just as confused as the others. The winds in here were masking the dark monster's movement and location.

Without holding the Wind Stone of Anaroc, Fenri focused on it enough to get the stone's power to activate further. The powerful wind magic within the stone came to life, and not too long after, the winds in the throne room began to slow.

It was at this moment that another bolt of dark lightning shot from the dark corners of the room. This one was aimed at Fenri, but he proved to be too fast and too alert.

"What's the matter, mate?" the werewolf mocked the shade. "Don't want anyone from the same league cutting in?"

Before the others could react to the situation, the Captain of the Wailing Wolf was already bounding away at the point where the evil magic had come from. The sound of twenty heavy claws tapped on the stone as the werewolf charged.

The wind continued to slow down, but they had not stopped yet.

The werewolf saw the target and immediately pounced upon an area near the throne. His frontal c;aws dug into the shadowy form, but the figure he had caught was just an illusion. It melted away into a misty cloud and disappeared out from under the beast.

"I had him," Fenri complained.

The winds of the dark magic came under the control of the Wind Stone and they came to a complete stop. Now it was just dark and silent. Right away, Yobo could sense the moving air when the shade sailed by.

"Do you see him, Yobo?" Henrick asked as his ability to sense the creature was still no good.

"No, but I can feel him," the monk said.

"Okay. When he comes out-" Henrick began, but was cut short at the sight of something.

The shade sorcerer appeared before them, and came out of its vaporous animation. It stood between them, and the throne. To everyone else, it seemed like a misty figure with white eyes, but Henrick was able to see past the smoke.

It was a hairless humanoid with sinewy black and gray skin that seemed like it was tight across its skeletal structure. It wore a simple black robe with a cowl that covered most of its head, and as the paladin stared into the white-orange eyes of the shade sorcerer, all he could see was hatred and malice.

The shade spoke to them in the common tongue. "I am called Scar-"

The shade was cut short this time as Fenri leapt out and attempted to wrestle the shade to the ground, but the werewolf tumbled right through the evil being as though he wasn't there.

"I am called Scarm and my title is Anima," the shade form reappeared, and finished what it was saying. "I, too, have come prepared."

Henrick, Yobo, and Samuel were confused by the nature of this particular shade. Each of them could see it, but as they saw from Samuel's attack, he wasn't really there. They all knew this shadowmancer had proven to be a powerful foe thus far.

However, with the stalemate at hand, Fenri's eyes began to wonder as the smell of the shade lingered from a few different directions. It was then that the wolfman saw the glow of something inside the darkness. He tilted his head a bit trying to figure out what it was, and then it dawned on him.

It was a window.

"...But you are too late," Scarm continued his prattling. "Our legion will be here in 13 days. Too bad you won't survive to see it. However..."

As the shade talked, Fenri returned to the side of Yobo and Henrick. "Let's break the windows," he suggested.

"*Windows*?" Yobo asked as he now looked up at the narrow panes of glass.

"The sun is still up," Henrick realized.

Before the shade finished his previous statement, the group of three suddenly split in different directions as soon as Fenri made the first move. Henrick charged at the shade, image or not. Yobo and Fenri went for the various dishes that lay upon the tables in the throne room. The two of them each grabbed a few items and made turns tossing them at the closest windows.

During the first moments of flight, Anima Scarm had unleashed a series of black lightning bolts at his foes. The targets were divided and it made him confused as to how best to deal with all of them. At first, the lightning was aimed at Henrick, but the rushing tactic made the sorcerer forget what kind of sword Henrick was holding. The magic became absorbed by the arcanium steel.

Yobo and Fenri threw more objects at the stained-glass windows of the throne room, but they were not successful as the darkness that filled the room seemed to reach out and swat the dishes away. Each failed attempt was met with the clanging sound on the floor.

The werewolf then decided on the only feasible action available to them. Fenri bolted out from the side of the room he was on. He charged up from behind Henrick, and used the paladin to cover his approach. On all fours, the wolfman drove forward before leaping over the paladin and the shade sorcerer. On the other side, Fenri landed on the strong back of the throne, and from there he jumped up at the window directly above.

Swiftly, he pulled out Betty from his waist. The head of the ax could not be resisted in the hands of the lycanthrope, and when the blade kissed the glass, it shattered into a thousand tiny beads of starlight. The shaft of sunlight drove a burning blade through the darkness and upon the image of Anima Scarm. The darkness that enveloped the throne room, and the entire keep, vanished like a flash fire tore through its very existence.

The image at the center of the room was not an image. It *was* the sorcerer. The body of Anima Scarm had disintegrated until there was nothing but a black skeletal husk.

The darkness was gone and the room fell silent.

Henrick looked around the room to account for everyone. When he realized that the battle was truly over, he dropped his sword and shield to the floor. His eyes fell over the body of King Marc Blade-Briar, then to Tyr Vicidian and Roland Hadoku.

His mind then changed to the thought of the King's son. He couldn't help but wonder how he would take the news of his father's truth and demise.

With the sunlight pouring in, Samuel Fenri was forced to retire into his human form. The pirate walked over to Henrick, and placed a hand on his shoulder. Without skipping a beat on his personality, he asked, "So I'm guessin' the bounty's off."

Henrick was still awe-struck from the victory. But in light of it all, he found the pirate's humor welcoming. A heavy sigh was all he could muster. He then looked over at Yobo, "Ye feelin' okay, lad?"

Yobo performed Hesin's Cure in order to get the Esfera de Luz to rematerialize, but after that he replied. "Yes, although I keep managing to damage my robe."

Henrick could only smile at the big man's fortune, and as he did, Melissa came to Henrick's side. The paladin was equally happy that she somehow survived.

"You challenged the king, Henrick. You slew him before the House Leaders," Melissa said with a hint of grief in her words. "You saw a threat to *this* kingdom, and you traveled half the continent to find a way to protect it."

Henrick knew where her words were going, although Yobo and Fenri were not quite sure until they heard her say it.

"You're the new king."

CHAPTER TWENTY-SIX
THE FIRST LAW PART TWO

Loria maintained her barrier spell during the charge of the Claymoran Army, and during the time that the shadows engulfed the keep. But now the shadowy veil was gone, and many minutes of quiet suspense passed by. The druids, the bounty hunters, and especially, Marc II awaited the outcome of the battle in the throne room.

It was then that Melissa walked through the door, and into the lobby of the keep. Henrick was behind her, as well as Yobo and Fenri. The four of them saw the magic barrier that held the crowd at bay.

Everyone that was from Claymore knew that the Fourth Law stated that magic was not allowed, and its only punishment was death. The bold use of it in the heart of the city served as a shining example as to why that law existed. A single person holding back their entire army was enough to prove that magic-users held too much power.

Marc II especially felt this way, but it was also demoralizing to think about it. At the present, he could see its necessity, and after what he, and everyone else, saw happen to the whole keep, he also couldn't disagree with its use for the time being.

Melissa stepped through the ranks of the druids, and didn't stop until she stood before the crowd. From here, she turned and waved for Henrick to join at her side. The Claymoran Army, in its entirety, silently paid their attention to the Darkbane leader, and the no-longer helmeted Henrick.

"The King has been defeated in honorable combat! And a usurper has been slain! The Odoku and Vicidian House Leaders are also dead; struck down by a sorcerer that had seized control over the mind of the king!" Darkbane yelled across the many heads of the crowd. She paused to let her words sink in. She then waved her hand at the druids as she spoke. "Because we knew that we were dealing with a sorcerer, we called for the aid of *these* druids! They are *not* wizards or witches!" She paused again. "I heed to everyone in the ranks before me to make haste through the city and the outlying villages!" She pointed her hand at Henrick. "The man beside me will be your new king! At first light, in the morning, he will speak at the Crown Balcony! Tomorrow is a labor free day across the whole kingdom!"

A short moment passed; it was another pause to let her words sink in. The many eyes before them fell upon Henrick in that moment. Some of them were numb to the shocking news. Some of them thought that Henrick did not have the 'intimidating' look upon him. Then, there was a very small number of them who actually recognized the man from his years as a sergeant.

"Now get going!" the house leader called out, and it was at that moment that all the troops scattered to spread the news of the tale they had just heard.

After the soldiers had dispersed, the barrier holding them back faded into nothingness. Henrick, Yobo, Fenri, Kamala, the bounty hunters, all the druids, Melissa, Marc II, and Sirus came together in a circle just as they had in Solace, but this time, the gathering also included many of the high-ranking officers of the army. Everyone looked at Henrick, but under a different light.

"I want to thank everyone 'ere," the new king said. He looked to Marc II in his eyes, "Fer those who were not upstairs, the previous king *was* manipulated against his will. He was the king that Claymore needed, but unfortunately, that sorcerer snuck his way in at some point." He continued as he scanned the rest of the party. "But that monster let slip that their forces are gonna be here in 13 days. With any luck, they'll be unaware that we have the tools we need at our disposal. We will fight back."

He then pointed to Serena with an open hand. "For those who don't know 'er, this is Serena. She has been at me side since the beginnin' of this. Her, and her druids, are free to walk the city, and until the shade are dealt with, magic will be allowed so long as no harm comes to the citizens." Everyone remained silent as Henrick continued to speak, "Fer the rest of the day, I think I'm gonna go rest."

Right after Henrick made his departure, Melissa immediately eyed Serena, but in reality, she had been looking at her since she was introduced. In the process of the group's departure, she approached the druid-woman.

Serena saw the blond woman beaming her direction, and she couldn't help but notice that she was the target. Their eyes met, and in that meeting a suspicious lump formed in the throat of Serena. She remained calm, but she couldn't understand the sudden nervousness building inside. She had been living among the wilds, among 400-pound tigers, but something about the Darkbane leader almost seemed *intrusive.* She suddenly felt her heart pound as if she was getting ready to fend off a pouncing predator.

"So, you've been traveling with *my* Henrick, huh?" Melissa started with a playful tone of ownership to the man. As the woman came to a halt, she placed her gauntlet-covered hands on her hips while offering a smirk at the druid. "How did *you two* meet?"

Even with the playful tone, Serena found the directness in the words. Even if the questions were out of curiosity, Serena found herself feeling defensive as her blood vaguely shifted inside her veins, but she still didn't show it. She decided to play along for now. "I found him after the shade ambushed him, and his group. The dryad with the hood saw me there."

"*Sirus,*" Melissa brought up the ranger's name. "I remember him telling me. I guess that would make you the Witch of Claymore?"

"I suppose so," Serena answered.

An awkward silence then took over as the women felt the air between them.

"Alright, then. Come on. You can stay in my house tonight," Melissa offered, but at the same time she nearly demanded it. Darkbane could sense the reservations from the druid, but she wasn't sure if those reservations were because of her or something else. She could sense something else from the druid, but that other sensation came through her nose.

Darkbane began walking away, and as she finished turning around, her eyes went wide with disbelief that the woman carried such an odor on her.

Serena, on the other hand, thought she would have to put up a fight, but then realized that that was never really the case. The druid already heard the woman's assertiveness in the way she talked, but now could also see the purpose with each of her steps.

Perhaps it came with the competition of being a leader alongside so many men, but the thing that threw the druid off was that she could not really get a good read on Melissa. Of course, they had just met, and it was that notion about meeting the armored woman that told her to follow before she would pass judgment.

Into the Darkbane mansion they went. As they came through the entrance door, the serf that stood by as a receptionist covered and pinched his nose as Serena passed him. From the other point of view, Serena could not ignore the smell of perfume and clean linens wafting through the air. The serf's reaction was not lost on either of the women.

"What's wrong with him?" Serena asked Melissa, referring to the serf.

"Hahaha. I hate to tell you this, but you're *no* bed of roses," the blonde woman admitted.

"Are you saying I smell bad?" Serena asked as they began to ascend the stairs to the second floor. Hearing such feedback was alien to the druid. She had been living in the wilds for most of her life, she bathed in clear, fresh, cold water when she was able to. Not once, not even on the road, did she notice any foul smells, especially on her body. Even now, the scent for which she was being accused of did not find her nostrils. However, and for some reason, it did bother her self-esteem.

"Ha. That would be putting it, mildly," Melissa scoffed.

Melissa led Serena to her bedroom, and once inside, the blonde woman locked the door behind them before going to close the curtains. The darkness that came over the room soon disappeared as Melissa lighted the candle sconces.

Almost immediately, she began the lengthy process of doffing her armor, but when Melissa saw the druid standing by the entrance, aimlessly, she had to say, "What are you waiting for? Take your clothes off."

The request was so direct and open that it nearly knocked Serena down on to her butt. However, she remained standing against her own flabbergasting. Not once in her life did she have to share privacy with someone, and because of all this, she wasn't sure she heard Darkbane correctly. "*What*?" she mustered.

"It's *okay*. No prying eyes of the men in here. It's just us women," the blonde assured.

While Serena hesitated to obey the command of Melissa, she couldn't believe how uncomfortable the woman was. It was in no time at all that Melissa's voluptuous, bare figure became caressed by the still air in the bedroom. Once or twice, the blonde woman would look curiously at the brunette, and she had to wonder what was taking the woman so long? Has she never done something like this before? Did that mean that her and Henrick never...? The thought of innocence almost made her laugh out loud, but she kept it to herself.

Nonetheless, Melissa walked to and from the bathtub, and to the surface of her dresser where she had all of her soaps, oils, perfumes, and lotions. At the bath, Melissa would use the hand-lever pump to draw hot water from the boiler downstairs, and into the tub. She would pour a couple of liquids from bottles until the steamy water was coated with fragrant bubbles.

Unknown to Melissa, Serena's heart was racing. The druid wasn't sure what to do in the situation, and she found that she was equally intimidated by Melissa's beauty. She was frozen in her own stupor and could only wonder why she felt this way.

When Serena failed to act, Melissa took it upon herself to break the druid out of her shell. She came over, still bare ass naked, grabbed Serena by the hand and led her further into the confines of the bedroom. The smell was atrocious, but it didn't matter. Darkbane silently vowed, one way or another, she was going to turn Serena into a *real* woman. She pulled the druid until she stood before a five-foot mirror in the corner beyond the dresser.

Melissa knew her way around a suit of armor, and the leathers that the druid wore would be no challenge for her. One by one, the blonde would undue buckles, straps, and tug at the limbs when she needed to.

Serena was still numb to the experience, and she just let the woman do as she pleased. Melissa silently scoffed at Serena's quiet, but couldn't help displaying a smirk that she was already winning this battle.

The busty blond finally became satisfied in her quest when she got the undershirt and pants off of Serena. The druid's body was riddled in scars, but the discomfort of the open air and the sight of the two women in the mirror struck immediately. Serena wrapped her arms around her chest in order to cover up her breasts.

Melissa couldn't believe the conservative nature of the young woman nor would she allow it. She spun the woman to face her, grabbed the druid's arms, pulled them out wide, and then embraced her in a tight hug. Serena could tell from the woman's figure that she was very fit, and that she would not escape the grasp if she wanted to.

As they stood there in a hug, Melissa could only silently mouth "whoa" as the smell of the druid's hair was not any better. If she was going to get to the woman's heart, she needed to survive this. With their mouths next to the other's ear, Melissa asked Serena, "Do you like him?"

Serena tightened her own arms around Melissa in order to not show her beat red face, but the druid had already given the warrior-woman the answer in doing so. The druid knew that Darkbane was referring to Henrick, but just as the realization of the reference had come, it also departed the druid's mind, defeated by the one thing she values more. In some strange way, Melissa asking that question, and hearing it out loud suddenly made her feel a little comfortable in the woman's embrace. She didn't want to let go of her at that moment.

"Even if I did, my station forbids it," Serena explained. There was a mix of somber notes and resolve as she spoke. "I have come to enjoy his company, though."

From one warrior to another, Melissa admired the druid's sense of duty, and she knew that if the druid was like *this*, Henrick liked her as well. Even though she had just met the druid, Serena's virtues of honor and discipline was worthy of her being in Claymore.

"You've known him for a while?" Serena asked.

Melissa narrowed her eyes and wanted to explode with laughter, but for the sake of the young woman, she would avoid any elaboration. She answered, "You could say that."

"What if he doesn't like me back?" Serena then displayed drops of doubt in her words.

Melissa then released the embrace and held Serena out at a half-arm's length. "If I know that man, he probably feels the same way about you." Melissa then dropped her hands down, but not before taking a playful swat and flipping one of Serena's breasts with her hand as she walked towards the tub. She followed it with, "Now, let's get those perky girls clean."

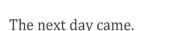

The next day came.

From atop the Crown Balcony, Marc Blade-Briar II and Melissa Darkbane looked down upon Rose Park.

The people of Claymore had gathered in full force.

The streets of the city were beyond capacity. Some of the people sat on top of roofs to get a better view. As the people awaited the arrival of the *new king*, those on the balcony could hear the indecipherable noise of a thousand conversations. The air grew warm as the bright sun rose above the east wall.

"I've not seen the people *gather* like this before, not even after the last Grand Melee," Marc II exclaimed. "It feels great to know the people still have hearts."

"Indeed. The weight of the shadows has been lifted. I have no doubt that Henrick will ignite the fire in our people once again," Melissa assured Marc.

Behind the two leaders, the druids, the bounty hunters, Fenri, Yobo, Kamala, and Sirus gathered. Some of them held side conversations, while some of them also awaited the arrival of the king in a patient silence.

Off to the side, Serena stood by herself. It wasn't her decision to do so, but rather, she became Melissa's personal social experiment. She wore a golden dress from one of Darkbane's handmaidens. The fit was *perfect*, or so that was what Melissa had told her. Her skin felt smooth and silky. It was unlike anything she felt before, but she couldn't decide if she was comfortable with it. Some of the lotions that Melissa used even covered up her scars. Her cheeks were dusted with a light blush. Her brown hair was combed and wrapped into a large braid at the back. Serena could still smell the powerful soap and perfume on her body; it was sweet and airy, and she could gather the hints of rose and lavender. However, it did seem a little overpowering.

Melissa watched the woman, and the others, and could only smile at herself when she could tell the others had no idea who she was. The experiment only had one last test. It was then that her thoughts acted like the cue as the two short bursts of the bugle announced the arrival of the new king. Everyone turned to regard the man coming up the steps from the inner city.

As with tradition, he wore the flamemail, even with its damaged links, and just like every monarch had when assuming command of Claymore, he had the flamberge strapped to his back.

Henrick shot a nod to the others as he passed them, he then set his sights upon Melissa and Marc II, and the balcony beyond them. Just as his shoulder became perpendicular to the person hiding at his side, his nose caught a familiar scent, and it made him flinch in his steps.

Most of them did not see the unusual movement, but Melissa stared at the man like a hawk with expectations. It was one more step before Henrick came to a complete stop. He narrowed his eyes at Melissa, who had suddenly crossed her arms, but the smell was not coming from her. It was coming from somewhere else.

He immediately looked to his side, and looked at the woman in the gold dress. His eyes were not narrowed much longer as he came to see the facial profile that hid among everything else. Henrick's mouth opened slightly.

"*Serena?*" Henrick stated with a disbelieving whisper.

Serena almost felt embarrassed to be seen in the dress, but Melissa had mentioned to her that if he stammered, he was interested. To that effect, Serena only returned a confirming smile.

Henrick's mind then fell on guilty thoughts as his focus came on to the color of the dress. He immediately came to the realization that this was Melissa's handiwork. *What did those two possibly have to talk about?* Just before his appearance to the rest of the kingdom, he became plagued with innocent paranoia, and it was something that he was alien to. Still though, he could not deny that Serena *was* stunning under the light of the morning sun.

"Hey! Are you ready for this?" Melissa called out to Henrick.

Before the new king could respond, he took the necessary steps to get next to Melissa. She wore a wicked grin as he approached, but he did not say anything to her. Instead, he only looked at the woman as if trying to read her mind, but it was useless.

Henrick took his first steps onto the balcony, and it didn't hit him until he was already at the edge.

There was an astronomical amount of people below him.

It *was* overwhelming, but he had already sold himself on the idea that he would own this moment. After all, these people were nothing compared to a dragon. He could hear the muttering of the people below come to a stop. The anticipation was unreal for most of the citizens of Claymore. Nearly everyone in the crowd did not know who this rogue kingslayer was.

He stood there in a brief moment of silence with his eyes closed. He reached out with his feelings. The citizens of this turmoil-stricken nation filled the air with drowned hope and forgotten strength. As they took note of his shadow above them, he could feel their energy. It was high, hopeful, and it was also electrifying.

He wanted to uplift the spirits of his people. Like he always wanted to. Assure them that he was worthy of standing before them. Henrick then opened his eyes and looked down upon the people of his adopted nation. Before he spoke, he swung the mighty flamberge off his back and held the blade in both hands.

He cleared his throat, and as clearly and loudly as he could muster, he began, "People of Claymore, your king is dead! I took his life before the council of the Four Houses, because I believed 'em to be an imposter, and a conspirator to the destruction of our kingdom! In both regards, I have proven to be right!" He paused to let his words sink in. "This conspiracy was orchestrated by a member of our most ancient of enemies! The shade!

"Durin' the last month, we have lost two of our House Leaders, our own General Hormac, Captain Spearfall, and a number of our own army at the hands of our enemy! At this very hour, they march to us! They march to us with a legion of dark fighters! They'll be here at the end of a tenday, and no other hold is likely to come to our aid!

"It has been seven centuries since the shade were tossed from this castle! And it has been nearly 300 years since we have fought a war! As yer new king, I stand before ye to tell ye this...

"War is coming!

"But all of us have been waiting for this! For the day that the red banner goes to war!" The crescendo climbed now, he held the flamberge in the sky, and Henrick managed to get even louder. "We will be known as the Sword Kingdom once again! This entire land is *named* because of us! This is Claymore! We will toss the shade from this castle again, and with the War-God's blessing, we will be victorious!"

Clapping and cheering roared from the people below. There was a new king, and a war was already on the horizon. There was nothing else the people needed to hear from their king. War is what the people of this land used to thrive on, and its hunger had been dormant for far too long. But then the cheering took a boom of gasps as the people pointed up to the balcony in awe as a cacophony took in the hearts of the people even more.

Melissa and Marc, who stood closest to Henrick, had to take a few steps back from the platform. Everyone, literally everyone, at the moment was in shock at the sight of their king.

Henrick focused on bringing forth the power within himself to conjure the moonlight upon his figure, but when he did he suddenly sensed that he had awakened something inside the flamberge. When he brought the moonlight to the surface, it never came.

Instead, Henrick became engulfed in an aura of green fire after a sound of ignition. The paladin did not know what was happening, but he, and the rest of the people of Claymore, knew only one significance behind the presence of green fire.

"The salamander is watching us," Marc Blade-Briar II managed to say with his mouth halfway open. Once he was a safe distance away, the House Leader fell to a knee in utter disbelief.

The others on the balcony, save for Fenri, followed suit.

Melissa Darkbane took a different action. She rushed to Henrick's side. She could feel the heat from her friend's aura, but it only worked to amplify her own heat in getting the message across. Across the Rose Park, and into the streets of Claymore, the people heard her sharp and fierce voice as she yelled, *"Hail to the King!"*

The people below got the cue, and all fell to a knee. The militiamen in the park looked across the crowds to ensure everyone displayed their loyalty. A single person at the head of the crowd in Rose Park stood back up and faced the population in attendance.

"Hail to the King!" the person yelled.

"Hail to the King!" came the roar from the people.

"Hail to the King!" the single person yelled again, even louder this time.

The people took the challenge and roared even louder. *"Hail to the King!"*

The hair on Henrick's body stood up as the tenacity of his new kingdom could be felt. Likewise, the reverberations in the air, and the renewal of glory and hope brought a tear to Melissa's eyes.

CHAPTER TWENTY-SEVEN
WAR COUNCIL

Several hours had passed after the completion of King Skullbright's speech to the citizens of Claymore. The king's delegation on the balcony remained until the crowd below dispersed. The people slowly departed the streets and began to mozy their way back home. It was during this time that Henrick explained to the house leaders that he wanted to summon all officers to the keep for a formal council in order to discuss the events to come. His mind was already on the war that was coming.

As everyone had departed, Henrick came to Serena's side. "Come on," he said.

Serena walked by his side as they departed the Crown Balcony. Together, they began their stroll through the streets of the city, and Henrick guided their path.

First, they headed south towards the Sword Gate and then they went through it into the Sword Ward. After that, they turned to the east towards Rose Ward. Along the way, many citizens passed by and greeted their new king with a bow or a salute. Henrick always returned the bearing in kind.

Along the walk, Serena was the one that started the dialogue, "So, you're the king now?"

"Aye. Although, I'll admit that was not me goal," Henrick admitted. "The laws and traditions took care of that." He then brought his attention to Serena's physique after a moment's pause. "I see Melissa *had* her way with you?" He could see the face of the druid was flushed with red.

"Yeah, but I don't know if I like all of this, though," Serena explained while looking at herself again for about the 30th time.

"I couldn't agree more," Henrick said. "I liked yer hair when it was all messy. Although, I'll admit Melissa knows what she's doin'."

"So I look okay like this?" Melissa asked for confirmation. Her ears picked up on the compliment from the man. Her heart palpitated on the notion. Standing there next to him after having to fight the shade made her feel good to share the private moment they now had. She felt like she was beginning to truly understand how she felt about Henrick. Especially, after traveling the continent with him, and Melissa getting her to express her thoughts out loud.

But her station as a druid weighed heavy on her heart and mind, it was weight that was always there now. It was a weight that she feared would endure their friendly relationship. However, she was nevertheless curious if Henrick was willing to admit the same, and she secretly hoped that Darkbane was correct with her assessment of the man.

"Bah," Henrick scoffed before he finished his thought. "How ye look doesn't matter. It's the kind of heart ye carry in yer chest that makes ye who ye are."

As Henrick walked with her, he could not deny the sweet fragrance coming from his friend. It was intoxicating, but the king was more than aware of the luring effects of perfume. As he had told Serena, he *did* prefer the woman in her normal get up. Something about the wilderness in the woman lulled him along more than the dress or her swaying hips. Of course, Henrick also could not deny how the woman *did* look in the dress.

But Henrick had reached a similar dilemma on his hands. He was now the King of Claymore. How weak might he appear if he was to take a magic user in his arms for all the people to see? How many challengers to the throne would he face should the citizens learn of his secret? He found that his new title as the country's leader would have to stay his hand in pursuing a deeper relationship with the woman. To that end, in silent suffering, he would have to enjoy Serena's presence, and nothing else.

Both of them felt the unspoken bond between them as they took their walk through Rose Park.

Deep inside, they wanted to let the words out, but each of them held responsibilities that required their attention first.

Serena spent half of the walk with her eyes down. It wasn't out of fear or embarrassment of her looks, it was the despair at having to keep her heart quiet.

Henrick forced himself to keep his eyes up and remain distracted by the exchange of courtesies he had with the people as he went by.

Time slipped by, and eventually, they ended up on the north side of town in the Coin Ward. From here, they used the Coin Gate to get back to the inner city.

They headed straight for the keep and went inside.

"I'd like ye to sit next to me," Henrick said to Serena as they crossed the lobby.

"Okay," she said with a smile and a nod.

On the first floor, at the rear of the keep, there was a dining hall. Henrick and Serena made their way there, passing through a couple of doors, and the king could only hope that everyone was already mustered.

As the two entered the rear hallway of the keep, Henrick saw someone that had been the furthest in his mind for as long as he could remember. That person was, of course, Cleric Landar. In an instant, the annoying cleric shot the king a grin as he approached.

"Ah, sire," the cleric said, his voice carried into the door of the dining room just a couple of feet away. The robed man opened his mouth to say something else, but he was interrupted by the quick, pointing finger of the king.

"Don't. *Even.* Say it," Henrick warned him. His voice also carried into the dining room.

Henrick knew what the cleric was going to do. He was going to tease the king about "Sol's favor", and how the cleric had been right about the man the entire time. Again, though, Henrick didn't want to hear it. The encounter made the cleric even more annoying to the king at that moment.

They entered the dining room, Cleric Landar included. The large room had a polished dark oak table that was long and able to seat 24 people. The walls were covered with red painted plaster and half paneled with oak. The ceiling was flat, and from it, several iron chandeliers hung with lighted candles. The place smelled of fresh red carpet due to its nonuse during the tenure of the last few monarchs.

All around the room, the various officers from the Claymoran Army stood with the collection that had followed Henrick from Solace. Standing before their seats at the table was Melissa Darkbane, Marc Blade-Briar II, and the commanders of the brigades, the city watch, and High Solian Morgan.

"All hail, the king," Melissa announced Henrick's arrival.

"Hail," came the reverberating response from everyone else.

"Be seated," Henrick commanded. He took the seat at the head of the table.

Serena took the empty seat between him and Melissa.

"Sire," Melissa began before pointed her eyes at two people across the table from her. "This is Beadu of House Odoku, and Garrick of House Vicidian."

Beadu was the wife of the late Roland Hadoku, and as the custom of House Odoku dictates, the most recent spouse of the House Leader acts as the replacement should something fatal happen to the current one. She was a well-built odum woman and she had a very muscular physique. Her arms protruded from the sleeveless blue robes that the members of that house typically wore. She stood just over six feet, and her hair was braided into very long dreadlocks.

Garrick Vicidian was not as weasel-looking as his predecessor, and in fact, he was just the opposite. He was a very heavy set sanct, and everyone knew that the man enjoyed food more than fighting. Even with that knowledge on hand, most did not challenge the prowess of Garrick as the man could swing a maul as if swinging a twig. The man had brown curly hair and a complementing mustache.

Both of the new house leaders offered a silent nod to the king to which he returned. After a second's pause, the war council began.

"Let's keep this as straight to the point as possible," Henrick began, his tone driving with seriousness as he scanned the room. All eyes were upon him. "The shade'll be here at the end of a tenday. Should they determine their pre-emptive strike has been discovered, they might try to come earlier. We cannot afford to waste any time in our preparation, and as the situation *is* dire, we're gonna need the aid of magic support in our war."

Almost immediately, the room became an uproar of mumbling whispers. The officers looked at each other, some of them shooting their eyes at the druids as they pleaded their disagreement with each other.

Marc Blade-Briar II stood up from his chair. It got the attention of everyone, and they grew quiet as the man prepared to speak. His eyes scanned the room as he said, "Claymore has always been a nation of warriors. To preserve our culture, I would disagree." He then pointed his eyes at the king.

The grumbling of agreement from everyone came, but it was cut short.

"But my disagreement will have to stay until after the battle," Marc II began again. He then pointed his finger at Loria. "Just one of these druids was capable of keeping *all* of your troops from storming the keep. I don't want it, either." He paused to make his notes more profound. "But after hearing about that thing in the throne room...we are going to need all the help we can get against Claymore's oldest enemy. I can't imagine how hard it was for my ancestors to remove the shade from this place, but with blades alone, it does not seem feasible."

"It's not feasible," Melissa agreed. "Contrary to what the common folk may believe, Claymore was cleansed of the shade using the artifact that our *now* king set out across the continent to find."

"Where is this artifact?" one of the officers voiced their question.

Those that knew of the artifact's existence turned their heads to look at Yobo. Regardless of the audience, Yobo went ahead and produced the dim-glowing artifact from under his saam.

"It is right here." Yobo said as he held the object out.

Henrick then added. "For those that don't know, the shade're able to vanish into mist under the cover of darkness, and they're very hard to kill. Some of *them* also wield magic that'll strike a person dead in an instant. This orb'll give us a fightin' chance. The previous owner of that artifact assured me that our friend Yobo here, is the only one that can use the artifact safely."

"What do you mean, *safely*?" Garrick asked.

"Anyone usin' the orb's power beyond a certain limit contracts a curse," the king explained. "However, I do not want to leave everythin' to our single trump card. The shade've had seven centuries to plan their invasion. We only have a tenday. Given what we already know, they'll most likely strike at night. We need to grasp every advantage possible."

Melissa had the first suggestion, "Given your previous concerns, we should bring all the transients back into the city, feed them really well, and get them into some of the vacant homes so that they can get their strength. The Gold Brigade will handle this."

Marc II then added, "The Red Brigade will visit the outlying villages, and conscript everyone that is able to fight."

"Should we reach out to other countries?" one of the red brigade commanders asked.

Yobo was the first to answer, "Telosa will not help us. However, I do know the headmaster at Planesgate. It is possible, he could aid us."

"Hmpf. Planesgate has had a distaste for us in the past. Even with the Sword Treaty, I don't think many magicians would jump at the chance to help us," Beadu argued. "The battles between us and the other countries, however historical they are, might be our undoing."

"That is why *I* will go and ask him myself," Yobo explained.

Henrick nodded. "Very well. Anyone else?"

"What about the catapults in Hel?" the voice of a really young woman piped in. Standing behind Melissa was her younger sister, Amelia.

"Now, *that* is a good idea," came the agreement from Beadu with a hearty smile. "Leave that task to the Blue Brigade."

Reeth was the next to speak, "There may be another druid that could aid us."

The comment brought in curious looks from everyone else, even the other druids.

Reeth elaborated, "In the lands called Ravenlock, there is a sandari who lives out there."

"*Ravenlock*?" Garrick cut in. "My ancestors fled from there. Our records tell of a wound in the world that opened up, and from that wound, giant bugs and spiders emerged to destroy our kingdom."

"Although unfortunate, if nature decides it's time to reclaim lost materials, it will," the large orc glared at the human. "The druid who lives out there is part of a blood line of sandari who keep those giant insects at bay. He ensures that the cycle of life remains *contained* in that...*wound*, as you put it."

"Where was that blood line when our people still lived there?" Garrick goaded.

Reeth was an orc, and he couldn't help but fancy the thought of jumping across the table at the pudgy man. But he was also a wise druid and saw right through the man's bluster. He responded, "Your people? It seems you fail to notice your own breathing, and that you are very much alive."

The druids each shared a smirk as the human sat back in his seat frowning with a disgusted look on his face. It was now Garrick that he wanted to jump across the table.

548

"I will leave the druid in Ravenlock to you then," Henrick said. The warrior-king then looked beyond the druids to the remaining members, Fenri and Kamala. "What of you, Captain? Kamala?"

"Ye know I can't be given an order to me crew from here," Fenri noted. "But should things get dicey...I'll bark. Hahahaha." The pirate drew weird looks from everyone, and he could not help but bust into a short fit of laughter.

Kamala scanned the room while she met the eyes that were upon her. Her sharp and lowered eyebrows toyed with the many minds before her. She smiled at the thought of spreading an ounce of fear among the hearts of the unknown warriors in attendance. She then took a small bow as she admitted to everyone in the room, "The Black Lotus is at your disposal."

All the officers in the room flinched and were flabbergasted by the woman's declaration. They all knew about the Black Lotus, and they all knew the assassins were close neighbors of theirs too.

That was just the icing on the cake, though. Many of the officers began to wonder what kind of king they had. A king who had brought a *circus* to this meeting of war. A small number of them, however, could see that King Skullbright had already been planning for this war long ago, and had already brought in the most unlikely of allies.

"Hahaha. A bloodthirsty nation siding' with murderers and summoners to slaughter an impending invasion from the forces of darkness?" Fenri then added to the lingering notion as the energy was building. "What're we waiting for?"

The comment sent a blood-warming sentiment to everyone in the room. No matter how they felt about anyone else in the room, everyone could agree to the idea of war. The muttering of side conversations and vibrant emotions fill the room.

As Henrick sat there, his mind turned numb as his thoughts fell upon the notion that many would perish in the coming assault, and that someone at this very table might not be here when it was all over. It was also possible that none of them would be. It left him in a somber place in the back of his mind.

He even found himself scanning his eyes around the room as if trying to guess or determine who was going to make it, and who was not. Of course, the answers weren't there.

It was then that he discovered something that he was afraid of...

...Telling others to go die for him.

He realized that his journey did not prepare him for this way of thinking. Not even on the balcony before his speech did it strike him. He wasn't normally an emotional person, but right now he could feel the tension inside. He assured himself that his turmoil would not be anyone else's. They were going to war either way, and that cold realization kept him from being sad.

He then looked over at the friend he had made at the beginning of this, and who had stuck with him this whole time.

It was Serena.

Serena smiled at him through the absence of words, and it took Henrick out of his somber stupor. He knew that he really cared about her, and he knew he would be torn if something happened to her during this battle. He didn't want to reveal that to her in order to keep her from worrying, but he could tell that he already gave that away from how she was studying his face.

Before he got too stuck in the mud of his mind, he returned his attention to the matter at hand. He stood up and everyone quieted down. "Alright. Let's make preparations, get the orders to the troops, and fortify the city. We're gonna send these beasts back to hell."

CHAPTER TWENTY-EIGHT
THE HIVE

The druids set out from Claymore the next day. They all had taken the form of birds, with the exception of Ti'or, who was an air elemental. Ravenlock was a neighboring kingdom to the northeast; long abandoned by its human population due to its historical calamity. The land itself, though, still remained a kingdom to other forms of life.

Kormanth, and the late Levinar, had been the only members of the Ember Grove to have actually met the druid that lived on the far east of the region. Before their departure, Kormanth had briefed the others on his past experiences when traveling to Ravenlock, and explained that the skies there were always plagued by an everlasting rainstorm.

The journey to the neighboring kingdom, even while flying, was four days. Over the course of their flight, all the druids had been scanning the ground below in an attempt to scout for any threats or shade gatherings. They all knew what the shade looked like, and they especially scanned at night for any signs. As each day grew into the night, the druids would descend and take rest as they needed to.

Each time Serena retook her humanoid form, she felt grateful when she saw that she was not wearing the golden dress. She felt more natural, and her hair did not hurt from being pulled back and braided. However, even without looking civilized, she couldn't help but feel a strange air among her fellow druids when they would look upon her.

She had remained faithful to her station as a druid, but she was aware that perhaps the others had already made their judgments. She knew that being a druid was the most important thing to her. Even more important than how she felt about Henrick.

But as the echo of her own self-assurance bounced around in her mind, she didn't know if she could bring herself to voice that admittance out loud. She could only feel torn about it, and because she felt torn, she became afraid of her own feelings.

The druids came upon the borders of Ravenlock on the second night, and down below, they could see a portion of the Sword River. Not too far away from the banks of the river, there was a grouping of stone ruins from a long-forgotten town.

Just as Kormanth had mentioned previously, the skies were riddled with rain clouds just as they had crossed the river. To avoid sleeping in the rain, Reeth used his empathic link to express interest in staying in the ruins for the night. The other druids unanimously agreed before following him down.

On the ground, they resumed their humanoid forms and quickly began searching the ruins for any potential dangers. Ti'or remained an elemental and swept through all the tiny cracks and crevices that the ruins harbored. With the shade potentially on the prowl, they did not want to take any chances.

The place was overgrown with clinging vines and six-foot-tall grass, and the soggy ground would make a mushing sound every time the druids would take a step. When the coast was clear, the druids regrouped at the edge of the village that was closest to the river.

Reeth pointed at some of the closer structures that still had a roof and said, "Let's hole up in these for the night. It should allow us to have fire."

The other druids silently agreed. They walked inside to get the places situated, but Serena did not join them.

Instead, she walked in the opposite direction and headed towards the edge of the river. Even as a human, the woman had eye's that could roughly see in the dark. The night sky was starless from the clouds above, and although she could not enjoy the presence of the Twins, she *did* enjoy the soothing feeling of the rain touching her face.

She then watched the river rushing to run southward, but even in the presence of all this beautiful water and the white noise it brought, she could feel her own doubts flooding back into her mind. She felt like her heart was strangling her and just wanted to breathe. She wanted to refocus herself.

Her own turmoil over the last couple of days had made her forget about an aspect of being a druid, and she had become completely oblivious to the empathic waves she was sending to the others.

It was on this second night that her mentor decided to intervene. Kormanth had approached Serena from behind, but because of the rain, and the woman's distracted mind, he was able to walk up to her without her noticing. Since Serena was a druid with feline affinity, Kormanth raised an eyebrow at her unresponsiveness.

"What's troubling you?" Kormanth asked.

Serena shot him an eye through her peripheral, but she was reluctant to answer.

"All of us have felt your despair," Kormanth admitted. "And I want to know if your head is in the right place?"

"The only thing I have ever known is being a member of this grove," Serena started. "It is all I have wanted, and I don't want to fail you, or the others."

"Fail us how?" Kormanth asked.

"I don't want to end up like my parents," she voiced her fear while turning to her mentor.

Kormanth needed a few seconds to contemplate what she meant by that, and had remembered everything he had told the woman about her parents, and their exile from the grove over two decades ago. He then connected the dots. "You have developed feelings for Claymore's king?"

There was a long pause, but Serena did not answer. This was also a realm of expertise that

Kormanth did not have much knowledge in, and it was the voice of another druid that broke the silence.

"Don't be afraid of how you feel," came the raspy, deep words of Reeth.

Serena and Kormanth turned to regard the orc as he approached, but as Reeth got closer, he turned around to see if another of the druids was around, and when he did not see Loria, he continued.

"Dryads are not known for their *flexibility*," the druid said, almost in a loud whisper, "They were once made of wood, you know, and Levinar was no exception. *I* am the arch-druid now, and while I do see the logic in creating druidic laws, it also inhibits the expansion of what life is."

Serena's blood felt lighter as she could sense where Reeth was starting to go.

The orc then provided more of his own opinion "Just between you and me, kid. As long as you don't forsake your vow to nature in your personal pursuits, I could care less about what you do with your time. Hell, you managed to bring to light the greatest threat the land has had in centuries."

Serena offered a smile to the arch-druid and simply said, "Thank you."

Reeth offered a toothy grin in return. "Anytime."

At the end of the conversation, Serena's mind was at ease. She had practically been given permission to pursue her own life. Of course, she reminded herself, that she still had to put her job as a druid first. She already knew that Henrick would understand that. Nonetheless, she felt the fire in her heart once more, and she was ready to tackle the mission.

The three druids returned to the stone structures, and prepared to get some rest. They gathered around the fires they had started, drank from their waterskins, and ate from the rations provided to them by Claymore. They took turns watching the darkness outside, hidden in animal form, and silently prayed that no enemies would find them.

———————— ◐ ————————

A couple days later, the druids found themselves over the ruins of Castle Ravenlock. From on high, they were witness to the aftermath of the raw might of nature. The castle was half-hanging, half-collapsed inside of a large, sloping, gray canyon, and to the north and south, the canyon ran the length of their aerial view. The miles of rain clouds were darkest above the castle, and the ground was shrouded by a light fog. The sight of it all was both terrifying and impressive.

In addition to these notions, Serena felt curious about the sandaran druid. Kormanth had never really mentioned this druid in his teachings to her, and given the landscape and weather, she could not imagine someone, even a druid, living out here. She also had to wonder if the weather was foreshadowing their meeting with the druid.

Kormanth screeched in his blood eagle form, and empathically communicated to his companions to follow him. He banked into a turn before swooping down to the ruins of the castle below. The others followed in pursuit.

A moment later, the druids came to land inside the square-shaped courtyard of the destroyed castle. As they all returned to their humanoid forms, they stood in the center of the drenched garden, but half of it was missing. Several yards to their right was the start of the sloping edge of the canyon.

Beyond the courtyard, and mostly in the western directions, the moss-covered bricks of the castle rose up to form the rest of the grand structure. There were large towers at the corners, square in shape, and the thick walls that connected everything together, held numerous doorways that led to other sections. Some of the doorways still had their doors, others did not, and the ones that did not, revealed the dark interiors in which the druids could not see.

"What a despressin' place," Kadrah said.

No one else made a comment, but they all felt the same way.

"The only way down to Sorin's lair is a tunnel inside the keep. From there, we can descend into the catacombs," Kormanth explained to the others.

"His *lair*?" Kadrah questioned.

"You'll see soon enough," Kormanth assured her.

The others did not question him further, but the wise and new arch-druid did wonder about something else, though.

"Is there any way we can alert Sorin of our presence?" the orc asked.

"No. He has his mind tied to the hive down there. If he were to ever let go of it, the bugs would surely get out of control," the human responded. "The outcome would leave destruction in its wake as you can see by this place."

"Nature has *reclaimed* this land. This is not destruction." Loria argued, and she was not far from the truth of it.

The keep was severely overgrown with vines. Every brick was green with moss. Torn banners with the House Vicidian raven logo hung from weathered posts. It was a humbling warning that if Terra wanted to take something back into the folds of her earth, there was little they, or anyone, could do to stop her.

When the moment passed, Kormanth led the way through the courtyard, and to a large archway that held two weather-stricken wooden doors. The doors led inside the four-story keep, and the bird-druid pushed them open with ease and squeaking from water-logged hinges. Droplets of water flew in all directions as the doors came crashing against the walls inside to reveal the dark confines within.

The druids entered the keep's lobby. There was a long rug that sat under an inch of water, and it ran the length of the chamber until coming to a large door on the opposite side. To their left and right, many other corridors led to other sections of the darkened keep.

"Wait," Ti'or whispered to his companions to get them to stop. His feline nose caught the scent of something unfamiliar as they stood in the center of the room. "The air is unclean. A predator, perhaps."

The druids looked around but they weren't sure what they were looking for. There were many dark areas of the keep, and the light from outside was not bright by any means. The ceiling was high and dark as well.

Loria whispered a small chant, "*Éadrom*," to light the tip of her quarterstaff with magical white light.

The dryad held her staff above her head, and then all the druids sought to look upwards. The druids were able to share a sense of uncertainty and dread as the ceiling was covered with a nest of monstrous spiders. There were six of the bear-sized arachnids, and all of them were as still as death itself as they were snuggled into their thick and slimy webs.

The doors behind the druids suddenly closed, and the sound of footfalls echoed off the walls. The echo begged the druids to look at the far end of the lobby. The light from Loria's staff showed that there was a grand staircase that wrapped over the large door in front of them.

A dark-cloaked figure stood at the top of those steps. Glowing red eyes could be seen beyond the veil of its cowl. The strange humanoid spoke some words, but the language was lost on the ears of the druids, save for one.

"Dryami," Loria exclaimed. The dryad druid recognized the language and its structure.

"*Dryami*?" Serena asked.

"A dark dryad," Loria translated the word with a face and tone of seriousness, "and it said *welcome*, but that word does not exist among their kind."

"*Oh*? So, we're not leaving alive," Kormanth mocked the situation.

The lone dryami served as a distraction while the spiders quickly descended upon the castle floor. Reeth noticed the movement from above, he turned to regard Loria as if he was about to say something, but he had no time for words. He pounced into a dive at Loria. With his heavy body, he tackled the dryad to get her out of the way just as a monstrous spider barreled down upon them with giant fangs. The other spiders followed suit, and now the druids were surrounded by the eight-legged beasts.

Reeth recovered to his feet, he instantly transformed into his fire-orc form. The spiders took note of the orc for they were not particularly fond of fire. Serena assessed the hesitation coming through her eyes, and she followed Reeth's example by taking her firecat form. Between the two of them, they had the attention of all the spiders.

"We'll deal with these, the rest of you handle that dark dryad," Reeth commanded.

Ti'or vanished as the huntari took to the wind.

Meanwhile, Kormanth rushed headlong into the fray as two spiders blocked his path. Loria and Kadrah were not too far behind. Kormanth closed the gap with the hideous creatures and whipped his eagle-feather cloak aside to relinquish his scimitar. He did not plan to strike at the spiders, though, because a powerful gust blew by and threw the spiders aside into a nearby wall.

However, one of the spiders was bigger than the other, and the big one was able to use the hooks at the end of its legs to hold firmly to the stone floor. Kormanth noted the beast had remained and he prepared to strike with a coiled arm.

The larger creature used its massive form, and the muscle of all eight legs to pounce at Kormanth with an incredible burst of speed. Fangs sank into the man's non-dominant arm like giant spikes. The pain overtook all other feelings the druid had in his body, but the sensation was gone as quickly as it came. Kormanth took his other arm, the one with the scimitar, and drove the blade in between the eight eyes. The spider fell dead in an instant, but he could also feel his legs becoming shaken. As the area of the bite became numb, he knew that he had been poisoned.

Loria saw her companion fall to the floor after being bitten. She thought to cast a healing spell on him, but she needed time to do so, and they needed to deal with the adversaries first. The dryad spotted the other spider that had been blown away, and she used her druidic magic to bring the vines upon the walls to life. They wrapped the spider until it was completely constricted, but her ever-fiery temperament amplified the strength of the vines, squeezing the arachnid until the bulb of its rear popped with blood and liquid webbing. The creature was still alive but it squealed in pain.

With her fellow druid distracted in the fighting, Kadrah rushed forward to meet the dark dryad on the stairs. In the dwarf's flight, the dryami brought its hands together and began to summon dark magic in the form of a sphere that swirled with dark blue and purple energy. The creature's eyes glowed intensely with red as the power came forth. It raised the magic upon its head as it prepared to launch the unfamiliar spell.

But then the spell fizzled.

Ti'or rematerialized from being an air elemental, and snuck up behind the dark dryad. The huntari flashed his razor-sharp claws from his hands before reaching up to the throat. In one swift motion, the claws tore through flesh and ripped out a chunk of the dryami's windpipe.

"Thanks, Ti," Kadrah said as she came to a stop.

Reeth and Serena danced with the other four spiders, but they never once attacked. Their fire forms seemed to be enough to corral the spiders rather than harm them. They were creatures of nature after all, and no matter how scary or menacing the creatures looked, they were still animals in their minds.

When the last whimpers of life had departed from the dark dryad's body, the spiders in the chamber reared back, and seemed to regain control of their own minds again as the druids could sense the spiders with their empathic link. The beasts were terrified of the fire, and because of this, the arachnids scattered down the hallways that branched from the lobby.

After a moment, the arachnids were gone from sight.

The druids regrouped, and Loria made no hesitation in coming to Kormanth's aid. She quickly began a spell that would work to seep the poison out of the druid's body. Waves of green and yellow magic washed over the human's body. Kormanth was still alive, but he was unable to move.

Reeth and Serena returned to normal.

"Until this poison is out of his system, he won't be able to continue," Loria explained to the others.

"How long?" Reeth asked the dryad.

"Maybe an hour," Loria answered. The others paused to let the information sink in.

"What do you suppose that dark dryad was here for?" Ti'or muttered while he attempted to lick the blood from his hands. He spit the disgusting liquid out to the side after tasting the rotten bile flavor. Afterwards, he went to stand outside in the rain to let the water wash his fur.

"It doesn't matter what they want," Loria spoke loudly so that the huntari could hear her. A concerned scowl was apparent on her face. "They are abominations."

"Do they travel in groups?" Reeth asked.

"The last time they were seen on the surface they led a war against Telosa. For one to be alone is unknown to me," Loria explained.

The dryad's knowledge did not leave a good notion in the minds of the druids. They stood guard in the castle chamber as Kormanth rested. Every so often, the man was able to move a new limb; proof that the magic was working. During this time, the druids continually thought about the possibility of more dark dryads lurking around. The rain outside made it difficult for them to hear anything, and so, they had to rely solely on their eyes to watch the dark hallways of the castle.

"Let us waste no more time. Sorin may need our help," Kormanth suggested as soon as he was able to stand on firm legs again.

"Agreed," said the arch-druid. "Lead the way."

Kormanth started through the large door at the bottom of the grand staircase. Beyond it, the druids descended the stairs and went deeper into the ruins of the keep. It felt especially darker down here, but with Loria's magical light, they could at least see a short distance in front of them.

The steps came to an end and they now traversed a long, dark corridor. Every now and then the corridor would branch off into other directions, but most of the side passages were caved in. It was at the far end of the passageway where they found a portion of the wall that had completely crumbled away, and there was a tunnel bored into the earth and stone.

The tunnel went straight for about 20 feet before it started to descend further into the earth, and as their path downward took on a curvy shape, they could tell they were spiraling down like a helix. The air was filled with the smell of earth and a small amount of moisture. The air grew bitter cold as they went, but after a while, the tunnel opened into a vast chamber.

The cavernous chamber housed an underground lake. They were on the only shore that they could see, and it sat a few feet above the water like a shallow cliff. The place was populated with many stalagmites and stalactites. Even though the underground landscape was a rare scene, there was another population that drew the druids' attention even more.

"Fire beetles," Kormanth explained to the others as he had been here before. "Very docile unless threatened."

The beetles' brown, bulbous bodies glowed with the chemical fire they held in their bellies. They crawled all over the cavern floor and on the walls, and with so many beetles before them, the entire chamber appeared to be covered with the glow of candle light. Loria picked this moment to let her magic light flicker and dissipate.

"I guess not all the wonders live above ground," Loria stated.

The other druids could only agree in silence.

They followed the shore of the lake for a moment. There were many outlets and side tunnels that led to and from the chamber. When the arch-druid looked back, *he* wasn't even sure he could tell which one they had just come from. The druids continued to follow Kormanth, and made sure not to get in the way as beetles walked in front of them.

"Which way should we go?" Reeth asked Kormanth as the anxiety of the maze came to the surface.

"The center of the lake," Kormanth replied. The human druid waved a hand at the lake. "There is a small island, and the tunnel we need is on there."

The other druids heard the words from their guide, but as they tried to peer at the lake, they could not see an island. The druids then came to a portion of the cliff-like shore that descended like a set of stairs that was built into the rocky landscape. When they arrived at the water level, their footfalls came to the edge of the water, and they could feel the wet, gritty, gravel-like sand beneath their feet.

"Shall we *fly* across the water?" Ti'or asked.

"We can't. The air is thinner down here. We would crash into the water," Kormanth answered, but followed with the solution. "We have to swim."

"I will not swim," Ti'or protested. "The rain was bad enough. We huntari prefer to stay dry."

A couple of the others managed a puff of silent laughter. The humor was because of the consistency of how much the huntari were similar to actual felines. The bouncing torsos from the laughing was not lost on Ti'or.

"Jest if you must. I will meet you over there," Ti'or said before transforming back into an air elemental and taking flight.

Without another word, Reeth was the first one to jump into the water. He was soon followed by the other druids, but Kadrah had to change into a beaver as she was not able to swim at all as a dwarf. The splashing of their movements echoed off the cavern walls in which they could not see, and it only took them a second to realize the freezing temperature of the lake. As they got farther from the candlelight, the druids then saw a light from ahead. It was Ti'or, and he had created a magical light to signal the druids of where he was at.

The druids were astounded by Kormanth's use of the word *small*. The island couldn't have been more than 30 feet in diameter. They came ashore and regrouped, and each of them could see that the island was made of melted rock and obsidian. At the center, they saw a small mound and a tunnel going into the island. As they took a closer look, they could see the tunnel went straight down. After some unimaginable distance, they could see light at the bottom, and the air coming from this tunnel was quite warm and carried hints of sulfur.

"A magma vent?" Reeth questioned aloud.

"Correct," Kormanth confirmed. "With the hot air blowing up through here, we can use our bird forms. Rest assured there *is* a landing directly at the bottom. It is also very hot."

"Why does this druid hide so deeply in the earth?" Ti'or asked.

"You will see soon enough," Kormanth said. After that, he brazenly hopped into the tunnel, and only after a quick moment of free falling did he take his phoenix form.

The other druids watched their guide go down, but they decided to transform into birds before going in themselves. Ti'or, of course, turned back into the air. The druids flapped their wings to slow their descent, but they found the air was still too thin to make any sort of difference. Even with the light down below, it was incredible at how far down into the earth they were traveling, and as the light got bigger and brighter in their eyes, the air got warmer until it was hot. Then the air got blistering hot, and the birds found it easy to flap against the upward pressure. It wasn't long after that the druids landed into the chamber below.

Before they could put their tiny bird legs on the ground, the druids could feel the intense heat of being close to molten metal, and they knew that they could combust at any moment. One by one, they quickly worked their concentration to transform into their own fire forms. Reeth was a fire-orc, Serena was a firecat, Kadrah and Loria used fire elementals, Ti'or remained an air elemental, and Kormanth remained a phoenix.

The chamber was large, and it took the shape of a grand underground chasm. There were other magma vents in the distance along the walls that actively poured lava. This lava flowed into a bubbling river of primal fire down below. The landing in which the druids stood upon was a large circular platform of stone and obsidian, and the landing rose up from the lava by about 50 feet. From this platform, a single pathway cut across the chasm and the river, and led to a dark tunnel.

Kormanth could not speak in his phoenix form, so he waddled ahead, and begged the others to follow him with a caw. Together they went into the tunnel. Once the air was cool enough, the druids released from their elemental forms. They followed the tunnel, and it must have been a mile long. When they came upon the exit, they discovered themselves stepping through an area that seemed like they were outside.

Before them was a natural stone bridge that reached across the bottomless chasm below, and on the other side of the bridge, there was another tunnel. Above them, the druids could see countless jagged stone spikes that jutted out from the cliffsides. Very small specks of the gloomy, rainy sky could be seen peeking through the stone obstructions. Kormanth continued to lead the party across the bridge.

"Is this the bottom of the canyon we saw from the sky?" Serena asked.

"It is," Kormanth responded. "But we are about a mile north from the castle ruins."

In a line, the druids crossed the bridge to the other side, and entered the next tunnel which seemed to be a straight shot. As they continued, the rancid stench of insects assaulted their noses. Loria made her opinion of the smell obvious when she conjured an enchantment that replaced the horrid aroma with the scent of fresh grass and daisies. The others were grateful, but Ti'or, and his feline likeness, found the odor to be less bothersome.

After a short jaunt, the druids arrived at the next cavernous chamber, but they slowed their pace when they heard the presence of voices ahead. They lightly stepped forward until they could see into the druid's lair.

The tunnel emptied into a giant dome-shaped chamber from above the main floor, and then a natural stone ramp ran down the left and right side along the walls. The druids who were not familiar with this place looked upward at the ceiling, and to their amazement they could see a wide-mouthed chimney from which yellow light poured down from. Inside the chimney, and all around it, there were hundreds of giant wasp nests that covered the ceiling. However, on the floor below, there were giant insect corpses: wasps, bees, beetles, scorpions, and spiders. That wasn't the focus of their attention as they scanned the whole room.

Below them, the druids could see five dark dryads, and they were accompanied by a couple of aberrations. The aberrations had the torso of a dark dryad, and the bulbous bodies of a spider. Their faces held eight tiny eyes. Although none of the druids had encountered or seen anything like them before, Loria knew the dire creatures to be known as dryders. The creatures were born of dark witchcraft.

The seven dark creatures stood before a peculiar sandari. It had leathery scales that were tan-orange like the sands of Sandar. But this was a druid known for his affinity for insects, and likewise, he had antennas protruding from its head, he had wasp-like wings sprouting from his back, and he had a scorpion tail in place of a normal sandaran tail. Between it all, he wore a suit of armor made from thick, bronzy, insect carapaces, and he held a trident in his hands.

 From what the druids could tell, the sandari was locked in a dialogue with the dark ones, but considering all the dead insects, they probably weren't here to play nice, but even in the face of overwhelming odds, the bug-druid remained in his wasp-sculpted throne of hardened clay.

"Those two big creatures; those are dryders," Loria whispered to the other druids.

"What do you know about them?" Reeth asked.

"Unfortunately, this is my first time seeing one," Loria explained. "Their existence is nearly myth."

The dark dryads had their swords and poleaxes pointing at the carapace-armored sandari. The dryders were also equipped with poleaxes. Between all the dark dryads, the one who stood in the middle rank wore a black cloak while the other four wore armor.

"I'm going to make my offer once more, lizard," said the dark dryad, speaking in the belluan tongue. "Vacate from your tunnels. Take the rest of your bugs with you or else we will burn the rest of your precious hive."

The sandaran druid struggled with his inner restraint. He was ready to unleash everything he had on the enemies that stood before him. He also knew the dark dryads would burn everything, anyway, whether he agreed to leave or not. He wanted to give in to his violent behavior, but he was also trying to stay connected to the hive. With the death of his many friends splayed across the floor, and elsewhere in his tunnels. The bug-druid tried to call others to his aid, but through the connection he could not hear any of them. The dark dryads had him outnumbered, he normally preferred his meals that way, but he wasn't sure he would be able to stay ahead of the dryders.

Before his feet, he looked at the fragments of a shattered purple crystal. It was something he needed to summon his loyal companion, but the dryads had broken it when they came in. He was running out of time to buy, but he would not entertain the dryami by losing his composure.

The sandari revealed a grin of dagger-like teeth, and stood up from his throne as he sensed a vague new movement floating through the air. His antennas sent vibrating signals to his brain, and that was all the confirmation he needed. It indicated that an invisible stalker moved about even if he could not see it. He knew it to be an elemental of some kind, but as he sensed the empathic waves in his chamber, he decided he would keep the dryads focused on him until the first strike came.

The bug-druid looked to the dark commander, and responded in belluan, "Fine. I will vacate my tunnels."

The dark dryads grinned, but they soon took it back as the sandaran continued.

"Over my dead body." The bug-druid made a ready stance with his trident.

It was as if the timing couldn't have been more perfect. Ti'or appeared out of the air elemental form and tore out the throat of the dark leader. Kormanth joined Ti'or and together they closed the gap with two of the dark soldiers. Reeth and Serena took to their fire forms and chose to charge one of the dryders. Kadrah changed into an earth elemental and exploited her stony body to occupy the other dryder. Loria remained at the top of the ramps. From there, she came to a kneel before letting the magic from her body flow into the earth.

"*Veri erek*," she incanted. When her spell was complete, the earth rumbled and came to life. It was another earth elemental that pushed its way up and out from the stone it was just cut from. It went to join the side of Kadrah. With that out of the way, she redirected her attention to see how she could support the others.

As the combat had started, the sandaran noted two of the dark dryads that were not being attended to. He charged forward, already he could taste the violence in his mind. The dryads saw him coming and prepared themselves. Sorin led with his trident and dove at the first dryad in a reaching jab, but it rolled out of the way. The other one took advantage of the lunging attack and saw an opening, but it had to backpedal and stumble off to the side in order to dodge the flash of a tail-stinger.

The dryads were equally hungry to skin the sandari and wasted no time in pressing back against him. They coordinated their attacks and fell into a flurry of attacks and parries with the lizard. One slash after another, none of the attacks were connecting for any of the seasoned fighters.

The druid then came in for a heavy lunge. The first dryad raised his sword to block the attack, which locked up the weapons. Stuck in place, the druid suddenly twisted to land a roundhouse kick to the second warrior who tried to take a cheap shot. The blow sent it reeling away after spinning in the air. The druid and the first one then locked eyes with their weapons.

"I'll squash you like the insect you are," the dryad said.

"Hollow words. Just like your existence," Sorin replied.

The dryad then pushed the druid backwards and out of the lock before charging after him.

Meanwhile, Ti'or stood toe-to-toe with the dark dryad in front of him. The thing had a poleaxe equipped, but the weapon was heavy and required more time to move around, and the druid was proving to be much quicker. The poleaxe came at the cat anyway with three quick jabs and then a downward slash. Each time the weapon came at the huntari, he slipped out of the way, and not even a hair was damaged as the druid moved. When the next jab came, the druid grabbed the shaft of the weapon, and extended a leg to kick the dark warrior in the face.

The blow sent the dryad back and forced it to leave the weapon in the hands of the cat. The druid wasted no time. He took the weapon and smashed the head against the solid stone floor with a crunch, breaking the bladed head off. The druid now held a weapon he was a little more familiar with: a quarterstaff.

The dark dryad was prepared for the situation, and relinquished a knife from his boot. It closed in and used its gauntlet to parry the anticipated jab from the druid. The knife moved forward and slashed at the face of the druid. The blade found flesh and orange fur as it tore a cut over the cat's left eye. The druid reared his head in response to the sudden pain, but the movement only allowed the slicing instrument to curve downward across his cheek. Blood moistened his white hair, but luckily the blade missed his eye.

The dark warrior chased the cat as the druid backed up to reassess. In that split second, the tip of the blade stabbed at Ti'or's belly, but the huntari had cat-like reflexes. He leapt into the air to cause the attack to miss.

On the way down, the druid's hands and feet bared claws, and he latched onto the torso of the dryami. The druid ripped the helmet off of the dryad, revealing its withered face and eyes that glowed red with hatred. Ti'or swiped up and down, left and right, while his feet held on to the body of his foe. Translucent red blood flew in all directions. The steady stance of the warrior quivered and it wasn't too long before the dark dryad fell limp due to hypovolemic shock. Ti'or stood atop the suffering body as it fell, and he licked his lips of the blood that now covered his own body.

Nearby, the two earth elementals fought a dryder. The massive limbs of stone came together to match the strength of the unnatural creature. Kadrah pinned the beast against the stone wall while the other used rocky punches to crush every bone in the dryder's torso. The creature stopped fighting back, and not long after that, the dryder was turned into a red pulp.

At the other side of the dome arena, Reeth and Serena battled the remaining dryder. The aberration did not appear to be impressed by the fire forms of the two druids, and it stood its ground in defiance of its two adversaries. Each time the orc or firecat came at the creature, it simply skittered away only to return and take a swipe with its long weapon. It knew it was quicker and stronger than the druids, but it was also realizing that the fire cat was a smaller target and needed to be careful with its strategy.

The monstrosity then witnessed its kin get pummeled to death, and it sent its mind into a shrieking fit of rage. After a glance between the orc and the cat, the dryder chose the orc. The larger target.

The dryder barreled towards the orc and danced with its eight legs in such a way that it made Reeth unsure of what it was about to do. With no more time remaining, and the dryad torso looming over his head, the poleaxe came up with coiled arms, and aimed for the strike. The orc rolled out of the way as the blade came downward, but in the midst of the roll there was a sound that became absent in the druid's ears. The dryder performed a feint and the orc took the bait.

Before the arch-druid could get back to his feet, the dryder used three of his legs in tandem to push the fire orc away and through the air. The strength of the creature was unimaginable, and the only thing that saved Reeth from bashing his head into the stone wall was the throne made of hardened clay.

The orc crashed into the throne, and it shattered into three solid pieces before the druid came to rest on the back side. Even though the orc's eyes were blurry and spinning, he could see that the magic of his fire form had dissipated.

The dryder's work was not done, though, and after it had made its successful attack against one foe, its ever-watchful eyes caught the movement of the firecat. Seeing Reeth go down, the firecat took off in a full sprint to take on the aberration. The rush of battle and adrenaline pushed Serena skyward as she leapt at the dryder in a high arc.

The dryder swung its giant form around in an instant, and made one devastating attack at Serena as she hung in the air. The large poleaxe cut across her belly and she reverted to her humanoid form before she could return to the ground.

Serena immediately laid in a pool of her own blood as the lining around her intestinal cavity fought to stay closed by a few tendons. She was thrown into shock, her eyes became dizzy, and her vision shimmered with black spots. She blankly stared up at the dryder who was rearing up to place the coup de grace.

As the vile creature brought its ax up high, it suddenly reeled back with a shriek as a trident sailed through the air and found its mark in the giant monster's chest. It was the moment that Kadrah needed to come bouldering into the aberration. The tag team elementals were back at work, and employed the same strategy as before.

But the dryder's strength was tenfold in its rage, and it managed to push both of the elementals back. With new targets before it, the dryder delivered another blow with its poleaxe, cleanly cutting through one of the elementals down the middle. It lifelessly crumbled into bits of stone.

The druids were overcome with the notion of losing another member of the grove, but the empathic vibrations from the elemental that still stood kept them from skipping a beat.

The dryder pushed forward again and delivered another slicing attack. The attack was slower than the previous ones. Much slower. The blade came crashing against the stone floor when it tried to swipe at Kadrah, but it missed, and now it seemed like the dryder couldn't pick it back up.

It was then that Kadrah saw the opportunity and delivered a giant, rocky punch that drove the trident further inside the body. The earth elemental did it once more, then twice. The drider was then pinned against the wall, the points of the trident digging into the stone. Kadrah did not relent, even after the eight legs had gone limp, and when the dwarf-druid was finally done, there wasn't much left of the monster.

Having defeated the dark dryads and the two monsters, the druids rushed to gather around Serena. Her breath was beginning to slow. She couldn't see anything. She couldn't hear anything. She had lost a large amount of blood through the wound she had received, and the other druids could see the evisceration.

"*Child*," Kormanth said through a grim visage as he came to kneel in the pool of blood at her side. "Loria?"

The dryad-druid was already kneeling at her side before Kormanth could say her name. She looked over Serena carefully, and she became very doubtful that a healing spell would fix this kind of damage. Loria found that she did not have words at the moment.

"Loria, should I cauterize her wound?" Reeth asked as he held a hand to his concussed head.

"No. Not this kind of wound," the dryad replied in a calm tone. After a few more seconds of inspecting, Loria lowered her head and continued, "Ending her suffering might be the only option we have right now."

"You surface druids rely only on yourselves," the sandaran criticized.

"What are you on about, Sorin?" Kormanth asked.

The sandaran worked to free his trident from the wall, and after a few seconds, he was able to pull it out. When he did, he inspected the tips, and grinned at his achievement of poisoning the dryder with his animal companion's venom. He would have to remember that for next time, he thought.

With the dryami dead, Sorin could sense that some of the insects had remained in the hive, but from what he could tell, there weren't very many of them left. In fact, there was only one species he was able to reconnect to. Somehow, it was the insects that were needed the most right now.

With two fingers to his scaly lips, Sorin whistled while facing upward at the chimney above. His antennas buzzed as he communicated to his insect-friends that everything was safe now. The sandaran stood there waiting, but as he did, he had questions for his guests.

"Hmm. Where is Levinar?" Sorin asked the group when he brought his eyes down.

"He's dead. I have succeeded him, but that's why we are here," Reeth explained.

"I see." Sorin did not find any interest in the answer. He did not care about who led the grove or anything of that nature. He continued, though, "It was fortuitous that you came when you did. But why did you?"

Against her own beliefs, Loria began to use healing magic to stabilize Serena as much as possible. She, as well as the other druids, thought Sorin's demeanor was odd, but they also weren't sure what the lizard meant when he referred to them as *surface druids*.

"Levinar is also not the only one that was lost recently. Those of us here are the remainder of the grove," Reeth said.

"Then dark tidings have brought you here," Sorin stated more than questioned.

"There is a foe on the surface known as the shade," Reeth elaborated. "They have set their gaze upon the Swords, and have a legion marching this way from deep in the Wastes."

"Yes. The Children of Abyss are on the move. I have *felt* the tremors," Sorin proclaimed. "Have you traveled here to see if my friends will defend civilization?"

Loria spoke this time, which took her away from her concentration, "I hate the idea as well, but victory against them will ensure the balance of nature in the Swords."

After two long minutes of dialogue and waiting, a response to Sorin's previous call came when the humming sound of large wings began to echo into Sorin's throne room. Five giant honey bees hovered into the view of the druids. Everyone but Sorin had to take a few steps back at the sight of the cacophonous squadron.

One of the bees landed and crawled on its six legs until it was standing over Serena's body. The bee scooped up the youngest member of the Ember Grove before returning to its hovering flight. The buzzing of the bee-wings shuttered as the insects lifted off the ground. It was not a moment later that the bees and their hum had disappeared back into the chimney.

"What happens now?" Reeth said through his toothy mouth.

"We wait," Sorin answered. After a short pause, he continued, "We must see how important that one is to Terra. If she is worthy, the queen will sustain her."

The other druids looked to each other as their mission had taken an unfortunate delay. As time was against them anyway, the druids returned to the reason for why they were here in the first place.

Sorin was beginning to wonder if they would ask the question that he voiced for them, but so far they hadn't said a word more. He could sense their reluctance, but the sandaran was unsure if he could actually convince the giant bees to join a war in which they really had no part in. They lived beneath the world, and he cared little for the dealings that existed above. Nor did he care about the sentiment of the druids showing up and helping him deal with the dryami.

Silently, he made the decision that he would not commit the last of his friends to the battle. There was too much risk, and he was not willing to accept it. Especially since his kingdom was already holding on by a strand.

The sandaran stayed inside his own mind when his eyes looked upon the shattered purple crystal nearby. He had to admit, the thrill of the fight with the dark dryads was invigorating, he enjoyed it, and he wanted more of it. Those thoughts got mixed with the violent memories of his lost companion, and his twisted mind began racing with the destructive solution that was before him.

Sorin did not face the other druids as he spoke, "I will not send my friends into your battle."

The decision brought concerned looks upon the druids for this was not the answer they were expecting. Reeth could only look at the sandaran with disappointment. He was a breath away from invoking the chain of command between them, but then the bug-druid continued.

"But," Sorin began before a short pause. "I need your help in retrieving my companion. Do this, and I will send *him* into the battle."

CHAPTER TWENTY-NINE
PREPARATIONS

The King of Claymore walked the streets of his city. The place was alive with the sounds of construction and the rumbling of heavy wooden wheels supporting the frames of catapults. He could see his commanders and lieutenants directing the citizens in the various taskings. They built barricades on the roads, fortified important structures, and converted taverns and shops into triage centers.

It had been close to three centuries since Claymore was involved in a conflict. The king remembered his history lessons well as he walked. The last conflict, the War of the Swords, ended with the defeat of Claymore at the mercy of Lumen, Planesgate, *and* Telosa. The previous war was a pre-emptive strike from those countries against the warrior-nation to keep Claymore from starting one. Needless to say, the attack worked, and since then, no warmongering ever came from Claymore following that event.

The king did not want a repeat of that war. He did not want his home to be caught unprepared. He wanted every resource available and at the disposal of his people. Over the last few days, he almost felt obsessed over the defense of the city. He wanted things to go his way, even though he knew that the chaos of war would not let him. If he could control the chaos by any means, however, he was going to try.

For the moment, the king was glad that the preparations seemed to be ahead of schedule, and reports had come in that *all* of the reserve siege equipment had arrived from the town of Hel. Through the mid-city, all the catapults were lined up to face east and north along the main avenue. The sight of the engines made it *really* feel like war was coming.

Claymore was no longer a sleeping nation.

Melissa and Marc Blade-Briar II were at the king's side as he toured.

"All this movement about the city really gets my blood going," Marc said with a hint of sheltered excitement. His face held an invisible grin as he watched everything going on.

"Yes, it's been too long since Claymore has seen war. It'll be nice to get the dust off the walls," the Darkbane House Leader shared her sentiment.

Henrick declined to add his own feelings, but deep inside, it *did* feel good hearing their words. He, too, was hoping to see battle during his tenure at Claymore. In reality, though, he had already seen battle.

His thoughts then went backwards in time again until he landed at the beginning of the timeline in his head. His mind reminisced of the cave in which Serena had taken him to when he was injured.

He recalled his encounter with the water nymph, the envoy of the Twins. This *war*. This *battle*. It was a test from the gods themselves. It led him to ponder on what could possibly be in store for him next should they be victorious. His insights drove his thoughts further, and he began to swirl the questions in his head.

What could be worse than the shade?

What was lurking out there beyond the walls that threatened all life on the planet?

The ideas shook the foundation of his mind, but he did not let himself fall victim to the despair of the unknown. Instead, he could only bolster his hidden tenacity. In that light, he came to the conclusion that the shade were nothing compared to whatever it was that waited for him in the beyond.

The thoughts of fighting the shade forced the king to spy his gaze upon Melissa Darkbane. Henrick knew that the Darkbane family had been training female warriors for countless years for the sole purpose of fighting monsters, and that they heavily followed the dogma of Lumina.

He had to wonder that if the other paladins were out there somewhere in the world, was it possible that she knew of Lumina's champion? He decided to table that conversation until later, and returned his gaze to the road ahead.

They passed the Church of Steel. Outside, they saw the clerics with their black robes handing out green flame pendants of the Salamander-God to citizens who wanted them.

From her, they turned around and made their way to the east gate. The three of them stared over the outer city and at the rolling green landscape as if imagining the shade were already there. It was a relief to see nothing but a blue sky and the summer sun.

"They will most likely come from this direction," Marc Blade-Briar II proclaimed. "Or at least, this is where they will put the most pressure."

"Sire," came the call from behind.

The trio turned to regard the young courier boy coming out of a jog. The young man approached the king, and then fell to his knees once he stopped. Before anyone could say anything, the runner produced a handful of rolled and sealed papers.

"Thank ye. Yer dismissed," Henrick said to the boy.

One by one, Henrick broke the seals of Undertrone, Lumen, and Lorewind. He read the letters to himself. When he was done with them all, he crunched them together, and tore them in half.

"Bah. Rubbish," Henrick scoffed.

"Unfortunately, peace between the countries does not mean allies," Marc II said. "We *will* remember this, though."

"They prolly don't believe the shade threat is real," Henrick added.

"What about the druids? They have not returned yet." Marc added. "We are going to need them if those catapults are going to have any use."

At the mention of Serena, Henrick's thoughts dwelled on her. He, as well as the others, knew that the druids should have been back by now, but they were unnervingly absent. They could not help but wonder if something had happened to them. Henrick was determined to not let his thoughts ruin his resolve.

The king decided to steer the conversation away from the druids, and said, "We have the favor of Sol, of Lumina, of Undine, and of Nielda. The gods are watching us. They need us to win. They will not fail us, and so we shall not fail them."

"Ha. Since when did you get so religious?" Melissa jested.

"Heh. The moment I realized Nielda chose me to fight this war," Henrick said as he continued to solidify the idea of his station. "I'm 'er paladin, and this war is me test. I can't say if we'll pass or fail, and I don't know what the future holds. All I know is that in me own heart... failure is not an option."

Later that day, the reds and violets of twilight filled the sky. The stars revealed themselves as the sun departed from the atmosphere. The red nebula above, the Scarlet Tear, complimented the heavenly scene. Of the two moons that revolve around Terra, only the first quarter of Nielda could be seen.

As Henrick stood on the Crown Balcony alone, he kept his eyes skyward, and he felt as though the moon goddess knew that he would be coming up here, and that the sister moon allowed them to have a private conversation.

"What'm I doin' up here?" he whispered the question to himself. He took a long pause to consider his words. He felt unsure of what to do, or how this sort of thing worked. He had never prayed to anything before. "I don't know if ye can hear me, Nielda, but I need to ask ye if Serena is ok." He paused as the absence of the druid bothered him. When no response came, he continued, "I've not realized how much I've grown to enjoy the company of 'er until she left for Ravenlock. She's helped me to better understand ye, but she's runnin' late, and it would help if I knew that she was safe."

He then sat upon the bricks of the balcony and patiently waited for a long moment as if expecting for something to happen. To his knowledge, he was doing everything that Serena had said to him: he was outside and the moon was out. Was there something he was missing?

He began to feel desperate for any kind of signal. His thoughts became anxious as the long moments passed, and his mind fell on a more logical answer. Perhaps Nielda heard his plea, and in the absence of this sign, it meant that Serena was not in good health. That idea did nothing to help his agitation.

His agony came to a pause as a call from behind reached his ears.

"There you are," Melissa said.

Henrick continued to sit, and he never turned to regard the all-too familiar voice.

"Talking to the moon?" Her words did not carry any sort of mockery. She then sat down next to him.

587

"There was something from earlier that had me thinking."

Henrick remained quiet.

"You said you had become a paladin, a paladin to Nielda. My family used to serve a paladin of Lumina before coming to Claymore. It's actually how our name came about. As far as our history records show, the Darkbanes swore an oath of service to the paladin, but we had been released from that oath at some point due to some calamity. The history records don't really tell of a major event during the time that was mentioned, so it's possible the calamity never came to fruition."

"How'd yer family *serve* this paladin of Lumina?" Henrick asked.

"As far as I know, we were the paladin's personal guards, we acted as protectors, peacekeepers, and when it was time for a new paladin to come about, we were charged with seeking them out." Melissa paused for a second while staring at her open hands. "My family used to be able to carry special powers, just as the paladins did, but I think those abilities disappeared after being released from the oath."

Henrick continued to sit, but he straightened his back and folded his arms as he dwelled on the information that Melissa had given him, but only for a second. He began to ask, "So, if yer to swear an oath to me service..."

"That's the reason I came looking for you," she finished his thought. The idea was that she could swear an oath to Henrick, and regain her long-lost family legacy.

The two of them stood up simultaneously and faced each other.

"That's not a bad idea," Henrick remarked.

"Tomorrow, then?" she asked. "I'll bring my sister too."

"Aye. If it works, perhaps there are others that will do the same," he added.

Just as they set their plans in stone, a sudden swirling of wind and dust kicked up all around the balcony. Melissa drew her sword from her waist, but Henrick had come to the balcony without a weapon or armor.

A magic blue circle appeared upon the surface of the balcony. The energy drew in the attention of four local guardsmen. They rushed to the king's side with their swords and shields at the ready. The energy continued to build for a minute until at last the spell was released in a flowering display of blue sparks. The guards charged, but their jabbing attacks were only met with the force of a magical blue shield. Inside the shield was Yobo, and he was accompanied by a robed, white-haired dryad.

"Ah yes, the ever-vigilant people of Claymore," the dryad mocked without a single tone of worry in his voice.

"Hold," the king commanded the guards. Henrick stepped forward. "Ye made it back, and with company."

"Henrick, this is Archmage Tigus from Planesgate," Yobo introduced.

The dryad held a confident smirk as he let the magic shield dissipate before reaching out with a hand to gesture for a shake. "I can assure you I hold no grudge like my kin in Telosa."

Henrick agreed to the gesture, but before the shake was over, the presence of seven other blue-robed mages were revealed as their invisibility effects fell off. The guards, and even Melissa, felt a hint of unease with the addition of these hidden wizards, but they made no move to attack as their king didn't either.

Tigus continued after the shake, "Yobo has told me about you. Perhaps with the concept of a new kind of king here, our two countries could become friends."

"I would welcome that," the king said while offering a smile.

"It is settled, then," Tigus began once more. "As Claymore's first paladin king, and the first king to openly worship the Twins, my students and I will humbly aid you in the coming battle. May this be the start of a new alliance in the Swords."

"Come then, we'll find ye a place to sleep," the king offered.

Together, Henrick, Melissa, Yobo, Tigus, and the seven other mages departed the Crown Balcony and headed towards the keep. The subordinate mages moved behind the main group, and did not make any noise or conversation, not even with themselves. Henrick and the others shared stories between each other as they walked.

The city was quiet on this clear night, and the lighted torches that filled the barricaded roads of the city were a comforting sign that the adversary was not upon them yet.

"Has there been any word from my sister?" Yobo stepped alongside Henrick to ask.

"Not yet," he replied. "Serena and her druids have not returned either. It's been almost eight days since everyone left, and yer the only one that's come back."

"Don't worry, they will make it back in time," Yobo assured him.

As the party approached the keep doors, the trotting sounds of shoed-hooves beating against the road came roaring into the inner city. There were three guards, and a fourth who appeared to be a scout. The horses came to a halt a few yards away before the scout dismounted and came to a kneel before the king.

"Sire," the young man managed. "Shadows are coming from the wastes. The shade. They are three days out, maybe sooner."

The group regarded the scout but quickly looked to Henrick as soon as the words left his mouth.

"Go rest in the barracks," Henrick told the man. He then turned to look at the others. "Looks like we're out of time." Henrick then stepped around the party and gestured to the guards at the keep's doors and three that had come with the scout. "You three, and you three!" The king yelled. "Do not ring the bells, but pass the word, and lock the gates! Claymore is at war!"

The six soldiers moved with a purpose. They quickly decided amongst themselves on which way they were going to go, and they were soon heading off in different directions. First the barracks were notified, then the officers on the second floor of the keep, and soon everyone else within the inner city was notified. More military members fanned out to the rest of the kingdom. The officers began to gather and muster their troops.

Within the hour, Claymore had been locked down, and all the exits had been barred.

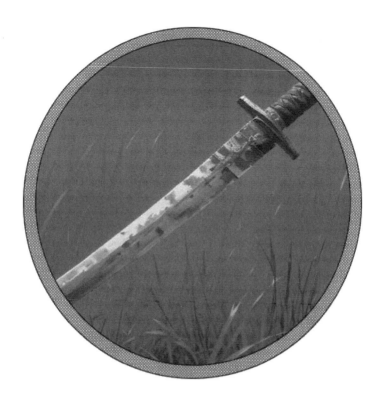

CHAPTER THIRTY
THE BATTLE FOR CLAYMORE

Over the next few days, the Army of Claymore stood watch upon the walls, feverishly, in anticipation for their foes to arrive. They watched the shadows rise up from the horizon to the east. The dark shroud that slowly engulfed the sky was like a clock that foreshadowed the event that was due.

At night, the march of the shade was invisible, but the patch of missing stars was no less disturbing. The people of the human kingdom would occasionally look to the west while the stars were still shining in that direction. It was the only sign that the shade were not at their doorstep, yet.

But the few days were over, and the twilight of the present day was here. The hours went deeper into the night, and it was during these dark hours that all of the stars disappeared. The shroud that covered the sky segregated Claymore from the rest of the world.

Inside the city, on the roads, inside the gate towers, and upon the walls, the soldiers were amassed. Every member of the Claymore Army was present. Every person conscripted from the outer city and the outlying villages were called to the fight. Their swords were drawn and their bows were ready.

The siege equipment was in place, but the druids still had yet to return, and without the use of their *daylight* magic, the effectiveness of the catapults were unknown.

The breeze that usually found its way through the avenues of the city was absent, and it was replaced by the echoing hiss of the shade. The flooded airways reached the ears of Claymore. The sound was disturbing, but not one Claymoran thought to flee.

They were all on call. They all stood next to each other to fight by their kin in defiance of the ancient enemy. Tabard colors meant nothing today.

The unseen approach of the Children of Abyss filled the entire night with agonizing suspense. The hiss grew louder and louder, but many hours passed before the white eyes of the enemy could be seen.

Some of the people of Claymore who had finely tuned internal clocks realized that the sun would be showing its first light at any minute, but it was alarmingly absent. There was nothing but darkness overhead.

No one knew how the shade was creating this sunless landscape. Some of the people looked to the east, and they could spot the glow of a distant purple light. They all had to wonder if that was the source of it.

The enemies of Claymore were not the only ones that had prepared for this day, or night, or whatever it was now. The king already had the answer to their problem. Atop Claymore Keep, and accompanied by some of Planesgate's magicians, was Yobo. As soon as the lamps and torches through the town began to go out, the last of the Gunn Drambor he used his martial arts forms to meditate on the powers of the Esfera de Luz to provide light to the entire city.

With the beacon of light over their heads, the people watching from upon the walls could then see the countless forms of the shade, and although the dark warriors stood ready in ranks, their misty aura made it appear like they were always moving.

Both armies stared at each other as the moment was at hand.

The Battle of Claymore was about to begin.

Runners were sent to every corner of the city to inform and cry that the shade were here. The people strengthened their resolve for the battle that was to come.

From atop the Crown Balcony, King Henrick Skullbright looked down upon his people. He could sense the darkness from all of them. The darkness they would need to become ferocious. The darkness to kill their enemies. He could feel their energy. He felt the same way. Of all the people that were here to fight, he hoped that he would kill the most of them.

The king was accompanied by the four house leaders, Captain Fenri, and Archmage Tigus. "The time has come," the king said after turning to them. He let out a heavy sigh. "I'm not sure what else needs to be said at this point. Let's give these demons hell."

Marc II said, "I've lived here my whole life, and not once have I seen the heart of the city so vibrant. It is good to be fighting again. Rest assured that the north gate will not fall on my watch."

Henrick's eyes then turned to Melissa. In the morning before the shade made their presence known, Melissa and 10 others, to include her sister, Amelia, stood before the king to make the pact of service to the Paladin of Nielda.

Based on the records of the Darkbane legacy, these oath-takers were known as crusaders.

With the oath taken, Henrick used the darkside of Nielda's energy to teach them about sensing the presence of darkness. With time short, Henrick had to train them quickly, but in the process of his mentoring, they discovered that when he brought his moonlight to the surface, that same light shined upon the others.

At that point, he showed them how to expend that power through their weapons, and he also tried his best to explain how to get it back if it went away.

But as they all stood at the precipice of the invasion, Melissa's face was half-turned, and her eyes were fixated on the dark purple light in the distance. She did not look away from it as she spoke, "I think the oath that me and the others took is working. I can feel them. Their malice. There's thousands of them."

At that point, they all turned to look at the beyond and the strange light at the back of the shades' ranks.

"We must kill them all," she continued. "It's the only way. It's our way."

"We must deal a heavy blow while they're outside the walls," Henrick said. "Should they get in, things'll go downhill."

"Have no worries, your highness," Tigus stepped in. "My students and I excel at the *heavy blow* topic."

Henrick put on the helmet to complete the lavender suit of armor. "Just don't hit me while I'm out there."

"No promises," the old dryad jested.

With that, the king and his companions departed the Crown Balcony, and they rode horses to their pre-assigned battle stations.

Henrick dismounted from his horse when he arrived at the east gate. The soldiers on the wall signaled the operators to open it for the king. Henrick met up with the 10 crusaders as the gears of the gate tower went to work to raise the bar across the back.

"You ready to do this, your Highness?" Amelia vibrantly questioned from under the helmet of her gold-trimmed armor.

"Heh," the king scoffed. "Let's go see if they are."

The paladin and the crusaders strolled through the break in the thick wooden portal. They looked out into the fields before them and saw only darkness. In the sky and upon the ground.

This was the picture that had haunted Henrick ever since having those visions so long ago. The only thing missing was Claymore being on fire.

As the King continued out past the wall, and beyond the outer city, the crusaders came to stand at his side. He called upon the moonlight inside his being. His armor shined with a divine presence, and the shimmering sparks showered over his escorts as well. He smirked at the endless warriors before them.

The king took up his sword and shield. His crusaders followed the cue, and brought up their hammers and swords. They were not alone, though. The east gate had remained open until nearly a thousand of Claymore's warriors stood behind their leader. Battlefield murder was the only thing on their minds as they faced the shade.

The bristling energy of the people fueled Henrick's own resolve. The people upon the wall had their attention drawn to the source of light on their king, however, the warriors down below kept their eyes on the darkness.

The time was nigh, and the king could feel the anticipation of the first attack in the air.

The king turned his head to regard his people. "Warriors of Claymore!" he began in a rallying shout. "This is a day of blood and death! The shade carry no sense of honor so do not show them any! Claymore *will not* fall!" The king continued while pointing a finger to the ground. "Everyone has a home here, we live here, we have children here! We fight for them, not for ourselves! We fight today because of the love we have for our brothers and sisters! We fight in the name of the Salamandar!"

"Fight! Fight! Fight!" The deafening roar came from everywhere.

Henrick turned to regard the ranks of the shade once more. They were not 300 meters away, and he noticed the light emanating from the Esfera de Luz shooting out across the top of the walls.

"Fight! Fight! Fight!" Henrick shouted back with the sandaran water blade held up.

"Fight! Fight! Fight!" Was the fierce response.

The king looked out past the dark legion with his divine sight, and narrowed his eyes at the distant purple light. It seemed impossible to reach. There were so many shade before them. But that was okay, he thought. He would play the attrition game, and as long as the light kept them from changing into mist, the warriors would be able to fight them man-to-man.

They could be defeated.

"Stay close," he advised his crusaders. "Our light will protect our warriors."

Atop the roof of Claymore Keep, Yobo still held the stance of Cova's Maw, and he continued to use the discipline of the form to stay focused on the Esfera de Luz to keep it brightly illuminated.

The monk was surrounded by a small group of guards and three of Tigus's students. This support group was meant to ensure that Yobo would not be interrupted during his concentration.

Yobo wanted to be the one thrashing through the ranks of the shade. However, his drive for bloody vengeance did not overcome his discipline. The fact that there were *a lot* of the dark warriors out there, brought him to the conclusion that he should leave the armies to fight one another.

———————— ◯ ————————

"It would seem that Anima Scarm has been defeated," Umbra Hadara said in the abyssal tongue. Although he spoke aloud, he was mostly speaking to himself. The shade general was astride a barghest, a large canine-like creature that had muscly-sinews exposed at the lack of skin and fur. The commander wore thick, jagged armor like the rest of his soldiers, but he carried a sword of stone that held the glow of a cerulean enchantment.

Umbra Hadara gazed at the source of yellow-white light from Claymore. He knew that to be proof enough that the insolent shadowmage was dead. The umbra then narrowed his sinister white eyes, and took note of the bright lavender dot near the head of his legion.

"*Nielda?*" the shade general muttered to himself in a curious notion. Hadara could sense the presence from across the battlefield, and even with his legion before him, he knew that small dot of light would be the most problematic. "That *conniving* bitch."

Umbra Hadara turned to face the three obelisks, and at their base was his second in command, Anima Apostun. The dull hum of ancient dark magic filled the air as puffs of dark clouds continued to get pushed up into the sky above. Dark purple runes glowed all over the obelisks, giving the structures an even more ominous look.

"I will give the order to attack. Get the rest of your shadowmages to summon Trestaliadoxen," the

Umbra commanded Anima Apostun. "Let's make this quick."

Umbra Hadara raised the warhorn up from his saddle and into the air. With a long and low tone, the signal to attack was given.

Both armies heard the sound of the horn at the back of the shade ranks. The dark warriors made no hesitation, and they were quick on the charge.

The time had come. Henrick was about to see what his whole journey across the region was all about. It was time to see if he had the favor of the gods.

The soldiers on the walls saw the enemies rushing in. Horns roared through the city in alarm for the battle. Every flag bearer sounded their horn as soon as the call came to their ears. Within seconds, every member of Claymore knew the impending doom.

The king rushed headlong to meet the shade and screamed, "Send 'em to hell."

Upon the top of the east gate tower, Archmage Tigus and three of his students were assembled to be part of the 'siege power' that the city was about to unleash. As the soldiers down below began their swordplay, and the archers flew their arrows, there was a small delay as Tigus had not given his students the order to attack.

"Master Tigus," one of the students asked in a flustered tone. "Should we not begin our attack? Those creatures are close enough."

"You are correct," the old dryad said. "Be very sure not to use pyromancy. None of you. We don't want to catch any of our allies in friendly fire."

"What about fulgamancy?" another asked.

"Yes, that will do perfectly," Tigus agreed.

As the first members of the shade legion charged in, the ranks behind them ran off to the sides. They maneuvered through the outer city to flank the troops coming from the east gate, but as they did that, they were also setting up a screen to hide that most of them were moving to other parts of the castle. Their ability to take mist form was being suppressed through the intangible power of light coming over the walls, but with the light, those same walls provided a weakness that perhaps the humans did not consider.

Some of the squad leaders from the Claymoran Army gave chase to the shade as they darted off in a dead sprint. Each of them was smart enough though to stop their own men from following the dark humanoids into the shadows cast by the city walls.

Inside the shadows, the shade instantly turned to mist and swam around in the air. They were completely invisible. Some of them reappeared and used their confusing tactic to gain advantage on their pursuers.

The dark warriors hissed and howled as they gained small victories over Claymore. They did not stand on success for very long, and as soon as their

601

targets were dead, they slipped back into the shadows.

———————— ☾ ————————

A rainstorm of arrows shot out from atop the city walls and into the open areas of the outer city. Even with the light, it was hard to track the dark humanoids with their smoky figures. Many of the enemy fighters slipped through and into the darkness below. Some of the archers shot blindly into the unknown, and even fewer were finding their marks.

What was the advantage they were looking for directly below the wall?

The soldiers soon ignored what they could not manage, and began to fire arrows upon the endless flow of enemies once again.

As the archers worked to find their moving targets, catapults from inside the city launched boulders into the outer city. The rocks sailed overhead with loud hums, only to come down on the other side, smashing through homes and structures. The sudden destruction of their own city caught some of the more-crafty shade by surprise which led to them getting crunched as well.

The shade that had reached the wall's shadow grinned in relief as they prepared to make their next move. They gathered in large numbers under the protective darkness, and they waited until their numbers were large enough to make the push they needed.

The shade would not obtain victory as easily as they would have thought. Just as the time for their maneuver came to fruition, streaks of flashing white lightning came crashing down across the whole front line. It zapped hundreds of shade, and arc off those targets to strike down many more. The resounding pop of shade exploding was reassurance to both armies.

With the shadow of the east wall compromised, the shade moved to the north and south walls. Perhaps there, they would be successful since the lightning was only coming from a single point.

Henrick roared as he and his crusaders tore a hole in the ranks of the shade. The people at his side on the front line all screamed with a fierce war cry. The battlefield was in complete chaos. The paladin king was the primary target in the fray. His glowing armor burned away the mist and smoke of the dark humanoids, revealing their dark jagged armor. He held the presence of the Twins' power inside him, and when he swung his curved sword, the moonlight carried with it. The divine power of the night would slice through the dark armor and purge all aspects of life from the shade targets.

Lightning blasts and arrow volleys continued to decimate the ranks still pouring in through the outer city, but the sheer number of shade that was pouring into this fight was beginning to seem unreal.

As the shade divided their numbers to the north and south, the mages and the archers were now dividing their focus. This left large pockets open for the shade to take the next phase of their plan, whether they were ready or not.

The shade morphed into their supernatural mist form before shooting up the vertical barriers with tremendous momentum. As their forms came to feel the warmth of the bright light on the keep, they were forced to revert to their physical form. The rest of their inertia carried them through the air until the dark warriors landed on top.

All across the city's outer wall, combat exploded, and many of the archers had to abandon their ranged weapons to draw swords and axes to meet the clever foe.

Down below in the streets of Claymore, the people and soldiers held their positions and watched as the grand melee unfolded upon their city.

On the ground at the north gate, Marc Blade-Briar II and Samuel Fenri watched the display upon the walls with ever growing fervor. The entire Red Brigade stood behind them at the ready. They also had one of the magicians with them as well.

"This is nerve wracking," Marc said aloud as he stared at the walls.

"Hahaha," Fenri could only laugh at the situation. "The shade're smart. Who woulda thunk?"

Inside the east gate, Melissa Darkbane and Garrick Vicidian stood their watch with their respective brigades. They all watched the walls trying to find the first signs of defeat at the hands of the shade. So far, though, it looked like the city was holding its ground.

"How long do you think we can hold this?" Garrick asked Darkbane.

"I don't know," Melissa replied plainly.

"Aren't Darkbanes supposed to be knowledgeable on these creatures?" Garrick mocked.

"I've only had the pleasure of reading about them, but they are among the worst kind of foe to have," she explained.

Since the eruption of the battle, the east gate had remained cracked open. Every so often, a shade would jump through and get annihilated by all the weapons waiting inside. Through that gap, though, Melissa and Garrick could see the light of their king, and they could see the warriors out there still fighting.

"If it wasn't for Henrick, we would all be screwed right now," Melissa added.

Garrick had thought to make an agreeable comment, but the moment vanished when a ruckus from behind them came about. A horn blast filled the air followed by the sounds of fighting.

Somehow, the shade were inside the city walls.

Melissa took off in a sprint, taking half of the Gold Brigade with her.

"Go get 'em," Garrick said while he remained to guard the gate.

Melissa, and her troops, took the road towards the Rose Bridge, and it only took a minute for her to realize what was going on. The shade were entering the city through the grating in the south wall; the one in which the aqueduct traveled through.

It was an unfortunate turn of events, but the wall had one weakness to which the shade had the perfect exploit. The shadows cast from the divisional wall kept the grating dark enough for the shade to get through with their mist form. As soon as the shade were clear of the shadows, they were forced to revert to their humanoid form. They took the fight to the humans from that point forward. The southern streets of the city erupted into an all-out skirmish.

The exploit was definitely something that was overlooked, or at least that was how Melissa felt at the moment, but having regained her family's oath to a paladin, she could feel the energy building inside her as she closed the gap with the shade. Her body began to shimmer with light as she led the charge into the ever-growing numbers of the dark humanoids.

She drove her longsword into the first shade that challenged her, and then she moved on to the next, and the next. The adrenaline of battle became mixed with the sentiments of her family's true calling. She felt obsessive to the rush, and the fervor she carried in defense of her home only amplified her animalistic instincts.

The king found a second's break, and he began to wonder how long he and the others had been fighting the shade outside the walls. Was it minutes? Hours? He had no way of knowing. The blackened sky above certainly wasn't helping him.

He knew the people of Claymore would not relent their aggressive defense, but every so often he would scan around him. He couldn't help but notice that many of the warriors had fallen, and the shade continually pressed their attack with sheer numbers. Even four of his crusaders had been defeated, shrinking the net of light that they had established.

The king was then filled with dread and concern as the sounds of horns echoed from within the city. All the fighters outside the walls suddenly knew that the shade were inside.

"Sound the retreat! Fall back to the city!" Henrick screamed to his troops nearby.

Not a moment later, horns blasted across the fields and the outer city. The warriors of Claymore changed direction and headed for the east gate. Some went into a dead sprint while their brothers and sisters covered them.

As the warriors made their way to the gate, Henrick made sure that he was the farthest one out, and made sure that his people made it to safety first.

As the number of Claymoran warriors diminished outside the city, the mages atop the east gate began throwing fireballs at the shade. The magical fire could not be turned by the dark creatures, and thus each sphere screamed through the air until it hit the ground. A rapid chain of booms and bangs rang out across the ranks. Not even their mist form could save them from the heat and flames.

The warriors entered their city, and they were immediately dispatched to go fight the shade that had snuck inside to the south. Once the king had made it through the gate, the warriors of Green Brigade forced the portal closed.

Henrick looked out beyond the shade army again as the gate came to a close; to the purple light in the distance. He wondered if there was a possibility his moonlight would carry him all the way there, but he also knew that he needed to be with his people in this time of need.

After Henrick found his bearing after coming through the gate, he turned to find Garrick standing nearby. "What's going on?" the king asked the Vicidian leader.

"The shade have breached the south wall," the heavy man replied. "We seem to be holding them on the main walls, but I don't know for how long."

Henrick stayed silent. He did not want to voice his agreement at that notion. Even as he stood there, he looked onward into the northern streets, and at the catapults.

Where were the druids? He had to wonder. The thought frustrated him, but it was soon lost as his eyes scanned to the battle in the city.

"Crusaders! With me!" the king commanded before rushing off to join the fray inside the city.

"Why have we slowed down?" Umbra Hadara demanded from his nearby commanders. The small dot of light had disappeared at the front of the battle. The general of the shade legion did not make a habit of assuming things, and so, when the small light was gone, he had guessed that the humans were finally being pushed inside their walls.

"The light atop their keep is slowing us down," one of the field commanders complained.

Umbra Hadara turned his barghest mount and charged at the commander. The giant, hideous hound took a massive chomp at the subordinate, but it quickly turned into mist to avoid being killed. Hadara's malice already saw through the anticipated maneuver, and while in mist form, the umbra swung his stone sword through the dark cloud.

The magic of his blade flickered to life and surged to all the tiny molecules. The dark cloud turned to a puff of dirt and dust, and then fell lifelessly into a loose pile upon the ground.

The other commanders witnessed the entire event unfold, but none of them were as stupid. They had no reaction. No rebuttal. They continued to focus on their own efforts of passing orders to the front line.

Umbra Hadara then trotted to the center of the three obelisks where Anima Apostun and his other shadowmages channeled a spell of summoning. The summoning circle was nearby 50 feet across, and it had to be for the creature that they were bringing forth.

It was a creature that the shade had pursued centuries ago, imprisoned it, broke its mind, and held on to it for this very moment in time. Already, its form was taking shape. Fading into reality as it passed through time and space to be transported here.

Its body was covered in glossy, smooth, deep purple scales with a leathery texture. It had alligator-like ridges that ran the length of its body from the crown of its head to the tip of its tail. Its head was angular in shape like a hydra's. It had a large and proud wingspan that would go beyond the diameter of the circle that summoned it. Its eyes glowed with a solid bright purple energy, signifying the corruption that had dominated it for centuries.

Umbra Hadara sported a sinister smile inside his helmet. The humans may have prepared for the shade, but they were not ready for what was coming.

They were not ready for Trestaliadoxen.

They were not ready for the dragon of shadows.

On the south side of the city, Henrick and Melissa led their people through the dwindling numbers of the shade as the creatures could not send their troops through the grate as efficiently as they first thought, and the battle on top of the wall was holding. It would seem that the battle plans that the leaders of this kingdom had come up with were working right down to their contingencies.

"The battle goes well, Henrick," Melissa said in between her sword strikes.

"Aye. Good thing the buggers didn't bring rams or catapults," Henrick added.

The Claymorans had taken heavy losses in the streets since the shade snuck into the city, but the damage to the shade ranks was being returned. The roads were slick with the blood of humans, and caked with the ashy residue left by the shade as they expired. It all got mixed into a black mud, but the suctioning of boots did not slow down any of the fighting.

Near the back of the shade assault party, the squad leaders directing the dark humanoids took note of the important players in the human ranks. Two of them had shining armor and those two stood out from everyone else. The shade leaders exchanged body language to give each other information as to who to take down first, and after the decision was determined, they slithered through the ranks of the shade and humans alike. They avoided each strike that precariously came their way and zeroed in on their target.

Melissa suddenly had to step back as she saw the blade come at her from the side. When she recovered, she found that the sudden attack was not an attack at all. It was a feint. A ploy. She discovered that she was being herded by a trio of the dark warriors.

They each had different weapons in hand: one had a greatsword, one had a greataxe, and the last one held a blade in each hand. She tried to look out over the battlefield to see where Henrick was, but they had become too separated in the fray.

The three shade leaders came at her simultaneously. She fell into a defensive stance with her sword and shield, and she knew that of all the weapons coming to her, the greataxe had to be avoided. The shade closed the gap. One went left, the other right, and the third remained at her front.

A three-way flank was a wise move she thought, but Lady Darkbane was a master of her craft. The woman with flowing blonde locks charged towards the one at her front. The one with the two blades.

The shade to her left and right chased the woman as soon as she moved, but she was upon her own target with swift and fluid movement. She came in with her shield forward and sword at a jab. The double blades came up to parry the incoming sword, but the sword was the bait.

In pure Darkbane style, the shield was the real weapon, and she drove it inward to bash against the dark warrior. She did not relent though, and before the other two shade leaders could catch up, she punched with the top-edge of her shield which further stunned her opponent. She spun around to completely face the other two, but as she came to a stop, her first opponent fell limp. In the twirling motion, Melissa had taken its head completely off.

The two remaining squad leaders struck with humming whooshes as their weapons came at the human. The fall of their comrade made no hesitation in their pursuit. Melissa shifted back to defense as she had to remain attentive to the following two-directional attacks. She would raise her shield to block the attacks of the greatsword, and in the same instance she had to side-step to avoid the hefty weight of the greataxe.

The attacks kept coming. The shade were very strong, physically, and the weight of their weapons did nothing to slow them down. One after another, the attacks from the two shade leaders came on continuously. With each block and dodge, the human tried to step in and gain an advantage, but the pair were synced in their movements.

Melissa knew she could not keep this up forever. Already, her shield was becoming heavier. Each second was turning into an ounce of added weight. With each maneuver, stamina became exerted. She continued to stand her ground, and as she did, she couldn't help but wonder if the shade ever got tired. But that did not matter. She was determined, and she silently vowed to not let the enemy get the upper hand. Blow after blow, she continued the bastion of defense that was famous in the Darkbane family.

The greataxe then came down again, and when it missed, it sank into the dirt, and it was that moment that Melissa was looking for. She completely abandoned the shade with the greatsword and pushed full force at the other. She set the warrior up just like she did with the first, and got inside the arc that the ax needed to swing again.

Darkbane was already coiling her arm for the sword strike. The shade brought up the haft of the ax to parry the blade at the last possible moment and it had to backstep to avoid the anticipated smack from the shield.

The attacks never came.

Instead, Melissa spun to block the blow from the shade behind her, and she carried her momentum into a deadly spin, before driving the tip of her sword skyward and through the bottom of the jaw. The greatsword fell to the ground.

But just as it did Lady Darkbane leapt into a diving roll forward to avoid the shade with the ax. She recovered from her flip, got back on her feet, and she readied herself against the single remaining foe.

The dark warrior never gave chase.

It didn't need to. The human felt a cold numbness radiating from above her hips, and she looked to see that the final leader was holding a bloodied short blade. It was the sting of that blade that pushed her into the instinctive roll. The pain became excruciating as she tried to remain standing.

The shade leader remained motionless as it watched the human slowly fall apart.

She cursed at herself in that moment, and she cursed at the shade. She cursed that she had yet to find a suitable man to bear children with so that they would carry her family line further. She almost laughed at herself for not pursuing Henrick further, but she had her fun with him.

Melissa tried to scan the blurry battlefield. She looked for Henrick and any of the other crusaders, especially her sister. But she did not find them. She hoped that Amelia was still alive, and if she was, she knew that it was now up to her to lead the house of gold.

All of the shade around her seemed like one large blob of black as the light around her body dissipated in that moment.

She was defeated. She knew there was no use in wondering if there was more she could have done to prepare for the battle. No use in wondering what waited for her on the other side. She was at least pleased that she would leave this world with a warrior's death. Growing old and fragile seemed boring to her. It always did.

Her shaking legs could no longer support her body, and she crumbled down to her hands and knees. She dropped her sword and shield on the way down. In that position, she closed her eyes and waited for the cold steel of fate to strike her down. She could sense the shade leader walking towards her at that moment.

The coup de grace would not come, though.

In that final moment of haggard breathing, she felt as if her soul was pulled out into a different world. A world that she didn't understand. It was a place of gray sand and red water. It was unlike anything she had ever seen. Unlike anything she had ever read about. In the darkness of her eyelids, though, that alternate reality was ripped away from her.

In that last breath, she felt another presence, and it wasn't the shade. It was warm, and soothing, and inviting, and it was strangely familiar.

Lumina. Melissa echoed the name in her mind.

She saw the spark of her own light within her spirit, and she reopened her eyes just in time to see the light cover her once again. But this was not Henrick's light. This was not the moonlight of Nielda. She could still feel the pain of her fatal wound, but her strength was returning.

The shade's greataxe descended through the air in a great swoosh, and the blade fell upon the neck to take off the human's head. The lust of murder from the shade climbed to new heights in that moment, and he was not about to let this human get back up for any reason.

But the moment was robbed as the ax struck against the shimmering gold field of protective magic. The head of the weapon shattered into pieces. The shade leader took a step back as the human stood upon her feet. It felt cheated by what it had just witnessed.

Melissa stood there looking at her open hands, and admired the golden embrace she felt. The embrace came with the feeling of warning, though. A warning that she was on borrowed time. Upon that declaration, she eyed the shade warrior before her.

She gathered her shield and sword from the ground, and charged after the creature before her. The dark warrior turned and stumbled over itself as it scrambled to get a weapon from the ground, but there wasn't enough time.

As the shade turned back to raise the greatsword up in defiance, Melissa brought down her sword infused with Lumina's holy light. The blade cut cleanly through the dark helmet and the rest of its body. The shade exploded when Darkbane's sword struck against the ground, but as it did, arcs of gold lightning traveled across the dirt and mud in search of more dark creatures. In the blink of an eye, 30 or more other shade became incinerated by the devastating smite.

The moment of reprisal was over. It was fleeting. But it was enough to get payback. It was enough time to let her know that Lumina had been watching this whole time, but that time was now over. The glow faded away with her strength. Melissa slipped back down onto the ground. Blood still flowed from her wound. She found it hard to breathe in those moments, those last moments, and it wasn't long until all her light was gone.

Marc Blade-Briar II and Samuel Fenri continued their vigil at the north gate. The two of them and the rest of their brigade could hear the fighting erupting on the south end of the city, but they had to remain vigilant should there be a breach in the north. The battle had already been underway for numerous hours, and the warrior and the pirate were growing restless. They were hungry for battle just as much as the rest of the soldiers.

The pirate smirked and placed a hand on his bearded chin. "Maybe we should just let 'em in," Fenri suggested.

"I'd be more than happy to let the dark bastards in here, but if we are to win this, we need our walls to do their job for as long as possible," Marc replied.

It was like the words of the late king's son were an answer to their bloodthirsty prayers. The north gate, and the entire north wall, seemed to shutter as a powerful blast worked to defy the durability of the huge wooden doors.

"Magic!" came the call from above right before an explosion obliterated the gate tower.

The reverberations continued. The magic attacks came again in rapid succession. The flash of dark purple magic arced through the tiny gap between the giant doors. Some of the soldiers standing near the entrance had to cover their faces as the wood began to splinter and give way to immense pressure.

Marc Blade-Briar turned to face his ranks, and stood before the soldiers he had with him.

"Warriors of Claymore, this is your defining hour," Marc shouted across the ears of his men and women. "You will bleed, they will die, do not mourn the loss of your friends until the day is won. We have a war to win here, and we will fight until they are broken, or until we are."

"Fight, fight, fight," came the rallying cry of the soldiers.

More blasts struck at that moment. Even with the breach of the north gate imminent, Samuel couldn't help but find curiosity in the student from Planesgate that was with them.

"Are ye ready, magician?" the pirate asked.

The hooded figure turned to regard Samuel. Its red tail stuck out the back of the blue robes. Fenri already knew the person to be a ru-era, but he did feel surprised to see one in the midst of helping a kingdom whose people were culturally closed-minded.

The ru-era locked its red eyes on the pirate. "The name's Moira," she simply answered.

"Fine, then, *Moira*," he half-mocked her. "Are ye ready for 'em?"

The pirate felt her eyes narrowing upon him. "I can assure you I am more prepared than an old, urine-stenched human."

"Buahahahahaha!" Fenri laughed so hard at the woman's fiery insult that he nearly fell down to his knees. The fit of laughter took the ru-era by surprise, but when Fenri was done laughing, he took a swig of alcohol from a bottle inside his coat. "Ahh. I like yer style, demon lady, but I must confess." He then stepped within a couple feet of the mage. "I'm full of surprises."

On his own cue, Fenri walked to the front of the ranks to join back up with Marc Blade-Briar. Once he was there, he took the Wind Stone of Anaroc off of his neck and put it in his hand with the chain wrapped around his knuckles. Grasping the wind stone tightly, he began to channel its power. Everyone nearby could all see the gem glowing with power.

"What is that thing?" Marc asked.

"Let's just say there's a storm a-brewin'," the pirate's amusing tone did nothing to ease the mind of the Claymoran warrior.

Fenri continued to build the concentration of power he was going to unleash, and he had to tap some of the inhuman strength to bolster himself. As the stone's power was reaching its peak, Fenri eagerly waited for the shade to break through the gate. The captain would soon get his wish. The bars that held the gate shut hung on by slivers and splinters.

The final blast came, and the giant doors buckled as the lockbar was split in half. A gentle breeze could have opened the doors at that point.

The shade did advance through.

The suspense began to confuse the warriors who waited for their foes. Why were they giving pause? They all wondered about it.

Fenri then caught the scent of ash. It was all around them. He looked in every direction, but the shade were not there. His memory then reminded him of the encounter in Rotor, and with that he realized that the shade *were* advancing.

They were being hidden by an illusion.

The pirate made no more hesitation at that point, and he unleashed the power of the wind stone to conjure a whirlwind aimed at the north gate. The bursting gale of air slashed across the road leading out of the city, and tore through the shade sorcerers that stood there.

The veil of the illusion faltered, and now all the Claymorans had eyes on their less-sheltered enemies. The troops did not need orders from anyone to start the foray of swords that followed. The shade were on all sides of the human warriors, but it would not be enough to shake the foundation of the Sword Kingdom.

War cries echoed off the walls of the city as the fury of the people found their purpose. In the middle of all of it, Samuel and Marc danced between each other as they hacked away at the opponents who dared to approach them.

Captain Fenri, amidst the fighting, looked out across the mass of darkened humanoids, and took note of a couple splinter groups heading off in different directions. The pirate could only imagine that they would try to breach the keep, and get rid of the magical light that was allowing the defense to be feasible. He knew that not even he would be able to fight these things in complete darkness.

The world suddenly went silent for the pirate captain, and the heart in his chest began to thump heavily. He decided then and there that he was going to stop the dark humanoids that broke off from the main group. He needed to. If the Claymorans didn't win, he wouldn't be able to extort them, or the throne, for services rendered.

In the blink of an eye, the extremely hairy aerin man tore away his human form, and became the animal that would rip through the shade. His shape contorted, bulged, and popped in disgusting fashion until he had transformed into the half-man, half-wolf being.

One by one, and sometimes three by three, Fenri slashed and clawed his way through the ranks of the shade. His strength was unrealistic, and most of the shade could do nothing to stop him.

The wicked blades of the Children of Abyss would slice and cut, but the reactions from the beast struck like lightning. Once the werewolf tore a hole through the legion of shade, he got down to all fours and charged after the first group of splinters. He never looked back as he dashed off, and so he never noticed that he lured many of the shade away from the Claymoran warriors at the north gate.

Meanwhile, Moira's eyes seethed with infernal flames as she called upon her demonic heritage. Beams of dark red fire shot from her fingertips and cut through the enemies, disintegrating all of them that she managed to hit, and when the shade replaced their lost numbers, the red woman would switch it up and let loose bolts of chain lightning.

The battle at the north gate, and throughout the Coin Ward, was holding the shade at bay, but they were not getting pushed back either. Marc Blade-Briar II knew that they had to keep them from digging deeper into the city. If the fighting here kept up it would be nothing more than a battle of attrition, but without knowing the true numbers of the shade, he surmised that it was a battle that they could not win.

Even with their endless numbers, the shade did not want a battle of attrition. They wanted complete domination of Claymore, and they wanted their castle back. They were not here to play games, and they wanted the battle over with as soon as possible.

The air at the north gate crackled and sizzled with the buildup of energy. All of a sudden, the magic of dark purple fireballs came screaming across the ranks of the Claymoran warriors. The heat could be felt on the skin of every humanoid there. That heat made some of the soldiers flinch as they were certain to find their demise in the form of their cindered corpses.

They couldn't have been more wrong.

Through the air, a meteor shower of dark-fireballs flew through the air at a high angle. There had to be more than 20 of them. They sailed over the wall that divided the inner-city from the mid-city.

The mages on top of the keep attempted to shield or counter the spells, but there were too many, and ultimately, they crashed against the top of the keep in a deafening cacophony. The explosion carried the first signs of dread upon the people of Claymore. Everyone in the city had their attention taken by the blast.

But they couldn't see anything.

There was nothing to look at except for purple flames in the starless environment.

The light of their defense was gone.

The light of the Esfera de Luz was gone.

Darkness consumed the city of Claymore.

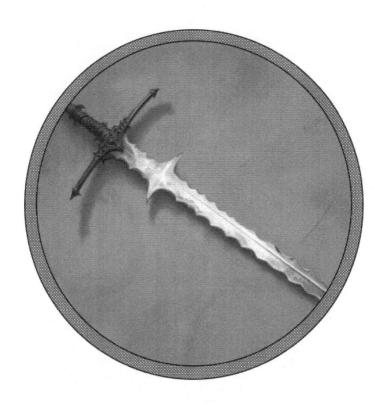

CHAPTER THIRTY-ONE
THE BATTLE OF CLAYMORE PART TWO

At the back of the shade legion, Umbra Hadara continued to oversee the final moments of the shadow dragon's form phasing into reality.

At last, Trestaliadoxen was fully summoned into the rocky grasslands outside of Claymore. The dragon of shadows stood tall and proud before its captors, but it had remained silent and unmoving in that moment as a command had not yet been given.

Umbra Hadara had planned to give the dragon the order to attack, but before he could, something else caught his attention. The grand commander of the shade looked out across the battlefield as his ears caught the loud, sharp sound of an explosion. Purple flashes flickered across the dark landscape, but when it was over, the light that held his forces at bay was gone.

"Hah," the shade leader scoffed at Claymore's inevitable demise. They never had a chance in the first place, he thought. Already, he could taste the fear and dread in the air. He already imagined smelling the coppery fumes of blood. His victory was at hand, and once they were established, they would start planning their assault on the rest of the region.

Chaos reigned in the City of Claymore. The town was completely blinded in darkness as the people's only form of salvation and survival had been taken away. The light produced from Yobo atop the keep had been snuffed out by the explosion that had taken place a few minutes ago.

Screams echoed throughout the unknown environment. The soldiers of Claymore attempted to continue the fight against the shade but they were no match against the vile creatures.

In the darkest of dark, the shade were invisible.

They were free to strike at their foes without reprisal. Jagged swords found flesh. Streaks of black lightning found their marks. The shade swarmed the city in their mist form, and they took shape only to slice down the warriors that still held life in their bodies.

The marksmen on the walls were overtaken. The battles at each gate were suddenly shifted to the favor of the shade. Even the light of the king and his few remaining crusaders struggled to keep the shade at bay. Against all odds, the warriors continued to fight the shade with blind, wild swings. They lived by the sword, and none of them would be taken as a coward. None of them would give up.

Trestaliadoxen, the voice echoed inside the mind of the shadow dragon as she came to open her eyes. She could see the landscape before her. She looked down upon her masters who had summoned her, and she knew that she was there to do their bidding.

You have fallen far, my sister, came the voice again.

The dragon was incredibly intelligent, but she suddenly became confused when she realized that the shade were not the source of the whispering.

Do not tell me that you serve mortals now?

The shade's magic strongly held the dragon's mind in place. The corruption of Abyss ran deep inside her scales. She could not break through the impossible enchantments placed on her through the binding of such powerful spells.

It was as if she was along for the ride. The unknown voice seemed familiar, but it was from an eon ago. The dark magic prevented her from remembering. Somehow, though, the sudden intrusion of the voice allowed her to see through her own eyes again.

How long has she been under the control of the shade?

Under the influence of the dryasaltu, and their dark god?

In the corner of her mind, she remembered her last moments. She had been defeated. Beaten. Imprisoned. Mutilated. Experimented on. She remembered being a dragon who lived under the sea, but her highly evolved intelligence knew that that was not the case anymore. She had been remade into the image of Abyss.

And all of that knowledge only worked to ignite her spirit of rage.

RAWR!!!

The dragon's cry of anger became unleashed. The volume rivaled that of the explosion at the top of the keep. The entire shade legion, and even the people left in the city, could hear the dreadful and frightening scream of ancient ferocity.

The dragon bellowed, and when she exhaled, she relinquished an enormous cone of dark blue and green flames into the air. She fanned her flames downward, and attempted to bring her breath upon the shade, but not even she could go against the bond of a summoner. She could feel the magic protecting the shade sorcerers.

So instead, she whipped her massive tail at one of the obelisks nearby.

The shade down below scrambled in a panic as they tried to find the spells required to dominate the mind of the great beast. They worked to establish control over her once more. One after another, the dragon could feel her weakened mind being pounded by psychic energy, and after each spell her mental defenses got weaker and weaker. It was not a moment later that Trestaliadoxen became completely docile and calm...

...But not before her tail would come to completely shatter one of the obelisks in a great explosion of magic and stone.

Inside the city, Henrick fought off the shade with the aid of his luminous armor. He looked all around him, and beyond his light, the heads he saw were the helmets of the dark warriors. He had no idea how many of his people were still alive. Their screams and grunts called out as they succumbed to the throes of death in an endless choir.

The king could feel despair and doubt making its way into his demeanor. The odds had become insurmountable. There was only darkness, and whatever that giant roar was a minute ago, he could only hope he didn't see it coming.

Then the whack of giant mace came slamming against his back. The armor kept the blow from his skin, but the vibrations that shot through his body felt like a shockwave of a thousand needles. Henrick held on tight to his weapon and shield, but he couldn't stop himself from falling down to his hands and knees. His head swam from the dazing attack.

In the following split of a second, the paladin sank into his mind. He closed his eyes, even though it did not matter considering the environment of the city. He continued to hear the cries of the people around him as they were struck down defenselessly.

"Nielda, Undine, Lumina, Sol. We need help. We need-," Henrick began his prayer out loud, but he cut himself short when something flickered through the veil of his eyelids.

He opened his eyes to see that he stood in a pillar of light. His blurry eyes began to refocus. He looked up, and noticed that all across the sky there were breaks in the shroud above. Sunlight had made its way through.

And from the looks of it, it was the late afternoon sun.

The fighting stopped as every single combatant regarded the strange phenomenon. Across the battlefield, many of the shade were instantly vaporized by the pillars of light, and because the city was now flooded with light pollution, the shade were not able to take their mistform.

Once both sides were able to realize the turn of events, the fighting began anew.

The hearts of the Claymorans had gained a second wind. Theier troops had been *dishonorably* slain in that short moment of pure darkness, but that only drove them to fight even harder than before. There was no time for exhaustion. They would all rest when they were done or dead.

That fury became stifled as a great roar engulfed the broken sky above. The enormous dark wings of the shadow dragon were spotted by all below, human, and shade alike. The dragon made a pass over the city, and gazed below as she traveled outward for a large banking turn.

On the return flight, she had decided on her first target. Trestaliadoxen bellowed on her approach and swept the inner city of Claymore with blue-green fire. Two entire infantry units were incinerated instantly, and there was nothing they could have done to stop it. The flames stuck to the keep, the barracks, the royal houses, and the corpses like napalm.

As the dragon passed by, archers and mages made their attacks when they could, but those that struck true did little to beg the attention of the giant flying creature. The soldiers did what they could in the face of this new enemy, but they also could not ignore the shade for very long.

The dragon made another pass over the city, and flew straight over the keep once. This time though, it could not have anticipated the defiance of a single person. Through the smoke of fire and war billowing up from below, Yobo leapt high into the air.

He had used Suldo's Stand to take on the power of the Esfera de Luz, and as the dragon flew straight at him in midair, the bold monk threw himself forward with a mighty fist.

His knuckles smashed against the snout of the dragon. Trestaliadoxen flinched and faltered in flight, and Yobo used her momentum to push himself upward until he grabbed a hold of the ridges on top. The flying beast managed to stay in the air, but now she had an unwelcome passenger.

Beyond the confined city, and above the legions of shade below to the east, the dragon attempted to dismount her unwanted guest, but try as she might, Yobo was not going anywhere. When the shadow dragon realized this, she came up with another idea.

Trestaliadoxen made a wide banking turn, and on her way back she kept her wings out straight and coasted as she angled her altitude lower and lower. When she came within inches of the ground, she tucked in her wings, rolled onto her back, and let gravity bring her massive body weight to come crashing down like a comet. And to create as much friction as possible, she dove down into the ranks of the dark humanoids, decimating many of the shade in her path.

Because she didn't care about the shade.

The earth was torn asunder as the dragon skidded to a stop. When the beast rose to her feet, she did not feel the presence of the insect anymore, and she turned in all directions to find out where the little snack had gone. She spotted the pest at the other end of her crash site, but for some reason she was seeing two of them.

Yobo stood firm in his spot, the golden light still shimmered around him, but after escaping the dragon's dive, he took a hard fall. He gripped his left arm, and he wore a snarl of pain on his face. Scrapes, bruises, and blood covered his left side, his saam was even more torn than it already was, and he was pretty sure something in his arm was broken.

The shade warriors weaved their way through the pillars of light until they had the monk surrounded. Yobo entered into a staring contest with the beast from more than three hundred yards away, and the monk hadn't noticed that the shade neglected to fill in the flank behind him.

But that was probably because he sensed the approach of something else.

Something hot.

"Seems like you could use some help?" Reeth came walking up from behind Yobo. He had already assumed his fire-orc form.

"You made it," Yobo stated without taking his eyes off the dragon, his breathing was heavy. "And yes, I could. That creature is very big."

"*RAH!*" The dragon growled as her giant scaled claws pounded the earth with drumming thuds as she charged after Yobo and Reeth. Trestaliadoxen completely abandoned any thought of the shade as she trampled over them. Two mortals stood no chance against her, and she was becoming hungry for their demise.

The dragon's senses were finely tuned instruments though, and she stopped in the midst of her trot to catch the glimpse of something coming from the east. Her eyes were capable of seeing great distances, and she could see the form of a flaming bird screaming through the air. The bird was aimed at her, and with great speed, the phoenix crashed into her with a great explosion.

Trestaliadoxen was not fazed by the blast, and she brought up her wing to slap the flaming bird out of the sky. The soul inside the dragon could only watch through corrupt eyes, but even her true self scoffed at the idea that such an attack would have worked.

The now-human form of Kormanth fell down and collided with the earth below. The druid did not move as he lay under a beam of light, stricken by the darkness of unconsciousness. The shade were anxious to end the druid's life, but they did not want to test the protection of sunlight.

Trestaliadoxen brought her attention back to Yobo and Reeth and went back into a run. The dragon was not a fool, and she would never deal with adversaries on the ground, especially if they were stuck there.

With great buffets of her wings, the shadow dragon lifted off the ground once more, and took to the sky. The incredible gusts of wind pushed aside the shade that were in the way.

After she was airborne, the dragon fell back into the instinct of using her fiery breath. She soared out for a distance and then circled back to make her return. She inhaled deeply and began to dive at the two miniscule opponents. The dragon was driven by madness and the inevitable victory over the insects. She opened her maw, the inside of her throat bubbled with blue-green flames.

In the air, the dragon had no idea that the earth had begun to shake and rumble. To Yobo, it seemed like a sudden earthquake, and both him and Reeth weren't sure if they would be able to dodge the incoming breath of the dragon as the ground vibrated their legs to numbness.

The tremors then ceased, and in the distance before them, the earth exploded into a ball of dirt and dust. Large chunks of soil shot in every direction like soft shrapnel. From the wake of this explosion, a beast of tremendous size rose up to snatch the fire-breathing dragon out of the sky.

It was a titanic purple-scaled worm, its enormous body was covered in thick hide that seemed like plates of armor, and its ugly, abhorrent maw sported giant, sharp teeth.

The purple worm continued to expend its long body up from the earth as its incisors latched on to the dragon. Its body then contorted and twisted until it pulled the winged-beast to the ground. The worm's spear-filled maw managed to puncture the scales of the dragon, but her meat was still too thick to chew through.

Trestaliadoxen turned her head to breathe flames on the worm, and the tactic got the giant earth-eater to let go. She immediately got on to her legs, and trampled in a circle to back off before staring down the beast for a destined grudge match.

The worm made no such hesitation as its own intelligence was limited. It was a creature that only lived to fight for its survival, and it darted after the dragon. The two giants were then locked into a wrestling match. They trampled over the shade as their battle caused them to toss each other over. The purple worm squirmed around like a fish out of water, and nipped at the dragon over and over. Trestaliadoxen fended off the disgusting face of the worm with tooth and claw.

Yobo and Reeth turned and began to sprint away from the battling titans. They worked their way across the battlefield as best they could. They fought off the shade where they needed to. Yobo punched and kicked the shade even though his left arm was useless at the moment. They wanted to get to Kormanth before he was flattened by the rampage that had taken over the scene.

Out of nowhere, Sorin came down from the sky with his insect wings, and aided the monk and the orc as they crossed the rocky grassland. His movements were fluid as he jabbed non-stop with his trident, but even as he fought the shade ranks, he could sense his companion's strength was beginning to wane.

"Krum is doing well, but he *will* lose," Sorin advised Reeth.

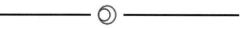

The sounds of utter destruction and chaos echoed across the city. The roar of the dragon loomed in the air, and sharp tones of cracking stone shot out as the two creatures took their wrestling into the outer city.

The warriors of Claymore never paid attention to those sounds as they had been pushed to the inner city. Even with the help of the breaks in the dark shroud above, the shade sorcerers and their death magic assured that the light was not the safest place to be.

And the shade still vastly outnumbered the defense that remained in Claymore.

The fighting was now right outside the keep. The battle was falling apart, and Henrick could sense the end. He was sure that the light from above would provide them with enough to push the shade back, but he realized that he was becoming mistaken. The unforeseen strength of the dragon had bolstered the shade and their resolve.

For the moment, Marc Blade-Briar II tried to direct the troops in the inner city, and so far, their final bastion inside the doors of the keep was working.

Captain Fenri was out in the middle of the shade ranks, and he was abusing the darkness that remained in the city to stay as a werewolf. He tore through the ranks of the dark humanoids, but their numbers were just endless.

Even though the people of Claymore continued to fight hard, they all came to the same conclusion that this was it.

This was their last stand.

Henrick did not see Melissa or Garrick. Marc II and Beadu were the only house leaders left. Amelia Darkbane was the only crusader that still drew breath. Sirus and Gunner stood nearby and continued to shoot their weapons into the crowd. Bertil, Moira, and Master Tigus supported the troops with their magic. Indra stood somewhere near the front and drew the attacks to her shield.

The king looked out to the sky above the city through the keep's doors. The late afternoon sun was close to setting, and he knew that if night fell there would be no stopping these demons from finishing their invasion.

Inside the lobby of the keep, Henrick stepped back, threw off his helmet, and fell to his knees and held himself up as he tried to recover some strength. There were many other warriors inside the lobby doing the same thing, but there were many more of them that were just too badly injured to continue.

For the first time during the battle...No...For the first time during his whole journey, he felt the weight of emotions swell up inside of him. He felt mentally numb as the air of defeat crept inside his brain. He looked outside the doors again. His people were still fighting. The ones that were still alive, anyway. How many people have died today? He had to wonder as the thought plagued him. He was not overcome with the doubt of his peoples' hearts, nor was it the fear of death.

It was remorse.

It was the remorse he felt for those that he led into this battle. He wanted to give his people a fighting chance against the shade, but it took him this long to figure that it really never was enough in the first place.

The shade were just too numerous. The moonlit glow upon Henrick's armor did not fade as the battle closed on its final moments. His mind wondered how much longer the war had left. He stared at the endless army of the shade.

It was then he felt the second wind refreshing his blood and muscles. The moonlight inside him sparked one more time. He sold himself on the idea of how the King of Claymore should die, and if it was going to end, he would end it standing alongside his people.

Henrick stood up, bringing his sword and shield to ready once more. He whipped his neck to get the stiff cracks out of the way, and then he took his march towards the doors of the keep.

"*Wait!*"

The familiar voice echoed off the walls from behind.

Henrick turned in joyful horror.

It was Serena.

She strolled up behind him with Sand in tow.

The other druids, Loria, Kadrah, and Ti'or, were there as well, but they rushed on ahead to join the fray outside the doors.

Serena came to stand before Henrick, and the welcome sight of her face distracted his eyes from noticing that she held the flamberge before him in offering. She then said, "Yobo and some of the others are out there fighting the dragon. We need to go help them. And you left this upstairs."

Henrick looked at the flamberge, but when he did, his eyes went beyond the greatsword and beamed at the huge and nasty scar tissue upon her stomach area from which a large section of her leather armor was missing. Serena noticed his eyes.

"I will tell you later," Serena said with a tone of confidence that Henrick had not heard from her before. "But right now, we need to go."

636

Henrick put his shield and sword on his back before holding the large blade up in front of his face. The silvery steel shined with brightness as he looked it over. For the second time, he could feel a spirit inside the greatsword.

It called to him. It wanted him to call forth the green fire. It wanted him to look within and find the Gift of the Salamander. It wanted him to know with the flamberge in hand, he was the Paladin of Sol as well.

He could feel all of his strength returning as he heeded the advice of the strange sensation from within. And while the spirit of Claymore still rang in the city, he knew the most profound source of his renewed might was because Serena was here.

As far as Henrick could figure, that's all he needed right now.

The King of Claymore fixed his eyes past the blade to meet Serena's emeralds. There was no lump in his throat. There was no second guessing, or second thought at this point. He let the moment of suspense take the air from his lungs, and then admitted it...

"I love ye."

The King of Claymore took the large blade up high and charged into the fray outside the doors. As soon as he found his first target, the green flames ignited to life across the metal of his armor.

"*Raaahhh!*" the king let out a blood curdling cry. The shout was so intense that the remaining troops in the keep suddenly got up and abandoned their lives for the sake of the war.

Serena was left stunned as Henrick went charging off, and she couldn't help but wipe a single tear from her cheek. The warriors ran by her as she stood there and watched the king return to his quest. She was just so profoundly happy to finally know, verbally, and from his own voice, that Henrick felt the same way about her.

She found a couple more tears of joy, but even with that, she managed to look down at Sand. She said, "Let's get 'em, buddy."

Both Serena and Sand took the form of firecats. They darted through the warriors of Claymore and began to blaze a path through the dark warriors. They tore the dark armor with their flaming claws and teeth. Henrick saw the firecats push forward as they played a giant game of connect-the-dots with the pillars of light.

"*For Claymore!*" the king shouted as he charged after the flaming felines.

"*For Claymore!*" came the echoing cry.

The remaining troops followed their king, pushing the shade aside, and killing the ones that dared to get close enough. The soldiers could see their flaming king charging headlong into the darkness with all abandon.

As the King led the army, he continued to roar and cheer. Constantly and nonstop. The singing drowned out the sound of battle, and his cry could be felt in the hearts of the remaining fighters of the Sword Kingdom.

Yobo and Reeth had managed to reach Kormanth. The human druid was still knocked out cold, but they were relieved that the man was not dead. Sorin had remained on the battlefield, and continued to fill his psychotic lust for battle.

The two giant beasts, the dragon and the purple worm, were still going at it. The outer city outside the east gate was all but destroyed, and there were a couple portions in which the wall of the city had collapsed under the massive weight of the creatures slamming against it.

Yobo and Reeth moved Kormanth to the south, and to avoid being trampled themselves, they moved south until they sat upon the beach of Starfall Lake. Under a pillar of light, the monk and the fire-orc took a moment to catch their breath.

"It's hard to tell how the battle is going," Yobo admitted.

"Agreed," the orc said. "Where do these things keep coming from?"

As they stood there and recovered, Yobo looked out onto the surface of the water. He was at least glad that there was one flank that the shade were not using. The monk had to do a double take though, and when he looked at the surface of the water again, he noticed many tiny ripples out in the distance. He kept his eyes peeled upon the water, and waited for the ripples to pass under a pillar of light again. When they did, he became strangely suspicious.

"Are you expecting anyone else?" Yobo asked Reeth while staring at the water.

Reeth didn't respond as he followed the monk's eyes. The ripples drew a direction as if they were heading for the shore a couple hundred feet away. As the strange movement got closer to the shore, the ripples turned into splashing, and it wasn't long before the figures emerged.

It was Kamala, and with her was the succubus, Severin. They rose up from the water of the lake. They were not alone, though. Rising up behind them was a swarm of dark figures. The dark figures were all too familiar to the monk and the druid.

They were shade.

But they did not hold the sinister white eyes as all the rest did, and they were not enveloped by dark mist either. These ones had glowing orange eyes, and strange pale green magic flickered from the gaps in their armor. Coming out of the water, there must have been a couple hundred of the dark humanoids.

The succubus adjusted her shoulders and wiggled her wings to get the water off them. Her and Kamala looked out to the beyond, and to all the forces that were on the battlefield.

"Seems the shade have proven themselves formidable," Kamala stated.

"Not for long," Severin disagreed with the sentiment. She then raised her hand into a pointing finger. "*Attack!*"

The green shade then turned to green mist before sailing away in pursuit of their former kin. Severin then flapped her wings as she took the sword and whip from her waist to follow up the charge of her *newly-recruited* assassins.

Yobo ran over to catch up with Kamala. "Where *those* shade?" he asked her with a pointing finger.

"No. They're the Black Lotus," she answered with a devilish grin.

CHAPTER THIRTY-TWO
THE TIDES OF KADAVAR

The King of Claymore followed the firecats to the east gate. The intense heat and flames from the felines incinerated the dark warriors as they attempted to stop the renewed spirit of the citizens.

The flamberge cut through sheets of armor whenever one of the shade would step in to challenge the Paladin of Nielda and Sol, and when the greatsword came down to strike, three more of the dark things would instantly combust from the splashing wave of green fire.

The warriors that remained of Claymore's defense stormed after their king like a stampede of wild beasts.

The abyssal warriors continued to be a force of endless numbers, but that did nothing against the hearts of men and women in this defining hour. Blades clashed and clanged as the two armies sought to defy each other, but the Claymorans did not relent on their pursuit. If one soldier got caught squaring off against a shade, another soldier would run right up to make quick work of the dark bastard.

Henrick continued to hack and slash with the flamberge, and he let the shade know of his wrath. His fervor parted the dark sea before him. The shade were nothing to him, and he would make sure they knew it well. It was in no time that he and his troops had made it to the east gate.

The purple worm struggled between the four clawed limbs of the dragon, but the earth-eater had gotten its share of bites on the ancient reptile. The worm's instincts could sense its poison was working on the dragon, but at the same time, the dragon's fortitude was god-like. Through all the battering and wrestling the two giants had been locked into, the match had so far been even.

That measure of power suddenly shifted as the giant claws and teeth of the dragon found their way under the armored plates of the worm. The dragon tore them away against the sticky resistance of attaching fluids and sinews. Trestaliadoxen inflicted heavy damage to the purple monstrosity through her actions. The dragon's giant razors found soft flesh as it continued to dig in, and the pain became more tender with each strike. And as the winged-beast got the upperhand, she followed through by grasping the grotesque maw of Krum before sending gouts of blue-green flame down its throat.

The purple worm writhed in agony. The dragon released its adversary as it made every attempt to slink away in defeat. The flames burned the creature from the inside, and the purple worm did the only thing it knew of to save itself. It drove its head into the earth, and it began to eat and bore a hole. The cold dirt was shoveled into its body, extinguishing the flames immediately. The worm dug deep into the earth, and the ground rumbled as it went.

The worm did not return.

Trestaliadoxen came to stand upon all four of its mighty legs. The bites she had taken from the purple worm nagged at her senses like a light buzz, but it would not be enough to sway her from her initial course of action. The dragon took a moment to scan the whole of the battlefield, but as she turned her whole body, she realized she could not feel her wings. They were completely numb to her. A *minor* setback, she thought.

As Henrick ran through the ruins of the outer city, he could not take his eyes off the dragon that lumbered in the distance. His eyes did not stay there forever as the shade continued to try and halt the advance of Claymore's final defense, but as he swapped his eyes to the dark warriors before him, he managed to look out ahead and beyond the legion.

He saw the back ranks of the dark warriors and the open landscape behind them.

The end of the shade was within sight, he thought. *They could win this war!*

The idea screamed in his mind, taking his fury to new heights, and taking his exhausted feet farther than they wanted to go.

Henrick's eyes found the dragon once again, and across the top of all the dark helmets between them, the king took note that the dragon moved in a parallel fashion as he was charging forward.

"Amelia! Stay here with the troops! Protect them! That dragon's comin' for me," Henrick shouted at the young Darkbane just a pace to his side.

"Yes, sire!" she confirmed as her figure held the green flames as well.

Just as the order came across, Henrick looked ahead and yelled again, "Serena! Get yer cat to cover me people."

Sand then broke away from his druid companion.

"Claymore! To me!" Amelia screamed to get the troops to follow her.

Sand charged up to the side of the last crusader of Claymore before darting ahead to dance circles through the shade, biting and clawing with fiery razors.

Henrick kept his gaze forward, and for a moment, he thought that his eyes might be betraying him. But they were not.

He saw the shade fighting other shade.

But these other dark warriors were unaffected by the sunlight, and the green magic that powered them allowed their supernatural abilities to function without the darkness. Fighting along the side of the green shade was a flying female figure with bat-like wings. Henrick was astounded by it all, but he had no time to worry or think about it.

Henrick and Serena broke through the rearward ranks of the shade, and they stepped out into the open gap of the battlefield. As they did, the quaking thuds of the dragon's claws resounded through the air as the giant winged beast came to meet them.

Henrick and Serena were not alone, though.

Coming up behind them was Sirus, Yobo, Captain Fenri, Gunner, Bertil, Indra, Moira, Master Tigus, Kamala, Reeth, Sorin, Loria, Ti'or, and Kadrah.

The dragon slowed down and then eventually halted as the ensemble gathered before her. The dragon stared down upon the defiant ones, and likewise, they took a measure of the dragon.

"Not even Krum could defeat her," Sorin admired the dragon.

"She *is* formidable," Yobo added.

The monk was still infused with the power of the Esfera de Luz, but as he stood there before the might of the shadow dragon, a familiar demonic spirit made its appearance.

The dread spirit of the Nessian Swamp Rose returned.

It wanted to fight the dragon. It wanted to see its power. It wanted to see it destroyed at the hands of its own power. The spirit of the rose had to time its grand reentrance so that it did not alarm the puppet it had been trying to use.

Yobo would have tried to warn himself, but the spirit was acting and knew what strings to pull on. It flashed the memory of his parents and the slaughter on Skyreach. The monk did not anticipate the return of the rose, especially now, and so it weaseled its way into his heart.

Besides, the dark energy from the Nessian Rose couldn't leave yet. It had a contract with the monk, and that contact was not fulfilled.

That was when the monk felt the heat inside his blood. That was when he saw the red shimmer flash from beneath his skin. The dark power began to send his inner rage spiraling out of control, and with the grand experiment of the shade before him, how could he deny the convenience of the situation. Yobo welcomed the red energy in, and he gave it permission to mingle with the Esfera de Luz when it asked.

Yobo then went into Cova's Maw, conjured the red Hesin's Cure, and performed Suldo's Stand. The glistening golden glow on his body mixed with the red. The shimmering of yellow sparks became arcs of flaming electricity.

Everyone took note of the change on Yobo. Tigus especially grinned as he realized that Yobo was still empowered by the dark flower's influence. Tigus silently patted himself on the back for getting the monk to go along with it in the first place, and he had to wonder how far it would string the half-dryad along before it got what it wanted. He told himself to be patient, and that time would provide the answer he sought.

"Any ideas?" Henrick asked everyone.

The dark energies inside Yobo's body quickly healed his broken arm, and as he began to get feeling back in his fingers, he knew more than anyone that he would be able to handle the most damage. He answered, "I will draw her attention."

"It will be best to keep all of her limbs as busy as possible if we are to have any luck in striking her," the archmage suggested.

Everyone else silently agreed to the advice.

The dragon found the prolonged suspense agitating, and without any more hesitation, Trestaliadoxen bounded across the battlefield at all of her foes. The adversaries instantly scattered in different directions, while one came directly at her. She knew the tactic in which they were trying to deploy, but she would not allow such actions to take place. She drew in breath, prepared the flames in her throat, and then swept flames across the battlefield before her.

The flames found the resistant sparks of four barrier spells blocking her flames from reaching any of her targets. The sudden event infuriated her, but she needed time before she could breathe fire again. She would play the mortals' game, she decided. It didn't matter in the first place.

She was the *superior* species.

Yobo ran full speed at the dragon, and his eyes never came off of the giant beast. In his focused pursuit, the distraction of the titanic foe made him blind to the fact that the power of the Nessian Rose was suddenly gone, and the power of the Esfera de Luz was gone with it.

The contract was complete.

The dragon came at the monk, but she did not use fire. She did not use a tooth or claw. Instead, she hopped and dove into a roll upon the ground. The massive weight crashed upon the earth, sending a shockwave out upon the surface.

The sudden force of nature was enough to make Yobo bounce off his feet, and it was there in midair that he noticed the magic from his body was gone.

The dragon steamrolled towards Yobo, and as the monk came to land on his feet he scrambled around for a safe spot. His eyes then darted at a small jut of rock coming out of the ground, but it was in the direction of Trestaliadoxen.

He had no choice.

He blitzed for the rocks, and he had to dive hands first upon the ground to get there in time. He slid and crashed against the stone, and as he curled himself into the fetal position, the large, titanic body of the dragon rolled over the top of him. He could feel the leathery scales touch his skin, but without any of the weight.

Off to the side, a division of the shade attempted to join the fray with the dragon, but Kadrah and Ti'or were there to meet them with their elemental forms.

Sirus, Gunner, and Indra also turned to meet the dark warriors.

Reeth and Serena came at the dragon from the side, but Trestaliadoxen's instincts were legendary and she was already aware of their approach when she was back on her feet. She spun and swiped at them with her enormous tail. The flaming druids were tossed away and fell into the middle of the shade like a couple of meteors.

The fire-orc and the firecat felt like they got smacked with a tree, which probably wasn't far from the truth, but they started to recover. They remained in their elemental forms, and began to fend off the jagged blades and black lightning of their enemies as they worked to return to the open field.

The druids had been handled, and now the dragon became unaware that Yobo was directly under her, but before she could react, the monk coiled his ice-crusted, iron-like fist for the punch. Frozen knuckles crunched into the joint of the dragon's foot. The shadow dragon flinched, rearing backwards from the sudden strike. She danced around until she had the monk in front of her, and by this time she was ready to breathe fire once more.

A large cone of blue-green flames spouted from her toothy maw, and there was nowhere for the monk to go. The dragon saw the humanoid figure disappear behind the veil of fire. However, she was far from satisfied.

From a long distance away, three beams of icy magical energy focused on the firebreath. The colliding beams fought the flames back and shot them in every direction except for where Yobo was standing.

The monk took only a second to look back and see that Archmage Tigus, Moira, and Bertil held the flames in place. The dragon looked at the magicians when she ended her conal attack. The staring contest didn't last.

Henrick came in at a sprint with the sharp point of the flamberge aimed at a hind leg. He sank the blade deep until the hilt would not let it go any further. He let go of the greatsword and worked to get his sword and shield out.

Rawr! The pain felt like an icy dagger, and it shot all the way up the dragon's spine until it made her bark in protest. Once more, the dragon hopped away from the source of the sudden attack.

In the distance, Sirius and Gunner took note that the giant beast stepped away from the rest of the companions, and that when they took the opportunity to change targets and shoot at the dragon.

Trestaliadoxen, even while getting pelted by the mundane ammunition, took the second she needed to remove the sword from her foot, and when she did, the dragon tossed it as far as she could.

The dragon turned to look, and she found the defiant monk charging at her once more, but this time she would not amuse the insect.

The time for entertainment was over.

She took her giant claw and swatted at the monk. Yobo's first instinct was to jump and dive between the dragon's fingers, but Trestaliadoxen decided to aim with her palm. Her giant hand smacked the monk and sent him flying away until he came down, splashing into the shallow water of the lake.

The monk did not get back up.

The dragon then eyed the magicians next, and as she did, she also took account of all the other combatants who still stood against her. Magic spells and ammunition continued to come her way. She danced with her enemies, her large form covered a lot of ground as she bounded about, and she fended them off with ease. Even with their numbers, she managed them with her highly evolved senses.

She would swipe with her claws, lash out with her giant whip-of-a-tail, she let the laughable magic of the mortals bounce and fizzle upon her scales, and with every passing moment, feeling was beginning to return to the wings of Trestaliadoxen.

But with the dragon so busy, no one had seen that Sorin was not there.

The sandaran had flown up high during the start of the battle. He used the breaks in the dark shroud to climb above it. Up in the sky, Sorin could see that there was maybe half-an-hour of sunlight left.

That meant there was no more time to waste.

He looked down and could see the dragon standing under the light below. The bug-druid then let gravity takeover. He plummeted back to the earth at great speed, and eventually his form reached terminal velocity. His figure fell back down below the shroud, and that was when he aimed his trident. He then threw his polearm at the dragon like a god was tossing down their judgment.

The barbed ends of the weapon came and struck the dragon in the back between its wings and front shoulders. The sudden, sharp pressure to its spine made the dragon lurch over to one side, and she fought to stay on her feet through blurry vision.

Now was the time to strike.

Kamala was already after the dragon. She leapt up and drove her enchanted daggers into the scales of the dragon, and she stabbed over and over as she used her weapons to climb on to the creature's back. Once she was up there, the orange blur of a firecat came zipping by her.

Serena used her claws to run up the dragon's tail, her spine, and then her neck. She rushed after the dragon's head, and when she got there, the firecat began to claw out one of the dragon's eyes.

Trestaliadoxen's demeanor exploded with rage. She writhed around as pain sought to overtake her senses. She thrashed about like a bull trying to expend the opponents on her back and head, but they did not go anywhere.

Down below, Captain Fenri, back in human form, lunged at the legs of the dragon. He swung Betty's head with all the feral strength he had, and sunk her notched blade into the dragon's meat.

Tigus, Moira, and Bertil assaulted the dragon with spells of fire and lightning. The spells began to deal their damage, and they left pock marks as the smoke cleared.

Loria summoned the latent power of nature in the ground, and brought forth an infinite number of vines to reach up and hold the dragon in place.

Unable to move, the dragon became an easy target, and the bombardment of anguish never ceased. Inside her mind, Trestaliadoxen could sense the power of the enchantments loosen as her life force diminished. She did not like the idea of being defeated by a bunch of mortal insects again, but at the cost of her spirit being free, she would agree to the terms of her destiny.

The pain then became too great, the dragon's body succumbed to shock, and Trestaliadoxen's legs went wide when they could no longer support her own weight. As her head came to slam against the ground below, her breathing was rapid, but it was also shallow.

She was dying.

"*Stop!*" Henrick shouted to the others.

Everyone stopped their attacks, and instantly put their eyes on the king.

The paladin walked up to the face of the dragon. Her one good eye was as big as he was tall. As he stared into her glowing purple eye, he could feel the darkness inside the dragon, but the darkness no longer shared the taint of Abyss like it did with the shade.

It felt more like the other dragon. Like Drextramlcrosis. It wasn't benevolent, but it wasn't villainous either. He continued to stand before her face and watched as her eye changed from a solid purple to a glossy, blue accompanied by a dark slit.

Captain Fenri came to stand by Henrick and witnessed the same thing. He then whispered, "I know how ye be feelin' mate. Their kind shouldn't suffer as such. They were born when the world was still young."

Henrick then stepped closer to the dragon's face until he could place a hand on her. He couldn't get over the fact of how large and terrifyingly awesome she was.

An impulse then washed over him. Was it his impulse, or something else? He tried to identify what was coming over him at that moment, but through all his deliberating, he kept coming back to one notion.

He was being given permission.

Permission to do what, though? He silently asked the Twins over and over about what he was supposed to do. He only realized the answer as he watched Trestaliadoxen's remaining eye begin to narrow.

And that was when the moonlight returned to his form.

"Everyone. Get back," Henrick told them.

"What're ye gonna do?" Fenri asked when not even his crazy mind could consider what was about to happen.

"Just get back," he repeated.

Once everyone had gotten back to what they deemed a safe distance, Henrick concentrated on the task before him. He focused his spirit and the moonlight that was within his core. With the power of Nielda at his disposal, he used his divine sense to feel the dragon's dark life force as he closed his eyes.

With everyone there as a witness, Henrick took all the moonlight upon his body, and shoved it into the dragon with one sharp pulse of magic. It was the dragon's body that now glowed with moonlight.

Trestaliadoxen's remaining eye went wide, her strength was returning rapidly, her wounds were closing, and by the end of the effect, her missing eye grew back.

Henrick neglected to move when Trestaliadoxen began to writhe around with her renewed life.

"What do you think you're doing?" Reeth called out.

"Release the vines," he demanded.

And that was what Loria did.

The paladin kept his fearless eyes upon the dragon as she came to stand up on fresh legs. She gave her wings a good flap to test their strength, and in truth, she felt vibrant like whelpling. Her scales returned to their original indigo color. She turned to take a few steps back before looking down to the paladin.

"Your actions are foolish, Nielda, but they will not be unrewarded," the dragon said.

Trestaliadoxen batted her giant sinewy wings before Henrick. The King of Claymore, and everyone else, fell to all fours to avoid being blown away by the buffets of wind. The shadow dragon got airborne and took off towards the city. The battered castle was not her target, though, nor was it the city.

Instead, she made a sharp bank and zeroed her highly attuned vision upon the obelisks at the far end of the battlefield.

RAWR!!!

The scream across the sky came as a warning to the shade, and to their dark god, Abyss. Trestaliadoxen angled herself at the magical towers, and as she descended, she flapped her mighty wings to gain even more speed. She became a 20-ton streak of lightning zipping across the view of everyone in attendance.

She was a dragon.

She *was* the very top of evolution.

She was hardened by thousands of years, and had a very distinct intelligence. She would make sure her captors would feel her wrath, and her wrath would serve as a warning to all mortal kinds in the future.

As she approached the dark glowing obelisks, she spun her body into a barrel roll and collided with the stone structures. The obelisks tore apart like paper under her weight. They shattered, and the magic inside of them released and dissipated.

The dark shroud that filled the air above completely disappeared, revealing the sun and its last 10 minutes of light. Those last minutes were enough as all of the shade became engulfed by the piercing orange light, turning them all to ash instantly.

The dark fog that plagued the castle-city of Claymore was gone.

The shade were defeated.

Henrick fell to his knees, and his mouth hung open as the realization came to his mind.

They won.

They achieved victory.

He could see the troops off in the distance throwing up their arms in cheers, but the king did not celebrate as much as he would have wanted, though. He looked upon the scene of the now-former battlefield, and all he could see was the bodies of the citizens.

It was a sobering moment for the king. With the destruction of the shade, there was nothing left to look at but the corpses of his people. He retracted his initial sentiment.

They achieved victory...

...But did they really win?

The population of Claymore was no doubt abysmal now. Henrick knew that this picture would be burned into his memory.

Tigus and Kamala went to get Yobo while Reeth and the other druids moved to get Kormanth. The monk and the human druid were still knocked out, but as they got picked up, everyone started to make their way to the city.

Henrick remained on his knees and continued to soak in the view of the aftermath.

Captain Fenri took note of Henrick, and the salty pirate knew more than anyone the kind of face that the king wore at that moment. Fenri didn't let the notion bother him though, and soon he was off to go raid the city while he could.

In truth, Henrick felt paralyzed while he sat there. Of course, the only thing that had a chance to break his stupor was walking up to him.

It was Serena.

He took note that she had gone to retrieve the flamberge for him. He offered a smile to her as she approached, and as he came to stand up, he noticed something else.

As the sun fell under the horizon, twilight was all that remained of the day's light. The sky was a mixture of crimson and royal. The stars above already began to show themselves, and before everything else, Nielda loomed over them.

She was at the fullest point of her cycle and her lavender light was like a promise being fulfilled. Undine sailed the sky as well while she was in her first quarter.

Henrick did not move from his spot as Serena approached. She came to stand before him, he returned his sword and shield to his back, and he took the flamberge in hand once again. He let the blade rest upon the ground by the tip while holding the hilt. The two of them stood there, and they stared at each other in silence. Then she stepped closer, and she placed his hand where her stomach scar was.

"I-," she began but Henrick's actions cut her short.

He pulled her close to him, and held her with the embrace of a single arm around the back of her hips. Their eyes met, and their faces intimately grew closer and closer with each second. After all they had been through, the two of them finally arrived at this destined moment. Henrick leaned his head forward, and Serena stood up on her toes. They came together to embrace in a kiss.

However…

Before their lips could become locked, Henrick suddenly sensed the presence of the shade…again.

But how?

How was it possible?

Serena then winced in pain as the sweeping of a phantom blade came to slice her skin across her shoulder blades. Henrick pushed himself back only to realize that Serena had suddenly been turned to stone.

The paladin ducked and rolled out of the way as he sensed the dark presence moving around him. He turned to face the lone shadeling with the flamberge held up in defiance. The shade made no hesitation, and drove his glowing stone sword at the human. Henrick brought up the flamberge to parry the blade.

At that moment, as the two weapons met, both combatants disappeared from reality.

Henrick and the lone shade found themselves on opposite sides of a round arena. The arena floor was like a disc floating in the air. Upon its face was the design of an unnumbered clock. The king looked at his surroundings above, but there was no sky. They stood inside a dusty, bronze coliseum. Giant chains reached down from the dark corners above as they held the round arena in place. Henrick could feel the air of endless generations in this old place,but the seats, the stands, and the multiple tiers of the grand structure were empty of any audience.

Directly above them, there was an amalgamation of gears that spun with their teeth interlocked. Some were brass, some were silver, and some were gold. The place was well lit, but there was no source of the light. The place was polluted with soft clicking noise as if time was being measured.

On one side of the arena, floating in the empty air was a large throne made of brass, and an intricate stone golem sat upon it. Its head was unmoving, and its face was plain.

Henrick didn't know what to make of it, but one thing was for sure, his opponent stood at the other end. Whatever the demon did to bring him here mattered less to him in that moment. First and foremost, he was going to make sure this one paid his due for what he did to Serena.

"Interesting," the shade warrior said in the common tongue. "So you're the paladin I saw. The one carrying Nielda's light, but you also carry Sol's sword."

The words of the shade grew Henrick's curiosity to the point that it matched his anger at the moment. Before the man could say anything, he watched the shade take his helmet off to reveal a humanoid face. It was a face that he had seen before, but only in a vision.

The creature had teal skin, sharp-pointed ears, and ridges running along the top of his head. Henrick also noticed that the shade was no longer billowing with smoke, and he could no longer sense it either.

"What're ye on about?" Henrick questioned through a snarl.

"Hahaha," the shade laughed at Henrick. "You have no idea what all of this is...do you? This is the Realm of Karnus. And the God of Time sits right there." He pointed a finger at the golem. "The rules are in the very fabric of the cosmos. When two paladins fight to the death, it shall be on level ground. In here, there is no light, no darkness, no magic, and no interruptions from the gods."

"What's that make ye? The Paladin of Abyss?" Henrick surmised.

"Hahaha," the shade laughed again.

The shade warrior then studied Henrick's eyes, and realized that he *really* had no clue about any of this. The dark warrior then began to pace around the circular shape of the arena, and Henrick made sure to stay at the far end from him.

"So naive," the shade mocked. "Each of the gods has their own set of rules on how they choose their paladins. In the grand and holy style of Abyss, the dark god takes what is already there, and remakes it in his own image."

Henrick remained silent as he assumed the shade was going somewhere with his explanation. The shade hoisted his stone sword up and rested it upon his shoulder.

"I...am Umbra Hadara. I am the grand military leader of the dryasaltu, the sea dryads," the shade proclaimed with a strong and confident voice. "And I...am the Paladin of Undine."

"*Undine?*" Henrick repeated in disbelief.

"I have been her paladin for countless ages," Umbra Hadara continued. "I have seen the rise and fall of all the dryad kinds. Do you think that because the tides of Kadavar are no longer flowing that my people do not flourish? Our city has never known such prosperity since we adopted Abyss into our kingdom. Your people have barely survived this battle. Will they be as lucky when we return after another few hundred years?"

"*Barely survived*? Yer head must be full 'o shite considering yer forces are dead," Henrick shot back.

"What! How dare you! Who do you think you're talking to, boy?" Hadara argued. "I have thousands of years of combat experience; you might as well just let me kill you quick."

The thoughts of the whole conversation fueled the fire building in Henrick's mind. His kingdom was decimated, and at the very end of his journey, at this very moment, he figured out that the Twins had set him on this path in order to restore the title of Undine's paladin to someone more deserving of it.

He was not going to disappoint them.

His thoughts were then back on Serena. She was within his grasp, and this demon stole her away. Hadara turned her to stone before his very eyes with that sword of his.

"I think I'm talkin' to a corpse, ye *bitch*," Henrick blatantly insulted the Hadara.

The cutting words of Henrick did exactly what he wanted. Hadara charged with his large sword in hand. Henrick met the charge at the center of the arena with the flamberge. The two blades came in with humming swoops and a sharp clang of steel. The two paladins gave no pause to their actions and they became locked in an endless flurry. Every swing of their greatswords would have been a deadly blow, but the two warriors continued to parry and dodge the attacks of the other.

Both of them then found the opportunity for a fatal swing, and the blades hummed through wide arcs only to meet again. A spark shot out as the weapons defied each other. Henrick stared into the orange eyes of Hadara with a snarl on his face. Hadara shared his own disgusting expression that only emulated his want for murder.

As the sparks flew out, the arena suddenly flashed.

The disc was then floating above an ocean, the sky poured heavily with rain. Henrick borrowed a split second to scan the new environment, but he would not dare take his eyes off Hadara. The two warriors then pushed off from each other.

Hadara turned his face upward to greet the rain. "You see this?" Hadara rhetorically asked. "This is what Kadavar used to look like."

"So why'd yer people abandon Undine?" Henrick questioned out of legitimate curiosity.

"You don't know what you're talking about, human," Hadara retorted sharply. "The ocean goddess...she left *us*. Our people were dying...And *she*! *Left*! *Us*! We had to sacrifice our ways in order to survive."

"So ye plunged yer own kind into darkness?" Henrick stated more than questioned.

"Your judgment does not matter. This fight is between us now," Hadara replied.

The umbra came at Henrick and closed the gap once more. The greatswords swished and cut through the drops of water as they sliced through the air. They hacked. They slashed. Neither combatant allowed the other to gain ground.

When the blades became locked again, the two paladins then began to punch at each other. Sometimes they would follow their swordplay up with kicks, but the result had remained the same. Both of them were ferociously eager to kill the other.

Henrick wished he had a long enough moment to get his sword and shield. Then he could control Hadara. The greatsword was not his most favorable weapon to use, but he was at least glad that the flamberge was super light, and the balance between the blade and hilt was perfect.

The two swords came to meet in a spark once again.

Just like before, the environment around the arena changed. This time it was a place that Henrick had been to. The disc of the arena disappeared. The warriors stood upon the surface of an endless body of water. The sky was a dark blue and filled with an infinite number of twinkling stars.

The warriors did not push off, but Hadara looked around. The sea dryad was confident that the weapons would remain pressed against each other as his thought came to the surface.

"You've been to Iname." Hadara said with surprise. "Perhaps you're not as new to this as I thought."

The dark warrior then pushed Henrick while the blades were locked. He followed through with a mighty kick that connected and took Henrick off his feet. The flamberge flew away from his hands only to land several feet away. Hadara chased after Henrick, but he soon stopped in his tracks.

Standing between Hadara and Henrick, the figure of a ghost appeared. The Paladin of Nielda recognized the ghost as the one from before when he was in Rotor. Hadara became irritated and confused, though. The battle between the paladins was a sacred rite, and there was not supposed to be any interruption.

The distraction allowed Henrick to scramble across the surface of the water, and retake his weapon in hand before standing back up. But he then took the opportunity to swap the weapons on his.

"*Nooo!*" Hadara screamed at the ghost. The dark paladin looked up as they went back to the coliseum. He looked up at the stone golem in the throne. "These are not the rules."

Hadara then returned his attention to Henrick before charging at him. The shade-dryad warrior stomped his boots as he moved to meet the divine challenger. The stone sword came across at Henrick in a deadly backhanded spin.

The Paladin of Nielda was proving to be a good fighter, but Hadara could keep this up for as long as he needed if it meant destroying his opponent. As the shade commander's blade came out of the spin, he anticipated the clang of the blades meeting.

There was no such clash.

In his rage, the Paladin of Undine was blind to the fact that Henrick had changed to a sword and shield, but the King of Claymore purposefully stood in such a manner that he hid the sight of the shield from Hadara.

At the last possible second, Henrick punched out with the symbol of the Twins and deflected the shade commander's blade upwards and away. The maneuver took Hadara by complete surprise and threw him off-balance.

The Paladin of Nielda followed through into his own spin and brought the arcanium blade into a low, backhanded uppercut. The curved sword sliced through Hadara's armed before meeting the corner of neck and jawline.

Henrick turned around to confirm his kill, but instead he stood in the former battlefield outside of Claymore. He looked upon his weapon, and saw it was stained with the golden blood of a dryad.

He then tossed the weapon aside as if it was a useless instrument. It wasn't so much that it was useless, but it couldn't help as he stood in front of a stone statue that held the face and figure of Serena.

Henrick thought that perhaps with Hadara gone, she would return to normal.

But she didn't.

The night sky was beyond twilight. The moons kept him company as he silently let the tears roll down his cheeks. Grief filled his heart. He had lost the most important person to him in this war.

He also lost Melissa.

He lost countless faces of his people at the hands of the Children of Abyss.

He could only step forward and embrace the statue in his arms.

To him, it was the only thing that would bring him comfort in that moment.

CHAPTER THIRTY-THREE
THE STONE PRINCESS

All of the survivors had forced their way into the Brew and Brand during the night, and took advantage of the *unattended* alcohol that was in the basement. They got drunk and wandered about the town, and through their singing and dancing, they all worked to organize the dead on the side of streets.

There were so many of them.

The dead greatly outnumbered the living at the conclusion of the battle. The warriors stole their minds and committed themselves to their song and their work. Through the buzzing of camaraderie, the still-breathing soldiers kept their emotions in check and focused on tending to their fallen brothers and sisters.

To their fallen family.

At some point during the night and under the comfort of lamp light, the warriors just found a spot and fell asleep. Their exhaustion had overtaken them, and the booze definitely didn't help them fight off their weariness. Some fell over in the streets. Some of them shambled over to the park, and found a nice spot of grass to lay on under the summer night sky.

For the rest of the night though, there was a stillness of peace.

Henrick woke up to the piercing rays of sunlight in his eyes. He lurched his aching body upwards to stare across the shimmering blue lake in front of him. The sound of lazy flowing water on the shore gave him some small comfort that he was alive, and that the nightmare was over.

But was it really over?

He reminded himself and turned to look off to his side.

The stone figure of Serena was still there.

She was still gone.

That didn't stop him from getting up and placing his arms around her. Even with the warm and bright sun, the day still felt darker than it actually was.

"You're here. Right in front o' me, but you're gone," he said as if she could hear him. "We did it, though. We stopped 'em." He paused for a moment as the grief came to hit him again, but he kept his composure as he continued. "The pain I now feel while you're gone...that's how I know I love ye."

Henrick stepped back and looked across the field leading to the east gate. He could already see a couple of figures outside the walls with carts collecting the dead. His station as king came back to the front of his mind. He recovered the sword of Thor Spearfall from the ground not too far away, and put it back in its sheath. The king then began to calculate the distance to the east gate from where he was and then turned his eyes on the petrified woman.

"The least I can do is keep ye safe," Henrick offered before getting down low to hoist the stone figure up and on to his shoulders. Across the field, Henrick marched with the extra weight upon his body, but he was not going to relent until she was secured inside the keep.

Upon his approach to the ruins of the outer city, he was spotted by some others.

It was Reeth and Kormanth.

"*Serena?*" Kormanth was probably the most in shock. "But how?"

"The leader o' the shade did this," Henrick answered as he walked by them.

"The grove continues to wilt," Reeth stated with gross concern.

"Both our kingdoms have been shattered by the sea dryads," Henrick's notes of defeat were apparent, but he let loose a bit of hidden truth to them. He didn't have to look at them to know their curiosity.

"*Sea dryads?*" Kormanth was puzzled.

"That's what the shade are. A broken echo of their culture," Henrick added with a hint of content in his voice.

The druids followed him through the east gate.

As Henrick carried Serena by the statue of Samuel Blade-Briar, he could only sense that the First King and his friend had met the same fate, only 700 years apart. That was probably why Simon Blade-Briar used the Esfera De Luz to destroy the shade back then. At that moment, Henrick knew that he would have done the same thing.

The king and the druids navigated the city streets. Word of the king's return to the city carried across the remainder of the population, and as Henrick carried Serena's stone body to the keep, he was followed by Yobo, Captain Fenri, Marc Blade-Briar II, Gunner, Bertil, Indra, Beadu Hadoku, Amelia Darkbane, Reeth, Kormanth, Loria, Ti'or, Kadrah, Archmage Tigus, Moira, and Kamala.

Henrick went through the doorways and up the stairs until he was in the throne room. Those who followed closest behind him came to assist in bringing Serena's statue down to stand next to the Throne of Claymore. Henrick, and everyone else, regarded the statue in silence.

Henrick spent the next morning gathering various materials so that he could make sure that Serena did not fall over and break. He ended up sliding her over to one of the pillars in the throne room, and used some rope to tie her in place. Satisfied with his work, he was finally comfortable leaving her to watch over the throne.

Minutes later, the king went outside and walked to the Crown Balcony. From up there, he got his first *real* look of his city after the defeat of the shade. Surprisingly though, a majority of it was left untouched.

There were areas in which fire magic had burned some of the structures and houses down, but the presence of the shade must have kept the fires from spreading. He could only shake his head at that notion.

The streets were still full of the dead, and the blood that they had lost beforehand. The sour lemon stench of rot was already fuming in the air due to the heat of the summer day. How many people were lost? He wondered again, but in reality he was always thinking about it. He would have to start a census between the city and all the villages to find out, but he knew it would be best to wait until the dead were buried.

The thoughts of loss brought to his mind the faces that had not returned from the events that led to the battle, and the battle itself.

The first ones were Thor Spearfall, and his friends and fellow soldiers that were a part of that unit, Lars and Kendo. He could see Melissa's face, and he could only shake his head when he remembered all the times he had snuck off to the woman's room as. The royal houses lost some good leaders, he thought, but at least they would be left in good hands.

Even with the loss, the people of the Sword Kingdom continued to work on getting their city back to the way it was before. The king held a proud smirk on his face at the sentiment of their dedication and loyalty to each other. He knew the kingdom would be as strong as ever before once repairs were done.

Upon the hour of twilight, the king had retired to the keep, but he was in the lobby. He met with Yobo and Kamala. The doors of the keep remained open and revealed the dark environment outside in contrast to the well lit walls of stone bricks.

"So the Esfera de Luz is really gone," Henrick remarked as Yobo had just finished trying to explain what happened to it. The king's eyes fell away in a second of silence as he tried to ponder on whether or not it was possible to get it back somehow.

The siblings joined in the silence.

"I guess we'll have to hope that we won't need it again fer a while," Henrick then spoke again.

"The druids have already taken their leave, as well as Master Tigus," Yobo reported. "I think that is a good sign that we won't."

"Yer friend from Planesgate were helpful in the battle," Henrick said as he came to regard the monk. "You as well, Yobo. Ye have me thanks."

"Do not thank me," the monk replied. "This battle belonged to all of us. The shade brought us together, and that was their undoing."

"Aye," Henrick agreed. "So, where ye headed?"

"I'm going back to Aero," Yobo answered before sporting an almost bashful smile. "There is someone there who is expecting me."

Henrick and Yobo then turned their eyes to Kamala.

"I'm afraid I can't answer that right now," was all that she offered.

The other two suspected that she might head back to the swamp and the Black Lotus, but their insight warned them against such a notion. Whatever curiosity they held for the truth fell away as they let the woman have her secrets.

"Very well," Henrick said to let the matter rest. He then offered a hand to Yobo. "Stay safe out there."

"You as well," the monk returned as he accepted the handshake.

Kamala bowed her head in conclusion. The two siblings then walked out from the keep, and soon they were gone into the night.

The next morning there was a cart that had been pulled up to the doors of the keep. Standing outside the doors, Henrick, Samuel Fenri, and Marc Blade-Briar II watched as some of the Claymoran soldiers loaded a chest full of coins into the cart.

The pirate had been wearing a discerning look on his face as he eyed the hefty wooden container. After it was loaded, Fenri was invited to hop into the cart, and when he climbed up, he sat upon its side to perform his own inspection of the goods.

He *gently* opened the chest as soon as his keen nose could taste the metal perfume in the air. He then looked upon the bounty that he was owed.

"5,000 dags. Just as ye wanted for the bounty," Henrick said before the pirate could say anything.

"Ha. Hahahahahaha," Fenri giggled inside, but he could not contain himself as his eyes went wide before the sparkling coins. Spit dribbled onto his beard as he tried to stifle himself.

Then, in the matter of a second, he became completely silent and his demeanor became nonchalant as he stepped down from the cart.

After readjusting his coat and tricorne, he said to the king, "Glad I could be of service to ye. Should ye need any more *criminals* apprehended...ye know where to find me."

The captain turned and got back on the cart without offering any form of courtesy. As far as the pirate was concerned, he was still above Henrick on the food chain. Fenri sat upon the front side, and ushered the two horses onward. After a few minutes the pirate was gone from sight.

Henrick then turned to Marc, and without any warning or prior notification, he offered the flamberge to the Blade-Briar leader. He said, "With the way things're now, and from what we have left, I can't think o' anyone else that'd be a better general to lead the army as it grows again. This blade was yer father's. Ye should have it."

Marc was almost taken back, but he immediately came to accept his new station. He took the sword from Henrick, and then rested the blade upon the ground by the tip. Marc stayed by the king's side as Henrick began to walk through the streets of the city.

As they walked, the citizens greeted them. Many of them held smiles to their king. To the one that led them to victory. Even though their population had been decimated, they still showed their loyalty and support for the king that brought the fight back into Claymore.

To Henrick though, there was still more fighting to come. He defeated the shade. The envoy of the Twins said that the path would be clear now. If a sign had presented itself to mark the way forward, Henrick wasn't seeing it. That notion toyed with the strings of impatience, but he was determined to wait. He knew Nielda would not fail her.

She hadn't yet.

Later that day, the evening hour fell over the city. Henrick returned to the throne room, and he spent hours staring at Serena's statue as if he was paying tribute to a goddess. Her gray form was cold to the touch everytime he would happen to check.

He then started to scoff at something as it appeared in his mind's eye.

That silly song from Furl Stonebrow. *Stone Princess* it was called. He heard it that day he went into the Brew and Brand before all of this started. He thought to hunt down that dwarf and give him a good slap for all the irony before him.

But Henrick accepted the romanticized idea in his head. He was the king after all. What better title for Serena to wear as she stood near the Throne of Claymore.

Through a heavy heart, he began to hum the notes of the song.

THE END

EPILOGUE
MOTHER OF THE MOON

The snowfall was heavy tonight. The crisp air bit at the skin of those who worked feverishly to unbury and shovel the white powder out of the tent city of Zahn. The whole community was out and about. Lamps hung from nearby posts, but with the large flakes, and the thick ice fog, blowing across their faces, it was hard to see the light.

The lifestyle was harsh in the northern region of Rignaul, but it also made the people hardy. Some complained about going outside in the middle of the night to work, but everyone had to do it in order to survive.

On the flip side, the snowy night was part of the beauty of winter. While the folk worked the avenues between their homes, they would occasionally pick snowball fights, and it was the best, most efficient way, to keep the joyful spirits high. For the adults, rounds of ale were available from the drinking tent.

As the snow got pushed out of town to the south, it was on the north side that a visitor wandered into town. Not more than 50 feet from the northernmost tent, there was a dead forest. Endlessly stricken by the drought effects of long winters over the course of a millenia. It was known as the Ice Needles.

The visitor stepped through the snowy weather. He walked directly across the top of the white powder, and not once did his body weight push the snow downward. He wore the darkest gray cloak, and it made his approach to the town completely unnoticed. He needed the invisibility though as his presence was not welcome.

Not here.

Not anywhere.

And he wore the face of a skeleton upon the mask under his hood, and he used his skull-topped staff as a walking stick.

Around the northernmost tent, he walked towards the entrance flap. He could see people through the fog not more than 10 feet away, but his presence was unknown. He stepped into the tent.

On a cot, to his right, he could see the only person in the tent, and she was soundly asleep at the moment. There was a small furnace standing in the center and it was currently radiating a comfortable warmth.

The dark cloak moved to the side of the cot before coming down to sit on the side of it. The pressure of his body disturbed the sleeper. She shuffled herself until she came to face the dark figure, but as soon as she flinched, he forcibly placed a cold, black leather glove over her face so that she could not speak, scream, or cast her magic.

Her hair was dark, like chocolate, and she had green eyes to go with it. She was approximately in her early 50s, and she wore a wooden token around her neck that had the etching and white-painted symbol of the Twins.

"Shhhh," the unmoving mask bade her quiet. His voice was trailed by the sound of an elongated whisper as he spoke to her. "I have. Found the chalice. I will end. The madness. Of the mate."

She stared up at the face that she could not see. Unblinking were her eyes. Her brows were lowered with sudden anger, but as the necromancer said his words, he could feel her resistance loosen through his gloves. At that moment, he removed his hand as if he knew she would be open-minded.

"Baron Tal," she called the necromancer by name. His words were not lost on her, but she also did not know how to respond. Her husband had disappeared some time ago, and she had no idea what he had been doing since he left. Some of the other druids in the Winter Grove had reports that they had seen him here and there, but they were never able to successfully trail the man. And now, for some reason, the *Scourge of the Swords* knew something about him.

All she could offer in response was her curiosity, "*Sagnis.* You know *where* he is?"

"Yes," the necromancer answered. "Into the Needles. I must go. Retrieve the chalice. He must not."

"I can go with you," the woman offered, but the open hand before her forbade her to move.

"No," the faceless mask advised. "Safer here. With the living."

As if on cue, there was a sudden clatter outside the tent. Both the woman and Baron Tal looked to the entrance of the tent as one of the citizens stumbled inside. There was a giant stab wound in the person's chest, but this person no more got inside before collapsing against the floor. Baron Tal stood up in an instant, and made his long, slow strides to go outside. The woman scrambled to get dressed, and get up.

Outside, in the night of snow and fog, Baron Tal was greeted by five members of the snowtooth orcs. Each of them had pale blue skin and orange orbs for eyes. They had black, gray, or blue hair, and they were all dressed like barbarians save for the one standing in the middle. That one wore dark leather and held two short blades. It seemed more like an assassin than a fighter, and part of his face was a scar that had been received from a burn.

"Go. Leave. Now," the necromancer demanded to the orcs.

"Stand aside. We're here for the woman," the orc leader replied.

It was then that the woman came outside to find the same thing that Baron Tal did. They were not the only ones, however, and from the side, two of the other druids came rushing over due to the commotion witnessed by some of the citizens.

"Celene," one of the druids called the woman by name.

"By the gods. Is that...?" the other druid said after noticing the necromancer.

"Stay back," Celena told them.

"Come along, druid," the leader said. "No one else needs to get hurt."

"I beg. To differ," the necromancer said. It was then that he channeled the dark powers inside his body and mind. He called to the dead spirits that lingered in the land, and to the vengeful ghosts that longed for violence from a dimension outside of time and space. He pointed his skull-staff towards the orcs as the wisps of white, spiritual energy...

...Came to life.

THE STORY WILL CONTINUE IN VOLUME TWO

The Stone Princess

Stone Princess, Stone Princess, how your vigil has been long.
Watching over the valleys, the weak, and the strong.

Silent and guarding, in the shadows I hide,
Waiting for cries, in the time that I bide.
With the fires of war, I am the speaker of peace
And through my voice, the sand I will crease.

Stone Princess, Stone Princess, how your vigil has been long.
Watching over the valleys, the weak, and the strong.

I cared for you once, and now you're gone.
The people you rallied, were a family of one.
But time has passed, your memory of none,
Now you're a part, of the mountain and the sun.

Stone Princess, Stone Princess, how your vigil has been long.
Watching over the valleys...the weak...and the strong.

Chapter & Illustrations by Page

About the Author

Carl E. Wooldridge Jr. has been a fan of the fantasy genre since his first experiences at a very young age. He grew up in San Diego, California, USA, he joined the military where he spent two decades working as a bomb technician, and he has been developing the World of Golterran, the World of the Twelve Paladins since 2011.